Close to Hugh

CLOSE
TO
HUGH

MARINA
ENDICOTT

Doubleday Canada

Doubleday Canada and colophon are registered trademarks of
Random House of Canada Limited

Library and Archives Canada Cataloguing in Publication

Endicott, Marina, 1958-, author
    Close to Hugh / Marina Endicott.

Issued in print and electronic formats.
ISBN 978-0-385-67860-5 (bound).--ISBN 978-0-385-67862-9
(pbk.).--ISBN 978-0-385-67861-2 (epub)

    I. Title.

PS8559.N475H85 2014   C813'.6   C2013-906368-4
                                      C2013-906369-2

This book is a work of fiction. Names, characters, places and incidents are products of the
author's imagination or are used fictitiously. Any resemblance to actual events or locales or
persons, living or dead, is entirely coincidental.

Book design: Kelly Hill
Cover images: (ladder) Aleksangel/Shutterstock.com;
(leaves) HelenStock/Shutterstock.com
Printed and bound in the USA

Published in Canada by Doubleday Canada,
a division of Random House of Canada Limited,
a Penguin Random House company

www.penguinrandomhouse.ca

10 9 8 7 6 5 4 3 2 1

Penguin
Random House
DOUBLEDAY CANADA

for Will and Rachel
everything always is

Deep in fall,
my neighbour—
how does he live, I wonder?

BASHO

MONDAY

🍁

Oh, the Hughmanity

dukkha, *suffering,*
or better, a basic unsatisfactoriness
that pervades all of life.

entry on Buddhism,
WIKIPEDIA

1. HUGH CAN TAKE IT

You can bear pain. Hugh can. But you can't stand to see it in others. It makes your hands and feet hurt. The grey room is full of grey people in various stages of pain. A little party: grouped by the window, sitting on the bed, ten or twelve of them. A woman kneeling by the nightstand says, *It's all up to you, up to Hugh*. Her cloudy hair, her dress in tatters. No.

No. It's a dream.

Eyes open.

Light? No. Three a.m. 3:02.

Okay.

3:07.

Hugh can bear pain. For himself it's not so bad, sometimes he doesn't even notice it. Hard when it's someone you can't help, though. Your mother. Cloudy hair all wisps and tendrils now. No. Don't think about Mimi, her hands, the pale phosphorescent skin of her chest, her searching eyes.

If you had a child, could you stand that? There's a question for you, for Hugh: why didn't you have a child? Okay, Ann had that abortion in the eighties. But that was somebody else's baby, Hugh is pretty sure. By then Ann was disconnecting herself from him by connecting with a few other people. You couldn't blame her, it was the times; women felt they had to be libertines in order to be liberated, and there was a fair amount of cocaine going around. He walked in on Ann once, having sex with some guy on a pile of coats at a party. Humiliating, titillating, to see her riding a set of naked limbs. Lots of reasons for shame. Hugh never even saw who it was—the guy pulled a coat over his face against the sudden light, and Hugh turned and left. That tawdry little pain hits again, a bee-sting of stupidity.

Why remember things at all.

Hugh lies in the dark, listening to the night's last rain falling straight into the basement of the gallery he lives above. Where valuable things are stored, furniture and boxes he ought to have moved, other people's art. He's tired of rain and basements and responsibility.

Della and Ken for dinner on Saturday, with Ruth—he should ask Newell too, but can't bear the burden of Burton, Newell's house guest. Della and Ken: that's a mess.

Think of something else: what to make for Ruth? Trivial, tepid, time-taking thought, a treat for old Ruth. She likes seafood crêpes. Okay, not rolled, but stacked like layer cake. Frozen crab, not that reeking stuff from the truck they had last time. *Fresh? Liars!* said Ruth.

The first time he was sent to live with her, four years old, confused, he thought they said to call her Aunt Truth. Newell waiting with him, waiting for their mothers to come back: two boys side by side at the long white table, watching Ruth laugh as she stood stirring at the stove, laughing at something Jasper said. Jasper flirting in his peacocky shirt, gesturing with his glass—he didn't even drink too much, back then. When was that? 1969. Warm and safe in Ruth's foster-kitchen, those boys, backs against fake ivy-covered bricks on washed-clean vinyl wallpaper. Ivy in pots too, growing, growing, shining green, kind and clean.

Almost asleep again, Hugh wakes. Clean towels, nobody lying, nobody angry, nobody going off the rails. Della waiting with them too, the next year, after her mother's breakdown. At the kitchen table, Della making a sandwich: square cheese, square white bread. The only thing she would eat at Ruth's. That time, anyway.

Ken didn't float into view till they were in university. Floating out again now? Doozy of an anniversary dinner, if so.

Yesterday at their house, Della was playing the piano. Hugh's mother's piano, already moved out of what will be, has to be—what turns out to have been her last apartment.

No. Go back. Yesterday, Hugh stood at the bottom of the short flight of stairs in Ken and Della's front hall, listening. Suspended rippling phrases. Schumann? Getting good again, now she has Mimi's Steinway. Della staring at the music, head tilted; the face of a dear horse, the same since childhood. From that low angle through the banisters, he could see her daughter, Elle, lying under the grand piano, painting Della's toenails with bright pink polish.

His empty life. Della and her daughter.

The woman and her little son; the funeral in the morning.

Hugh has pretty much stopped sleeping. He naps in the evening, put down by half a bottle of wine; wakes at midnight. Up for a few hours, naps again around four a.m. The phone alarm shouts him up at six. Every morning he thinks, behind glued-shut eyelids, you should change that setting. Every morning he lies there saying no, no. You have to get up.

There's the gallery to attend to.

At night the apartment above the gallery is a ship in fog, a Swiss Family Robinson treehouse. Wooden shelves and floors, plank deck stretched out over the framing room roof at the back, overhung by trees. In the early morning it's a form of tree-burial, and he gets out fast.

The espresso machine stands by the sink in the framing room. He gimps down the back stairs on stiff bare feet, pokes the button. A grinding noise. The red light blinks: out of water. Always something. The stupid thing cost more than a fridge, and now he has to keep filling it up. He takes the latte (milk only faintly sour) to his desk and sits staring at the earth's crust of bills, papers, orders. Dusty red files with pathetic labels like NOW! or DO THIS WEEK.

He has to get moving. At least get dressed. The sun has come out. At FairGrounds, the coffee shop next door, a shining young girl is whacking mats against the porch post, sending dust whirling up into a devil. Della's Elle? Or one of the friends. She can't see into the gallery, he hasn't turned on the lights. But he can see her shadow perfectly: a perfect shadow. Elle, yes. Aureole of pale hair in sunrise, sunrays. Another one joins her— they lean on the railing, nymphs just out of the larval stage. The other one is dark, makes Elle look like a negative. Savannah—no, this one's Nivea, Nevaya, something invented—it's Nevaeh (middle name Lleh ha ha). One kisses the other's cheek. Their limbs are long like the lines of broom and rail. Diagonals, perpendiculars.

Della will be in soon to thrash out the text for January's class poster. Kids' classes, et cetera, *Introduction to Watercolours*. Okay, but Ian Mighton's collage master class starts next week—get the flyer finished for that. Hugh himself is doing *Self-Portrait*, again.

And the funeral is at ten.

Well, that's okay, he hardly knew the woman. The little boy, though. Sad.

The empty room, the cup in front of him, his feet on the worn boards, the blinding window hiding him safe from view, his hermit shell upstairs: Hugh feels dizzy, as if the building is his mind, as if the whole world around him—the dead woman and her little son, Mighton coming, Della's Elle, non-Elle Nevaeh—all these who ought to be tangible are only instances of his ingenious mind inventing ways to occupy itself.

Last night until it rained he lay out on the deck above the framing room, wrapped in the old afghan Ruth made, under shifting shadows of branches, imagining a painting he will never paint. He can still see, or sense, it: the scale of it, the intricacy of the thinking. But he will not be able to execute it in paint or in collage, or by the xeroxing of the great.

The coffee is gone, it's eight. Get dressed. Grey tie, jacket.

Ruth's stomp on the front step, her key in the lock. Hugh is already hidden, hurrying halfway up the stairs. Can't bring himself to call out good morning.

The funeral, okay. Time to go. Here's Della, climbing the gallery steps in her good black coat, bright paisley lining firmly unrevealed. Sober, not distressed; black chiffon wrapped round her neck, black hair bound up above it. Fine funereal turnout, for someone they hardly knew. Two years of Saturday parent/child painting classes—the mother seemed very nice.

"Such a bright little spark, Toby," Della says. "He'd try anything. Not even five yet. Never minded glue on his hands, as some do." Her expressive face falls into a clowning sadness, but not to mock. She pulls her coat sleeve across the morning-dusty counter, then slaps at the sleeve. "Ken can't come—he's team-building, a couple of days rappelling down Elora Gorge or some fool thing."

Uncomfortable, knowing more than she does, Hugh doesn't answer.

He flips the sign to *Back Soon* and locks the door. Ruth has run over to the Mennonite Clothes Closet to check on the coat she wants; they'll go on ahead. It's okay, there are no customers.

"How did Gerald find them, did you hear?" Della asks Hugh as they go stride for stride.

"Ruth says he came home from work and opened the garage door as usual. The groceries were still in the back of the car. Melted ice cream."

"She never seemed anything but cheerful, in class."

Hugh tries to remember the woman. Brown hair, worried eyes, a tidy little bundle in the back of the classroom, a fond hand on her son's head.

"They were old," Della says. "She was nearly fifty. They tried for ages to have Toby, Gerald told me once. He looks terrible, I saw him in Lucky Foods yesterday, wandering the aisles."

"Ruth cleaned for them—she says it was postpartum, only it never stopped."

"Gerald had no idea, none in the world."

"You know him outside of class?"

"We bought the car from him last year, I guess that counts. And he came to class, about half the time. He was so proud of the shared parenting thing. She's from—she was from Iowa. Missed her family, maybe? Or just tired of always coping . . ."

They turn up Oak Street.

Della slides her hand through Hugh's arm. "It might have been an accident . . . She gets home from shopping and stops for a little nap, forgetting all about carbon monoxide. I did it myself, when Elly was little— sat in the car for a while when we got home, because she was asleep and I knew if I took her out of the carseat she'd wake up and start crying. We just didn't have a garage to get gassed in—"

She breaks off as they join a small stream of walkers funnelling into the churchyard. Leaning closer to Hugh, she whispers, "He was such a nice little boy. Not difficult at all."

Inside the church Gerald lurches down the aisle, huge in a grey suit, the too-friendly salesman's cheer ironed out of his eyes. Sedated, Hugh supposes.

Gerald kisses Della's cheek, shakes hands. "It would mean so much to her that Hugh came," he tells Della.

Hooked on his own name, Hugh's ear checks, then fixes his error: the poor man only said "that *you* came."

But his mind sticks on it as he follows Della along a pew. How much would it mean to her? Did she close the garage door thinking, *This will be good, Hugh will come. They'll all come to the church, Gerald will be such a great host . . .*

Stop. They don't know that she did it on purpose. Maybe she was just tired. Drove into the garage and dozed; didn't sit there thinking, I can't, I cannot do this anymore. Maybe she was not in terrible, terrible pain, the kind of pain that cannot be endured, the kind that you beg your son for release from, over and over.

(DELLA)

over the lawn beside the gallery (last shadows of last leaves shudder in
small wind, ashes) will they burn the boy's body? (small ash grit)
into FairGrounds, say hi to Elly
(my mother's twelve identical canvases lined up around the room, strict
economical palette, fishing boat after boat after boat after boat after boat
after boat after boat after boat boat boat boat—is that twelve yet?—all
those boats paid the mortgage, who knows how they managed,
Dad sad in the Barcalounger all night, unable to shift or go up the stairs)
                                        at least Elly never has that to deal with
sad smell of his clothes the pity of him   eyes closed in late afternoon
a cup of tea for his throat with whiskey in it
can't even look at poor old Jasper now   close my eyes against it
              nothing could have made me close Elly's eyes forever, nothing
Elly at the counter, who loved me more than anything,
nothing in her eyes for me now
how can love be gone, that giant ardent unbearable passionate love, gone?
the light in her face under the skin when she talks with Nevaeh, smiling as
she pulls the lever, the scream of the frother covering what she says
turn away so as not to read her lips, she deserves a private life
how rough a time she's having—is the pain only from living, the pity of
it, or from some failing of mine or Ken's?
dear love, the mouth tugging at the breast and smiling, dancing in the
bedroom, nothing sweeter, so open between us it could never be closed
      and yet here it is, gone
(hollow piece under the breastbone, how to do that in clay? how to get at
that pocket of air there. . . . identical, symmetrical, twelve boats, hull and
prow laid down in a figure eight, pencil on blue-washed canvas, paint in
patches, paint-by-number, torn postcard)
                              and Ken—where is he really? has he left us?
never mind never mind
if he is gone I will have the bed to myself and my thoughts
what passes for thoughts
nothing in my head but eyes

2. FALLING FOR HUGH

Hugh lives his life in the second person, never quite sure whether it's *Hugh* or *you*. Either one demands, accuses, requires responsibility. You'll do it—or was that Hugh'll do it? You/Hugh said everything would be okay. Why did you leave? Where did Hugh go?

It works the other way, too. Ruth, who works mornings as the gallery assistant (ostensibly so Hugh can spend time at the hospice), answers the phone on speaker, and a man's voice says, "May I speak to you?"

"Go right ahead," she says. A short silence. "Who's that?" she asks.

"Uh, Mark, from the Ace?"

"Well, how can we help you?"

"I'm looking for Hugh?"

"Oh! I thought you said *you*." Ruth laughs to herself as she moves to the window to yell out to Hugh. He is listening from the porch, where he's been untangling strings of firefly lights he thought might brighten up the gallery sign.

The Ace Grill wants their staff awards certificates framed, Mark has a few concerns; Hugh will pick up the certificates, and can you get them done by . . . ? Yes, Hugh can, for Saturday, for sure. The yellowing cream plastic of the receiver is heavy in his hand. The phone is almost as old as Ruth is. It's after noon already, and she only works mornings. She's getting her coat on, an old navy pea jacket. She pulls a red knitted hat out of the pocket. Still only October, but she is always cold. Her eyes are huge behind her glasses. He loves and is irritated by her in almost equal halves. He is stuck with her.

Trotting off for the day's second visit to the Clothes Closet, she calls back, "You be careful!" Old bat. Hugh taps his teeth together gently to keep from growling. Alternating sides, a bit OCD. His teeth are hurting. He has to shake off this bad temper.

He reaches to hook the lights over the sign, steps up to the next rung of the ladder, and misses it.

His foot slams down on nothing.

He falls.

Twenty feet, a long time—down onto a slumped bank of cedar chips. Lies on his back, stars (look, pointy stars!) circling in his vision. When he closes his eyes he sees op art, distorted checkerboards melting into Dali, so he opens them again.

Wind bellowed out of him, he lies there, unable to gasp for the longest time. It becomes clear, in a sunburst of cheap pop epiphany, that he has been this way his whole life: unable to breathe, lying as still as possible to avoid pain.

An ant on a leaf of grass in front of his opened eye, clouds in the baby blue sky, small people and their children going about the streets on their little paths like ants: all of them in pain all their lives, all dying. Mimi in the hospice, Ruth on her way to the Clothes Closet. How the clouds too can be in pain he does not trouble to sort out.

Then his ribs creak open like a rusted umbrella and the blood comes drumming into his ears and eyes. A stroke? Fiftyish, he's about due. Nobody comes to help—nobody could have seen him fall from the ladder perched at the end of the porch.

For five or ten minutes he lies alone, dying or not dying, in a lot of pain. Then he gets up and puts the ladder in the shed again. Never mind the lights for now.

His head buzzes or blanks, something electrical wrong in there—he cannot stop thinking about Ruth, out of all the people around him who tremble on the edge of falling, ladders poised over the abyss, nobody to notice when they fall. Ruth, who should not be living alone on the OAS. He does her taxes, he knows she doesn't have enough money even with what he pays her at the gallery (two hundred a week for five mornings so he can go to the hospice; she's up early anyway) and the occasional cleaning job. She won't take his advice, clear out her cluttered house and move into an apartment. She wants to stay independent. Which she's not, anyway; she's entirely dependent on him continuing to hire her and pay her, even though she can never remember to say "Argylle Gallery" when she answers the goddamned phone. She is not an ideal employee.

But the fall is forcing empathy upon him. As he hangs the *Back Soon* sign in the window he figures out—and this is a real epiphany—that if she moved into a pleasant apartment with less stuff and less to worry about, she would actually be pre-dead.

He should be picking up the certificates from the Ace. But here he goes instead, ducking into the Mennonite Clothes Closet.

The trotting tassel of Ruth's red hat moves through close-packed aisles on the other side of the store. She plans to offer them less than the posted price for a corduroy jacket that has caught her fancy. She's been checking it every day. Hasn't quite worked up her nerve to suggest $5 instead of $15. "Strictly speaking," she told Hugh this morning, "I do not need a jacket. My navy peacoat's still good—*that* was a find—but the coppery tone, this wide-wale corduroy, just matches one I had when I was a girl, and I've got my wanter turned up loud."

No good for Hugh to buy it for her. She would whip out her little purse (pouched pink leather, like her mouth) and pay him back.

So he sidles down the aisles outside her narrowed peripheral vision, as she pretends to look everywhere but at the jackets. While she examines shoes, Hugh slips a sharp-edged, brown hundred dollar bill into the left-hand pocket of the corduroy jacket, from the opposite side of the musty-smelling rack. Ducks along behind the racks and out of the store.

Watching from the gallery he is rewarded, ten minutes later, by her squat copper-clad torso swanning along George Street, on her way home. Beyond his hope, he sees her shove her hands into the pockets. He can almost hear the crinkle. She pulls her left hand out, and her look of thrilling glory is enough to fill his cup forever.

You did it. Good for Hugh.

3. HUGH BELONG TO ME

There isn't really time, but Hugh stops in at the hospice on his way to the Ace. He runs up the shallow steps, nods to the nurse on duty (Judy, not the sourpuss), up the two flights of steep stairs. He walks down the polished hall, feeling the living strength of his stride under him. Spring even in his fall-jangled legs; the opening and closing of his ribs, still breathing. Unlike these fossils parked in wheelchairs along the hall walls, strings of oxygen whispering into nostrils, glassy-eyed, lopsided stares.

Mimi's room. Door ajar: an aide is turning her onto her side, nightgown gaping. Hugh waits. Through the narrow opening he watches the nurse's burnt sienna hands on his mother's skin. Alabaster shot with cerulean, lemon; patches of almost alizarin. If you painted her. Poor body.

The nurse is Nolie Suarta, he sees. She comes out on silent feet. A smile, a little duck of her head to apologize for being in his way. Which she wasn't.

Chair by the bed. To sit, sit. Sitting, watching. This is all there is to do.

Mimi's hair clouds on the pillow, the white of it a surprise every time. Her hair must always have been what you saw first, Hugh thinks, each time she came back. Abundant chestnut, moving of its own accord, almost like snakes. Part of the exhaustion of being a good son: thinking good thoughts about the mother, keeping thoughts good when you branch off into memory, what was real and what was not. Snakes, ladders.

Her eyes are shut. She's had her dose, then. His head hurts, his teeth hurt. Back molars, both sides. Don't clench. He feels in a pocket for blue gel pills, pops two. Okay, three. The skin under her jaw begins to tremble. What does she dream, inside there? Dreaming of doors, a long corridor, a way out.

People who are alone sometimes get a dog. So they have a reason to get up. To bathe it feed it talk to it play fetch chase sticks run with, to love.

If you cannot get love you can at least give it.

(DELLA)

holding it off all day   Ken—why is he—
can't breathe   breath gone   is he dead?
                                                 has he ceased to love us?
                                     no there is not much question there

listen! there's some explanation
he's broken his finger   bitten his tongue
no crying in the grocery store   Kleenex in the freezer how kind
Gerald at the casket   he must have loved her
unless they had run down   unless that was the problem
she killed herself because she was alone   was going to be alone
but Toby, the darling

              chicken, eggs / milk, cheese, yogurt / grapes, raisins
                 everything on this list becomes something else
                 everything that is becomes something else

Toby and his mother   *Hugh and his mother*
no wonder Hugh and Ann were together   Ann is like Mimi used to be
all melodrama   just because it's icy doesn't mean it isn't   overblown
how is Jason coping—tough to have
Ann for a mother   anything left to sit on in that house?
I can't fix this   Elly can't imagine
I can't jump in there with furniture   Jason could live with us
Ann wouldn't let him, she needs an audience   and now she's got a boarder?
Elly says there's never anything to eat in their fridge
can't see Ann stoic in the grocery store
like ever-loving Saint Me
and Jack gone now gone since Xmas, ten months   *and Ken*
but even then, Ann has not died of it
                                                      is it the same
                                     no there is not much question there

4. HUGH WILL TAKE CARE OF IT

The basement has to be faced. Climbing the porch steps Hugh sees damp edges on the boards and remembers the night's rain, the sluicing sound. He goes straight down the cellar stairs, not letting himself pause or turn to paying bills or other also distasteful but less horrible tasks.

It's bad. The floor is wet. In the permadusk—have to get a better light down here—dark patches stain the sides of cardboard boxes, tidemark or spongemark.

Della's stuff: he moved it up a shelf last time, it's fine. The Parkers' boxes, ceramics and soapstone; the stuff will be okay, but they're heavy, the cardboard will give if he tries to move them. His mother's extra furniture. Why is it down here, he asks himself unasking. Because the things are too good to give away; because she may still ask, What have you done?

What has Hugh done? The rosewood Eames lounge-chair ought to be upstairs, but the leather reeks of fifty years of Joy and cigarettes. Hugh hates it. Sell it, then! She'll never know. He shifts it out of the path of a streamlet shining on dank cement. Boxes of china, old clothes: reshuffle, clear a wider path to the drain.

At the wall, Hugh's heart sinks. Mighton's boxes. Why did you leave them over here? Right in the line of damp down the wall. There will be mould. Awkward—the boxes will have to be opened to repack them. Even knowing Mighton for twenty years, thirty years, it will feel odd to paw through his things.

To paw, period. To own, to care for. To be a caretaker, to hold on to for others. Hugh steps in water and feels the slick slide of it, falls to one knee—saves himself, hurts his leg. Pants black-smeared. Now he'll have to climb all those stairs to change. Twenty-eight stairs in all. This, it seems, is what sends him over the edge. He is separately dismayed, out-side himself, to hear the sob.

Della's long pale face peers down the stairs. "Yoo-hoo!"

"Don't come down!" he shouts up. Wiping his face.

"Hugh? You okay? Hugh?" Della calls down, keeps calling, until he comes to the bottom step. "Did Ken call? Or text? I'm just wondering—I'm supposed to pick up Elle but . . ."

He tries to think. Ken. Can't pull himself away from all this wreckage to remember what he's supposed to know, supposed to say. Impatience sprouts like mould in his mind, fractalating, pixilating what he was thinking.

"I'll be up in a sec," he shouts. "Don't come down, it's a mess."

He empties and replaces the buckets that stand under the windows, and goes up to get on the blower, on the horn. Get Dave the fuck over here to do something about the cracks, it's got to be now, not next spring. Give him a piece of your mind, or get Ruth to. Ruthless.

As he emerges from the basement Della says, "Have you checked your upstairs phone?"

It so irritates him that she treats him this way, like a baby brother, like a son who needs reminding about every tiny thing—he can't even answer. Has no idea what to say, anyway, not knowing whether or what exactly Ken has told Della about wanting to quit—

Her eyes, beseeching.

Why is it him who, he who, *yoo-hoo*, Hugh who has to deal with this?

"I haven't done the poster copy," she says, after a minute's silence. "Or Mighton's flyer. I will. Today. I'm going now."

He hates that meekness of hers more than anything else.

But she can't let it go. "I'm just—Ken—"

He is already up the stairs, motioning to his black-streaked pants.

"Have to change!" he calls backward, vanishing around the turn. "I'll check, I'll check."

L leaves FairGrounds to run to school for Studio class—her mom forgot to pick her up, again. Late, going to be late, run. Frick *frick*, flick *flick*, legs click off distance, glad to go after too much pulling espresso, ex-presto, perfecto. Frick, school is weird, after homeschool, even only doing art and algebra. But one does need to get into art school next year, to get the hell out of here, and IB marks will make applications easier than a vomiting cascade of parent-based evaluations. Only, even with one's coterie, getting to/hanging around at school sucks.

And always always always the panicky urge to go home and work on the *Republic*. At school she does not talk about it. Only Jason has seen it. She hasn't even let her mom go through it and she believes, she does believe, her mom would not unless invited. Because it's her work, her self. Her mom would not. Her dad would, probably, but he's not that interested in art and probably fears to find what hellish interior thoughts she harbours. The nudes would make him stop looking, even though they are mostly just repro Voynich Manuscript–type ladies. Not all of them drawn from life. Only Nevaeh.

Last night, Nevaeh—can't even talk even inside about that. Like fire, like dry ice, wanting to touch it, to see if it will burn you. To touch her mouth. A great canyon gapes between wanting/doing. If one does one small thing, or set of things, in a doze, in a daze, does that mean—? Silk armskin sliding, foreheads touched in fond embrace, is one then—?

Languid, head lolling over the edge of the bed, Nevaeh's mouth upside down looks like another, other person's mouth. Just as beautiful, but lighter, happier. (Onion-skin portrait for the *Republic*, upside down/right side up, two of them side by side. Or negatives . . .)

N—let N stand for the unknown—is what one wants *that moment* but but BUT. Then could one still talk to her? Or Jason? And Savaya, what about Savaya?

A wind, and Orion zips up beside L, slowing his silver bike to match her stride.

"Carry your fucking books, miss?"

L laughs and shows her empty hands, her douche-pack with brushes and pencils and phone.

They move on together, Orion balancing, easy. He is the easiest to be with. Knows himself, maybe. Orion is like Newell—who's back in town, doing the master class.

"Excited for the master class, and Master—Burton?" she asks Orion.

"—bation," he says, in unison. "Yeah. I have to pick up the lady, who-ever, Mrs. Lovett. She's staying at Jason's."

"I'll go with you. We're doing the cyclorama for the backdrop, me and Jason."

"Art, Art! How lucky we all are," Orion cries, going into paean mode, a long hand flung out over path and river. "To be at our glorious school—when compared to all other schools, even that ruling-class übermensch-haus Sheridan Tooley went to—really working, learning stuff that will be useful. Assholery and tomfoolery is everywhere, fine, that's an education in itself. We're good, we're so *good*."

Yet he looks keyed up, fearful underneath the joy. Underneath, every-body carries it. This earthcrack the voices come out of, this crater of sadness. Everyone does.

At four p.m. Hugh pours himself a glass of wine, a civilized thing to do at a small gallery without much hope of selling anything on a Monday afternoon. Maybe he should get back on the ladder, do those lights.

Ruth walks in. Outside her working hours.

"Look what was in here," she says, pulling a gloved fist out of her pocket. There's that bright brown hundred. "I'm going to have to take this back. It's too much to keep—I'd be stealing it from the Clothes Closet. Those Mennonites do such good work."

Hugh pours a little more malbec and offers to make Ruth a coffee. He drains his glass, standing at the espresso machine in the framing room.

"Nice jacket," he calls back into the office.

"Well, it does fit," she says, smoothing her cuff. "Lucky day already, even without the extra."

"I don't know," he says. "I think you ought to keep that." Spurs his sputtering brain to think of why. "It's like it was meant. You've been looking at that jacket for so long . . . It was your luck, waiting for you."

"Lucky for the Clothes Closet it was me that bought it, because *some* of the people in there would not think of giving that money back, and you know who I mean."

He knows, he knows exactly who she means. The *Asians*, the *Natives*, the *blacks*. Here's where he wants to smack her upside the head, but she's an old woman. How do you go about changing her now?

"I thought of giving it to the Conservative Party," she says. "They really need it."

Hugh's teeth tap together tenderly. It makes him feel like a dragon, a tempered, brutal force that helps smaller beings, but someday might eat them. Or burn them to ashes.

"*You* really need it," he says.

She pulls the hundred taut between her fingers, staring at it. You don't see a lot of those around. "What would Hugh do?" she asks.

No, that's his own ear's *Hugh*. Ruth's just saying *you*.

"Take us out for dinner, is what you'd do," he says. "If I were Hugh."

She shakes her head, says she'll think about it. What would be best. "I'll go to the hospice now, and I'm working tonight, catering. Must be off!" Out she goes.

Okay, next thing. Over to Curios & Curiouser, old Jasper's antique/ junk shop, next porch over on this touristy, flower-hung Main Street, Yourtown.

Jasper is hanging his own lights, birdlike on the top board of a worn stepladder. He should not be up there, not after a long, late lunch. He's brought his wineglass out onto the porch with him, forgetful of yard-arm convention. Watching Jasper's thin limbs tremble on the ladder is physical pain; hurts you in the head, the hands, the legs.

Hugh can't remember when Jasper did not drink. Was a time, Ruth says. Long ago, she and he were almost, or sometimes, a couple. Jasper at the stove in Ruth's kitchen, wineglass in hand, telling rude jokes that Hugh and Della did not get—later, Newell explained them. Jasper's shop is in trouble, that troubles Ruth. Hugh too. The old guy can't be allowed to sink. The cheque is ready. Hugh wrote it out first thing and put it in his pocket with Ruth's hundred dollar bill.

A frail grey hand quivers, stretching out and searching behind him, and Hugh takes it. Jasper descends, legs not shaking so much once he's on the ground. They go through to the little cash desk at the back, Hugh tripping on Jasper's heels past jars and tea-chests stacked on brittle chairs; sliding pyramids of boxes, mahogany and ormolu, ivory-inlaid and trick-trapped, Jasper's specialty being things in which to put other things. A litter of orders and accounts and bills crowds the clear desk space down to six inches at the drawer's edge. Jasper doesn't sit at his desk anyway, even when drinking. Always agitated.

Hugh takes the cheque out of his shirt pocket, neatly folded in half. Unfolds it, still warm from his chest, and puts it on the desk.

"Pay me back when you can." (Jasper wouldn't take it if he didn't say that.)

Jasper's wattley throat works. "Ten thousand—you—it's too much."

Hugh can't be bothered to argue today. Trots out the unassuming smile, the shrug he learned from Newell. That will win Jasper over. "Cluttering up the bank. Useless unless it's used," Hugh says.

"You—you can trust me for it."

"I know, but don't be worried. It's nothing. I like your store, that's all. I need to buy my curios somewhere, and you're handy."

Out of the store again before Jasper can cry. That would be unpleasant.

6. GUESS HUGH'S COMING TO DINNER

Heading out onto the porch, look, there's Newell himself, crossing the street. His head lifts to the evening breeze, hair swooped back and cheekbones strong—matinee idol superimposed on a ten-year-old boy, to Hugh's eyes. Hugh's oldest, dearest friend, his Ruth-brother.

Seeing him, Newell calls, "Hugh! Just who I want. Help me pick a bottle of wine."

Hugh looks back at Jasper's window. The old guy seems not to have heard that Pavlovian *wine* bell; his stiff arm comes up to salute again, waving the cheque in thanks.

Turning away, Hugh quickens stride to catch Newell on the doorstep of the new wine shop, a fancy place people still eye with suspicion.

"You okay?" Newell's attention, a strong beam, focuses on Hugh.

Hugh shakes his head, then nods. "Squandering my inheritance."

"Slipping Jasper some cash?"

"Tell me, does money fix everything?"

"Physician, fix thyself. That Largely woman is not answering my lawyer's calls."

Hugh does not want to talk about all that. "Late for a wine run. Emptied the cellar again?"

"What are you doing for dinner? Come eat with us."

Newell puts an arm round Hugh as they duck through the door, hung with blinking pumpkin lights and mini-nooses. Friday is Hallowe'en. How often does it fall on a weekend? Never, that Hugh can remember.

"Yes?" Newell checks the stacked cartons, the specials, waiting for an answer.

Hugh's been stalling. He hates—*hates*—Newell's current houseguest and old mentor, Ansel Burton, a plump and aging queen who hates Hugh right back in spades, doubled and redoubled. But Hugh loves Newell, his oldest friend, and derives comfort from his company. He could use some comfort. And a good bottle of wine, since he's spending all his money anyway. If Newell will let him buy.

"Pinot," Hugh says. Clarity, that's what he needs this evening, and a decent meal. "And if you're cooking, yes." Burton's cooking is ghastly, all veal and cream.

Ten thousand was too much to give to Jasper, but it will get the curio shop through till Christmas, maybe prevent him selling his half of the building to Lise Largely. So you had, Hugh had, an ulterior motive. It was only going into the RRSP anyway, to lose value in a sinking line. Jasper can be the bad investment this year.

Newell breezes around the store, chats up the pretentious clerk, charms the girl restocking the beer fridge, finds a thirty-year-old port. Spreads his effluence effortlessly to make the world a better, more flowing place. And buys the wine. He always, always buys.

Hugh watches this performance, not at all for the first time, and compares it to some of Newell's best work. Not *Blitzed Craig* or *Catastrophe*, that's just formula TV stuff. But earlier, when he was a smart, hilarious japester kid in New York. Or Henry V, the years at Stratford before he went to pieces. *Once more into the breach, dear liquor store girl! A little touch of Newell in the night* . . . An older king, these days. Now when Newell stops smiling, lines still fold his eyes, skid down from nose to mouth.

They climb the single long flight to Newell's condo in Deer Park, the new building on the river. There is an elevator, of course, but Newell has outside stairs as well, up to a rooftop patio with a glossy border of dark green hedge. A tree up there. Money is its own reward.

From Newell's open black-lacquered kitchen bulges a great white toad, bulbous head squatting on a pair of drooping Victorian ladyshoulders cased in mauve cashmere. As always, Burton combines the gross and the dainty.

Hugh knows his physical revulsion has always been plain to Burton, and causes most of Burton's hatred for him. Honestly, why has he come? He can't be that lonely. He pauses on the threshold, thrown into gloom by Burton's rich vowels.

"Why, Boy! You didn't tell me we were having guests—I have not made my toilette!"

He is meticulously dressed, as always. The archness, if not soured by such sharp dislike, might be funny. Some people do like Burton. Does

Newell? Not really, Hugh believes. Is indebted to him, tied to him by a purple string of mutual obligation and shame.

"Hey there, Burton." Hugh makes a small production of wiping his clean shoes on the coir mat. "You're in town?"

"*Patent*-ly," Burton says, an actual sneer developing his lip.

You'd think Newell would stop putting himself through this, but it's one of his little innocences: he can't help believing his two closest friends will someday be friends.

"Now, what have you brought me?" Burton asks, burying his nose in the bag. "Lovely! I do relish a good Pinot—ooh, port! and it's prim*eval*!—must I wait for après-ski?"

Newell pulls the port's cork and pours, a gentle slide into each heavy glass. "It's an occasion, Hugh—Ansel starts his master class at the performing arts school tomorrow. Scenes from *Sweeney Todd*. He's the master, I'm just a ringer, brought in to play Sweeney."

"I cast my pearls," Burton says, calm after a long swallow of mahogany port. "We're to Meet the Creatures tonight, you'll have to come help Newell remember who's who. And whatsie, the broken-down one they've brought me for Mrs. Lovett—Ivy. Ivy Suet, is it, Boy? She was a fixture at I of O."

"IFO?"

"Idea of Order," Newell says. "Experimental theatre company, big in the nineties." Burton sneers again. "Not Suet. Ivy Sage," Newell tells Hugh. "Nice, intelligent. Eccentric."

"Pudding face, that must be the connection." Burton waves his hands in a self-forgiving swaggle.

"Good casting for Mrs. Lovett," Newell says.

The port calms Hugh, too. In a high leather chair at the counter he prepares to watch the dinner show. Burton, swaddling a huge white apron over the mauve cashmere, stations himself at the other end of the long black slate counter to chop for salad, playing the humble prep cook with a running commentary and a tea cozy squashed into a porkpie hat on his head.

Newell cooks fast and fluidly, like he does most things, relaxed and at peace; Burton boasts about the beef, organic wagyu (his choice, no surprise), and the truffle oil tater tots now sizzling away, which he made and froze last week. "Merely choux paste with riced potatoes in the batter, but between Hugh and I, ha ha, I dispensed with the black truffles. It's the truffle *oil* that gives the true *tendresse . . .*"

Truffle oil, the biggest scam perpetrated on the dining public since artifical vanilla: pale chemically induced resemblance to truffles fading quickly into gasoline and damp rot. But Burton likes to be an expert. Hugh nods into his port and lets it go.

From time to time, in the inexplicable good mood that settles over him whenever he has manoeuvred Burton and Hugh together, Newell breaks into a line of song, "*. . . the trouble with poet is how do you know it's deceased? Try the priest—*"

The third time, he checks himself as Burton pokes the button on the iPod. Paul Simon fills the room instead, *"The Mississippi delta was shining like a National guitar . . ."*

Burton stops the music. "How can that be glorified with the term Music? If you must have rock, where do I find Pink Floyd on this thing? You find it, Boy. *Dark Side*, now *that's* an album." In an egregious gangland grate he grinds out, *"Monee-e-ey! It's a gas . . ."*

Hugh watches with a schooled expression; he feels painfully old, but considerably younger than Burton. Wiping his hands on a linen towel, Newell slides the iPod to something Cuban. Burton swishes off to the washroom, in a huff.

Exhausting, really.

"Sad this morning," Hugh tells Newell, while they're alone. To explain away his glum face. "Della and I went to the funeral, the woman who killed herself and her four-year-old."

"I knew them," Newell says, surprising Hugh. "I bought the Saab from Gerald, he had to import it. You knew that."

Hugh can't remember if he did.

"The kid was great. Toby." Newell has immense capacity for sadness. More than Hugh, by a million miles. But he's cooking now, at the apex: steaks sliding onto warmed plates, pretentious tater tots jostled and nestled, every move skillful and graceful. Newell's hands are beautiful.

Returning, Burton tosses his exquisite salad, teak claws clap-clacking in his clutching old paws. It is Hugh's job to be civil and pour the wine, and when they sit at table, to enjoy the steak and swallow the potato things whole. He hears himself say, "How long are you visiting, Burton?" The plaguing question he had not meant to voice.

"We thought you'd never ask!" Burton puts out a fat hand and covers Newell's, which lies discarded beside his still-full plate.

Newell seems not to be eating, but has opened the second bottle of Pinot. He looks up and meets Hugh's eye. The frank, unfamiliar shock of contact makes Hugh realize they haven't talked in a long time. He finds his breath constricted.

"I've asked Burton to stay here for good," Newell says.

Fucking fucking fucking hell.

Newell's face is a mask. Only his mouth moves, as if there's a person under there somewhere, in the dark. "We're both alone, and neither of us is—"

Burton simpers. "Oh, I'm an old crisis, Hugh knows that! But I think there's something to be said for returning to safe harbour, don't you? After life's journeying." The port, the steak, the wine have made him expansive. Powerful enough, here, to lie back in his chair. "I see myself as Newell's—what? His elder brother." Burton's pasty hand squeezes Newell's, which does not move. Then it does, turning to clasp his kindly.

"His loving introducer to matters of the heart." Burton's eyes are downcast, his mouth a reflective rosebud. It's a pose out of an old acting manual: emotion recalled in tranquillity.

Every time, every time Hugh sees the toad Burton, Newell's voice comes back to his ear from years ago, saying, "I was twelve, but he knew already what I was."

What, not who.

Back then, when they were twelve, Hugh knew who Newell was. Not Burton's pet. Newell was an open heart, an open face; a boy as unhappy as he was himself, but without the sideways look he acquired after Burton introduced him.

Hugh remembers feeling it even in childhood, the powerful fury rising in his chest, his head, into his jaw, and gently turned aside by the control of delicate tapping.

Ivy stands in the empty living room. Four French doors (three French hens) open onto a garden pavement that leads over to a low wall, and the river flowing gently along. It's pretty. They go upstairs, turn right, and the woman opens the door.

A beautiful empty room. Silence.

Ivy takes a breath.

She's so lucky to get this, a broad, airy bedroom in a pleasant house by the river. For a month-long artist residency, the school won't keep her in a hotel. The other offer is the drama teachers' spare room, but their marriage is coming apart and Ivy can't bear fighting. This place is perfect. An old family house built in the thirties, substantial, stained glass, inlaid floors, front and back staircases. But only two people living in it, a woman and her son, in grade twelve at the school.

The woman, the owner of the house—*Ann*, and Jason is the son—Ann walks to the window and tries to open it; for air, or to show Ivy a silver knife of river coming up beside the house, but it seems stuck. Ivy's window (hers already) looks over the short driveway. The tree outside has lost half its leaves, but the black branches are pretty. The glass is spotless.

Perfect, Ivy thinks. Her ill-arranged life back in Toronto is dirty, upsetting, and crammed full of stuff. This is so clean and bare—an empty bookshelf, an empty dresser, an empty bed.

"There's an ensuite," the woman—*Ann, Ann*—says. She opens the door to display white tiles, a bevelled window over the bathtub. "This used to be the master. Before. Jason's dad left us, last Christmas, but we're getting over it." She's blonde, a bob cut straight across and dragged behind her ears. Minimalist hair. "He was in management at the Quaker plant, he ran off with his secretary. Like a fifties movie."

She draws her thumb along her bottom lip to lock her mouth closed. Then she says, "It's a new mattress."

"Well, that's—perfect," Ivy says. "Ann."

Ann takes her cheque and goes away.

The inlet of river spears right up into the side garden. Here, close by the window, Ivy can see it lapping, happy at the brink. Yellow kayak belly-down against a silvered old stepladder, black steps cut into the green bank of grass. The boy must use it. Or maybe that's Ann's shirt flung to dry across the yellow. Ivy tries the window again, but nope. It is painted stuck, three inches up. A flap in the storm window lifts to reveal three round ventilation holes, a slight breath of air. Ivy presses her face against wavering glass to see the real river's edge. Railway ties brace the bank; the river floods every year, Ann said. Perfect, Ivy tells herself. If it floods, the kayak will float up to my sill—I need a chisel to pry this window open—and I'll paddle away. Somehow managing to screw myself into the kayak without flipping upside down.

She lets the curtain fall and listens. Down the hall, the boy, the son is laughing, cackling. Sounds like he's practising laughing. Not much to laugh about in this strange vacant house. The living room downstairs is entirely empty. No chairs, not even a carpet. Bare fireplace, hearth and innards stark black. Not one picture. Ann's aesthetic "embraces austerity."

In her hollowed-out, hallowed-up bedroom, the empty space, the holy, Ivy sits on the bed for a little while—planning, in spite of herself, what to put on the empty shelves.

Next, back to the school office to sign forms and get keys. She walks along reading *Arms and the Man*, for relief from *Sweeney Todd*. A car horn blats beside her, and she jumps.

It's the school principal—Rosy, Jeep, Cherry—Jerry Pink. "Want a lift?"

"Oh, thanks," Ivy says. "That would be—perfect." She feels sad to leave the leaf-strewn sidewalk. "Pretty town," she says, with some idea of flattering Mr. Pink by extension.

"Full of divorcées." Eyes on her, not on the road. He laughs. "You always read a book while you're walking? Better not let our parents see you doing that."

Ivy does not need to ask why not: it looks weird. She doesn't mind.

"Party at my house tonight, after Meet the Teacher—we hand out the teaching awards from last year. Newell is coming, and the great Ansel

Burton, all you drama types. Come along and get acquainted. I'll send a kid to pick you up."

He swings into the drive by the portables. Pats her leg, staring to see if that causes trouble. Ivy stares back at him using her Downs' syndrome face, borrowed from her last gig, an interactive improv workshop production for the differently abled, one of the best things she's ever done in her life. I am completely unaware of you as a man, and therefore not prey, her face says. Plus, see? I am ugly. She steps out of the car.

He laughs again. "No more reading books while you walk!" he shouts as he pulls away.

The world is so full of men, no wonder there are so many divorcées.

Ivy walks home in the late afternoon. A long walk in sprinkling rain; she should have taken her car after all. The woman (Ann, *Ann* is her name; and Jay?—no, the son is Jason) is moving a big armoire out of the living room. The last piece of furniture left in there. With a mat under one end, Ann is yanking it along foot by foot.

Ivy can't get up the stairs until the thing is shifted. "Do you need help?"

"I learned how after the divorce," Ann says. "You can move anything you want to by yourself."

"Where are you putting it?"

"Out."

Ivy steadies the other end and pushes. Not too much, so she's not butting in and helping. They make some headway.

The son—*Jason*, yes—blows in like leaves drifting through the front door. He slides through the armoire gap and up the stairs, completely silent, dragging a gym bag, a naked dressmaker's judy, and two neon-orange puffed down jackets. The kind that make Ivy look like a cozy beach ball.

"I cleaned out a shelf of the fridge for you," his mother says.

Jason ignores her, rounds the stair-turn, vanishes. Are he and Ann not talking? Oh, wait—she means for Ivy, for *her* food. Ivy has not bought any yet.

"Where's the store?"

"Three blocks west to the Lucky Dollar, or drive to the mall for Superstore."

"I'll shop tomorrow," Ivy says. Feeling forlorn.

"Eat with us tonight, if you want."

Ann is not asking very nicely, but Ivy says thanks, perfect—then goes up to her room to look at her empty shelves. The lovely emptiness, bare wood, clean walls. *So unlike the home life of our own dear Queen.* The thought of her apartment, and its tenant, makes her feel sad and sick.

When Ann calls up the stairs, "Dinner! Jason?" there's no answer from the boy's room. Ivy sticks her head out into the hall and waits. Smells like spaghetti down there.

No response, nothing.

"Jason!" Ann's voice comes shrilling up again. Then, "Ivy? Will you tell him dinner? He's got his headphones on."

Ivy slips down the hall and knocks on Jason's door, too lightly. Again, louder, to penetrate the headphones. Still nothing.

She hesitates, not wanting to find him in an embarrassing situation, then turns the knob and opens it into a blizzard of white, a floating storm of airy nothing swirling away from the door's gust of air. Jason gapes, delighted, head up and mouth open as if to catch a snowflake of down.

"It just—it just—!" He pulls the white lines and pops his earbuds out, trying to tell her.

"Exploded?"

"Ex*plo*—*!* I just, I slid the knife—" He motions with an X-Acto knife along the orange nylon of a jacket, and another eddy of down swoops up in the breeze the motion makes. "I didn't know—I didn't think it would do this!"

For the first time he looks alive. Down begins to settle on his dark mink hair, on the brightness of his suddenly open face, and Ivy cannot help but be uplifted.

8. HUGH GETS EATEN

Hugh walks over to Meet the Teacher with Newell and Burton, although it nearly kills him. Strung up with the strain of dinner and Newell's announcement, he finds it hard to endure Burton's self-important spiel to the drama students' parents, all seeking reassurance that the master class is worth the after-school hours and the two hundred dollar fee. A précis of the brilliance of Sondheim, the use of Stanislavskian ensemble in musical theatre, tra la la, history of Burton's brilliance, theatres he's graced, actors privileged to have worked under him, more on Burton's brilliance. Questions?

Parent after parent stands to ask if their offspring will have a significant role, or a solo, apparently not listening to Burton's repetitive ramble re: *emphasis on company*, collaborative philosophy, exploratory work, and "nothing set in stone."

Newell is not contracted, except as eye candy, for this parent event. Once he's been introduced, and has waved and grinned for the crowd, he slides away and stands with Hugh in the shadows by the back wall. Just like junior high. "He's happy," Newell says.

"In his element," Hugh says. It's hard, but vital, not to sulk.

"You surprised?"

What can you say to that? Hugh tries, "I hadn't realized he was looking for a harbour." Even that sounds petulant.

Newell leans closer. "He's had a rough couple of years. His lover, a— well, they went to Bali for treatment, but it didn't work. Not AIDS, some kind of cancer."

Hugh assumes that Newell helped to finance that.

"It went very badly at the end and they were stuck there because, oh you know, all the shit and horrors. He died in June. It was a fish cure or something spiritual."

Newell's brown leather bomber jacket smells good. Old, real, like himself. The Hermès cologne nobody else wears. Alexander the Great also smelled good, apparently. After he died men fought over his clothes. At least, so Plutarch says. Newell is fastidious and definite about his person, but not vain; the cleanest human being Hugh's ever known.

"Anyway. He's happy now." Newell knocks the wood panel behind them.

Hugh ought to have said that. He ought to agree with it. His teeth are bothering him; his tongue searches for a lodged scrap of wagyu beef.

At last, speeches over, they proceed to Principal Pink's palace. The streets are dark, heading into the older, richer neighbourhood along the riverbank. Cold late October wind cuts the evening air and from time to time Hugh catches a gold leaf falling from the maples overhead. It's quiet here, empty, Monday night.

He ought to be with Mimi at the hospice. Turn left at this corner. . . . But he trudges straight along anyway, beside or behind Newell and Burton.

Mincing on subtly heeled boots, zipped up tight in an unbecoming black leather jacket (which—here's one consolation—is too ill-chosen to have been a gift from Newell), Burton is elevated, excited to be the Master of the Class. His old conceited self, only more so. Burton sucks up intimacy. It's not enough for him to walk with his arm through Newell's, he has to be in on every moment of conversation, vitally involved, or else he pouts and pulls away—but he pouts without letting go that arm, so Newell still has to soothe him. All the walks with Burton Hugh can remember. When they were boys at drama camp, Burton the Artist in Residence. Even then. Burton in those days gleaming, hard-bodied, like a shining tropical turtle, knowing and talented and bold, on his way up. Before the Public, and the thing at Yale.

"*The history of the world, my sweet, oh, Mr. Todd, ooh, Mr. Todd,*" Burton carols, crack-tenored, zimming along the leaf-strewn sidewalk, "*is who gets eaten, and who gets to eat!*" He skips. "Won't we have a magnificent month," he says, clasping Newell's arm tighter as they turn up the walk of a large Victorian house.

Pink's place: peach paint, picked out in peony, and yellow gingerbread.

Hugh stays out on the veranda for a few minutes, hoping his temper will cool down. It's hard not to think that Burton ought to be killed. But of course that's not a useful thought, so you stop yourself. Hugh stops.

Jason goes to answer the doorbell, bowl of spaghetti in hand. Ivy guesses he doesn't dare put it down or his mother will clean it away. He looks like he never gets enough to eat.

A boy he calls Orion comes back with him. Orion is courteous, explains himself: sent to escort Ivy to the drama party. He must be one of *them*. Touchingly good-looking, in an unfinished, over-exposed way. Flax-blond hair cut over his ears to odd effect. A princeling.

"Orion, like the constellation?" He nods, politely patient, and Ivy is sorry she asked. She might have joked about his belt; that would have been worse.

All the boys are tall these days, she feels like a pigeon walking among them. But having recently realized, at the age of forty-six, that she looks like Queen Elizabeth the Queen Mother, she decides to feel good about that. A jewelled pigeon on a mild strut.

Jason tells his mother, "We're supposed to help at Pink's for work experience."

"Oh." Ann looks put out. "I guess. I'll pick you up at nine."

"Might be later. Elle's going too."

"You have a bio quiz tomorrow."

"Ten."

Ivy finds this telegraph bargaining fascinating: the longest stretch of words she has yet heard them exchange. Ann concedes. Her head bows over her spaghetti. She twines two strands on her fork, threading round, round, round, without lifting it to her mouth.

Jason flies up the stairs. Ivy follows, needing a better coat. Not for warmth, for armour. Ansel Burton doesn't like her, and besides, he's crazy, maybe even psychotic. Newell is kind, but only an acquaintance. Not a night she's looking forward to. Not a *month* she's looking forward to. But the four thousand bucks, yes—more godsend than windfall. And the solitude. She could stay up in the empty room, say she's sick. A migraine. She closes the closet door on her few things and looks around at the nothing that is not there. The nothing that is.

Three teenagers fill the car, a battered Civic hatchback, pretty much to bursting. Jason gives her a quick glance as she opens the door; the other two stare straight ahead. The young know: eye contact contaminates.

"Perfect—so, I think I'll take my own car," Ivy says. "I'll follow you."

All three of them nod. Then the girl in the front (Elle?) unfolds herself, plucks a bag from between the seats, and scrambles out. "I'll go with you, so you don't get lost."

More good manners. Ivy is a bit surprised, but nods. "I'm Ivy Sage," she says.

"I know," the girl says. "I'm L. The letter L." She looks around for the car.

Ivy points to her very old Volvo, slumped beside Ann's new Subaru. "Are you wearing anything precious?"

L looks down to check her clothes. "Guess not," she says. But she is in unrelieved black.

"Because the dog hair is dreadful. I have to get it cleaned out. I was dog-sitting all summer and I still haven't faced up to it."

After a look at the fur-snowed seat, L takes off her black wool coat and puts it on inside out, cream satin lining gleaming in the streetlight. She waves to the boys and slides, or satin-glides, in beside Ivy.

"The letter L, that's unusual."

L looks blank. Bored? Ivy can't tell. She snaps her seatbelt buckle, waits for L to snap hers. They trundle off in convoy down the street, and L's nice manners reassert themselves. "My mother—her name's Della— called me Ella, as in Cinder, but that seemed like an error in judgement, so then for a while she said I was named after Elle Macpherson. Which is crazy. I used to say it was El, short for Electra."

"At least in the morning," Ivy quips. Then, at L's raised eyebrow, "*Mourning Becomes Electra*, a play I did when I was young. Never mind." Sad to be old, Ivy thinks. Nobody gets her jokes. Well, they are not good jokes. She drives.

L points. "Down here, left at the lights—so anyway, my mother's crazy." She gives an indulgent hoot for her crazy mother. (Ivy laughs too, in honour of her own.) "So we sent away to have it changed officially, but it turns out she never registered me properly at the hospital, so I'm Baby Girl Belville. Talk about a stripper name. I'm tempted to leave it like that."

"Well, yes! Are you in drama?" she asks L.

"Orion is. Jason and I are painting the sets. We're in visual."

Too bad. Ivy needs a few friends. Burton is such a weasel. Four thousand bucks.

"That's the house," L says. A big old pillared place, front porch bulging out. Too many cars already parked along the street. Orion zips the Civic into a dubious spot, half-over someone's driveway.

Ivy pauses for L to hop out, saying, "You go in with the guys. I'll find a spot." She drives happily down the block into the dark. A few extra minutes before she has to be public.

"Maybe she needs to toke up or something hippie," Orion says, watching the tail lights of the Volvo diminish. "Chew nicotine gum. Chant."

"Light a sweetgrass, do a mantra, man."

The boys think they are very funny. "I like her," L says.

"Ivy, though?" Jason says. "Like, *Soulcalibur*." Orion laughs, loud in the darkness.

L bats at the dog hair on her coat lining and turns it right side out. Black again, she climbs the half-moon porch steps, not kicking the pumpkins all to hell, though that would feel good.

Orion and Jason trip along behind her on big feet, gawky. L is so glad not to be male.

Newell Fane is coming, he's probably already there. She doesn't want the flutter in her belly when she thinks about him, it's juvenile. She's always known him, he's best friends, like, brother and sister with her mom and Hugh; there's nothing to flutter about. There he is, Newell, haloed in the hall light. His hair. But it's his eyes, tired and kind, that kill her. Knows all your flaws and loves you anyway. He's like thirty years older than she is, plus actually gay, everybody knows, although he doesn't make a public deal of it. But that doesn't always—look at Orion. Gay, except that Savaya experiment. And look at Savaya. It's a continuum, a spectrum, a *raiiin-bow connection*, right. Anyway she herself probably likes Nevaeh best of anybody, but that doesn't mean you don't flutter flutter flutter. The problem of love. She starts a butterfly thing in her mind, a paper thing, mobile, to work with the ladies in pots from the Voynich, fluttering from their chrysalides to the light-haloed, shadow-eyed face of him.

Hugh's hanging around on the veranda, as if he didn't want to go in. But it's cold. Hugh hugs her, then Jason. He salutes Orion, who's been in pretty much every art class Hugh ever gave. Jason too, and L, because of not taking her mom's classes. Every class for ten years, ever since Hugh came back from wherever, some other life he'd been living. He is probably her mentor, if you have to give it a name. But she has not shown him the *Republic*.

Parked beside the pumpkin punchbowl, Hugh holds a half-glass cupped in his hand. Students and teachers hover, waiting for the old prank where some joker kid adds bottomless bottles of vodka. Maybe it's already been done. You'd have to taste the punch to know, and Hugh can't bear to. Such a headache. Can't be the wine, must be the fall from the ladder this morning. Stand up straight, man. You ought to head for the hospice. Or wait till the awards are over, then go. She won't know Hugh, she's been wandering in crazyland for days; harder to go there than to stand watching Newell's progress around the room, with Burton as tug.

Jason and Elle—unexpected treat, to see them here. Their set design, a painted cyc, a gobo London Bridge from die-cut Mylar: he takes their word for it. Elle says Della's coming. Hugh feels some relief. Burton is easier to bear when there's someone to mock him with.

Here's Jerry Pink. Tight, rose-tinged asshole that he is. Hugh wishes he was at home, climbing the wooden hill to his treetop house and pulling the stairs up after him, alone. It's not lonely if you like being alone. Jerry Pink is all hail-fellow et cetera; Hugh endures it. The school gets their certificates framed at the Argylle Gallery and they won't if Pink takes a pet. Pink is in plaid, he's a joke of a guy. One arm round a student, Savaya or Nevaeh, Hugh can't remember which the tall blonde one is. Pink's other arm snakes out to snag a woman, a shortish, plumpish person. Thick eyebrows give her a look of surprise, or attention, when she turns her eyes on you. She turns her eyes on Hugh.

A nice look, actually. That's a nice face. Intelligent, sweet. Exotic but plain.

This must be the I of O actor Newell brought in for the master class scene work. She looks back at him, straight back; their eyes focus and lock crosshairs, as if they were spy cameras. Actually seeing each other, on first meeting, in all this punch-drunk crowd.

🍂

Ivy likes this person. His height and breadth fit the imaginary stencil in her mind: "Man."

Out of her league, of course, because she is dumpy and hidden and nobody ever knows her at first. She always has to translate herself, insert herself into people's consciousness. *Then* they like her.

But here, look: at first blow, first glance, this person, this man looks back at her and sees her true self. Nice.

Then Burton, sensing something happening that he's not in on, bustles over. "Eye, *Vee*." he says, two words in all. He holds her off and looks her up and down. "*How* sweet. Mrs. Lovett as the Queen Mum." That's the worst of Burton—he has a sixth sense for everybody's conceits. Ivy feels herself blushing. Or maybe this is a hot flash, because she is getting old, very old, it's true.

Newell, strolling along behind, grins at her beautifully and lifts his hands in apology. "Really good to see you, sweetheart, I'm so glad it's you. Un*bear*able," he says into her ear, hugging her, "if it had been anybody else."

Oh, why did she agree to do this? Newell's pity is almost more than she can take. He must know about her trouble. *Four thousand, four thousand*, she says to herself, and she smiles at Burton with just the degree of respect tinged with challenge that he tells himself he likes. Actually, he likes you to kowtow, but he wants to pretend that he's an equaller equal among equals. It wearies her very much to know so well how to pander to his measly soul. He's spouting off about *his* Mrs. Lovett— how he wants her: solid, fleshy, gap-toothed, definitely middle-aged. Which is so flattering. Plus, she is not gap-toothed.

Newell interrupts Burton. He hands Ivy a small pie and a glass of punch. "*Mrs. Lovett, how I've lived without you all these years I'll never know.*" She's forgotten that trick of his memory, knowing all the lines, using them in conversation to create intimate understanding, trusting that you will know both the surface meaning and the lurking ironic undertone, undertow. Trust is Newell's coin.

"Anyway, one thing I *can* promise you," Burton says, grabbing their attention, annexing Newell's untouched pie. "No performance! We won't stage this for an audience, I've made that clear to Pink. Master class means just that, *class. No* performance. All righty?"

Ivy's bite of pie was a mistake. Barbecued duck, when she thought it was cherry. But it allows her not to speak, to put up a hand to cover her mouth. She smiles and nods over the hand, coughs, looks around for the bathroom. "Under the stairs," Newell says, and she bolts.

"*That's* Ivy Page, Hugh," Burton says behind her, perfectly audible. "Not entirely . . ."

"Ivy Sage," Newell sings, over whatever Burton was going to say.

Across the hall, under the stairs—first door opens to steep stairs, basement. Next one, there we are. As the door closes behind her, Ivy hears Burton: "*Blank page*, I must have been thinking."

In the tiny bile-green washroom the mirror gives her back a flat white face. Small eyes and a sorry expression. She spits the pie into the sink, then cups up the whole mess in her hand and flushes it down the toilet. The taps gush a stream of hot water to clear the dribs out of the sink, but she can't wash her face for relief. Her mascara (pathetic attempt) would make a mess of her face and the towel. She leans against the door for a while. Like in an airplane washroom, she can't bear to go back to her seat, a middle seat too far back, between oily, patting Cherry Pink and that poisonous duck Burton. *Four thousand, four thousand.* Money is a bugger. If she wasn't so weak and stupid and broken she wouldn't be doing this, she'd have gone to law school, or gritted her teeth, gotten her goddamn MFA, and be teaching in some cozy university on the other side of the country.

❦

Hugh drinks punch. It doesn't seem to be affecting him, in terms of making it easier to be here, but his teeth have stopped bothering him. He tried to leave after Burton was stupid about Ivy Sage, but Newell looked at him and smiled, and he can't leave Newell. Is that what Newell would say about Burton? But Hugh loves Newell.

The punch might be getting to him after all. Obviously Newell loves Burton in some way, some awful Stockholm syndrome way. People are the death of each other all the time. The funeral was this morning. He ought to be at the hospice, not that Mimi will miss him.

"I don't have a lot of time for that Burton," someone says, right behind him.

It takes Hugh a second to shift contexts: Ruth, here at Pink's. She's setting another tray of hors d'oeuvres on the table, making room, clearing up. Copper coat off, white blouse and black slacks. Server uniform. It kills him that she's still working all these jobs.

"Are you getting paid for this?"

"I am, don't fuss. Fifty for the evening, and Jerry Pink had it catered! Everything came from the Ace, all I have to do is set out and refresh."

"If you're going to be late, take tomorrow morning off," Hugh says. He loves to give her days off. The morning gallery is so peaceful without her.

"No need! I'm out of here by ten, I told him that, it's a school night and he has no business letting the party go long. Did you bring the certificates?"

"Took them to the school on Friday," Hugh says. He needs and appreciates her nagging.

Ruth gives him a nod and sweeps up three scrap-littered platters. She marches off to the kitchen. Fifty bucks, for what, five hours? Okay. As long as it's cash and she doesn't have to declare it. But if Hugh knows Jerry Pink, he'll have a school cheque for her with her SIN number on it. Anal asshole. That makes Hugh laugh to himself, ha. Can't it be time to leave? He looks through the crowd for Burton's mauvery, thinking Newell will be near.

But Burton is in the nook by the fireplace, glass in hand, talking animatedly, in an intimate undertone, to a blond boy. Orion.

Orion's mother, Mona, was one of the questioning parents at the meeting. The father has never been in the picture. Mona is a drifty-scarved, half-starved sessional in the dance department at the university. Religious about furthering Orion's artistic education. Dance, of course, modern, tap, ballroom. All those art classes. Orion: clever, odd, likeable, a sharp-edged, fragile/tough boy whose work is always interesting. No visual talent, but himself visually pleasing; a serious actor. Newell might do him some real good.

Burton leans closer, close enough to speak into Orion's ear under the eccentric stab of golden hair. Where does he get that haircut? Not here. Mona must take him into the city.

Hugh's eye is still on them when Orion reacts to whatever Burton is saying—a quick jerk of the head, eyes staring up in one short glance, and then down again, a brief flush of colour. Tendons tighten in Orion's neck and he bends his head away like a bird's, the whole line of head and spine curling away, the soul sent into hiding.

Hugh looks around, checking.

Newell is at his side and, yes, has seen this interaction too.

Burton lays a well-groomed hand on Orion's sleeve, and Orion looks up, smiling carefully. He says, as if he's guessed the riddle, "That's Blanche, right? From *Streetcar.*"

Burton gives himself up to a wild guffaw, shouting, "A scholar! Newell! We have a scholar of the drama here!" He turns back to Orion. "And to finish the quote: *Run away now, quickly—I've got to be good and keep my hands off children.*"

What, what will Newell do?

Nothing. His flat-lidded eyes flick from Orion to Burton, then back. His mouth moves, tightening downward, but he says nothing.

Okay. Okay, what would Hugh do? This is not a court of law. Who knows what Burton said. Or what Orion is reacting to. Maybe Burton asked if he contributed to the Conservative Party. If he did make a pass at him, what's Newell supposed to do about that? Orion's eighteen, for one thing.

Newell grins at Hugh, holds his empty glass up, and turns to the bar table.

Hugh slides back farther into the alcove and occupies his mind with a familiar substitution: if Newell had an older, awful wife, and that awful wife was whispering to boys, would it be any of Hugh's business how Newell dealt with Burtina? No, it would not. He finds the image of Burtina restful.

Gay and straight, he thinks: like listening to a speech in French when you don't speak the language well, when you're still hearing the French words, translating them, then receiving the meaning.

Tiring.

(DELLA)

promised not to be late—
stupid to wait and wait for a call / a text   *nothing*
in the door at full gallop

                                                                              Elle, Elly
there in the back corner   fine she's fine   back to back with Jason
Hugh and Newell and a woman watching them
Mrs. Lovett: drunk, slightly sexy, superior, like what's her name
who played the Queen Mum she's all lit up
        what's so interesting?
booze in the punch
Jerry Pink runs close to the   edge
sweet Savaya also runs close   right on the edge
Pink: pasty smugface plaid   a cartoon of himself
                                                                       we hate him

        where did Hugh go?
shadowy in the alcove by the sunporch   watching unlovely Burton
lovely Newell   our hearts go out to him   the little brother
he looks so sad   why does sadness make us love?
true sadness
not the slump of depression   that makes us hate the person
                                                                like Ken hates me
                                                                    and I him
Pink surging up to speak   ditching Savaya
ought to talk to her mother   that will be a rough conversation
        Hi, April, your daughter is slutting around with the principal. . . .
and what it would betray   Elle's confidence
things overheard and seen   impossible

        Elle, Elly, are you all right, with everything that's been going on?

More punch will get you through this. "The list of those teachers who've gone above and beyond is really long this year." Every syllable out of Pink's mouth sounds smeared. "Lead us in the quest for excellence, we're here tonight to celebrate enthusiasm, commitment, the achievements of this great school. Vision revisioned, following twelve months of review and consensus—" Pink does not even bother to finish the sentences.

Hugh's heart is full of hate these days; head pounding too.

"Today we honour those who asked those questions and committed themselves to finding the answers. Worked late into the evening and early in the morning, winners who wouldn't take *No* for an answer. Support and encouragement of family and friends. Through the years, enlightenment and inspiration. Sponsors, encouragement, support . . . start every day with Quaker Oats." Had to get product placement in there. Pink gives a rich, corporate laugh. "Finally, I would like you to take as your motto the words of Pearl S. Buick, who said, *All things are possible until they are proved impossible and even the impossible may only be so as of now.*"

What the hell did that sentence even mean? And did he really say . . . ?

It seems so. Hugh looks up—Della is far away, staring at Elle. But Ivy Sage, by the stairs, catches his eye. Pearl *Buick?* Her own eyes wide, registering, laughing with him—then sliding down, her face ironed out to decorum.

The awards go fast, eight of them given out splat-splat-splat. Best this, best that, none of Hugh's pals in the art department recognized, including Della in her part-time class—par for the course, part of the core beliefs. Burton drifts over and maintains a snide commentary during the outflow of plaques and certificates: "The Argylle Gallery's finest work," he says, in vile congratulation.

Hugh edges delicately out of his earshot, again and again, but Burton tags right along, until they're out of the drawing room and into the wide hallway.

"You're looking hearty, healthy, hale, these days, Hugh," he says. "Looking after Mimi hasn't got you down, I hope?" As if they could have a real conversation.

"Glad to do it," Hugh answers, pointedly watching the current award recipient.

"Oh yes, I *know*. I myself . . . " Burton begins, eyes going wet. Dank pools of sentiment that Hugh honestly can't stand to look into, rude as avoidance might be. "It is the last honour, to be the handmaid of the beloved."

Hugh downs his punch to drown Burton's words, but chokes—can't stop himself: "Don't compare some casual boyfriend with—" He chokes again, coughing, dismayed by the venom in his own voice, the contempt contained in *boyfriend*.

With poisonous deliberation, Burton turns away and begins remarking on the crowd, the bad perms, the fashion sense, the relative slackness and fatness of the teachers. "You'd better watch out too," he says, patting Hugh's belly. "There are getting to be two of Hugh."

Possibly having heard some of Burton's epithets, Newell slides through the crowd and puts a hand on his arm, not so much comradely as controlling.

The last award: long service, for Ms. Blaikie from the library. A generously girthed, kind person, she crosses the carpet to Pink, who is holding out the last framed certificate. Burton seems to loathe Ms. Blaikie most of all. "Look at the waggle on that ungirdled rear—feminism has a lot to answer for . . ."

Hugh taps his teeth together, but can't wipe dislike away, though he knows it will only egg Burton on.

It does: "But she's *somebody's mother*, men, as the corporal would say. My own mother, ungirdled as all get out, God rest her, God rot her, gave me love and cigarettes and booze, and a fantastic succession of stepfathers, back when a father's step really meant something!"

Hugh makes an involuntary noise, and Burton turns to look full at him. "Don't like a slur on the mothers, do you, Hugh? Humorous, *Hugh*-morous to think it—when your own is such a piece of work."

Newell's lids lift to stare down at Burton.

Who shakes his head and elevates his chin. "No, no, we mustn't speak ill of the ill, the semi-deceased, the decently near-ceased her exit so long anticipated—" Newell's grip tightens, but Burton rattles on, "Fragile Mimi! That hideous strength, even in affliction, oh, Oedipus was never so pussy-whipped as you, Hugh."

Hugh finds himself again making a noise in his throat. Like a growl.

"Burton, quit," Newell says. "Hugh's taken care of his mother for years."

"He's taking care of her, all right," Burton says. His eyes brim with joy. "Helped her right into the hospice. *I'd like to help you out, which way did you come in?*"

Only Newell could have told Burton that old joke. A vision of them laughing together about his mother makes Hugh dizzy. He reaches out blindly for Newell's shoulder, to demand satisfaction, or something—but Newell has turned away, not wanting to take sides. Hugh's head pounds.

Burton is still smirking, still scoring some point: "He's cleaning her clocks. He's cooking her goose. He's saying, *Here's your hat, what's your hurry?*"

"You fucking—"

Hugh doesn't bother saying anything more. He hits Burton with his fist, as hard as he can, straight in the face. Burton looks surprised and pleased as he falls. *My mother and your mother were hanging out clothes, My mother punched your mother, right in the nose.*

Burton lies splayed on the gleaming wide-plank heritage floor. Newell kneels at his head and checks for damage.

Reeling away from the two of them, Hugh falls backwards against the door behind him—a door that pops open and decants him down the cellar stairs. A short flight, four steps to the landing, and the stairs are carpeted—but his head hits the wall and Jesus, it hurts like heck.

Dizzy, Hugh staggers to his feet and struggles up the stairs, through the doorway, off balance, falling again.

Newell twists to grab for him, but Ivy Sage's strong little hands are already there, easy on his elbows, bending herself to take his weight without fuss, as if they were doing a trust exercise.

"It's you," Hugh says, relieved. "I was looking for you."

"Oh yes?"

"Well, I . . ." Nothing comes to his mouth.

She looks at him, not smiling but not at all sad. Even in his haze he is struck by her eyes, clean and young in the squashed face. Shining like aggie marbles, greenish, with a dark ring round the iris.

"I—you, I—wondered where they've put you, where you're staying. Or—" Why be floundering? "You seem to be new to town, I thought I'd talk to you some more."

The clean eyes assess him, sparkle at him. "And you are who?"

"Yes, yes, I am." Dazzle, shards of light.

"Who?" she asks again. Then he hears it: *who*, not Hugh.

"Oh! Sorry! Hugh, I'm Hugh Argylle, the Argylle Gallery." He has a card in his pocket, it's a miracle. "Not hard to find. Beside FairGrounds coffee, if you drink coffee."

Ivy laughs, her face folding into a pleased crumple that makes him happy.

"Ivy." You name people to put them in the world, in your own world.

"Hugh," she says. Putting him in hers. "Nice clean hit there."

"If you're not busy, dinner tomorrow? Seven thirty? There's a nice— the Duck and Cover."

Ivy nods, once.

And then Burton is up on his feet, shouting for revenge in a gleeful have-at-you tone, quite the commotion, so Hugh slips down the hall and out the side door Della is holding open, and is gone.

(DELLA)

blood is always so red! so much redder than we think
what is to be done? oh Newell
this boorish impossible bloodsucker you're stuck with
you know how we all hate him   Hugh most of all
Mimi will die soon, Hugh will get better
or what if Hugh kills himself
what if he—
he doesn't have a garage door, just the lean-to
the funeral was only this morning   we'd feel so
if he did

                                                    if Ken
                                    if Ken was so fraught, so sad,
                                        so unhappy to be leaving
                                            to be unfaithful
not the car, the garage   what a word
but a bridge   exhausting
or a baseball bat picked up in one swift movement
or a gun in our
what we imagine   if we stop if we stop for an instant

                                                    Elle
                                                if she did

Damp, velvety darkness confuses the streetlights, each pale head in a mist. The river flows turgid, slower than summer, settling iceward. Hugh walks along, thinking not about Burton or Mimi, but about the basement of the gallery. What else has to be shifted down there, in case the foundation crack widens over the winter, floods in the spring.

Slow night-silence parts for his footsteps. As his steps change, mounting the old bridge, he begins to hear a second, syncopated set. He lifts his head to glance behind him. Newell, following.

Hugh stands still.

Such a pretty night, now the rain has let up. The mist, the shining pavements, shining leaves. A moon has risen—*a* moon? *The* moon.

Newell reaches the bridge.

"It's always the same moon," Hugh tells him. "Are you looking for me?"

"For Burton," Newell says. "Della's out here somewhere too. He tore off into the night to catch you, shouting about Hemingway and Wallace Stevens in Florida, about Rimbaud, Gore Vidal—you name it. Hard to say which literary figure he imagines himself to be. Tennessee Williams, maybe. He's roaming around shouting Blanche's lines through the blood, and he doesn't know the town like you do."

Hugh walks on.

Newell waits for a minute, then runs with long strides to catch Hugh's hand, his arm.

"Don't be angry with Burton. He's such a mess. Can you let it go, for my sake?" His eyes so tired in that noble face.

Impossible or needless to ask why Newell couldn't report Burton, charge him, even after all these years. All the intimacy of friendship adds up to nothing, except that there are questions you know not to ask, even though you do not ask exactly why you must not ask.

"Can't live with him, can't shoot him," Newell says, and Hugh can't help but nod and promise, even if it's not out loud. Newell nods too, and sets off back toward the school.

Hugh carries on across the bridge, to the gallery, home.

Up the porch stairs, key in the lock; up the back stairs, the landing; down the hall to the bathroom.

He vomits for a long time, feeling strangely happy to get rid of everything, everything. If only he could throw up everything that ails him. He washes his mouth, his face. In the mirror, his eyes are bloodshot. He turns off the light and sits on the side of the tub for a moment, happier in the dark.

Happier in his house, his treehouse, than out in the world.

Cleaned her clocks. He ought to have gone over to Mimi's room. Or go now. But she'll be drugged out for the night now. He gets up and walks through to the living room, turning off lights as he goes. The afghan Ruth knitted for him when he was twelve. He wraps that around him. The chaise longue is mostly under the half-roof of the deck; he kicks it sideways and climbs into it. Only the footpad is really wet.

Rain falls on the small remaining leaves and on the asphalt surface of the roof. The yard light behind the coffee shop, the one that bothers his eyes, has burned out. That small happiness means a lot.

(ORION)

In bed at the midnight hour, Orion rethinks.

"*You look like a young prince out of the* Arabian Nights *. . . I want to kiss you just once, softly and sweetly on your mouth*."

Old Burton doing Blanche, mouth smelling like the end of everything. Lying in bed beside Newell by now. Or on the pullout couch in the guest room, if Newell was as mad as he looked. Poor old guy, thinking over what he's done with his life and the end of it coming, thinking that he will always be able to depend on the kindness of strangers but in fact no, we can't. All us strangers, strange as anything in individual beds, all thinking like crazy. Newell in the huge bed under the blue silk duvet, thinking how to stop his old pal from coming on to boys in the master class, master of his domain. Or maybe lying spooned behind Burton, comforting the old guy, soft dick pressed against him kindly because he can't help being kind all the fucking time.

We have to be *less kind*.

Orion thinks about what he can make out of all this mess: a good part in *Sweeney* now, a leg up later. That's it.

He needs more to think about, to find a way into sleep.

He thinks of L, lying in a square of pale light from her attic window, knowing that her father has split, and like Savaya, calculating does she or doesn't she, re: Nevaeh. And of Jason wondering, wondering if there will ever be one for him, and if he will be ready. Jason's mother, hands folded on her chest, a raging, corpse-like Sleeping Beauty; his own skeletal mother lying like sticks under her pink blanket, crying, tears sliding down her nose and her yellow cheek. Farther out in the city, rooms full of fathers who have done something awful, something unforgiveable, and have not yet told anyone; men who have a minor operation in the morning and believe they won't live through it, all the ordinary shallow pains.

Each one of us lies sleeping not sleeping thinking thinking a thousand things and the frets form a net of fears, a net that lies knotted under our continuo humming as we go about the day, and at last the spread wings of dreams release us from the net and take us unto the forbidden country.

TUESDAY

❦

Hugh made me love Hugh

the origin of dukkha *is craving,*
which leads to renewed existence,
accompanied by delight and lust,
seeking delight here and there

> *entry on Buddhism,*
> WIKIPEDIA

1. IF IT MAKES HUGH HAPPY

Hugh can't sleep. You never can, after you punch somebody. Forced inside by real rain at one, he takes a hot shower to settle down, to drowse into something like unconsciousness. At two, pillow crammed beneath his neck, still lying there. Head hurting.

Greyish light murking the room—oh, you left the blind half-open.

Awake. At least he's not dreaming other people in the room this time. No Mimi.

He can't go over there. When she is wandering, not herself, she begs. More pills, morphine, do something, do something. You ought to. But she wants to live, when she is herself. Dutifully sipping a mango smoothie, a spoon of yogurt. Obedient, hopeful, droll. Sores inside her poor mouth: take a swab to wipe them clear, to give her some relief. Everything in the world narrows to her mouth.

He closes the blind and goes to the fridge. Sometimes food helps. Cheese smokies—not all that old, although one side is leathery. He cuts that part off, turns on the frying pan. But then the house will stink, and so will the gallery. On the deck, the barbecue shines in the rain. Eggs? Or toast, toast is not a bad smell. Hugh's four-slice toaster is very old, left over from—wow, from the apartment he shared with Ann before they bought the house. Plastic breadbag melted onto one side of it, but the crumb tray slides in and out smoothly. Best toaster he's ever had. Age does not ruin everything. It's so old the plug has two equal prongs. Honey or jam? Both jars dry, empty. He pulls out a black garbage bag, cleans the kitchen and then, awake anyway, makes the tiny meatloaves for Saturday's dinner party. The toast waits on the bar, limp by the time he's done. He eats it with a tester meatloaf, then vacuums the whole apartment. Then gets into bed, virtuous, old, alone.

He plays *Call of Duty 4* until the unkillable twelve-year-old online gamers drive him crazy; after that he switches to solitaire on his phone. He lies in bed, thinking stopped as long as the cards flip sound-lessly into place.

The alarm goes off at six.

Dark autumn morning, waiting for light. Not going to be light. This sadness is no joke. Burton is no joke. Have to do better, find some way to get along with—

No.

Downstairs. No need to lie there thinking of Newell or Burton, of his mother, of Ruth (who often leads off from his mother, as a more fixable bucket o' woe to mull over), of Jasper, any of these sadsack disasters he's saddled with. And some he refuses to be saddled with: Della and Ken in unspoken flux—not talking. Has Ken told her yet that he has to quit? Nothing Hugh can do about all that.

More, more of them: Orion being ogled. People you can't bear to think about: Gerald, wifeless and sonless. Ann—she's well rid of that stilted jackass; but Jason, skinny to start with, must have lost twenty pounds. Hard to be ditched by your dad. Caught, framed, in the mirror by the fram-ing room door, Hugh sees his own sloping shoulders, his defeated stance as he waits, blinking, for the green light to blink on the espresso machine.

In the silence he whistles a soft non-tune. A moth clings to the wall in the first damp morning light: *Is the moth dreaming or is Chuang TʒHugh dreaming?*

Ah—the grinding noise of beginning. Just in time, Hugh remembers to pop a paper cup under the spout for the self-cleaning water to flow out. Here's a question for you, for Hugh: in spite of everything, why such a good mood this morning?

It comes back to him. Ivy. Right after punching old Burton in the piehole. Hugh said dinner, she said yes. At least, she nodded. How is that even possible? Along with a pretty big headache, Hugh is surprised to discover that somewhere underneath, his heart is singing.

The morning is cool, misted. Girls will wear sweaters. Is he still a man? Still capable of desire, still subject to it? He asked Ivy out and she nodded. Her eyes clear as water, river water, grey-green. Rain is good for us. Wine is not. Sorrow is not. He changes that to *sadness*. Sorrow is like *solemn*—too fat and self-satisfied a word.

You must be climbing out of it, Hugh thinks. Or you would not care what word it was. If you could paint, that would be good.

He takes his coffee to the front window, whistling . . . *the trouble with poet is how do you know it's deceased? Try the priest.* Newell, singing Sweeney's song last night. Before the (his heart stops singing) punch. Don't think about Burton, how he will sue you.

There's Ruth in her new corduroy coat, out on the sidewalk talking to Dave, her cousin's son. Not at all a bad guy, gets a ton of quick-fix work from realtors and does longer projects too, but he's taken his sweet time figuring out what to do about the basement. Old Dave. Works with his sons, four of them, heights descending like steps on a stepladder; Dave's not getting any younger, in fact. He's got a new worker with him, a black guy carrying a big old toolbox, looks familiar. Oh, it's one of the porters from the hospice.

At that, bolt-from-the-blue like it sometimes comes, a wave of gasping nausea pours over him. Mimi in the bed, her velvet eyes, begging to go, to go, as she—now that he comes to think of it—as she always went.

That thought cools his head. He stares down at plaid pyjama bottoms, remembers that he's not dressed. He heads back through the shop and up the stairs.

It's so unfair.

It's not a question of fair. You'll miss your mother, fine. Everybody does.

Ivy. What the hell was he thinking? He is incapable of anything, any relationship beyond the surly bond with Newell, the snarled strands of obligation to Della, the loose truth of Ruth. Ivy must have been drunk, to nod. Even his name is hard to say: Hugh Argylle, no turning-post in the middle. He called himself Hugo Argylle for a while, in university, but then it started to sound like Hugh Gargoyle. He's pathetic! He always has been!

But still, quietly, his heart is singing.

(ORION)

Too early in the morning/too late at night. Sixth boss, a troll, *the most dangerous ogre in all of Outland*. White, fat thing bumbling out from behind mud-splashed mirrors in the Hall of Gruul: single-target damage 7,000 crushing with Improved Demoralizing Shout-up; Arcing Smash, 5,000-6,000 damage on plate; when debuffed, cleaves.

The pickup raid is a clusterfuck, too many of them cratered already, this probably won't work, but still, this boss is not a serious threat and—*O my beautiful blood elf, take him down!* Because Burton doesn't have enough money or enough power to be a serious threat. To what? To my integrity? (Alone in the basement, Orion laughs.)

People have to look out for themselves. What's the problem with having a champion?

People need real love too, that's the problem.

Kill kill kill kill kill, Lanjasa Elfkine grappling, moving, jerky slip-sliding and whacking, fingers flashing in the apex the acme the epitome of deathdealing killkilling . . .

Dead enough? Oh, back for more. Die, feisty-ferocious mallrat Maulgar.

Look at my mom, at how she is: a detached retina, dangling, and she's roaming semi-blank/semi-hysterical through the landscape, hands fluttering at the end of her long, long arms. Eye mask and ear-plugs as she sleeps.

Here's the real problem with Burton: he's not good enough. Neither is Newell, because he has Burton hanging around his psychic neck. I want to be better.

Maulgar dies. Orion throws the controller against the basement wall.

He reaches for his phone and texts:

> one kiss

A pause.

< ?

> I want to kiss you just once, softly and sweetly on your mouth.

A pause.

< . . . x

Here's Gerald Felker, the bereaved, climbing the steps of FairGrounds, his usual stop before heading to the Saab dealership. Hugh knows that office coffee: bitter and prolonged, like death. Opening the gallery door he hears Gerald ask for "an extra shot in the morning jolt!" Sounding manic.

As Hugh finishes sweeping the steps and flips the gallery sign to *Open*, Gerald comes out again onto the FairGrounds veranda and sees him. Bulging muffin sack in one hand, Gerald raises his cup in a salute, a toast. Hugh lifts an imaginary cup back. "Good to see you yesterday," he says, before he can pull back the words. Gerald's face crashes from cheer to painful shame, caught having fun behind his dead wife's back. It's just habit, Hugh wants to tell him, to comfort him. You don't mean it, I didn't mean it. You didn't mean it even in the old days, the ol' glad hand, it's just Chamber of Commerce, just business sense.

Off goes Gerald down the street, around the corner. Hugh is suddenly afraid that he won't make it, will park himself in his garage and die there one day soon. He can see Gerald's office window—it will spring into light in a moment. Hugh stands in the shadow of the gallery's porch, waiting for the light to come on. Willing Gerald to get there, to live.

When she arrives (ten minutes late, because he told her to take the morning off), Ruth starts right in. She's in a mood. It's age or something, calcifying her mind, Hugh tells himself. She's the most sane and helpful person, except for this crazy awful stuff.

"Dave's got a new person working for him, moonlighting from the hospice. Dave lets him drive the truck! I didn't like the look of him. I always think he seems lazy, at the hospice. You can't be too careful. Everywhere you look these days—well, you can see the difference. In the faces. At the hospital, too. Many, many more dark faces these days, you see it."

Oh, you do. Hugh sees it. One thing about his mother: never any of this, even on her worst days. Bile rises in his throat but he looks away, studies the place where he will hang the big Mighton.

"It wasn't like *this* before, that's all I have to say," Ruth says. Liar. She has much more to say. "In my days in this town, you knew everybody and they didn't have the kind of strange ideas that you find now."

And what can you say to that? Anything Hugh could say would be politically correct and practically false.

Even Ruth can hear her own incalculable wrongness, and it bulldogs her jaw. "These people—"

"Please, please, stop," Hugh says. Not sure if he has said it out loud or not.

She stops, adjusting the front blind: "Look, here's Newell, with his friend!"

Funny that she doesn't have the same trouble accepting gay people. Ruth adores Newell. She has DVD sets of all his series. Of all her part-time kids, Newell's her baby.

There they go. Newell and Burton ranging down the street to FairGrounds, Burton's arm tucked into Newell's bent elbow, his head up, catching the breeze of a cool morning. They trot up the steps in unison, almost a shuffle-off-to-Buffalo; musical theatre being much on their minds of late. Newell sports a goofball grin and Burton an eyepatch and a slouch hat. And what looks like concealer and foundation.

You realize he's going to sue you, Hugh tells himself.

He leaves Ruth in charge and walks round to the hospice. The son, as required, going to sit by the deathbed of the mother.

Stairs stretch endlessly upward like a video game or (back to his own childhood) the *Sorcerer's Apprentice*. Mop and pail, mop and pail, endless stairs and water, all out of his control.

The hall, the quiet corridor. No bodies laid out there today. Nolie is just coming out of her room. Always better when she's on duty.

From the bed, eyes open, Mimi smiles for him. About the eyelids, much sweetness. Still eighteen, at seventy-eight. Hard to believe some days that she is dying. Her face is peaceful. The drug cocktail mutes or translates pain, makes it unintelligible.

"You, did you, busy. Have you have, Hugh?" The darling husky voice is hazy these days—hurry, answer before she realizes that she is not making sense.

"Phew, busy, yes, I had some running around to do. I can't remember—" Hugh runs his fingers through his hair, a thing he got from her. "Oh, I went to Della's. I found her playing your piano—she loves it." That was days ago, but it doesn't matter. Days and nights have no more meaning here.

"*Her* piano," she says, and seems to know what she's approving of.

"Yes, she loves it. It means a lot to her that you gave it to her. She's coming to see you this afternoon."

Mimi's eyes light up. "Ken?" Always a man's woman. She likes Newell best, though. Like Ruth does.

"Ken's away," he says. Her eyes close, she is drifting. Keep on, a mild gossiping tone will ease her way.

"He's having a mid-life thing. Wants to quit his job, or take some kind of a leave from the firm. Not good timing, though. I think money may be—" No. Don't talk about money. Background, not foreground. "They put the piano against an inner wall, as you suggested. It sounds great."

"I'm sorry," she says, eyes up, open, searching. For him?

"I don't play. No sense me having it."

But that is not it. She is shaking her head, fitful on the propped-up pillow. "I'm sorry, I'm sorry—sorry, sorry—" Half sobbing, "I'm so sorry," in a child's voice that pierces him to the quick. She puts her hand on his. Papery, pale, silky with sickness and age. She looks at him, looks, looks.

Sometimes *forgive me forgive me forgive me* is in everything she says. Sometimes, *it's all your fault*. Remembered from her violent childhood, things she has let slip or that he guessed.

It kills Hugh. You can't do anything about it; she could never set it aside. In a long, privileged life, she only ever felt betrayed and beaten and bad. How long life, how long childhood lasts. Mops and pails, water everywhere.

He wipes her eyes, careful with the cobweb skin, and slides an arm behind her shoulders. But she turns away, maybe pretending that he is one of those who hurt her. Maybe thinking it, or knowing it.

(DELLA)

he's in a fugue state
he smashed into a tree   rapelling in Elora Gorge
and they don't dare   can't bear to tell me

                                      I think that was a lie   Elora Gorge

he won the lottery   can't decide what to do with it
he's shopping for a present   for our anniversary
                                      can't find one   can't face me

his other wife is sick   he's got to look after her   his secret wife

he got religion
started speaking in tongues   at a Kinsmen's breakfast
                                      like Dad's friend Phil Millman
                                      burly in a brown 50s suit
                                      then a clerical collar   struck

he hates me   can't bear to tell me   he's left me

no
none of those   please

Okay, away from the hospice, running over to Della's to get the January flyer settled. And for the collage course starting next month. Ian Mighton arrives tomorrow—wait, Thursday? Lucky turn of events, Mighton able to teach the class because he's got to be in town to sell his old place. The house he let Lise Largely live in, while they were dating. You'd think (Hugh'd think) Mighton would have more sense than to fall for full hair and an empty, roaming eye.

Hugh veers across the street in body, veers his mind away from Lise Largely, the realtor-slash-developer who has a bid in on Jasper's place, who wants to buy Hugh's too, who wants the whole building for a naturopath/allergy spa. Hugh could find another venue, or give up, give up, give up. A gallery is a mug's game at the best of times and now is not the best time, no. Who's to say she shouldn't have it.

Hugh's to say. He says *Never give up. Never give in.*

And Echo replyeth: *Give up . . . give in.*

He strides along anyway in the fresh tangle of leafsmell, rainslick; the sun sulking, slumped behind a bank of fog climbing off the river. Red flash—a cardinal, flying low across his path. Another follows, a pair of bright crimson males. Some note from Audubon or *Birds of North America* slides into his mind, that males with brighter red have greater reproductive success than males that are duller in colour. Mighton is as bright a bird as you can get, except for Newell, the brightest, yet neither of them has had reproductive success. Does Newell mind? Does he mind the way Hugh minds? You never know. Newell is detached.

At Della's corner lot, a dash of coat out the back door—red and gold paisley lining flaring, not the solid funereal black of yesterday. Well-kempt, unkempt, *verklemmt*. The car, Della's green Mini, flicks out the side drive and off downtown, without a glance behind to Hugh, jumping, waving his arms, a mad puppet dancing to yanking, tangled strings.

He gives up. Goes to the house, to wait till she gets back.

"Your mom on her way to see me?" he yells as he opens the front door.

Up the short flight of steps, Elle's head appears around the louvered kitchen door, nods. It's nearly ten, don't people ever go to school?

"Does she have her phone?"

Shake of the head, after a quick look at the kitchen counter.

No, she never does. "I watched her drive off," he says, begging pardon for busting in. "It's the Mighton flyer. She knows his stuff better than I do." He doubts Elle would know that Della and Mighton were once *an item*, as Ruth says.

Elle holds up a coffee cup, queries. He nods and follows her into the kitchen. Which is a worse shambles than usual: dishes piled along the counter, long sideboard stacked with piles of papers, photos, brushes, books bristling with bookmarks, three unmatched shoes.

On the built-in dinette table Jason lies flat on his back, considering a feather held up to the light. He drops his head to see who's here and jumps up in one elastic burst, skinny legs wheeling briefly through the cool kitchen air. Colour flares around him in streaks and flows, weird, migraine-like— what's that thing, synaesthesia? Then Hugh sees the colour is real, is cloth and feathers. "Hey, Jason. What's all this?"

Jason stares at Hugh, as if not understanding the question.

Elle hands Hugh a cup of coffee, holds out cream; he dollops in enough to calm the black, to quell the bile.

"Fashion project," Elle says. Maybe her first words of the morning.

"No FairGrounds this morning?"

"Tuesday—school in an hour. I work tonight."

Elle's schooling is complicated. Home-schooled for years, now in her grade twelve year she's taking courses at the high school to get credits. AP Art, Math. She's been doing Option Art there for years, all the extra-curricular stuff and projects, because Della teaches at the school too. It occurs to Hugh that Della is a bit too thinly spread. Why all the jobs? Ken must do all right, lawyers—But he was a sessional at Trent for years, went to law school late, on student loans. And he's expensive, all the hobbies. Wine, sailing, etc. Hugh remembers Ken on Friday, heading into the bank, looking hounded. Is money every trouble, for everyone?

Elle is talking: "—first-unit project, he's doing birds and virtues. Down is for November."

Hugh nods as if this makes sense. Down, *down* . . . ?

"Give me mine," Elle says. Jason bends to his overflowing baskets. Like a magician slipping silks from a sleeve, he strings out shattered, glittery shreds until Hugh rubs his eyes, seeing each thing as feathered— more, plumed.

Arms full, Elle vanishes back into the bedroom hall. Moved by avuncular over-politeness, Hugh looks the other way, and his eye hooks on an easel just inside the dining room.

And another one, and another. He goes through the arch and finds two easels, three, six, seven; the art-class kind. Canvases propped on chairs and bookshelves, tacked on the wall, trailing into the living room. The pieces normally hung there stand stacked in the dining room arch. Hugh follows along the line of work. Each one is the same, or nearly the same, a series of seascapes, harbourscapes. A boat, a wharf, rocks roughed in. Charcoal, smears of tempera colour, glossy paper (cut from magazines?). What's this—playdough? Pie crust? Some have small nudes in the boats, figureheads perhaps; some boats are strangely built. One is a whale.

Twelve canvases march along the wall and into the living room, past Mimi's piano, the last three crowded onto the mantelpiece.

"What's your mom doing with—" He stops. Elle is changing, she can't hear.

Jason slips through the archway, arms full of slick-sliding silks in orange, green, bright blue. "It's—she says her mom says it's homage."

Hugh turns to look at Jason. Why so shy, after all these years? When Hugh and Ann once were . . . what, Jason could not know. Can't know, how Hugh knows Ann's body so well, still, can see the skin under her clothes no matter what she wears, can feel the slight weight of her left breast in his hand. No matter how married she was, or isn't, now.

"Um, homage to *her* mom." Jason looks at the pictures. "Was she a fisherperson?"

Della's mom was a hack painter who turned out seascapes a dozen at a time, factory-style. In between bouts of ferocious depression. Homage, right.

The back doorbell rings. Jason lets Orion in.

Hugh watches from the dining room as Jason works, draping Orion's straight shoulders with more confections, concoctions, a concatenation of bird and person.

"This one looks backwards." Jason is serious and concentrated. "Tuck, see, the tail comes around, wraps twice and then—unfolds, explodes—I'll fix it when it's on."

Orion disappears, Elle emerges, coated or clad in something black, blue. What's the word—neoprene? Wetsuit stuff. Scales, sequins. Fish or bird? She turns, reveals a coxcomb hood with long blue feathers trailing down the back. Her legs appear, revolve, beneath the abbreviated hem, thin as Barbie legs. Too thin, he thinks. Pretty as all get-out.

Disturbed to catch himself eyeing Elle's pretty legs, Hugh recedes into the dining room to study Della's array. But glances through to the kitchen from time to time. Observing teenagers in the wild.

A girl slams through the back door and leaves it hanging, the screen door bangbanging behind her. The big girl, the blonde from the party last night. "Savaya!" Elle cries, clearing up that small puzzle. So the dark, thin one at the coffee shop is Ne-something, Naraya, Nivea . . . The blonde is headed for a fall if you ever saw one, and Hugh hates falling, in himself or others.

They chatter as they try things on, Jason pinning and snipping with a pair of lefty scissors. Hugh approves. Saves the fingers, saves the wrist; everyone should have a pair. He wonders when he became such an old maid.

Elle gives Savaya a pair of boots. "The boots you bought at Value Villa*zh*?!" Savaya shrieks, train-in-tunnel, but a melodic, feminine train.

"Too big," Elle says, tragic. Savaya starts to put them on her bare feet. "Remember there's that yucky yellow stuff in them that—oh."

"What yellow stuff?" Savaya asks.

"The stuff that got all over my socks. Now it's all over your feet, dude."

"Oh *that* yellow stuff. How cute are these boots!" Hikes her skirt way up, showing shapely gams, then drops it in a series of frills and fillips. She cries, "Oh, see my skirt hoist itself up like that. How embarrassing!" and Elle shouts, à la Harry Belafonte: *"Hoist those skirts up a little higher!"* and they're all singing "Jump in the Line."

Flying back in a sleek black suit like Lucifer, or a very *duende* Puck, Orion demands their input: "Hey, in *Streetcar*, do you think Blanche is Tennessee? Or is Stanley him; is he trying to macho up and kill off the weak, crazy part of himself?"

Another girl dances at the door—Elle's friend, Nev-what? Nevaeh. Sharp angles, soft skin, a sulky or unhappy look. She looks around the unkempt kitchen, the dishes, the shoes on the counter, and as Elle kisses her she says, "What is *wrong* with your *family?*"

Elle, shocked upright, blanks for a minute, and then says, "We're just . . . busy, I guess?"

Orion waltzes the girl away, saying, "Are you *judging* my *friend*, Nevaeh?"

Nevaeh's laughing. She says, "No, no, that's what my *father*—ugh, never mind!"

She has long hands, long feet that turn independently; she is a dancer, gravely graceful or giddily gawky, depending on the tempo of the moment. Hugh remembers her: grade eight Kiwanis Remembrance Day art project—Nevaeh ordered to take part by her father, heavy-faced, sombre, a renowned international academic. Hers was an interesting piece, cable typeface on white slips, a chunky blue-grey background, the text some complicated cipher that Nevaeh declined to decode. Second prize, maybe should have been first.

A waltz-dip finish, and Orion says, "Imagine the joy of having an artist mother."

Jason hands her a blue feathered thing. "Hope."

Nevaeh sighs and takes it away, plumage trailing behind her careful-stepping feet.

Tiring, youth. Hugh stares at Della's boats instead. He leans in: yes, Savaya stands at the prow of this one, hip tilted, arms akimbo, almost a figurehead; behind her, sketchy, reaching men and girls. She's a piece of work, all right. He searches the boats for other people he knows: there's Ruth, crouched on the rocks above the tidemark, scrubbing a boat clean of barnacles. Some pictures are only roughed in, some beginning to take real shape. In one, an empty boat called *Beyond My Ken* has drifted away from shore.

Conversation comes from the kitchen in snatches as Jason shifts and pins his models, happy and at ease. Tucking up a shoulder seam on Nevaeh's tight, seams-out bodice, stapling the neoprene, Jason says, "It's just, Shakespeare is so overrated. I feel like he's like the Beatles—it was, like, right place, right time."

As if in answer, maybe continuing an earlier train of conversation, Orion says, "Bikes are like part of my soul. I have a weird romantic love affair with my bike. It's crazy."

Jason: "I wish I could ride a bike, but when I was little and I tried to ride bikes I got really frustrated and my dad said to quit."

"It's not all that hard—it's just—you've just got to go for it."

Gesturing with the scissors at Orion, set to trim the bottom edge of his glistening beetle-carapace vest, Jason asks, "But don't you have to have a little bit of balance?"

"Well actually, I don't know—I've just always known how. I don't remember learning. It's the one thing I know I can do brilliantly, no worries, you know."

They are so serious. In his eavesdropper's nest, Hugh finds himself on the verge of—what is this, crying? What is wrong with him?

He looks up and sees Della, just outside the screen door.

Her face is so sad. One finger scrapes the bottom of her eyes before she reaches for the handle. So it's not just him. A rush of kindliness spills upward into his chest, his throat. Old Della. He calls to her across the kitchen, gesturing behind him to the long march of canvases—*"The water is freezing, and there aren't enough boats!"*

Elle doesn't notice her mother, but that line from *Titanic* is a family joke, and she swirls herself into a figurehead, arms outstretched, calling to Jason, "I'm flying, Jack!"

Della has pulled the screen door open, red leaves of ivy framing her. Hugh sees her eyes close for a measurable beat, and open, and then she turns away before Elle sees her. Down the back steps and out of sight, crying too hard to come in to a teen-full kitchen.

Many things might be the matter. The funeral yesterday upset her. Or Ken—Hugh never did check the messages on the upstairs phone. Or maybe just that Elle is the pearl of Della's heart, and will take all this happy bustling life wth her when she goes. Very soon.

Last week Della laughed about the pain, how unreasonable it is. "I *want* her to graduate, I want her to go! It's the best thing in the world that she's almost ready to leave." At their regular table in FairGrounds, eyes welling then too. Cold morning sun lit the papery, welted skin around her eyes, small new lines above her mouth. Crying a lot these days.

The kids are going upstairs to look at shoes, but Elle comes to the dining room arch where Hugh still stands, abandoned.

She takes his empty cup. "Like my mom's boats?"

"I think they're the best work she's done in years."

"Me too. Is she any good, or anything?"

"Elle. You know she is." It comes out tutelary. He makes a face, as if that will fix it.

Elle says "You know, it's *L*, the letter L. Not *Elle*. I can hear the *Elle* in your voice, but you can't seem to hear the *L* in mine."

At this little note, this slight correction, Hugh feels more abashed than he has for a long time. He nods, doesn't say "*L*," but forms it with his mouth.

She grins, in both forgiveness and apology. "I'm still crabby this morning. Hey, I meant to say, that was a good punch you gave Newell's old boyfriend last night." So she saw that. "Orion liked it too. And Jason."

"It was a stupid thing to do," Hugh says. "I'm ashamed of myself."

"Would you like to see the stuff I'm working on?"

That surprises him. "I'd be honoured," he says.

She goes first down the basement stairs. Talking, although she's got her fingers laced across her mouth. "I call it *The Island Republic*," she says. "It's just a set of—an atlas or—maps, or it's just— Shit, I wish I hadn't asked you . . . "

They stand at the bottom of the stairs. A sign directs him, under a decorated arrow:

THE ISLAND REPUBLIC OF L BELVILLE
DO NOT ENTER

"You can, though," L says. Hugh reaches out to the light switch.

The large rec room is festooned, the whole space is occupied by paper, too insubstantial to fill it, exactly: lines strung in a maze, above head height, hung to varying depths with sheets of varying size. Many very small, some foolscap width but longer, a few much larger. Some strands of line are decked with tiny lights, but the room is bright enough to see the drawings, the—maps, L said.

It's not a maze, exactly, but a shape.

Hugh stands still, looking at the whole thing, and then enters. He moves along the alleys between the paper. Every step makes them shake and move. Lines and colours sharpen, recede as he goes, even though he goes slow.

First: a series of large maps on tissuey translucent paper. Street maps?

Clean drawing on tracing paper, on onion skin or rice paper, sheets taped or sewn together to make larger sheets. Each of these eight or nine has a title at the top, or a name, in indecipherable script. But as Hugh looks at the first he sees a house emerge and a face in the house—and a street on which the house unfolds, an exploded 3D diagram that has been subtly translated into Della's face, the planes and angles he knows very well.

Then Ken's.

Jason, and that one Ann? And Ruth.

This one: dark face, the paper dark, the ink silvery, the house a shadow, only one room truly visible above the eyes/the entrance to the house. An unmade bed.

He was afraid that was Newell, but here's Newell now. His soul in his eyes, in the sad set of his mouth, glossy box hedge ringing his mansion round.

These are—Hugh feels a bit dizzy. These are strange. This is like—like the first time he watched an art video and saw the point of it. Filmy paper overlays the dark face (Nevaeh?) and Newell's too. It's almost transparent. Frail, weightless. Drifts upward in the small breeze of L moving into the maze behind him. This series ends. There is a gap, a blank space on the line where strange symbols have been drawn directly on the wall behind. Two columns, sketched literal meaning on the left, brush-stroke symbol on the right. Like a legend.

Second: the next pieces are small. Drawings, images on white space, unanchored. A girl's body standing in water, her top half reflected, redoubled. He moves to the next one. A woman floating in clouds, palely outlined. Taupe and blue for the clouds, which are circular suggestions rather than conventional childish billows.

Then the sequence changes back to maps, or diagrams, interspersed with full-blown adventures, almost Bayeux Tapestry in their movement, people and events unrolling like a graphic novel on unwound scrolls. He is walking through a story, or a history.

"I like this—" (pointing to the circular, what, city walls? broken by gates) "repeated . . . "

"Yeah, it's not wombs, just so you know. I'm not interested in wombs."

"I didn't suspect it."

"Oh you know, I'm just— Or in feminism by itself. Or political— I don't want to do the same— It seems so useless, even when I know it's *not*, but I just can't. I want to see inside people, people's lives, and that's small. I'm not doing the big, you know, I'm not, you know. Fighting Kony and the Lord's Resistance Army, stopping hate speech against LGBTQIA and you know, queers in general. Slutwalk. And veal—I don't know. I hate porn and so on but I don't mind porn-porn; I mean, I'm using nudes all the time, it's just the bad stuff . . . which is everywhere."

"These are—these are—" Hugh is in the centre of the maze, the map, the world, by now.

He stops talking. He turns in a slow circle, making the forest of sheets around him tremble. He doesn't speak.

"You have to get out by, sorry, by crawling," L says, after a while. "Hunker down." She squats to knee height and walks that way out of the tangle. "I wish— I can't, but if it was in a show or something, I'd try to make it all swoop upwards when you've gotten through to the centre, so it would kind of disappear. I've drawn a thing, a machine for how to do it, pulleys, so the pieces all get closer together as they go upward, like the world is whirling away from you in space, all getting smaller, getting smaller, small, small."

Hugh stands there, silent and looking.

(DELLA)

all I have left undone
and the bank now   how can I have   spent so much
on nothing   on bills   that I always   we will never
we own nothing
nothing to look forward to but this   for ever
my mother's unsellable china   my mother's linens and chairs
everything she slaved over   kept perfect for so long
                                            useless in the current crisis

I hate this house and everything in it
and Elly will leave and it will just be us

                                                            Ken

                    not us

                                                            me

the boats   those barren vessels
nothing in my basement but
Elle's eyes mind heart   don't look don't look
                                        let her make her own work
                                            keep doing mine

the basement will empty of her unwinding mind
and these children now not children
and I not myself again or now or ever
me   *Ken*

4. I MASTER THE CLASS

Eerie. The smell of a school still has the power, the power of voodoo, to make Ivy feel like she's got bad cramps and ugly clothes and no lunch money.

She got up early and dressed with care, but now—semi-costumed in a lantern-shaped black papercloth skirt (forty-eight bucks on eBay!) with a wide black belt, a shawl in her bag to bundle in when they start work— she sees the folly of herself in the double glass fire doors. Tiny squares of wire inside the glass divide her into a plump graph of old and hopeless.

"*This is none of I,*" she thinks. Then, yipes, hears herself saying it out loud.

I am short and eccentric, she says to herself interiorly: yes, old. But that's no reason to squirm or shrink. Her carriage corrects and she enters the long hall feeling buoyed. Her boots help. Nice little lace-ups, just enough heel to give a person a boost.

The hall is crowded, full of kids writing and painting on the walls. No curse words or blatant nude parts, although from psychedelic-hued mayhem the odd cock-and-balls or parti-coloured breasts emerge, and Dinner Party–type vaginas. Ladders line the long corridor. Ivy is careful of aluminum legs, jutting higgledy-piggledy. Children of various sizes and ages swarm up and down, lithe and loud. A graffiti festival, or impressive mass disobedience?

Here's the window to the drama lab. Bare fluorescent brilliance. There's Newell's head of burnished gold. Perfect. She takes a quick breath to feel air flood into her back, bobs her head like a horse accepting the bridle, and goes in.

Burton on the left, deep in conversation with drama head guy, Terry. Newell on the right, being swooned over by drama sub-head, Terry's wife, also named Terry. *Terry & Terry,* they used to shout in the dressing room at the Equity Showcase Ivy did with them at Harbourfront in the earliest nineties. *TerryTown! Two-gether, Four-ever!* Not for actual ever, though, turns out. They'll be divorced by Christmas, if the paperwork goes through.

Ivy resolves, in the instant before truly entering the room, to have a great day. This skirt really is ideal for Mrs. Lovett. "I love it," she says, as an affirmation.

"We love it too!" Burton cries in welcome. His punched eye is a putrid shape, a puffed, purple pear. Now he will have no choice but to look askance, so she won't have to hate him for doing it for effect. "Dear Ivy—already in a garment! But you won't get to work for quite some time yet," he says, patting her arm.

Early this morning, lying peacefully awake in the solitary whiteness of her sloping room, Ivy resolved—strongly resolved—to be kinder. To treat everyone around her with respect, to find what good there is in people. So now she brings her gaze to bear on Burton's puffball eye and thinks kindly and respectfully of Hugh popping in such a solid juggernaut of a punch. She gives Burton a wide, loving smile meant for Hugh and sits at the empty space mid-table, where a folder awaits her.

He-Terry explains the entrance chaos, condescending yet hiply enthusiastic. "Not an insurrection, ha ha. The front half of the school is being demolished next summer, so we've got a mural project on to paint it up. A fundraiser, of course."

She-Terry: "Each and every student is participating, not just the art students, it's truly, *truly* exciting. They've been tweeting the whole thing and the Facebook page has over eighty Likes, and we've got CTV coming on Friday to—" Burton's tidy tamping on the table stops her. She sits, stage-whispering, "*My hobby horse!*" and lets the meeting begin.

Terry Mr. starts it off: agenda, schedule, tech details, pausing for questions from Burton. Terry Mrs. breaks in a couple of times to assert her authority over movement/voice/dance matters. She's gained and lost a good deal of weight over the last few years, and Ivy thinks (finding the good) that she looks *just great* right now. Misery being the best diet. Even Ivy herself is on the downward slide these days, though technically, factually single. And soon to have her apartment all to herself.

As will Mrs. Terry, unless she keeps the house. Ivy's seen their house. Leaded panes and a frothy, grownover English garden, which seems to be Terry's obsession. What he probably calls his *passion*. No doubt Terry will insist on him moving out.

"Do you think?" Burton says, louder, as if he's said it before. Is that a stink-eye he's giving her, or just the swelling? Oh, he's asked her a question. She's got nothing—not the faintest tinge of an idea what they've been talking about. She looks sideways to Newell, but his eyes are downcast. Ah, he's texting below the lip of the table.

Back to Burton. "Perfect," she says, nodding, as if after quiet consideration.

That seems to do the trick. They ramble on, this teacher/artist session going till three, when the students will arrive for the first master class.

A very faint crease lines Newell's cheek, barely deepening. The smallest of smiles curves his perfect mouth, and his fingers work again on the hidden phone.

Burton's satisfied voice glides on, slippery cadences skating over the polished table. Ivy takes the cap off her highlighter, ticks items on her agenda, starts with well-acted dismay, and checks her bag. She lifts her hand in delicate supplication, and Burton pauses.

Slipping into the pause, almost mouthing it: "Sorry, I've left my —in the car—I'll be—" She's out the door. She has a gift for mobility, for sudden, courteous vanishings, refined over thirty years of rehearsals and calls and tech dresses and casting conferences.

Out, out, outside, out the side door with the bar on it. Although clearly marked ALARM WILL SOUND, she noticed kids going out this door last night. It opens in silence.

Her car, half a block down, is perfectly safe. Her phone (a mere excuse) is here in her bag. But she has nobody to call, nobody to text or dimple for.

Only Hugh. Dinner. That's going to be a treat.

Patient, distressed eyes, the plane of his cheek, the open smile that seemed a little under-used. That punch! A gallery. *I don't know much about art.* But she knows what she likes: she likes Hugh. If I had his number, I'd call, she thinks.

Deeper in her bag, his card.

ARGYLLE (and below, the same letters rearranged, spidery traces showing how)

GALLERY

She laughs as the phone rings.

"Hello?" A woman. Dang.

"May I speak to Hugh?"

"You may!"

Then nothing. What? "Um, is this . . . the gallery?"

"Oh! Yes, *Argylle Gallery*!" The woman sounds bothered, as if correcting a fault.

"May I speak to Hugh? to Mr., um, Argylle?" Ivy feels her cheeks heat, blushing. Once in high school she called a boy, got his Ukrainian grandmother instead, and couldn't make herself understood. She is swept back to seventeen.

"To who? To Hugh?"

"Tu-wit, tu-woo!" Ivy says, idiotically. Swept back to seven, now, and Brownies.

A pause. "Hugh's at the hospice," the woman says, without reproach. "I could take a note?"

"Perfect. If you could say we're still on for this evening, that would be— He said the Duck and Cover, but I can't find it on Google."

"Oh *hoo-hoo-hoo!*" the woman says, her laugh just like that. "*Hoo-hoo!* No no, that's the Hooded Falcon, the pub over on George, by the river, but people here . . . "

"Oh! Right, I've seen that sign."

The woman is still talking. "I could get him to give you a call when he gets back?"

"I'm afraid I'm working and I can't . . . It's all right, now I know it's the, the Falcon, so if I—" Inside Burton will be coming to the boil. "Goodbye!"

The alarmed door will not open from the outside. Ivy has to go all the way down the block to the front door. But it is a lovely day for a walk. Even Pink, pouncing out of the office to show off the mural, can't prick her mood's balloon. She wards off a tiny teenager swinging around a long-legged ladder, and heads back into purgatory.

The community league is sending flowers to Gerald Felker. That will fix it.

Ruth shows Hugh the sign-up roster for delivering dinners to Gerald, alone in his giant white house, his haunted three-car garage. Hugh says no, no thank you. Ruth writes both their names in several slots anyway.

Hugh can't argue. He's ten feet up the indoor aluminum ladder, adjusting the top rail for hanging *Dark Gates,* the new, very large, mixed-media collage that Ian Mighton sent dimensions for, and is bringing with him on the train. Mighton sells instantly; several people are on the list to be informed as soon as any piece comes in. It is—as much as anything can be—surefire; the commission will cover the gallery overhead till December, maybe January. But being collage, it needs a good light.

"Won't be your turn for three weeks at least, the length of this list," Ruth says.

"I'm not doing it. I hardly know the guy."

"You can take him to the Duck if you don't want to cook."

So proud of her work. Busybody. And not finished with interfering: "You need to go to the doctor," she says. "Your eyes are different sizes. Your pupils. I noticed."

That's a little alarming. From the cash desk Ruth looks at him. "Was it just that fall down the basement steps last night? That didn't look too bad."

Hugh grunts. Refusing, pettishly, to answer her. What she doesn't know she can't bug him about.

The phone rings.

"Oh! I forgot," Ruth exclaims, not answering the phone. Hugh begins to climb down the shuddering ladder. "A lady called for you. English. She said she was meeting you at the Duck, she didn't know where you meant."

Inside his trembling, childish, ladder-descending belly, something delicious turns over, a beautiful fish in cool water, a sliver of light. "Not English. She's an actor."

He picks up the phone. "Argylle Gallery," he says pointedly, taking this opportunity to demonstrate for Ruth how to answer a business call.

Not Ivy. It's Newell.

Hugh's heart clunks, missing a beat. For a minute he'd forgotten punching Burton.

"Hugh, listen—Lise Largely wants a meeting. You know I have an interest in Jasper's place. She's talking to the lawyer, trying to set up a deal for the whole building. Can you face it?" It's like Newell not to refer to, or seem to recall, last night. His voice is clear and buoyant, with the usual electric charge running under his calm.

An interest in probably means Newell owns most of it. "I can if you can," Hugh says.

"That's what I said to Jasper," Newell says. "I can if Hugh can."

"Today?"

"Tomorrow, I think—Hendy will let us know when it's set up. Why she's so all-fired I don't know; Hendy thinks she might have another real estate deal on the blocks."

Surprised to know more than Newell and his fancy-pants lawyer, Hugh says, "She and Mighton broke up in July. She had to move out of his house, he's coming here to sell it."

"Wow. She's been there for years. I'll tell Hendy, might be useful. We like a lever."

Hugh bats away Ruth's sign-up sheet. She is poking it at him, miming an offer to write Newell's name in. "He's not doing it either!" Back to Newell: "Ruth's got a roster for feeding Gerald Felker, the poor guy whose wife—you know. Look, when are you done at the school?"

"Five, today. They just get their toes wet."

"Listen— Look—" He sounds like an idiot.

Newell waits. Some sensation of a laugh comes over the line.

"I have to come over and apologize to Burton," Hugh says. He stares out the window at the cedar bed he fell into yesterday morning. His head hurts all over again, a troubling buzz behind the eyes. "I shouldn't have hit him."

"Good old Ansel. Can't live with him, can't kill him," Newell says. As warm as if he's standing beside Hugh, arm round his shoulder. "We'll be home by six."

As Hugh hangs up, the gallery door slaps shut.

Gerald.

He comes in, and drifts to the rack where the prints stand, ranged in sliding stacks. Flip, flip, flip, Hugh and Ruth hear. Pause, flip. Pause. Flip, flip.

"I mean it." Ruth pins Hugh's eye. Getting her *piece of my mind* voice on. "You need to let Conrad Frey have a look at you." Their doctor is South African, an Everest climber, a crazy man. Hugh avoids him like the plague he might prevent; only sees him out running late at night, in a trance of bliss, with a strange, lolloping, low-knee gait. He actually wears blinkers when he runs, that can't be safe. And earphones. After midnight he pads by on the rainy sidewalk below the gallery, a regular tramp-slamp-shuffle of expensive shoes with ten individual toes, running for the river path as if pursued by a slow bear. The bear of age and infirmity and, let's name it, death.

"Death?" Gerald's head rises, slow as the moon, above the rack of prints.

Hugh goes back, horrified, over his thoughts—did he say that out loud?

Gerald nods, head dipping, taking great effort to frame the words. "D— Deeth? *Wounded Child*, there was a print here, by Deeth—do you have any more of his?"

"Hers, actually, Ingrid Deeth, local artist," Hugh says, swinging around the counter to help Gerald. In any way he can. "Large format photo, her take on Hugo Simberg's *The Wounded Angel*. We might be able to order a giclée print of the original. . . ."

"I'm making an appointment for you," Ruth says quietly as Hugh goes by.

He waves a hand at her and gestures Gerald back into the print stacks. To talk about Ingrid Deeth, okay, but not, not about death.

Hugh looks up at the door-slap: Elle—L and Jason. Semi-drowned, happy.

L pulls a paper out of an inner pocket, unfolds it on the counter and smooths it out, talking all the time to Jason. "They were like, yeah, we're going to paint the mural in our own blood, and I was *seriously*, people— good thing they're pulling that wall down."

"Never have that problem in Fashion," Jason says. "We are mostly not organic, and hardly ever conceptual." He goes from piece to piece around the shelves, examining the ceramics gravely.

"From my mom," L says to Hugh. Della's mockup for the flyer. "She says if you check the text she'll get the real one done tonight."

Okay. Hugh takes it to the window to cast an eye over it, listening to their commentary on the master class. Burton's eccentricities make them laugh, that's a relief. The flyer's type size is small—too small? His eyes don't want to focus. His head hurts. No Advil left.

L jumps up to sit on the counter. "Sheridan Tooley was hanging around waiting for his ride to Toronto—what a poser that guy is, even more now that he's got a gig. I showed him the costumes on your Instagram and Sheridan goes, I don't have Instagram, I'm off the grid."

"He doesn't even know what that means." Jason scorns both Luddites and posers.

Hugh hands the poster back. "Nothing wrong with that," he says, going with them to the door. Rain dashes down, making endlessly reborn, re-widening circles on the rain-soaked sidewalks. Jason and L stand looking out, forlorn and skinny, overburdened with neoprene, until Hugh offers them a ride. A reason not to go to the hospice.

At Jason's house, he goes in with them out of habit.

They dart up the stairs, nothing but a floating *Thanks!* behind them.

Well, of course. It's not like he's a friend of theirs. Too bad it was Jason who had to go home. At L's house, he could go down and look again at her—what is it?—installation. He wants and doesn't want to think about it. About what he ought to be doing, talking to Gareth Pindar about getting her in to his gallery. Stop thinking. The paint smell is strong in here.

Hugh stands there, blank-headed, in the living room.

Seems like there's a lot of stuff he isn't allowed to think about. His head hurts.

Where's Ann? He hasn't seen her for a while, he should at least say hello.

The empty house rings. She's gotten rid of a shitload of stuff, you could swing a lion in here. The vacant walls make his eyes yearn for something to rest on. A line of black squiggles, there, snaking along the top of the freshly white mantel, down the line of wood to the white baseboards. Step closer:

no lies no lies no lies no lies no lying no lies no more lying no lies none no lies no lies no lies no

Black Sharpie, looks like. Small printing. It takes a while for the shape of the words to resolve into sense. *No lies.* He and Ann haven't talked about anything but Jason for years. He wonders why Jack left, what he was lying about. Just the girlfriend?

A noise, light tap of shoes: Ann, back. Hugh's thoughts feel as loud as words. He turns to the window to hide them.

"I've been clearing the space," Ann says behind him. "Energizing."

"I like the—the—space," Hugh says, wanting to cheer her up without entangling himself in responsibility for her cheerfulness, or for Jason's safety. Except he feels sorry for Jason, because Jack is an asshat. "It's elegant. Suits you."

She almost, almost smiles. "I needed a change. This whole house, just me and Jason? So I took a boarder. I gave her our old room, with the ensuite."

Does that *our* mean hers and Jack's, or hers and Hugh's? Because this house, this place was his and Ann's once, thirty years ago. Twenty-five, even. That wide, low-ceilinged, open-windowed bedroom was their room. Her hand on the slanted ceiling over the bed, pressing there as they made love. He shuts his inner eye.

"I haven't slept in there since Jack left anyway," Ann says. She's staring at him. Her eyes like hooks. Seeing that same moment? A shudder passes over his mind: that she might, she might be thinking—she could not be thinking that they could, that she and Hugh could . . . that you can sometimes pick things up, old loves. Or you think Hugh can.

"Good, good," he says inanely, to no point at all, trying not to be unkind. "Good to get yourself some company." He is as big an ass as Jack.

There's a space of silence. "Nobody loves me now," Ann says.

Oh for pity's—for *fuck's* sake. Hugh's inner eye sees a black-and-white photo of his mother, shadows of bare branches on her dress, lying in a chaise longue in the backyard at the house here in Peterborough. Although you can't see it in the photo, a word bubble comes out of her mouth: *Nobody loves me now.*

A tear falls out of one of Ann's diamond-shaped, diamond-sharp eyes. Unfair—she's been a brittle barb for years and years, and now she's *vulnerable?* But she's got a Sharpie in her hand. She flicks the tears away and kneels to write along the baseboard:

Any intelligent woman who reads the marriage contract,
and then goes into it, deserves all the consequences. Isadora Duncan

Watching the angular script form, Hugh thinks, what's Jason doing with all this?

I know enough to know that no woman should ever marry
a man who hated his mother. Martha Gellhorn

You do not owe him anything, Hugh tells himself.

I saw that nothing was permanent. You don't want to possess anything
that is dear to you, because you might lose it. Yoko Ono

Okay, maybe some—not responsibility exactly, but some—fellow feeling. Jason could have been his son. Interiorly, Hugh debates. Let him have the spare room at the gallery.

"Why don't you guys, you and Jason, come to dinner on Saturday?" he asks Ann, wishing he was not asking her. "It's Della and Ken's thirtieth anniversary—you know, the dinner I do for them every year."

Ann is crying now. Her pale lips clamp, an effort of control. "Yeah, sure, fun," she says. Six or seven pulled Kleenexes lie on the floor beside the baseboard. She blows her nose with one, then pots it into the empty fireplace grate. "I'll bring champagne."

"No need to—" Okay. "Maybe flowers?"

She blows again, the small, pointed nose he knows as well as his own. "Yes, yes, *great*! A big bouquet of blood-red roses to celebrate their wonderful constancy and love. Why didn't I think of that myself?" Her voice is rising, pitching, as Jason runs down the stairs, L beside him. "I love to celebrate the longevity of marriage, the *faithful fucking husband*."

Jason heads for the front door. Not to run away. He holds the door to let L and Hugh escape; with a courteous little salute, he shuts it behind them.

Hugh stands outside the door for a moment, unable to turn from the spectacle of his own adolescence replayed; then he walks down to stand with L by the van. They're silent, listening to what might be going on inside the house.

After a while L asks, in a quiet voice, "Couldn't she just Facebook all those quotes?"

Ivy gets home early. At the master class Burton went straight to work with surprisingly little bombast, assigning scenes: all young lovers and Sweeney. He gave Ivy a fairy-wand wave: "Goodnight sweet prince, stand not upon the order of your going, when shall we three meet again? Two tomorrow, the drama lounge."

Dismissed. Perfect. Home by four, with time to wash her hair.

But Ann is in the living room. Paint pot in hand, uncapped Sharpie abandoned on the floorboards, she is frescoing the stair wall with a small brush. She reminds Ivy of the paperback cover of *Famous Last Words*, the Findley book where the guy writes his tale all over the wall. A tale that was, as she recalls, a sordid tabloid royalty-gay-BDSM exposé. That can't be fair, she thinks, I'll have to go back to that one—Mottyl the Cat in I of O's psychedelic *Not Wanted on the Voyage* being her favourite role ever, after all. The play, the movie, and ten years later the opera. I was famous, once. Back then.

Ann straightens up and smiles politely, vaguely. Black lines of text run along the walls.

"May I read?"

Ann nods, and stands back, almost shy. She tucks in a strand of hair and the brush stripes her cheek with black. The first is standard-issue feminist rhetoric:

When a woman tells the truth she is creating the possibility
for more truth around her. Adrienne Rich

Oy. It's going to be a long month.
The second is odder:

Of all things upon earth that bleed and grow,
A herb most bruised is woman. Euripides, Medea

The last one (at least, the one Ann has just finished) makes Ivy laugh: a pair, written on the doors of the cupboard under the stairs, so the two are framed together.

The great question that has never been answered, and which I have not yet been able to answer despite my thirty years of research into the feminine soul, is "What does a woman want?" Sigmund Freud

I want to drink your blood. Dracula

A laugh spurts out before Ivy gets her guard up, but it's all right. Ann lets slip a short, tart smile. "I'm being filmed this weekend for a magazine. My decorative aesthetic," she says, smile growing though she tries to stay cool. "Challenging the hierarchy through minimalism."

It would be kind to sit on the floor, to enter into the spirit of all this and help Ann look up quotes (as she evidently has been, laptop open on the empty floorboards). But Ivy wants to keep herself to herself. To stay open to Hugh, just for tonight, in case. In case there's something, some quiet, blue, Bunsen-burner flame that might have been lit.

"I got off early, I'm going out for dinner—I thought I'd take a shower?"

Ann's face goes blank. "It's your bathroom," she says. She kneels again.

A breeze. Ivy turns to shut the front door tight, but it's someone coming in. A tall woman with deep-set vivid eyes high up in a long, kind face. From the party last night. "Hey, Ann," the woman says.

Ann gives her a cool look and carries on with her paint pot.

To Ivy, the woman says, "I'm Della Belville." Her dark hair slips from a low-knotted chignon, too calm a style for the disorder she carries: restless eyes, the suspicion of a tic. But kind, yes. "You gave my daughter, Elle, a lift last night?"

"Oh, L! She's lovely."

"I think so too! Friends for life, then," Della says, taking Ivy's hand.

Ann shifts along the line of writing, then grunts and rocks back from her knees. "Shit, I knelt on the Sharpie. *Shit*, that hurts."

Della goes to look at the lettering on the wall. She reads in silence, no reaction on her face. Like an art teacher, Ivy thinks, waiting till she has seen before she speaks. The contrast between Della's exterior face (stable, thoughtful) and her perfectly visible interior self (torn, wild-eyed, mobile) fascinates Ivy.

"Nice," Della says, in the considering way that makes a student keep working. "Love the Dracula. And the *Medea*." She turns to look at Ann, takes a breath. "But you're not actually bleeding, right? Or a 'herb most bruised'?"

Oh dear. Tension. Ivy makes a delicate move for the stairs. Della sees and nods, releasing her; Ivy nods too, and is up the first flight almost instantly. That acquired gift for going.

Ann sits up on her heels. "Don't—"

"Because Jason . . ." Della says. Dogged, intent.

"Don't," Ann says again.

Ivy rounds the landing bend and vanishes. But at Della's next words she stands still, halfway up to the second floor, curiosity wrestling with cowardice.

"I can't help but think of Hugh's mother."

Silence.

"Seeing you down there, so taken up with the work. A bit obsessed."

"Shut up," Ann says. There's movement—Ann getting up?

"I'm just saying," Della says. "Let me know, I'll get Conrad to do a house call."

"Don't."

"The thing is, Jason looks like death on two sticks. Last night at the party I thought, now *who* does he remind me of? Oh, right—Hugh, when he was a kid."

Ivy sits on the bare wooden step, very quiet. Hearing Della's deep, unemotional voice break higher—crack, almost, with the effort to be calm—Ivy holds her knees to keep the papercloth skirt still. Taking (forgive me, God) acting notes, getting important clues to Hugh and the reason for his sad mouth.

After a silent moment, Ann says in a reasonable voice, "That's mean. Mimi's crazy. I'm just, I'm just *mad*."

"I know." Della half-relents. "And sad. I'm sorry, I know. But I think it's time to cheer up. It's hard on boys to see their mothers so sad—"

"Quit saying that! You don't know Jason, what's happening with him. He's fine."

"Elly's worried about him. About you. I came to see if you're okay."

"I'm good. I've got a magazine shoot on Saturday, I'm famous. I'm really so, so good." Ann is losing the reasonable tone. Ivy leans forward to see down to the landing, to Ann's hunched back, arms wrapped around herself, Sharpie clenched in one hand. Is she crying?

"Funny," Della says gently. "Because you don't *seem* really good."

Into her elbow, muffled by her arm, Ann says, "Don't say I'm like her."

Della sits close, touches Ann's bone-sharp shoulder. "Honey, no, she was bananas half the time. You're not crazy—that's why I thought I could talk to you."

This is painful and private. Ivy ought to go away. And yet, fascinating. She stays put.

Ann says, "She saw ghosts. I don't." Tears shine on her cheek.

"Not necessarily ghosts."

"Visions, whatever. The people who would come and sit on her bed at night."

"I mean, not necessarily dead. People she knew, I think," Della says, matter-of-factly. "They had parties in her room sometimes. Just dreams."

Ivy's interested in this: the same thing happens to her from time to time. *Visitors*, she calls them to herself. She is careful not to mention them to others.

Ann wipes her face with her sleeves. "Anyway, it scared the shit out of me. The whole time Hugh and I lived together, all four years, we only stayed with her once. She was shouting and walking around all night."

"Poor Mimi. She told me that the people asked her whether she wanted to live or die, and she said, *I'll live*. But she had to keep remembering what the right answer was, each time."

"I'm not like her," Ann says. "Not in every way."

"You've had a rough year." Della is all warm good sense, one arm easing around to comfort Ann. "Jack's a jerk, that's all. You're not wrecked," she says, stable and kind. Ivy wants to lean on Della too for a while.

Weeping, weeping, Ann says, "Hugh loves her so much."

"Yes, he does. You want Jason to love you like that, so it's—a burden?"

"No, no—I'm so much like her, though, I *am*. She was more my mother than my real mother ever was, and now she's dying—" Ann bursts out again, real carrying-on sobs now. She catches herself back from hysterics and grabs one of the loose Kleenexes lying around on the floor. Which she provides herself with in advance because she knows she's going to woo-hoo-hoo within a few minutes of settling anywhere. A sad, semi-freddo state of affairs.

She blows her nose, and Ivy can see her strain away from Della's kindness, brittling up again; but Della's arm stays firm. "Honey, I hate to ask, but where's all the furniture?"

Ann says nothing. Then—this is strange—she laughs. "I'm just trying to figure out how to carry on here, and I'm not at all happy."

Ivy wants to laugh too, but at the same time she knows that state, that stretched-out time of not being at all happy, not ever, no matter how much cake you eat.

"Nobody is," Della says sadly.

And that snaps Ann's fragile temper. "Oh, fuck *off.*"

Della straightens up herself, sits apart. Seems like she too felt a need for bracing. "For example, Ken—"

But Ann is on her feet, and flying up the stairs. "I don't want to hear a word about what *Ken says*, you *wife*!" she flings back at Della—and almost falls over Ivy, whose knees unfold too slowly to get out of the way.

Ann grabs the banister to steady herself and stands, staring at Ivy. The pause, or the surprise, gives her back some poise. She calls lightly down to Della. "Or what *you* say either. Look at Ken. How happy is your own husband?"

Self-contained again, she glides up the last steps and down to the end of the hall, to her new un-master bedroom; she does not even slam the door.

Oh, impossible. Ivy hopes with all her heart that Della has not seen her hiding there. Humiliating, to be caught eavesdropping, and when she liked her so much, too. She hears Della clamber to her feet and stand, breathing, in the living room.

On the stairs, Ivy stays still, waiting her out, invisible.

It has to be done, but Hugh can't make himself shut up the gallery and walk over to Burton's. To *Newell's*, he corrects himself. But no: Newell's place no longer.

He hates Burton. The feeling shocks him. Come on. He's just an old guy, just an old—

An old molester. Stop. You can't keep thinking like this unless you're planning to do something about it. And there is nothing to be done.

A relief to see Della climb the steps, one hand rising automatically to stop the bell from tinkling. "Hey," she says. "I thought you might still be here."

"It's like you're psychic," he says, his mood improved. Della gives him the opposite of the heebie-jeebies. Her eyes are red, but she seems to be over her earlier spasm of sadness, or whatever drove her away from the teenage costume try-on. Is Ken being a jackass? Then Hugh will have to punch him too, which would be sad because he likes Ken.

"Thanks for proofing the flyer text," Della says, giving him a sideways look, a fond horse, examining.

"Come for a walk?" he asks her.

"At your service," she says. "Elle's out with her peeps and Ken's still away."

"But not dinner."

"No, so I gather. Ruth tells me," she says, lightly, "that you are having dinner with Mrs. Lovett. Some people might hesitate."

"She's not doing the cooking," he says.

"I met her. She seems very nice."

"That's tepid."

"Just careful of you, that's all. Assessing the minefield."

"How did Ken's rappelling go?" (Speaking of minefields, Hugh thinks.)

"I guess they'd have told me if he fell off the cliff." Her tone, her face, precludes chat re: Ken. "How's Mimi today?"

"Pretty good, we talked about you, the piano—then she went to pieces."

"I'll go over at dinnertime, keep her company."

"You're kind. She— I'd be glad." Hugh flips the sign and twists the key, and they walk along the early evening street in good companionship, through the misty air.

"I was at Ann's this afternoon," Della says. "Interfering."

"Hard to imagine," he says, and she swats him.

"Telling her off. I didn't intend to, but she's covering her walls with black marker."

"I saw." Hugh slips up onto a low stone wall to avoid a sidewalk puddle.

Della takes the low road, down into the street. "Marker is a bitch to paint over, that's all I know. But I didn't say that."

"Old Ann. Can't live with her, can't tell her anything."

The spines of yellow leaves show red against the concrete sidewalk. From square to square the markings vary, official stamps or twig-dragged lines; very occasionally, a small handprint. Hugh could draw a map showing all the handprints in town. One day jackhammers will tear them out for something new, moving sidewalks or jetpacks or hydraulic tubes to swoop you from place to place like in old department stores, everything old new again.

"I'm a fogey now," he tells Della. "I call everybody Old So-and-so, now. Like goddamn Holden Caulfield or something."

"Makes you sound like Newell. It's just a tic, or a phase."

"Or aphasia. Brain rust of some kind. I've got to go apologize to Burton."

"What are you going to say?"

Hugh wheels their formation to the left, into the Bloomsday flower shop. "Here are some nice flowers, Burton."

"Good plan."

They pick through the stock. While Della buys some dried orange lanterns, Hugh ponders roses and their meaning. Yellow, according to the card, conveys friendship, jealousy, infidelity, apology, a broken heart, intense emotion, dying love, extreme betrayal.

"Okay," he says, and takes three dozen.

It's only another block to Deer Park, Newell's condo.

Della refuses to come up, but she takes his hand. "They get along pretty well, don't be so mad," she says. "Look at Ann—an object lesson on how not to take a breakup. Don't you be the lesson on how not to take a hookup."

"You see things so clearly," Hugh says. Respect for her good sense in his heart, even if it doesn't make it into his tone.

"Wish I could see Ken so clearly." She turns down to the river with her arms full of orange bells. "Wish you could."

A tickle of worry scratches Hugh's ear. He brushes it away.

Up the long flight of private stairs to Newell's shining kingdom. Glossy hedge like a maze shunts him along the wall of glass, great panes flaming in the setting sun. Hugh can't see whether anyone is watching from inside as he comes forward with his suitor's gift.

In fact it's easy enough. Burton has worn pale yellow to accentuate the brilliant blue-black of his eye, swollen to magnificence. Hugh schools himself to civil contrition, unless there's talk of suing him for assault, but the plum-black mess of that eye makes the words honest: "Burton, you look— I don't know what came over me. I'm sorry, I am really sorry."

There's a pause, just long enough for Burton to measure the truth of that, to judge it. Then he swings an arm wide, and takes the flowers. "For *me!*" He smiles, showing all his yellowy teeth for once; by that Hugh can tell he really is pleased. "You are a rascal, first to use your fists, instead of your words, and then to bribe me so magnificently. *You* know, as not *everybody* knows, that a mere dozen is stingy. Let me see to these right away. I feel, dear Hugh— an increased friendliness toward you after our altercation, as those who engage in prizefighting tell me is quite common."

Not much of an altercation, Hugh can't help thinking as he moves with Burton to the sink in the jet-black island. All that happened was I knocked you down.

But he doesn't let that loose, and Newell comes back with a bottle and three glasses. "Almost as if you knew Hugh was coming," Burton cries archly. Or maybe that was " . . . as if you-know-who was coming!"

Newell is in running gear. Burton displays him: "Boy's off to do his daily ten K. The obligations of success. You could do with a K or two yourself, or do you scorn the physical entirely, Hugh?"

Nothing to say to that, Hugh thinks. A) it's true, and B) he's still on sufferance, being re-accepted into the circle of intimate inferiors to whom Burton doles out pinpricks.

But A) it's certainly true. He sits in his slackness.

They give Hugh the rundown on the master class: how little talent there is, from Burton; from Newell, how surprisingly good the kids are. Burton rails about the impossibility of musical theatre. "Not a voice among them! I'm seriously thinking *Streetcar*, an avant-garde imagining, thirteen ways of looking at *desire*—a tantalizing one-two, a switcheroo."

Newell looks patient and partly amused.

"None of them can *sing*, Boy! I can't, I cannot spend a whole month working with clodhoppers who can't dance, don't ask them, who will *not* open their mouths, and couldn't hold a tune with a pair of filigree sugar tongs."

"Aren't you contractually obligated?" Hugh asks.

"I'm changing the scenes, that's all. We do have some talent—the boy Orion, for example —although not, dear *God*, in the musical theatre line. Light years from what these children should be working toward. *Glee*'s an aberration. There's not the smallest chance that any of these tykes will be asked or expected to sing or God knows *dance* in their future lives, whether packing groceries for the A&P or in some regional summer repertory theatre troupe-slash-commune in Pisspassthequodit, Maine."

"We are contractually obligated," Newell says. "Yes." He ties his gel-packed, light-filled silver-sided running shoes, a B-list god, going for a run.

Burton puts a loving arm around Newell's bent neck and squeezes, hard. "*Streetcar*—I've got such a vision! We could do these students some real good."

Hugh thought those same words last night, that Newell could do Orion some real good. But not Burton— who's getting excited, enlisting Hugh in the new idea. "To explore what Tom was really getting to the root of!" (Calling him Tom, not Tennessee, as if he knew him. Maybe he did, he's old enough.) "I'm thinking of an X'd cast, you know: male Blanche, Stella—that giant girl Savaya, what is she, six-two? Contemplate the violence inherent in that system!"

Perhaps there's something actually wrong with Burton, Hugh thinks. Beyond the usual psychosis; maybe he's sick. There's a weird dark smudge across his eyes, his temples. Or else, okay—that's probably bruising from the punch. Hugh drains his extremely good scotch in one swallow, and gets up to go. "Appointment," he explains, not wanting to say more.

Newell must have heard him talking to Ivy last night, but says nothing.

Burton, though—damned Burton never misses a trick. "An ap*point*-ment! Well! Give the lady our best regards, and make sure to ask about her recent performances. I understand there was a request for a remount of her one-woman I of O show, an Elizabeth Bishop bio-epic, at the National— ask her how *that* went." No attempt on Burton's part to disguise his own tone: malicious, leering, greedy for the mortification of others.

Hugh has no idea what he's talking about, but doesn't need Newell to say, "Leave it alone, Ansel."

Burton giggles and leaps up to rearrange the yellow roses in the great square crystal vase. *Friendship, jealousy, infidelity, apology, a broken heart, intense emotion, dying love, extreme betrayal.*

"Okay," Hugh says. His apology is over. "I'll be sure to report back any personal agony she may confide." He kept his shoes on, he can walk straight out.

Newell follows him onto the terrace, though.

Now, out of Burton's gravitational pull, Hugh is ashamed. But won't apologize again. "Don't bother excusing him," he says. "I don't like people who like humiliation."

It's a short walk across the sifted stones.

"Everybody has hard stuff," Newell says. "Everybody is stupid sometimes."

Hugh reaches the stairhead.

Newell tries again. "Everybody has bruises. Not just him, me too. And look at you! Your mother when you were a kid—even now! That didn't get better, but you've never cut her loose, have you?"

"She is my *mother*," Hugh says. (Not my molester, he wants to shout. But still, always, knows he must not say.) He starts down the stone steps.

Newell stands there at the top of the stairs. "Maybe you just don't like gay people. Did you ever consider that?"

That hurts Hugh. "I don't know how you even dare to suggest that. For example, however little at the moment, I like you."

"But you only like the parts of me that don't seem really gay."

Hugh says, stiffly: "I like the parts of you that are human. I don't care about your sexuality."

"Weirdly, all of me is human. Including my—sexuality."

Hugh is almost at the bottom of the stone steps. "I like everything about you, I always have. I just—don't—like—Burton."

"Well, you've got to," Newell says. His voice is not raised, but its skill and beauty carry it down the stairs to nestle in Hugh's ear, beside the gadfly Della set there earlier.

Got to like Burton, can't like Ken.

(ORION)

Down along the grey path by the river, tiny pebbles moving sliding underfoot, the best bike in the world and the long ride, mind into rapture, everything in the body awake and moving, mercury sliding, bones and sinew triumphant. No boss can best this breasting of the autumn air. Leaf mould, water, silver air that slips through cells, the whole body breathing *fall, fall, fall—*

At the corner of the river road, ahead, a silver shoe flashes a green gel glint.

The green rises into the still-green grass at the far gate, a path flagged, flared through the rhododendrons.

As if it might be chance, might be accident.

The mist of this strange planet is filling my head with such thoughts . . .

The loved one.

In secret. What is more intoxicating?

9. I.O.HUGH

The curio shop closes at six, but not the gallery—Tuesday is class night. Old Jasper drifts over, glass in hand, pie-eyed. He's got someone in tow: Gerald, the widower.

The day has wound down. Hugh is cleaning up the back room before Della's class.

"Here's Hugh!" Jasper says. "*Yoo-hoo, You-Hugh!*" he sings. "Come eat with us at the Ace—*I. O. Hugh*, after all!"

"Hey, Jasper." Then, hating himself for a wet blanket, Hugh asks, "Good day for curios?"

Wrong thing to say. Jasper's face twists into a familiar knot. "Three people asked my advice about silver and decided not to sell or buy; one of them dropped a Sèvres box and neglected to mention the chip. A man pulled out a phone and bid on a Cattelin music box online, the very one I'd offered to get for him." Then, pathetically, he turns that frown upside down: "But otherwise, wowzers! A large order for tchotchkes from a show-home designer, and the Byersville museum curator called me *sweet-cheeks*. And she's a hard nut to crack."

Gerald sits in the basket chair by the ceramics. He glistens, pearlized with grey sweat. Not okay, after his day back at the dealership. His wine-glass is empty. He sets it carefully among the pots. Hugh does not have a single useful thing to say to him. All the time they've been acquainted, they've never spent ten minutes talking together before today.

He takes the wineglass and sets it on the cash desk. "Long day, Gerald?"

Gerald nods. "Sold a pre-loved to Lise Largely. A sympathy sale, but I'll take it."

"Can't call it sympathy, from that fiend." Jasper raises his glass in a toast, and settles on the bottom shelf of the magazine rack, folding his legs like an elderly cricket. "She wants my store, Hugh!"

"Okay," says Hugh. "First, I only know her through Mighton, but she worries me. Wasn't there some kind of scandal? And second, are realtors allowed to speculate? I thought there were rules."

"Poor creature, she still has to make a living." Jasper says with a hic-cuping laugh. "But she can't really realtor, real-itize, since she lost her licence—that's why she wants the place, to open an allergy/aromather-apy clinic. Largely Allergy." In case Hugh has missed it, Jasper waves his hands helpfully: "She can just rearrange the letters on your sign!"

Looking up, Gerald says, "Her sister's a naturopath, the sister's hus-band is a chiropractor, and Lise trained in flower essences. She told us all about it, she's a pal of my—"

He stops, a cliff opening in front of him. "My—wife—" he says, and stops again.

They sit quietly, the room suddenly full of the dead.

"Come, Gerry. To the Ace!" Jasper says, stick legs jerking upright with false spryness. "I'm on your dinner roster, it's my night."

Della arrives for class as Gerald pulls himself out of the basket chair, and at the sight of him she gives an involuntary sighing cry. A warble, a *woe-is-me*. He smiles for her and processes carefully out with Jasper as the gallery fills with a parrot-flock of small children for the evening class.

Toby not among them.

How is Gerald supposed to live with this?

Della holds Hugh's jacket out to him over the flood of children.

"Get out of here," she says. "You have a date with density."

(DELLA)

at last
a text:
        < I'm all right. Just so you know.
            > Any idea when you're coming—
                                back or home? erase erase erase erase erase

            > I love you

                                        erase erase irrelevant

type again:
            > All right. We're all right.

                                    not the best answer either
                            which non-existent we is that?
                                        me and Elle
                                        me and Ken

phone open again again again
while the children paint
stare at the unblinking screen

10. I PUT A SPELL ON HUGH

The Duck & Cover glows in the twilight, every window golden. Pumpkins crowd the stairs; precarious to climb past them. Stumbling on a tricky step, Ivy wonders whether her expensive new rose-covered shoes really work, as per shoes. But they look so pretty on the hoof, they make her love herself.

Through the glass door she sees midnight blue walls, small tables. The room looks like the interior mind: candles set in the windows, darkness within. That's all right, darkness is useful for thinking.

Hugh falls up the stairs behind her, sprawled full length this time, like he's crawling up on his hands and knees. His self-appalled/self-amused, mainly tolerant eyes look up from the long tangle he makes on the pumpkin-riddled stairs, and Ivy experiences a pretty good swoop in the lower regions. Who'd have thought, at this late date?

"Nice of you to drop by," she says, giving him her hand.

The hostess is Savaya from the master class. Hugh introduces her as L's friend, but Ivy already knows her. She sits them at a table in a small bay window, shielded from the street by a Japanese maple, leaves like fire in the dusk. Ivy lets Hugh have the door-facing chair she usually takes herself. She doesn't need time to recognize anyone here.

"Crab cakes?" Hugh suggests. "Fish is good here. They bake their own bread."

He's stopped looking at her—he seems to be having an attack of shyness. She sends X-ray eyes through the back of his menu, but he does not move it.

She tilts. "You there? Hugh?"

He looks up, caught, and half his mouth smiles nervously. The waiter comes and they order. Not a bottle of wine, because Ivy says she can only drink one glass.

"It gets worse if I have a hangover," she says, once the waiter is gone.

"What does?"

"I thought you'd have heard about my—my current—" Oh boy, now she's stuck.

"Heard from Burton, you mean?" Hugh's whole face grimaces. "I just took him three dozen yellow roses. But I left before he could get gossipy."

"Yipes, three dozen! Were you afraid he was going to sue you?"

"Yellow roses, as perhaps you know, are the roses not only of apology, but also of *dying love* and *extreme betrayal*."

"In fact, I did not know that."

"No, well, not everyone has the language of flowers at their fingertips. It was on the card at the florist's."

"A subtle dig, then. Do you think Burton will perceive it?"

"If it advances his purposes, I'm sure he will."

The wine comes, the waiter goes again. A private spot, this window seat.

"What is your, your current—?"

Ivy makes a face. "Nothing. I just have a gapping problem. I forget my lines."

Hugh looks interested rather than pitying.

"I forget things in general, too," she tells him. He might as well know.

"Yet here you are, at dinner."

"I remembered you." Then that seems too intimate a thing to have said. "Mind you, I couldn't find the restaurant, but that was because you said the funny name."

"I wasn't remembering very well myself. That was the second fall of the day—I fell off a ladder yesterday morning." He blinks, shakes his head quickly. Touches his forehead.

"How far?" Her arms prickle with worry. Weird.

"Maybe fifteen feet. I was trying to put up Hallowe'en lights on the sign at the gallery."

"What did the doctor say?"

Hugh rubs his eyes. "I haven't seen him yet. Ruth made an appointment, but I hate going in."

"Ruth?"

"The woman who took your call. My gallery assistant."

"She seemed perfect."

"Gallery assistant is too grand a title. She helps out. She's okay with the ladies who come in to buy cards." Saying that, Hugh looks ashamed. Interesting.

"Where did you find her?"

"She looked after me, on and off, when I was a kid. There's no getting rid of her." He drums briefly on the table, pours more wine. Knocks twice on the table to discharge bad luck. "I don't want to get rid of her," he says.

"No, I know. I have a mother or two myself."

"Ha!" But he looks miserable.

She waits for him to begin again. Well, she can carry on. "Who do you eat with usually?"

He looks around the restaurant, as if his friends will materialize. "Newell, when he's here. When he's here without Burton. But I ate with the two of them last night, now I think of it. Della and her husband, Ken, but he's—away right now. Ruth, I guess, not often. Although we sort of ate together too, last night. She was the server at Pink's place."

"I remember her, she's a sweetie!" Perhaps a bit overblown, too much happiness. Ivy tries to explain. "L hugged her. And I met Della today, she's L's mother, right? She came to the house where I'm staying. It's such a relief when I remember people."

"Your difficulty, does it affect—does it make it hard to work?"

Ah, her turn for misery now. "Since my work is entirely memory-based, yes, it does."

They sit silent for a moment. Ivy wishes she had not said that so baldly.

"I'm sorry," she says. "I'm not good at talking about it."

The invisible waiter slides a long plate of crab cakes onto the table, smelling of ocean and a fire on the beach. Hot in the mouth, temperature and spice heat, pico de gallo cold and sharp beside them.

"Sheryl Crow has a benign brain tumor," Hugh says. "It makes her forget her lyrics when she's singing."

Ivy looks down. She fills her mouth with crab again.

"But I suppose she can tape them to her guitar," he adds. "Awkward with the longer songs. That's why she doesn't do *Now I'm a broken man on a Halifax pier, the last of Barrett's Privateers.*"

She laughs. "Fine! I do not have a brain tumor. I did find the courage to go and see about that. No aneurysm, no Alzheimer's. It might be, I might have a stress problem, or need, what is it, ginkgo biloba. Or I might just be, well, old."

"Burton knows? And makes a little hay?"

"Yes, he does. Everybody in theatre knows. I had a big blow-up, a one-woman show, it was a disaster. The show was good. Elizabeth Bishop, I'm perfect for her. But I just couldn't, I couldn't. So after a few, after, oh, three bad nights, they found a replacement."

"Oh no." He looks honestly empathetic. Usually people are trying not to laugh, because it is pretty funny, the actor's nightmare.

"Somebody gave me my script and I read from it, the first bad night. After eight or nine terrible pauses. I thought I could keep doing that, reading the script. But eventually, no."

"Does it matter for film?"

"If I know the line and then I get up and don't know it, that wastes a lot of money."

He nods. It's nice that he's not saying too much.

"I'm still good for workshopping—I do voicework, audiobooks, anything where you keep the script in front of you. Whatever radio is left, with the cuts. It's not like it's the first time in history. Ellen Terry couldn't remember lines for *Captain Brassbound's Conversion*. Richard Dreyfus: his London opening kept being delayed, a few years ago. Et cetera. People tell me all kinds of helpful stories. When I was young I worked with an awful old woman. She wrote out her lines and pasted them around the room on the mantelpiece, the picture frames, an antique box of soap. She'd pick it up in the scene and read the lines right off it. I was disgusted with her. Serves me right."

"No it doesn't. The young always think the old are pathetic whiners, that's the deal. Then we gradually find out."

"I find that so often! Whatever I despise, I eventually have to experience myself. It's a dark little sidestreet of karma."

It is satisfying to make him laugh, to talk to him. To feel known. The way his eyes are set in his head, the lines of his mouth, please her.

The fish arrives, with fresh thick bread, and arugula salad.

"Do you have family here?"

Now Hugh looks guarded. New friends: such a process of what to tell, what not to tell—Ivy feels tired, for an instant. But curious.

He says, having thought, "Ruth, she was my foster mother."

"I heard L's mother talking about your mother today. I forget her name, shoot."

"Mimi. Oh—Della, you mean. L's mother is Della, my—foster sister, I guess. Ruth looked after us all, Della, Newell, me."

His pinched face says, can she not see that I do not want to talk about this stuff? Yes, yes, but she wants to know, she needs to pull down the social barrier that prevents strangers from asking about your intimate life.

"Mimi—my mother—is in hospital." He catches himself. "In the hospice wing. Dying."

"What does she have?"

"Everything. Bone cancer, diabetes, heart disease, pneumonia. In the old days, she had various episodes and excitements. Now, basically, she has death." His hand rests on the white cloth. "It's hard to talk about her. I listen to myself, wondering how long it takes to learn how to tell the story of the sick person: what words work, what is a lie, or a fiction."

"I'm sorry," Ivy says. "You must be so sad."

He laughs a little. "I am, but I'm used to it. Della may have told you, my mother was—she suffered from depression, manic episodes. Bipolar, probably, but they could not seem to— Shock therapy in the seventies, et cetera. That made her more careful. She didn't want to fix it. It's not a problem, now that she's immobile."

Ivy doesn't ask anything more.

Looking at his plate, Hugh says, "She's a—she was a lovely person, a fiery . . . a flame. But not easy, you know. I'm sure I'm, I mean, you can't be brought up by— Well, I wasn't. Ruth took me over from time to time, whenever the downslope hit."

It's heavy going, Ivy can see that. But she can't do anything to help except sit with him.

He smiles at her, sudden sun through clouds. "It's probably good to love your mother. Even if she was batshit crazy half the time, she was always a beautiful nut. She's finished with acting up now. And since I've looked after her for the last few years, I don't even have to feel guilty, right?"

At this point, feeling Fate's cartwheels trundling over her chest, Ivy's chief sensation is dismay. What fresh trouble is she getting into here?

"Right, right," she says. Her hand crosses the table to touch his fingers. Straight, smooth-skinned, plain, over-sensitive. Such a nice hand.

(L)

Hope. L letters it carefully, behind the muffin case. Tuesday night is always dead. Thinking of Nevaeh's beauty in the black-and-blue Hope dress, stalking off to change again because Jason didn't like the way the crest emerged. He's fussy about the lettering too, and L's already thrown away too many of these little cards he made for dress labels. Perfectionist. But in her opinion there is not enough perfectionism in this world. People having the gall to decide to make things properly, to insist on things being right.

Nevaeh leans on the counter drying cups. Superimposed, L sees her leaning on her bedroom chair, explaining just how it came about that she and Savaya were necking. How Savaya got a text and said, *Wait, that's Jerry, I've got to go;* how it would always be that way, and how it hurt her *so much.* And how she needs, needs, what? Maybe me, maybe?

But it is not real. What is between them, what delicate things they, delicately—oh, swoop, the rush of feeling comes once again. But still not real. It was not good enough that night, it is not now. There is some barrier, some dissonance, not between them, maybe, but where they come from. Money, partly, Nevaeh being rich; Nevaeh's famous, ferocious father, scary slow-speaking guy, asking "What is *wrong* with your *family?*" L's own father being basically the opposite of ferocious.

Maybe solitude is best.

She could talk to Orion—but Orion's distracted, off on a stratagem; making the best of Newell and managing Burton very well. An education just to watch him. It's a strange burden, to look at him. Newell has the same quality. Draws the eye, and shakes it off.

Maybe I am too much of a perfectionist and there is no perfect, only a sequence of making do. What is attraction, anyway? The dent over Nevaeh's upper lip, her collarbone, the slender turning of her upper arms. Her wide-open, flame-throwing heart. Or Newell's wide-spaced eyes, is that it? Or else it is how sad he always, always is, beneath the charm.

Orion is not sad, not yet. But his mother, hokey jeez, *she's* a mess. And my mother too. And where is my dad?

Into the labyrinth, lost like I am, in *The Island Republic of L.*

Ivy is the kind of person you can talk to. Hugh can. You tell her things you should keep quiet about: "It's the automatic actions that worry me. For instance, I didn't mean to punch Burton. My arm just came out. I hate him so much."

"Why?" He looks at her. "I do myself," she adds quickly, "but why do *you* hate him? He doesn't tease you like he does me, and he doesn't have any power over you."

He adjusts the candle, which is guttering. "I don't like . . . how he is with Newell."

"Jealous?" She blinks, as if wishing she hadn't gone that far. "I mean, I only mean, yes, Newell is the best. And you're obviously very good friends. It's hard to have to share him."

"I've known Newell all my life. All my conscious life. I've known Burton as long as Newell has. And he's——"

A brief silence.

Ivy smiles at him. "You can tell me. I'm safe, because I forget everything."

Some cautious or honourable streak stops Hugh from spilling his suspicions of Burton. Or some desire to protect Newell. But he says, shamefaced for himself, "Newell said today that maybe I just don't like gay people."

"Do you think that's true?"

"No."

"No hidden prejudice? Nothing in your subconscious's, um, closet?"

"No!" He laughs this time. "I just really don't like Burton."

"Well, that's a big club, you can share my annual membership."

"I would like to belong to all your clubs," Hugh says. "If you will have me as a member." That came out a little forced, a little lame. He sighs to himself and tries to smile.

She is looking thoughtfully at her butter knife. She polishes it on her napkin, and puts it in her purse. Is this part of her forgetfulness, he wonders, or kleptomania?

Purse shut, Ivy looks up into his eyes. Her own are surprising, liquid and bright in the candlelight. She asks, "So here's a question for you, for Hugh: is life a submitting to fate? Or do we have to decide, have to choose what to do?"

"You have to live the life you have," Hugh says. "Except I haven't." He has done nothing, nothing good.

"I always want to be somebody else," Ivy says, ashamed too. "But it's good for work."

Except she can't work now, he thinks. Terrifying. "Okay, how about improv—lines don't matter there, right?"

"Yes, except some days I can't remember what people were just saying." Ivy leans her head on her hand. "Can't follow a conversation."

He looks at her sane, sad face.

"Well, never mind," she says, straightening up. "Tell me about your life, your lives."

"I had a couple of other lives, yes, away from here. A couple even while I was here, going back and forth between my mother—crazy, glamorous—and Ruth—ordinary. I went to art school; then I came back here and lived with a woman for four years while I taught art at Lakefield, and tried to paint. That didn't work. We split up. I went out west to be an artist full time. Didn't work. I'm just not that good, I'm better at teaching. So then I took over a small-town hotel in Maple Creek, Saskatchewan. Whole other life, hardest I've ever worked."

Her mouth can't seem to stay straight while he reels off his CV. But as far as he can tell, she is not laughing *at* him. Happy to be here, or something. That makes him happy.

"After ten years without a day off I sold it, went to California, made jewellery with a silversmith from Peru; I painted portraits on the beach for a year. Twenty bucks for a single, fifty for the whole family. Not good portraits. I lived in a strange motel, full of druggists. Not weed or cocaine— pharmaceutical dispensers, cheap drugs from Canada and the UK. People trooped up and down the halls all day getting their Dilaudid and their blood pressure pills. Okay—then I came back to Canada; I cooked for a while, short order not haute, wrote an art criticism column for the Halifax paper; on the side I did some book design and worked for an auction house—"

"You're like one of those invented author bios on the back flap: 'Neville has been a brain surgeon, lumberjack, car thief, tango dancer and cowpoke.'" She makes him laugh, internally, a pleasurable effervescence. "Are you a good cook?"

"More cook than cowpoke. I cooked breakfast at the Waegwoltic, posh country club in Halifax. I make the best omelette you'll ever eat. After noon, I mostly eat out."

"So why are you here?"

"At the Duck? It's after noon."

She cocks her head, patient, and he laughs.

"Okay, Peterborough. Ten years ago my mother got sick, and I came back here and opened the gallery." That sentence covers an awful lot of ground. He won't be fool enough to unpack it for her tonight. He can't even talk about Mimi, her present state.

"My parents are eighty, still going strong," she says, as if understanding that he's done in. "My twin sister lives next door to them in Thornhill, so it's like I never left at all. She gets a medal when they croak, boy." Her eyes are agate-coloured, dark grey-brown. Grey-green? Shining in the candlelight. "They're self-sufficient, interesting people; gave me everything and so on. Both lawyers. They wear the same clothes."

He laughs. "Always Toronto?"

"Mostly. School, theatre school, et cetera. I travel around for work, a lot, I guess. I have an apartment, College and Spadina, a loft!" Proud of it. Then her face twists up, she is sad. "But I haven't been—well, somebody's living there. Jamie, a friend's younger brother. Sort of looking after the place while I've been in Banff, and up north." Her voice peters out.

"Parked on you?"

"The poor guy, he's not very well, it's complicated. I don't know how to go back."

"If you can't live there, where do you live?"

"Oh, with my sister. Or I house-sit, or I get another gig. Like this one."

"You don't seem like a twin. You seem like yourself."

"Well, that's not really how it worked with us, but I will take it as a compliment—"

Catching his eye, she looks down, and the heavy creamy lids stay lowered. She looks at her plate, adjusts the knife and fork to less-perfect parallel. The fork crosses the knife, tines engaged. Like legs entwined.

The dark eyes come up again. Her mouth twists, she knows his mind. But there is still coffee to come. "Well then, tell me about your childhood. Your earlier childhood," she says.

"My parents separated when I was three. Divorced a year later. Which may explain her really difficult breakdown when I was four. I went to Ruth's for a year or so. My mother would never speak about him again."

She looks troubled, sorry for him.

"Don't worry. I don't really remember him. From time to time I used to get an urge to Google him, but I suppressed it." (Over and over, feel and stop feeling.) "A lot of stuff in life seems to be like that—like being an alcoholic. Or eating too much." He pushes the bread basket away, signals to the waiter for another of the red.

Ivy says, "Aldous Huxley said most of life is one prolonged effort to stop thinking. Is he still alive?"

Hugh doesn't pretend it's Huxley she means. "No."

The waiter fills his glass and goes.

Hugh hasn't thought about his head for a while. The ache is still there. "Okay, there were a few of him on the internet." He puts his glass down.

His father, somewhere in the world, not ever thinking of Googling Hugh. Hugh is filled with knives and pieces of glass; furious with Ivy for making him dip down into childish disappointment. "Once I found an obit in the *Vancouver Sun*—died in 1987. Two daughters, wife, extended family, Rotarian Award. Dry cleaning business." (Where's your special-ness now?) "So for a long time I thought he might be dead. There were others, a Henry Argylle the right age in New Brunswick. One in New Jersey, two in the UK."

She's watching him. Her mouth is a pleasing line, her face open. A loving face.

"But in fact I was sent ten thousand dollars from his insurance money last month. He died in Winnipeg, he'd been living with a married step-daughter and had no other family left. She wrote me a letter."

"Maybe kind of a relief?" As if she can't even tell he's angry. Or is choosing not to let him stay angry. "You don't have to talk to him, now. And you won't have to stop yourself from looking him up all the time."

"Either I was the dry cleaner's boy, or I am my self."

She looks at him, autumn-eyed. She says, "You are your self. You are Hugh."

They walk home in the cool night. Fall sharpening into winter. Glad of her warm coat, Ivy tucks her arm into Hugh's without even thinking, without wondering if she should. His good, warm arm.

As they pass the gallery they hear a grating thunk: L, locking the door of FairGrounds. She and the thin dark girl from behind the counter embrace—then with a wave of one long arm the other girl slips into the passenger seat of a waiting car. Getting off work at ten. Late for a school night, going to walk home alone now? L's mother's name has slid out of Ivy's mind again; that makes her fist bunch tight inside her jacket pocket.

"Hey, Hugh!" L says. "Oh, hi, Ivy—I mean, Ms. Sage."

"Oh, Ivy, please, *Ivy*," says Ivy. Besides liking L for herself, Ivy loves girls at this age, girls going wild, going like roller derby girls, each one a firecracker, a graceful, mad bacchante flying toward you in a violent swirl of eyes and arms. They make her think of the girls she hung out with, nights in swimming pools behind rich people's houses, sneaking from yard to yard all night, each new pool still as heaven, blue-lit from below. They make her remember dancing, and walking through dark streets with people you didn't know. Being in hot smoky places, never going home, being up all night at a party with hot knives cooking in the kitchen at the Delta Phi. Various, oh various, various people, and never any reason why not to. Delta Phi, *Della*, L's mom is Della. Phew.

L and Hugh are talking about her work, a series she's doing, has done? Hard to piece together from the scraps of their conversation, which might as well be semaphore or Morse.

They walk down London, Harvey, streets Ivy is trying to learn. She can see how much L likes Hugh. Trusts him. Her art teacher, her half-uncle. They have a world here, a life, a long community. For the first time in ages, Ivy thinks about how it would be to belong to some people, some place.

Dublin Street: and here is L's house, evidently. Green, spreading, odd. Big old trees. Hugh slows, clearly expecting L to peel off, but she says, "I'll carry on with you—I have to go see Jason, he's got my *Charity* dress almost ready and he wants me to try it on."

Hugh gives L a strange look, and then looks at Ivy, as if this is not fitting. But of course it is, it's a fitting.

Ann's house is across the street from L and Della's, farther down on the river side.

Just as they get there, Jason opens the front door to peer out and sees them coming up the walk. "Quick, the glue's setting!" he shouts, darting down to grab L's hand. The loudest and the fastest Ivy has heard or seen him yet. Behind him, Ann is kneeling by the stairs, intent on her work.

L and Jason go inside, and the door shuts.

Hugh looks down at Ivy, who sees now that she is quite a lot shorter than he is, darn it. Too short? He seems disconcerted.

"You're staying *here*? With Ann?"

"I am, yes."

"Ah," he says.

But now he smiles, very warmly. Heating her whole chest with it.

Hugh says, "Funny thing, it never occurred to me, when she said— Or when you said you were boarding, that it was with someone I know."

"The world is small."

They stand on the walk for a while in the early darkness, smell of smoke in the air and of dying leaves on the sharp, burnt edge of winter.

Then they say goodnight, grave, courteous.

(ORION)

Inside the hollow of rhododendrons, roofed with curled leaves, in the oldest place in the world now old in season, the young god Orion lies sleeping and waking, knowing he must move soon or his mother will freak, all Greek drama in her motherliness and panic, will run through the streets shrieking with her hair streaming behind her, her mail-order Hanro nightie flowing like a chiton and blood dripping from the finger-ends of her thin thin arms. He has to get up.

But he could lie here on the bosom of the earth forever, replete, on the soft litter of leaves left year by year to dry and crumble into silt. He stands, one movement, pleased with the motion of limbs, the strength and grace of his long, useful legs.

Lonely—all of a sudden. Left.

We all have someone to go home to.

He's starving, and there will be nothing in the fridge. He picks up his bike where it lies in leaf-litter, flicks leaf-shards from his sleeves and shoulders. The rest will fly off as he goes. He goes.

Ladder, up. Quiet. Only the river sipping at the grassy bank. This is the best back yard in town.

Don't slip. Okay. Now up the ladder to Ivy's window.

"It's Hugh," Hugh says, through the narrow opening. "I mean, it's me."

She gets out of bed. Almost 1 a.m. He can see her moving through the dusky room, in pyjama pants and a loose top.

Light? No light.

She kneels at the window's edge, bends to talk to him through the three round air holes in the storm window. "It's stuck, it's painted shut. I borrowed a butter knife from the restaurant to jimmy it, but it wouldn't work. I need a real chisel."

He holds up a container of the Dairy Bar's mango ice cream, two spoons. Feeling a bit precarious, perched on the old boathouse ladder. "I wasn't finished talking yet."

The pretty gold cardboard is frosted over, slippery.

"Don't fall, please?"

"Okay. I'll be careful."

Juggling spoons and container, Hugh hands the spoons through the peepholes to Ivy, one at a time. He props the ice cream on the top rung of the ladder and pries off the lid, which releases at last with a rude *pop!* that nearly kicks him off the ladder.

"Careful!" Ivy cries, as soft as a pigeon.

He puts out his hand for a spoon, which she slides back through the peephole. He scoops it full of ice cream, says, "Come close—" and threads the spoon through the wooden O again, into her waiting mouth.

Ivy's eyes are bright, her mouth full of spoon and mango. In the low light he could put his hand through the glass, as if it was water, and touch her face.

WEDNESDAY

❦

When life gives Hugh lemons

Craving to be (bhava-tanhā)*: this is craving to be something, to unite with an experience. This includes craving to be solid and ongoing, to be a being that has a past and a future, and craving to prevail and dominate over others.*

from the entry on Buddhism,
WIKIPEDIA

I. HUGH CAN'T

What do you think about as you lie in darkness? How do you keep your mind from eating itself? Hugh examines the corners of the room. The corners of his eyes. Not weeping, good. Yesterday, he didn't go to Mimi in the evening. Again tonight. First time in—oh, in the whole of life's great pageant. You could get dressed and go over now, 4 a.m. Hospice hours.

She'll be asleep, drugged out for the night.

It's not that. Can't bear to, that's all. She is the complicated bane of his entire existence; any day, any moment, she will have the final gall to die. Hugh can't bear to look at her.

You can stave things off with music. Sometimes. *The Mist Covered Mountains* used to work pretty well on a dark and rainy night. The Knopfler version, starting with a long, winding scree-whine of tide and squeeze-box. *Local Hero*. A movie probably nobody remembers. Ivy might. They could watch it again. He looks the DVD up on Amazon—$154.39! Okay, soundtrack on iTunes, $9.99. His Visa might not let even that go through. He's not allowing himself to buy anything online anymore. Just the one song, then. The waves pounding the shore.

Could have made a dent in the Visa with the ten thousand you gave Jasper. Should have.

A tear drifts down his cheek, catching the light in his reflection on the dark computer screen. His father's money doesn't matter because soon he will have his mother's. If she's got any left. The tear slides into his mouth. Behind the tear he can still taste mango ice cream.

The Mist Covered Mountains is now unbearably drawn out and boring.

Okay, okay.

He stands up, pulls on yesterday's clothes. One decision not needing to be made.

The streets are black-wet: more water in the basement. Change the bucket when you get back. Check the messages upstairs too, for Della, for

Ken. Hugh blinks light rain out of his eyes and refuses to think about Ken—it's painful to know when Della doesn't. Ken's probably not serious about quitting anyway. He's just in a slump, in a slough. Like you, Hugh.

One acquainted with the night. With the luminary clock on the Hudson Tower.

The stairs seem steep at the hospice. Too early/late for his legs. Kelly is on the desk, tubular and calm. She walks over to fasten the lock behind him, but doesn't bother with small talk. Something comforting and kind about the hospice in the middle of the night; even the staff seem meditative, close friends of death that they are. The air is still, the stairs to Mimi's room uncreaking; the door opens with proper weight, with gravity. Oiled hinges.

"You came!" Her voice as he enters, not a beat wasted.

"Of course I came, sweetheart," he says.

She is sitting up in bed, awake in the dark. Alert. Hands folded at the sheet's edge. Her reading glasses flash, bug-eyed, as her head turns. The curtains are open, clouded moonlight coming in; a nightlight somewhere low down gives the floor a pale glow.

She doesn't have the energy to speak again. He sits on the bed, takes her eggshell hand and talks about nothing. What he did all day, the rainy weather, the grass still green even though the leaves are going, gone . . . leaf-shadows falling across her eyes.

Go away from that: "I came in early, before all hell breaks loose today. That crazy Lise Largely—she did your lease, remember?—is trying to buy Jasper's place and mine. We have to turn her down. Did Della come in today? Ken's in a state, can't stand his life—he borrowed a cabin out by Bobcaygeon and went away to think for a few days. I don't know whether to tell Della where he is, or leave it the hell alone."

She turns the big glasses to him. Has she been listening? Hard to tell. She says, "Joseph said he had to tell me that heaven is real. Isn't that a strange thing."

Joseph. A chaplain? Hugh made sure not to tick that box on the visitors-allowed form. Hating anything that smacks of visions, or imaginary friends, or what might come next.

"The little boy said it was real, he died, and it was real, he went, it was real."

Hugh feels the same sick desperation, revulsion, the longing to go, from childhood. That hatred coming up in his throat like bile. He lowers the bed for her to sleep, until she puts her hand on his. Papery pale, silky with sickness and age, still her hand.

She looks at him, looks, looks. *Forgive me forgive me forgive me, it's all your fault.* Eyes monstrous behind the magnifying lenses; pale, frail moonface.

"I'm afraid."

"I know you are," he says. "I know."

"I'm afraid."

It is never less than terrible to hear. Now she will say it, over and over, for a while. He sits back in the bedside chair and listens.

Walking home, Hugh wonders where he should live when she dies. And why.

(ORION)

Man, *have* to start getting more sleep. *Man.*

Because his mother is pretty honourable, or is afraid after their last big fight, and no longer comes in here unless he asks her to—and he will not ask her to—

Because of all that, his bed is an armed fort, a rat's nest, barricaded by towers of empty cans and bottles, chip bags, pizza plates, bowls with last curls of macaroni fossilized where they died.

One of these days the metabolism will give up and he'll get fat, look at Burton. And it will all be his mother's fault.

Orion stands in front of his closet mirror, comparing himself to naked photos of Prince Harry on Twitter. Heavy, swinging, a nice silky giant of a thing. Mouth on mouth, mouth on cock, everything rising. Everything that rises will converge.

The virgin convergences. He is sick of AP English and Honours with Distinction and scholarship apps, the constant yearly tide of this and that, then the paper to prove it. Why not just leave this place, leave school, go straight to GO and do not pass Jail?

He turns, he sways. Arms up in the mirror.

Handsome man looks good in anything.

He falls to his knees, falls flat on the futon, sets the alarm for 8:30, and slides instantly into sleep.

2. HUGH CAN'T DO EVERYTHING

The rain lets up as Hugh reaches the gallery porch. Five a.m. No sun yet, but a lessening of the dark. Hugh goes downstairs to repack Mighton's boxes.

Six damp boxes; six new plastic totes Ruth got at Home Hardware yesterday. She is an angel, she's the only reason the gallery still functions at all. She needs a raise. But Hugh is not thinking about money today, at least not till after Lise Largely. Not thinking about her yet either. He slits open the first box, the least wet one: looks okay. Pieces wrapped in plastic, in cloth, in clean newsprint, with cardboard between them. No need to unwrap those that are dry. He takes his time, feeling for damage and damp.

Mighton, bloody Mighton. Della and Ken, thirty years this Saturday—before that, Della and Mighton were together for a while. Hugh slits, checks, rewraps, transfers.

What happened to Mighton's painting of Newell and Della and Ann wound together in a knot? Not in these boxes, it was big. He should paint it again, now, unknotted: Ann on the bare wood floor, black Sharpie in hand; Della checking her phone for a text from Ken; Newell looking off to the left, at Burton curled on the stairs like a bad conscience. Ann still the same, uncracked porcelain, like an expensive sink. Newell tired. Della suddenly old. It would be interesting to see how Mighton sees her now. Thank God she didn't stay with him, because although he's a genius he's also a slimeball. Lise Largely deserved him—how did she hornswoggle her way into Mighton's house? By being a champion hornswoggler.

Third box, fourth: water damage only to the cardboard box itself. Five, and here comes trouble. This box stinks. Hugh's heart sinks. It's getting lower and lower every day.

Upstairs, a noise: Ruth opening the front door. What the hell is she doing here so early?

He shouts up the stairs, "Go home! Go back to bed! It's not nine yet!"

"Oh, I was up," she calls down, all chipper. "Too old to sleep these days."

She's almost as old as his mother, hard to remember that. Who had the harder life?

Coffee will help. He climbs the stairs with depressing effort and goes back to the framing room, where Ruth is at work on a new set of certificates, this time for Home Hardware's regional awards night. Except for healthy corporate staff relations, the gallery would close in a week.

And except for Ruth. He pushes the button on the espresso machine, and walks over to give Ruth a quick hug.

"What's that for?" she wants to know.

"Star loyalty certificate, for coming to work early whether you need to or not."

"You're going to Conrad today, don't forget. Did you check your messages? Della was in asking."

Hugh reaches for his phone. Upstairs is far too far away.

Her bird eyes assess him. "You repacking Mighton's things?"

"I am so."

"Don't let it get to you. Dave's coming this afternoon, he promised me on his mother's life. He'll fix the crack, fifteen hundred, and he said he'd give a twenty-year guarantee."

"I may only need six months," Hugh says glumly.

"You have that meeting with Mrs. Largely today?"

"Yes, yes I do."

"Well, don't do anything drastic there either. There's many a slip twixt the cup and the lip, and she's too big for her boots *or* her britches, pride cometh before a fall."

"Whatever eldritch thing any of that means, I will not sign over the building this morning."

"I don't like that woman. There's something *off* about her."

"Yes, there certainly is." When Ruth's prejudices agree with his own, Hugh doesn't mind them. "I went in to check on Mimi this morning."

"Aren't you the early bird! And was she well?"

What's the answer to that? He turns away, to make coffee and go back down. Concrete, cardboard, Mighton's boxes are easier to deal with than his mother.

And he wants to text Ivy.

(DELLA)

Mimi's piano   she remembers I loved her
                        loved her playing   Elly won't wake
                                        Ken not here to wake
            Mimi's note: *Chopin often saved me when I couldn't cope,*
                        I hope he will you too.
Schumann   saves me when I cannot cope   Satie, sometimes
I could finish a boat   or twelve
stand looking at them   blind cross-eyed double-visioned
deal with this today   go to his office   see my lawyer ha ha ha
Jenny sitting there   his assistant she must know   must be arranging
                        makes blood run loose in my veins
                                                    she must know
                        he isn't speaking to ~~us~~   to me
maybe she's gone too   maybe she needed a kidney
                        Ken too shy to say anything   too noble
team building   rappelling in Elora Gorge
                            and then——a sickening——
                                fall   and they not telling me
but that is not it because he texted us
   < I'm all right. I'll let you know.
~~we~~ I texted back   ~~we~~ me there is
no we now
   > all right
                    up, go, go
                            running water helps a little
                                shower hot as can be borne
                                            hotter

Pearly early light wakes Ivy. She pats a hand on the bedside table for her phone. It's 6:52.

Hugh. Hmm. The window is open, cool morning air. The top of the ladder no longer shows above the sill.

Text? Email? Nothing. Half-propped on the pillow, her chin feels uncomfortably doubled, but nobody can see. She hits refresh and a text appears. From him, from him.

< awake yet?

One eye shuts, to help her focus. She types with one finger,

> coffee?

< sorry, meeting, then doctor—lunch?

So Ivy goes down the back staircase (claustrophobic doors at the top and bottom) to the empty kitchen. Not entirely empty. Ann stands by the back door holding a cup of hot water with lemon. Honestly. But the smell is not lemon—putting on her glasses, Ivy sees that Ann holds an uncapped Sharpie; now she's writing something on the door in a cramped hand. Letters too small to read from this distance.

Hoo-boy, Ivy thinks. Everywhere. I wonder if I should try to get her some help?

Jason comes running down the back stairs, hair gelled up in a quiff, à la Tintin. He jumps the last two stairs and grabs a clean glass as he goes by the gaping dishwasher. "I had the weirdest dream, it had you in it," he tells Ivy. "It was, like, a thriller, you know—starts with this truck going down an underground parking ramp—it's full of water but the truck keeps on going, the guy drives really well, it's, like, the beginning of a thriller movie."

He yanks the fridge door open and pours juice, talking all the time. "Not Tom Cruise—more like Clive Owen, somebody like that. So that's the credits, then there's this strange shot where I'm—you know, the main guy—is looking down into the water of the river, down by the water-steps." Jason's face tilts to look down onto the tiles. "Creatures, like otters, or, but with fanned tails, stare up at me—at, you know, the person who is watching them."

Ann just keeps writing, so Ivy takes her cup to the dinette bench (built in, otherwise there'd be no place to sit in this hollowed-out house) to sit across from Jason, who plunges on: "Everybody starts getting sick, it's an epidemic. An *underwater* plague, these, um, intelligent beavers give it to us—they have these—fantails, like mermen—I don't know. This plague makes people insanely violent, they try to kill themselves and other people. To stop it, you have to hold them tight, like you're doing the Heimlich manoeuvre on them, and you have to—to *love* them, to tell them over and over that you love them. Some people are better at this than others, right? But everyone has to do it, you have to love people or die—eaten or clawed to death."

Ivy does not have to pretend to be interested.

"This one guy, the driver from the parking lot—hey, it must have been him who started all the infections, because he was underwater!—he's really good at it, he's the first to work out the loving technique. There's this woman in a restaurant having a plague-fit—it was you! And he stops her. He holds the pressure point and loves her like mad, like crazy, with all his heart, and everybody else sees this happening and they copy it, and the woman he fixed helps too. A little baby is taken with the plague. The guy says, 'Babies are easier'—he means easier to hold on to, to find the pressure point . . ."

"But they really are easier to love too," Ivy says, loving Jason's sudden volubility.

"I think it was Hugh in my dream. Weird. He was hanging on to an old wino for dear life, telling him I love you I love you I love you."

Ann has been staring at her tiny printing. When Jason stops speaking she caps her Sharpie and says, "I think leather's coming back. Mimi had a leather maxi, a Halston, with an asymetrical zipper. I'm going to take my leather coat in and have a skirt made."

Ivy says, "That is a weird, good dream, Jason. I love dreams like that." Because she's trying not to like him too openly, with his clueless mother right there, the words come out patronizing or condescending, and Jason looks up, disappointed. For a minute, it seems, he thought she was somebody worth talking to. But she's not.

Ivy ducks her head in shame. "I *love*— I get thriller dreams too. I love the *love-you* thing." He's embarrassed now, and she's a doofus. She takes her cup and goes upstairs, checking her phone. No new text—but email, yes. Happiness rises.

But falls. It is from Jamie. Her squatter, her tenant, her burden. Flooded, what?

Dishwasher broken, water— two more frantic emails ping in while she reads. A cold knife of despair stabs her chest. She's been living in a dream, in a clean empty room with enough money and a true love. Here is the real world.

Now a text, this time from Alex, shouting in caps:

> WATER TURNED OFF. FUCKING DISSASTER JAMIE UPSET. NOT COOL. DEAL WITH PRONTO.

Pronto. Perfect.

4. HUGH CAN'T IMAGINE

Gerald is back, flipping through prints. He shouldn't be, it's ten in the morning. He has a Saab dealership to run. Hugh watches as he straightens up and wanders through the two long rooms of the gallery, hands locked behind his back. Nosing close to some pieces, standing back from others—the connoisseur at work, determining value and possibly, God knows, cadence.

Della dives in the back door, straight to the espresso machine. "Want one?" she calls, before she realizes that there's anyone else in the gallery. Her voice changes, major to minor. "Oh, hi—hi, Gerald. Do you . . . coffee?"

Gerald looks up, his eyes not focusing. "No," he says. "No thanks, no."

They regard him.

"No," he says. "I've had my java for the day. I know my limit. Joe's a good servant, but a bad master." Dissociated, almost disembodied.

Della nods. Gerald nods. He turns and goes out the door. Back to work, perhaps.

She turns to look at Hugh, who shrugs. "Is that happening often?"

"Twice yesterday, Ruth says. First time this morning."

The grinding noise, the coffee machine starting—Della races to put a cup under the spout for the self-clean cycle. "They were always so happy, it seemed to me. With their last-minute surprise. Maybe it was too much, physically. She was forty-eight when Toby was born."

Mimi was twenty-eight when I was born, Hugh thinks. Pretending to be eighteen.

Della is still talking about Gerald's wife, whose name Hugh has forgotten. "She was so good, so patient. I just don't understand it."

Hugh says, "Don't have to understand it, because we are not responsible for Gerald. He's not a friend of mine. I don't want any more friends." Any more grief.

Della comes back with an espresso in a glass. She raises it, to ask if he wants it.

He shakes his head. "He keeps coming to the gallery last thing in the evening."

"Every day?"

"If he wants to buy art, as consolation, Hugh am I to say no?"

She is pulling out her phone, checking, blanking it again. She is always fucking doing that while you're trying to talk . . . Hugh stops.

You can't be angry, not with Della.

"I looked at my messages," he says. He lies. "None from Ken."

The phone rings. He stares at it. Ken? Well, he can leave another message.

But Della picks it up. "Argylle Gallery," she says, in a professional way; too bad Ruth is not there to hear. Ruth is upstairs giving Hugh's bathroom a serious clean, her mission for the morning. He fights with her about this, but the bathroom shines—he just deposits an extra cheque in her account. So far, he's getting away with that.

Della hands him the phone. "Ann," she whispers. "On the warpath."

Must have figured out about him and Ivy, Hugh thinks, blushing. Into the phone, expansively, he says, "Hi, Ann!" Bracing himself.

Della rolls her eyes and ducks out the door, goodbye.

"You have to talk to him," Ann says. He knows that hysterical note. Talk to Jack? Hugh's insides twist at the thought. But that's not it. "I went into Jason's closet to find my leather coat, and there was a magazine. More than one, a stack of them, all—"

This is uncomfortable. "You know, that's what teenage boys do. Look at magazines."

"Hugh, you don't—the degrading—you can't *imagine*. Listen, listen to me—some of these are—I can't tell you— I don't know where he even got them, they're old, they're filthy. Ugh! *Playboy, Juggs* with two Gs, *Modern Man* . . ."

"Really? I thought that one was—"

"Twelve issues, in plastic sleeves."

"Well—" (Vintage. That figures. He's a little surprised, in fact, that they are hetero mags. He had wondered which way Jason's cat would jump.)

"It's not, they're not—the whole— How any boy, any *son*, can look at those disgusting images, those obscene, filthy, those—"

She's going off the deep end, it seems to Hugh. "Ann, Ann, wait—they're not that bad."

"You don't know. You can't imagine."

"Actually, I can."

"My father—my *own father*— You *know*, Hugh, you know what this does to me. I have to— I can't, I need you to talk to him. I need a man to talk to him."

"Not this. I can't do that. I'm not his dad, Ann."

Her voice rises to a half-shriek. "And where is his fucking father?"

"Look, it's just not something you can do to a teenaged boy, you can't—"

"Hugh, you *can*. Please. Jason needs you," she says.

"What am I supposed say to him?"

"Tell him that men—that loving, good men who love women don't need those things, that they're creepy and disgusting, that pornography is rape, is abuse, that the women in them are slaves to the patriarchy, that—" She stops herself.

He waits. She can't keep silent for long.

"Are you saying no? You won't?"

"I can't. You can't do that to him," Hugh says. "It's a delicate thing. It's something private. You— I'm sorry, but you shouldn't have been in his closet."

"My coat!"

"You shouldn't keep your coats in his closet. You've got lots of room in your own—" He stops, remembering that she's moved out of the master bedroom.

"You and Della! You think you can come around here and tell me how to live, how to raise my child," she says, a low, concentrated fury.

"No, not at all."

"Hugh, I *need* you. I ask you to do this one, this one important thing for me. Because I don't have anybody else. Because you used to love me."

"You have to let him keep his dignity. He's a teenaged—"

"You're all treating me like an air-headed, panicky *mom* because, because I've been making a—making an authentic statement with the house. I'm not—"

He breathes away from the phone so she won't hear him sighing.

"I can tell you, Hugh, there's not much about porn that I don't know, I know way more than you do about it, for one thing, and *I know* this stuff is bad for him."

"Listen," he says. "I know you want to do what's right. I'm telling you, in this case you don't—you can't humiliate him this way. It's just not fair."

"Fuck you, and fuck Della too. Is she listening? Tell her that for me."

Hearing the dial tone on her end, he hangs up.

Phew.

The bell tings on the door: Gerald, back? Hugh honestly can't look at him again. No, Newell comes through the door, tinkling the bell again with a graceful swat above his head. "Coffee, need coffee—"

"That's FairGrounds you're looking for. Next door," Hugh says.

"Need company. Need you."

Ruth comes down the back staircase, always alert to Newell's ins and outs. She gives him a big smile, but shows Hugh a stoplight hand. "You can't. Hugh can't, Newell! You have to see Conrad, Hugh."

Fuck me, Hugh thinks. Please. Just hit me on the head again and let me rest.

"Coffee," he says, and ushers Newell out. But he throws back to Ruth, because it is not fair to tease her, "Conrad is later, there's time."

He still has the last box of Mighton's stuff to go through, too. This madhouse.

(L)

Jason's mom texted him , < COME HOME.

Dunh-dunh-*dunhhh*.

When they get to his house after second period, Ann is in the back yard, calling to Jason to come out. L for some reason—oh, wait, could it be experience, or good sense?—stays in the kitchen.

Ann's smoking a cigarette, in a lounge chair. She doesn't smoke. In a psychedelic sixties tea gown—that's Mimi's gown. Where the frick did she get that? Wearing a wig, some kind of vintage pageboy thing, the same colour as her hair but not her hair. Weirdly fake-looking, like the later Warhol wigs.

She's got a little fire burning beside her in the bowl of the copper Turkish grill. Beside the fire, a stack of magazines. Oh boy. Mammoth set of boobs on the top one.

L watches, the horror of the moment burning her eyeballs. She can't hear a thing. Jason bends—for an awful second, L thinks he might be bending over for the strap, but no. He takes the top magazine and flips through it while his mom continues to talk. He's so brave.

He looks up, and her mouth moves again. A trap-mouth.

She's tricky, L thinks. Especially since Jason's dad left, yes, but she's always tricky. She's why Jason is the way he is. Shy, miserable. Maybe his dad is partly why too.

Ann lifts her hand and says one last thing, and then Jason starts to feed the fire with the magazines. A small bright fire, in the bright copper grill that Jason gave her for Christmas after his dad left, using $300 of the money he'd been saving for AutoCAD for his laptop. The grill she never used once, all last summer, but just left sitting there in the rain "patinating."

L does not let her head show through the kitchen window. She is not going to witness Jason's shame, and make him even more miserable from now to eternity probably.

Hendy lies back in his office chair, almost prone, fingers tented. He sits up quickly when they arrive, greeting Newell with the easy warmth of long-time associates. To Hugh, he's cooler. Since Hendy is also Mimi's lawyer, this makes Hugh feel uncomfortably suspicious about his mother's will, or maybe he means her estate. What does Hendy know that Hugh ought to know? Nothing to interpret in the lawyer's lack of expression; his face is flat, his even voice perfectly pleasant.

Lise Largely sails in. Newell gives her the same impersonally loving hug he gives to everyone. Lise *adores* Newell, she signals it with her saturated-blue eyes. She's wearing casual luxury—jeans that cost five hundred dollars and fit like kid gloves, boots with heels. A scarf in muted colours that don't wash out her ash-streaked hair. If you like that sort of thing, gorgeous: those overblue eyes under heavy lids, heavy lashes. Hugh watched Lise operate with Ian Mighton. Moving into his house while hers was being renovated—then after the reno, oops, her house got sold, so she had to stay in Mighton's. But he's finally pried her out. Whatever lever he used must have had a pointy end.

"*Hu*-ugh!" She has a habit of drawing one syllable out into two, her head cocked. She gives him a limp paw. Nobody's ever taught her to shake hands like a human being. "You haven't been answering my *ca*-alls. Never mind! This is exciting. Don't worry, I'm going to look after Jasper! Can't let him go bankrupt, when responsible development of the property will mean a comfortable old age for the poor old guy."

Stiff with dislike, Hugh nods twice, then shakes his head. "Jasper's friends understand that his shop is his—is his whole world."

She makes the sound of a laugh. "Jasper's an old curio, just like his store."

If the price is high enough, Jasper will have to cave. Will Hugh? Mimi is dying, there's the terrible legacy of her estate. Maybe. Who knows what's left, after balancing her secret extravagances and secret stashes.

"We—those of us—" Hugh stops, tries to regroup. "You should understand that Jasper's friends are ready to support him however we— with whatever makes his life worth living. When the people who—who *are your life* are in need, you step up."

Newell touches his arm, and cuts in gently. "With financial support, in other words."

"You *step up*," Hugh says, sounding like a nut. Exactly how a pathetic old man is his life seems urgently clear at that moment: Jasper laughing with Ruth by the stove all those years ago, the ivy wallpaper, Hugh and Newell like white mice along the wainscotting.

He looks up. Newell is watching; but his eyes always look partly desperate. That heartfelt understanding made him a star, that pity for pain. He sits beside Hugh as if his body is ballast.

Lise has an agenda. Not as in something she wants, but an actual paper agenda in her hand. "I find things go more smoothly if we know what we're going to address," she says. A copy for each of them. The heading: *Purchase of Retail/Gallery Properties, L. Largely.*

Hugh stares at it. Seems to be a done deal.

But Hendy has an agenda too, just not on paper. "A few points to take up," he says, putting down the sheet. "Re: the Statement of Adjustments: credits to the purchaser include arrears in taxes up to and including—" His voice steams on into jargon, regulations, this holder of fee, and that party of the second part.

Hugh drifts off, a figurehead anyway, only the titular owner of the gallery-half of the building she wants. He owns nothing. He is perfectly placed to be ousted, in a sea of debt. The Visas alone—the three of them put together add up to $70,000 now. Every sale goes straight to interest; he is behind the proverbial, mystical, physical eight ball.

But Newell is beside him on the black leather settee, while Lise Largely sits alone on a spindly chair. Hendy goes up one side of her and down the other, his smooth, shuttered face—he's on Hugh's side now. Although Hugh cannot fathom how, it seems that he may escape from this business with his hide, with his home. That even Jasper might escape too.

It's a short meeting. Hendy rises, flicks Largely's disused agenda into his recycling basket, and offers a hand to Newell and then to Hugh for a quick, manly shake. Okay.

Newell turns to Largely, clasps her hand, asks after Mighton. Being cruel? Hugh checks his face, but can't tell. "He's coming home this weekend," Lise says, as if they're still together. Knowing that's not true, Hugh feels like he has a slight advantage.

Which she then takes away: "Before we leave, I need to talk to Hugh."

Hugh realizes it's him she means, not one of the others she's calling *you*. Lise's smile creases her skin in hairline cracks. "I've left six messages—of course you're back and forth to the hospice. Which is why I felt I had to get hold of you. Assuming that your mother—that you—won't want to extend the lease on her apartment for another year, of course the owner really has to get another tenant in there, *whe*-en . . ." Leaving off the *when your mother dies*.

A photograph of Mimi swims into Hugh's mind: in a ballet tutu, eight years old, chin lifted and feet turned out, pink tights casing legs that are so tense they seem to tremble. Her fingers, each blessed finger delicately and artistically bent. Alive, alive in every tendril.

Hendy asks, "Has the owner requested—is it urgent?"

Who owns the place? Some company or other, Hugh can't remember.

"*Sort* of." Largely swoops her shiny eyes. "November first is the new lease year. If you'd *like* your mother to sign another year, that's fine!" (squint-smiling to beat the band) "But I thought I could do Hugh a favour. In the circumstances."

Hugh can't think. Mimi's apartment: main floor of a nice house on the river, near Della's. Fully reno'd, brick kitchen, expensive. A year's lease—$30,000. You could save Jasper's life with that. Give it to Della and unstitch her worried forehead.

"I can't get the place cleared out before the first," he says.

Largely smiles. "I think I can request an extension from the owner. November 15?"

If he accepts her offer, he owes her, and somehow she will get the gallery.

"No," he says. "I'll get onto the movers. November 1 is Saturday. Say Monday the third." Emptying Mimi's apartment, arranging for storage, sorting, selling—how is that going to fit in with Della and Ken's anniversary dinner on Saturday night? It will just have to. Ken may not turn up anyway.

Hendy interrupts. "Did your principal send a registered letter to inform Hugh?"

Largely has that one: "A registered letter went direct to the leaseholder, of course. Mrs.—Hayden? Or is she Argylle? I'd have to check the file—I presume power of attorney covers Hugh picking up her mail, and reading the letters?"

Ruth runs by and picks up the mail every morning. She puts it on his desk every day, every fucking day. Hugh feels the weight of unsorted mail, the blue basket on his desk, like an old woman's body settling over his shoulders. Two old women: Ruth pointing out the basket over and over; asking him, like Della is always asking him, and his mother's sunken eyes and sunken voice asking him: *Is there mail?* He's seen that letter, he just didn't look at it.

"Get me a copy of the lease, will you, Hugh?" The first time Hendy has addressed him.

Hugh is in no shape to do anything but nod. Hendy must think he's an idiot.

Newell is beside Hugh, gently pointing at the antique Patek Philippe on his wrist, the best thing to come out of *Catastrophe*. "Doctor's appointment?"

"Right!" Hugh leaps at Largely's hand, shakes it. Anything to get out of there.

By Monday. And this is what—Wednesday.

Out of the office and on the street in a single breath. Down the street to the gallery in six more. Hard-drawn, ragged breaths, because you can't cry in the street. It's bad enough at the movies. People here would see, would notice and think Mimi's dead, would come to console, to condole.

He opens the door and stops, breathing again.

Ruth is about to order him to Conrad, but he holds up his hands. Not to stave her off, just giving up. "Largely says I have to have my mother's stuff out of the apartment by the first. I said okay, by Monday."

Ruth jumps up, like she's going to whip over there right now and start working.

"No, no," he says. "Ruth, you're the best. But wait."

He can hear Newell coming in behind him.

And Della will help, and you could pay the kids to—okay, you'll need to rent a bigger van. And a storage space, okay.

He breathes; you can breathe, if you remind yourself.

"Okay, okay. Ruth, I can deal with it. We knew it was coming, I just have to face it."

Ruth starts to weep, silently. Her dear little face in a screw.

"She's not going back to that apartment," he says. "Not ever."

"I know, I know," she says, all water.

You just don't want to know, that's all. Hugh doesn't want to know either.

6. CAN HUGH FEEL IT WHEN I DO THIS?

"Remember the fall? All about it? When did it happen?" Conrad's always doing that, all the questions thrown on the table at once, like a card player in a tantrum. Game called on account of earthquake!

Hugh takes a breath, stays calm. "I fell off a ladder." He hates being medicoed. Especially by a bullet-headed lunatic with a machine-gun voice and a sense of godhead.

Conrad swivels back to the computer to enter the data. "When?"

"Monday morning. And then I fell down some stairs, on Monday night."

"Two. Ah . . . And how long were you out?"

"Well, three or four hours. Dinner, then the party at Pink's, and then I walked home—"

"No, *out*. Unconscious."

"Oh." Hugh thinks. Swings his black leather stool right, left.

"Were you alone?"

"Yes. I don't think—I don't know if I was out at all. I might have been." He can't figure out whether the safe answer is yes or no. "I don't think I was out at all. Just winded. I thought I was having a stroke."

"How far did you fall?"

Twenty feet. "Maybe ten feet."

"Stupid."

"I have put up those lights every year for ten years."

"Here's a piece of medical advice, I give you gratis, for free, thrown in on the public dime: don't climb a ladder without someone there to hold the legs."

"Okay." Hugh does not wish to hate anybody else in this town. Conrad means well.

"Did you vomit?"

"No." Then remembers that he did, didn't he? He threw up red wine, all over some sink or other. He looks out the window.

"You're not taking warfarin, by any strange chance, are you? Double-doctoring?"

"What for?"

"Oh, it's a blood thinner, also a rare treat for the rats. Poisons them dead, I promise you."

"No."

"No allergies, and you're not a bleeder." Conrad gets up from the computer and comes at Hugh, flashlight pointed. "All righty," he says, jabbing the light in each eye repeatedly. "Sore neck? No? Honestly, I can't think you need a scan, you're talking well and it's been what, three days. Why didn't dear Ruthie send you in sooner?"

Hugh remembers the casual formality of his old roaming days, when doctors hardly knew him, when they did not sit on arts boards with him or report to town council on the downtown rejuvenation project. When there was never anything wrong with him.

Conrad presses his head all over. Gentle fingers, taking his time, like the children's aid nurse with her freshly picked toothpick going through his head for lice, or Ruth's fingers, washing his hair in the kitchen sink. His own fingers, rubbing his mother's head when she was forlorn. When she lay on the bed sobbing quietly or frantically, the only thing that soothed her was a slow, repetitive pulling of fingers, combing and combing through her pretty hair. Hugh passes a hand across his eyes, waiting for Conrad to finish.

"No bumps. Good job, you. If you notice a bump coming up in the next month or so, come back and see me. That'll be serious. The thing that worries me"—Conrad spins Hugh round to face him— "is that second fall."

Hugh is surprised. "Oh, that was nothing. Five steps, maybe. Conked my head against the wall, but it was a carpeted landing. Soft."

Conrad shakes his head. "It's twice in one day. Two falls, ten times the danger." His eyes are sharp, so Hugh struggles to perk up. "Some subtle problems don't show up right off the bat. Memory deficit, changes in cognition, obsessing . . . personality changes."

Hugh nods, looking away.

"Experiencing violent tendencies lately?"

"Well obviously Ruth told you about the other night. I can only assure you, doctor, that Burton had it coming."

Conrad nods. "I've met the man." His lips pooch out, pooch in. "Look. What I'm worried about with you is PCS, persistent concussion. In some, the symptoms of concussion last. Past six weeks, those patients are almost always treated with antidepressants. In my own view, I'll tell you what, they were depressed already, their brains already in a depressed condition. The standard thing is to put someone on antidepressants and bedrest, absolutely no exercise. No exertion, no excitement; no snakes, no ladders."

Hugh thinks of last night at Ivy's window, the old ladder wobbling as he went up, shaking badly as he went down. His feet cramped as he reached for the ground.

"If you ask me, Hugh, your brain was—you were already, before the fall, the *two* falls—already a candidate for antidepressant medication."

Hugh swings his black leather stool back to looking out the window.

"As we discussed, last time you came in."

The leaves, fading from the first red down to burnt-out cinders, to yellow ash.

"But you refused." Conrad taps his pen on his table. "So what's the unbearable part of it? Why are you here now?"

I think about suicide all the time, with longing, he wants to say to Conrad. I can't let myself yet—but after my mother dies, I can. She can kill me and herself. Like a leaf detaches, slips to the ground. Autumn is what happens. Everything dies.

But you don't say those things out loud.

"Can't sleep," Hugh says at last. "Not sleeping. Never more than three, four hours. I've gained weight. Ruth nagged me till I agreed to come."

"Headaches too?" Conrad puts the pen under his nose, a black moustache. He twirls it.

"Okay, no, I don't have headaches. I just can't sleep." That sinking feeling, quite literal, as he falls asleep—sinking into the pillow, the pit full of all the things he doesn't let himself think about all day. So many!

"I can give you sleeping pills."

"I don't want pills."

"Fine, I'll give you ten of them."

Hugh takes the scrip, pockets it. He is very, very tired.

"So no exercise, no stimulants. No alcohol. Nothing. No ladder climbing."

He's going out the door.

Conrad adds, now jovial: "You're old, Hugh. You don't want to let this get out of hand." As the nurse comes in, Conrad shouts, so that the whole waiting room must hear. "There's nothing shameful about being depressed. If you'd broken a leg, you'd fix it."

"Not depressed," Hugh says. To the room.

On the sidewalk outside the Argylle Gallery Ivy feels absurdly shy. Maybe he won't like her today. This has been known to happen, in the firmament of first dates. But the taste of mango comes back to her, gold melting on her tongue. The spoon through the ventilation hole, Hugh standing on the silver stepladder. She laughs and opens the gallery door.

No Hugh. Humph.

"May I help you?" It's a little older lady, trim and pert-faced, coming out from the back. The one who was the server the other night. Her name. . . .

"I'm here to see Hugh?"

"Well, here I am," the woman says. Ruby? Trudy? She lifts her eyes and hands upwards, tsking. "No, no—you mean *Hugh*! I'm always doing that." Rueful.

"You must be Ruth," Ivy says. "I'm Ivy. Is he—?"

"Oh! Off to the doctor. That bump on the head, you know."

"Good thing you made him go."

"I watched it happen."

"You did? You were here?"

That seems to give Ruth pause. "I saw him fall down the basement stairs over at Mr. Pink's. You were right there."

Oh, he hasn't told her about the ladder, putting up the lights. "Right! It didn't seem too bad. He got up right away. But he wasn't quite . . . lucid." Neither is Ivy; she makes a face.

"You're the one with the trouble over learning your lines, I hear?"

Everybody knows. Everybody. "I am."

"I wouldn't be surprised if that passed off. Once you're through the Change."

Ivy looks at Ruth. Unable not to hope, it's the saddest thing.

"I had an awful time myself, but I'm back now, sharp as a tack!" Ruth gives Ivy a self-delighted pat, then turns and heads back into the nether parts of the store.

The door sounds, and Ivy turns.

Hugh, back. "Hey," he says. She is so happy to see his face!

He looks miserable. Afraid her smile is too big, she tries to tone it down, fails, smiles more widely. He gives her his hand, or takes hers. Both.

"Hugh came back, did you?" Ruth calls, coming in, face bright as a new penny, copper jacket snug around her, red hat clapped on. "Then I'm off like a dirty shirt. Conrad give you the all-clear?"

Hugh rolls his eyes. "I'm fine, I'm fine. He says I'm not concussed and Burton had it coming—thanks for that."

"He had to know," Ruth says, defending herself. She gives Ivy a conspiratorial wave.

The bell tinkles her out.

"Thought she'd never leave," Hugh says, still holding her hand.

They stand there for a moment. Even with his face so drawn, it's quite exciting to be beside him—what will happen?

Hugh releases her hand to take her elbow (as if he still wants to be touching her, as if they cannot come unglued) and steers her through the arch into the other gallery showroom, saying, "Come, come see the place."

Perfect. It's a gallery, sure enough. Tables with ceramics, moveable screens holding smaller pictures, a few stone carvings; one big fabric mishmosh that Ivy can't figure out at all. The discreet price tag says $13,000. She gasps. The artist's name: Della Belville.

"Yeah," Hugh says. "She's not a fabric artist, turns out—an experiment years ago, she went back to painting. It covers a big crack in the wall. I put the price high on purpose."

"You know one day someone is going to buy it."

"And then the crack will show. But the world may end before that. Lunch?"

There are things that Ivy wants to look at longer, but she nods and he leads her to the back, and through into a back hall. A big darkened room ahead, through another arch: Hugh says, "Framing in there. Where the actual money comes from."

Stairs go up on one side, turning the corner. He ushers her up, so she arrives at the top before him, and can take a quick glance around. Wood floors, wooden kitchen shelves. Books along the walls. The oak all gleaming clean. Does he live like this, or did he clean for her?

She moves forward to give him room at the top of the stairs. Past the long counter of the kitchen, into the living room. A fireplace, glass doors to a roof deck. Old brown leather couch, amber striped linen curtains. It's surprisingly nice. Surprisingly. Is this the inside of Hugh's head, like Jung says about houses in dreams? She likes it a lot.

Hugh lets Ivy roam and goes to the kitchen. You should have thought about what was in the fridge before offering lunch. You just wanted her to come upstairs.

His eyes hurt. He rubs them, stares past his fingers into the fridge. "Omelette?"

"Yum," Ivy says, looking at books. Okay.

He cracks, chops, whisks, dots butter into the hot pan, toast into the toaster, calls her to the counter—sets in front of her a perfect omelette. She is properly impressed; she eats with attention and pleasure.

"I seem to know you," he says, looking at her face, her little teeth.

"I know," she says. Grey eyes lift and light up. Green or grey? They must be her main asset in the theatre. In life, too.

"You have beautiful eyes," he says. He is surprised to hear it coming out of his mouth, and it hangs there in the air between them for a moment.

Then she sighs, crosses her eyes wildly and takes another forkful, and he breaks more eggs to make his own. He is happy. And still miserable. Which lies deeper?

"You all alone up here?"

"What?" He turns from the stove, then back—eggs require attention. "Yes! Alone. I redid it when I bought the place. I'll show you in a minute. It's small. Two bedrooms, but they're small. A mess."

Only they aren't, Ruth did a quick tidy while she was up here. It's safe to give Ivy a tour, to open doors and show her his white bedroom, the shipshape bathroom. She talks nicely about the space, the light. In the empty guest room they look through the windows onto the street: FairGrounds, the Saab dealership, the Ace, the river. Seeing the little neighbourhood at its best, from above the fray.

Back in the main room Hugh opens the sliding doors to show off the deck. In semi-warm sunlight, under die-cut shadows of bared branches, they sit on the chaise longue because it's all there is: Ivy curled up in the seat, Hugh on the leg-half.

"Like the Friendly Giant," she says. "*One for two more to curl up in.*"

"Della and I watched that every day at Ruth's," he says. "However old we got."

"Is she—is Della your, what, cousin? I'm sorry, you probably told me, but I forget."

"No relation. Ruth babysat us, and Newell, whenever our families collapsed. Della's mother was sick for long periods; my mother—" There he halts. Then he goes on. "Went off the rails from time to time. Nervous breakdowns, they called it. She'd have a few months in the hospital, and then she'd come out, pick me up from Ruth's, and we'd start off again."

Ivy nods, not interrupting.

"My father—I told you about him. So just me and Mimi, driving off in her little yellow Karmann Ghia. I was always relieved when she came back. Always relieved, next time, to go back to Ruth's."

Ivy takes one hand off her ankle and puts it on his arm.

He smiles at her. "Nothing to feel sorry about. Newell stayed with Ruth a lot too—his parents were well off, they travelled. He and Della and I rode our bikes around town, out to Bobcaygeon, wherever we wanted. We had a club, we had siblings for a while. Good for all three of us. And Ruth got paid, and that was good."

Except that it was awful. Pain that never can be told. For a second Hugh wonders what Ruth did with that hundred, whether she gave it to the Mennonite Clothes Closet—that'd be fine, he tells himself. *They do such good work.* Better them than the Conservatives.

"I like you so much," Ivy says.

Saying it right out like that—easy, or brave? He has chocolate ice cream—he could— The phone starts ringing inside.

Or he could kiss her. No glass between them now.

"Hm," she says, grinning at him like a kid. Then, "Should you answer the phone?"

"Come in, I'll make coffee." He takes her hand to pull her out of the chaise. It's still going, still—Hugh makes it to the kitchen counter, sure the ring will quit. He hits the speaker button. The ringing stops.

"Hey, Hugh!" Ken's voice, distorted by the speaker. Or is he crying? The voice wobbles into the room, too loud: "It's you! I thought you weren't there."

"What's up?"

"Della's not answering her cell—"

"Okay," Hugh says. "Everything's okay, as far as I know. I know L's fine."

"Della's phone is turned off, I can't get through. Is she teaching tonight? I don't have my calendar, I can't remember if she teaches Wednesday— I need to get hold of her, she's—"

What the hell is all this? "You okay?" Hugh asks.

Then there's a silence while Ken breathes. Like a man between bouts of vomiting, breathing to hold off the next painful rush.

The back door slams downstairs. Hugh sees L's pale head, Ken's colouring, at the bottom of the turn. She's coming up.

Before his mind even frames the thought, his hand takes the receiver from the stand and hits the speaker button to shut off Ken's voice. Into his ear, unstoppered, Ken floods a ranting stream, so unlike his usual reserve that Hugh feels some alarm, which he conveys to Ivy by wild eye-rolling— she goes to the top of the stairs, gives L a big happy greeting, and draws her into the living room to look at something on the wall in there, allowing Hugh time to listen to Ken. Which he does not want to do. He takes the phone, nodding to Ivy, and slips off to the bedroom.

While L wanders around the room touching things, Ivy wonders what Hugh was going to say, or do, before the phone rang. That must have been L's father on the phone. What's going on there? Della seems pretty conflicted—her layer of warm calm is like custard skin, gently set over a seething mass beneath.

L stops jittering around and stands in the middle of the room.

She says, "I have this, you know—I've been making . . . an installation, I guess you'd have to say, because it's *installed,* but that sounds so precious. It's just a big thing that has to—that needs a lot of space, and it's like—like this one thing my mom did when she did her MFA exhibit, she did this thing with gold leaves on a huge piece of wall that was so great. You know, it looked really good, but the deal *was* that each leaf had a tiny red loop of thread glued to the back—she pounded in a thousand tiny tacks all over the wall and we hung all the leaves so whenever anyone moved in the room, the leaves moved—but, but they didn't just move, they—" Her arms waft, graceful, she cannot keep herself from dancing. "They fell, like fall, like autumn. It was *so great*, except that, so—so she ended up paying me ten bucks an hour to pick up the leaves and put them back on the little tacks, and it was *non-stop*, I made like two hundred bucks."

Ivy enjoys her babbling and Della's leaves; and enjoys feeling like they are her friends.

Hugh comes out of the bedroom. "Well!" Over-jolly, faintly fake. "Great to see you, L! To what do we owe the honour?" He stops, resets his tone. "Lunch?"

L stares at him, sensing something weird. But she lets it go. We must all be so weird to her, Ivy thinks. How to tell what's off, in an off world?

"So I was thinking," L says, jumping into it, braced. "I wanted you to forget about the thing, the thing I showed you. It's not—it's not ready, or anything, I know that. You know, *shitted is not painted*."

Ivy's face must show surprise. Hugh explains for her: "When Turner showed his work in 1828, another artist sneered, *cacatum non est pictum*: shitted is not painted. L, L, you've been listening in class."

L glares out the glass doors to the deck, out to the branches leaning closer.

Hugh goes over to her. "Your maze, the *Republic*—" He breaks off, starts again. "I didn't say enough the other day. I didn't know what to say. I was afraid I might burst into tears, standing there." (L stares through the glass even harder.) "Teaching is tiring: it takes a long time of looking before you see something really good, before you find, are shown, the thing you've been looking for."

"I have been here all along," L says. Dignified. She's only young, still.

Hugh shrugs. "I guess you were too close for me to see." Giving the side of her face a suddenly wide, unreserved, beaming, face-altering smile. L looks at him, suspicious. But what she sees must ease her fear. She does not turn away again.

Ivy watches them, the bodies turned toward each other, wondering if L's work is actually extraordinary, or if it's just that she's so pretty. Shocked by a stab of jealousy: this nice girl, daughter of a friend, Hugh looking after her interests. Ivy remembers Burton staring at Orion, herself watching Jason this morning. The older and the younger, the unbearable point of—is it of conquest? Not Hugh—would Hugh? Then she shakes herself, mentally. Nonsense.

But L's poor face. This degree of wanting is like pain. For the work.

Yes, in Ivy's experience too, work is more important than love.

"Let me figure it out," Hugh says. "I want to talk to my pal Gareth Pindar, about your options. The thing is, it's too good for my gallery, too big, it's too—" He breaks off. Now it's Hugh's turn to stare out at bare branches. A second, another few.

The pause brings L's eyes back to him, as Ivy watches. There's always this problem: the young loving us, briefly, as they launch. Ivy thinks about Orion's arresting beauty, Jason's dream.

"Well, it's really good." Hugh turns back to L, who nods, as if this is some kind of contract.

Ivy's pleasure and confidence, her connection with Hugh, drains away. The young have all the power, and she is, let's face it, a dumpy, awkward, nondescript woman with a muddled mind and a tedious past.

But Hugh says, "Lunch, okay," and he takes her hand as he goes by, pulling her to the kitchen to help. The pressure of his hand says, *Help me, I'm a mess*, and she presses back.

Orion sits on a high stool in the old Home Ec kitchen in the basement, which nobody besides them ever goes into. "Those old guys were all bent out of shape pretending to be straight, or trying to be. Like Cary Grant. Rock Hudson, Marlon Brando, James Dean."

Jason is cutting Orion's hair with ultra-sharp scissors borrowed from Fashion.

"Okay, Marlon Brando was not gay." Savaya is definite about that. Waiting next in line, she uses the countertop for a fulcrum, long legs swinging under the table and back out, hands clutched on the edge to keep her more or less balanced.

"He was, he was bi."

"Don't move your mouth for a sec," Jason says. Orion stares up at his pale eyelids, the red lining of his bottom eyelid. Crying all afternoon about his cold and crazy mother finding his fucking porn for fuck's sake. How is he supposed to grow up, drowning in bile?

Savaya scoffs. "You always say that. According to you anybody good in the movies was good because he was gay."

Mouth stiff, like a ventriloquist, Orion says, "Because he was gay *and couldn't admit it*. It's the tension that creates the dynamic."

"Bull, shit," Savaya says, sings. "Some of them were straight and some of them were gay and art struck them all indiscriminably."

"Fred Astaire, probably," Jason says, judicial with his scissors. "But not Bob Hope."

"It's easier for us. It got better." Orion turns his head, obedient to Jason's fingers. "Too better, maybe." The scissors snick, snick; Orion's profile poses. Handsome man looks good in anything.

Savaya swings her legs, light-minded, distractible. "Where's L?"

Jason pulls the sheet off Orion, gestures Savaya to the stool. "She had to go to Hugh's. She freaked out because he saw her *Republic* install, and he didn't say much."

"She shouldn't care so much about what he says," Savaya says.

But we do care, the mentor is the arbiter. Until we're done with him. Orion checks his hair in the black glass of the wall oven.

Yes. This works.

8. HUGH MAKE MY DREAMS COME TRUE

The hospice steps get longer every day. Illusion, illusion. Hugh plods or strides down the hall, eight or eighteen hallways, longer every day. Lise Largely chasing him from door to door, bills in white envelopes flap-flapping just behind his head, Gerald's hound eyes watching from the lintel of his mother's door, naked Voynich ladies from L's maze shrouding every window and peering through the keyholes—

He's gone mad, maddening more with every step.

Here, trapezoidal, as proper in a German expressionist film, looms Mimi's door.

Dear mother. Whom he always loves. Who is always holding his hand, who adores and adored him, to whom he is always tied with bloody silver cords and hot pink velvet ribbon.

Hugh opens the door. Mimi is awake. Her head turns, anger sparkling in the deepsunk eyeholes, in what's left of her gaze. "You! *You* come here?" she says, gaze flicking away.

"Here I am," he says, not bending to kiss her. She will only pull away.

"I am disappointed in Hugh," she tells the wall. "I thought of all things of all people Hugh would not desert me, Hugh of all people."

(What is *wrong* with your *family?*)

"I'm here," he says. At night she is drugged calm, or at least remembers night's natural state is sleep. During the day she talks in spates, in flourishes, often angry.

Her eyes are huge when she looks back at him. "Nobody thinks of *me*, banjo eyes on the ceiling day and night, a burden to myself and others— hands all over me, turning me, patting me when I do not want to be touched. What's left me if my self my home is gone?"

Yes, long shadows go out from the bales, and yes, the soul must part from the body: what else could it do? Hugh sits on the bed. "Listen, Mimi, I want you to move in with me. It will be good for both of us. I'll—no, listen, Dave is coming to fix the basement, there's room to store your things. I'll paint the spare bedroom pink, we'll be cozy up there, like birds in the nest. I don't want you living on your own anymore. You need company, and so do I."

She cries and cries, then. Weeping is hard on her.

Sometimes it seems like the world is trying to speak to Hugh. Birds appear singly in front of him: one for sorrow. Five or six ones, at intervals. Some people might count cumulatively, tot them up, two-for-joy, but Hugh knows better. *What are you trying to say?* his mind shouts. As he sets off down the sidewalk, a magpie, most potent bird portent, flies straight at him. He dodges, bruising his arm on a parking meter.

The world won't shut up, sending him messages he wants no more than he wants Ken's. There are things he has not done, things for which he needs to atone. He hasn't been a good one to love, whether or not he was a good lover. Mostly he was not. Ann, others too. He did not love them except in a selfless, monkish way, knowing they needed love. Which now strikes him as condescending, distant, detached. He does not feel detached about Ivy. Children too: L, needing to be shepherded, to be properly represented. Maybe that lost one of Ann's *was* his. Maybe she thinks of that baby when she talks to Jason now. That baby would be old now, thirty, Jesus. Jason—do not talk to Jason about porn, for God's sake.

Old errors, new ones. Hitting Burton. Not kissing his mother—not kissing Ivy when he had the chance. Another example: not kind enough to Ruth, who will probably be the one to find him lying in the framing room dead and broken one of these days, when she brings him a badly wrapped, over-mayoed, canned pink salmon sandwich at lunchtime.

Hugh's tooth hurts. Maybe it's jaw cancer. Started the other morning. Don't think about it. Plus, you're clearly a hypochondriac. Irritating to be in pain all the time, pain of a tooth, irritating not being able to close the jaw in the ordinary way. Every mouthful pain, every breath, not knowing when it will stop—or really, knowing that it will get worse and worse, that this is the downward slide, the snake. The back right molar is giving up.

It's hideous, unbearable, that we age, we fall apart. Just when you know what you want (*Ivy! Enough money to get out of this hole! Mimi young again, happy, not crazy!*) you are too old to make use of it or can't get it anyway.

Back in the framing room Hugh puts on Borodin—not the usual, but a sad winding, clarinet-heavy one, like someone noodling on the organ after church. Then the strings barge in, too sweet. He switches the music off.

It's impossible, this thing with Ivy. People can't do this kind of thing, at this late a date. Find each other. *Hook up.* Anyway, his obligations.

Not that Mimi will be moving in upstairs, because she is not moving anywhere. She is dying. She will be dead.

(L)

Finishing is the boring part, L hates it. But Jason revels in it, perfectionistly. In his company it's almost enjoyable. At least here in Fashion they have a serger, a big press, and a good steam iron. Four boards in the alcove; even a sleeve board. And Betty, who talks most of the time, when she's not going out for a smoke. The costumes are mostly from Stratford, Betty being connected. She used to be head seamstress at Stratford, but then one day—she'll tell the story—her life fell apart. She went to Toronto to buy fabric and, surprise!, she sees her salesman husband walking along the street in front of her. She calls, but he doesn't hear her. So she runs after him and turns the corner just in time to see him walk in the front door of a house. She runs up the walk and knocks on the door, not thinking anything but that she's happy to see him because he travels a lot with his business and it's been a few days.

And the woman who opened the door had never heard of Fred, but called into the kitchen to ask Rick, and there he was. Her husband. *Fred/er/Rick*. Four kids! He'd been married to the woman for eight years. Another whole family. How many other men—her own dad—

That must have been back in the eighties or something. Now, they'd just get a divorce.

But there is something going on with her dad. Obviously.

The iron hisses.

A brief tap-tap: L's mom is at the door, trembly fake smile on, ha-ha, like *Can I dare come in?* Behind the alcove wall, L's heart or lungs sink. She motions to Jason to be quiet, stay hunkered in this little bunker. Her mom will say something to Betty, too personal or too generous, and if she sees L she always gets weirdly worse, just out of nerves. Jason shrugs, bent over his work, attaching giant, exact eyelashes to the shut embroidered eyes on Nevaeh's Hope costume. Blind Hope? It looks really good on. Nevaeh's small high breasts look exactly like protruding, clamped-shut eyes, like for example when you are hoping against hope, praying that your dad has not killed himself or otherwise gone off the deep end.

"Hey, Betty!" her mom goes. "I promised to help with the Hallowe'en costume sale." Anyone who leaves their costume until two days before is not really bothering. But the sale is a good way to get rid of stuff—that costume room is a museum of tattered dreams. Her mom says, still apologizing, "Ann came too—she's looking for some vintage clothes she thinks might have ended up here by mistake."

Jason's mom, too? Shit. Jason has gone invisible, ducking silently under the big press. L takes her hemming and joins him. Nobody needs to know they're there.

Burton's flutiest voice catches Ivy on her cell. He orders her to run down to the basement costume room before the master class. "Shoes, hats, gloves, bags to strew on the table, you'll know what I want. Silk night-wear, fifties elegance. Tat."

Is Burton repositioning *Sweeney Todd* to the fifties? Ivy does not ask, but trots down the stairs to the cool, aqua, concrete-walled basement. At a bend in the hall, there is Ann, her landlady, at a long mirror beside a rank of padlocked doors. She's wearing a silvery pageboy wig and an op-art dress that vibrates in the shadowy corridor. Ivy's stomach jumps. Well, for perfectly good reason. Down in this low-lit cement world Ann exudes a powerful ambiance, tension and rage waving off her like too much perfume.

Placate her: "Love your dress! Fab! Is it vintage?"

In the mirror, Ann assesses her pink/orange paisley. "It was Mimi's, Hugh's mother's. But she said it looked better on me. She said I ought to have it. When Hugh and I were lovers." Her voice is aerated, barely audible. Or maybe Ivy just doesn't want to hear about her being Hugh's *lover*, stupid seventies *Joy of Sex*-type word. Like calling a girlfriend your *lady*.

"Mimi had rooms full of clothes. The school borrowed some for a show last year, so I'm getting them back. Hugh doesn't know what's valu-able." Ann shakes her head, the too-big wig slipping on her narrow head, a beat behind. "I found these . . . ugh, these *magazines*."

She seems honestly distressed, unlike with the whole epigram-writing feminist indignation thing, which felt kind of fake. Askew, the wig makes her look sad. She stares at Ivy in the mirror. "I can't talk about it."

Ivy can't get past her to go into the costume room. "No—perfect. I'm bad with secrets."

"Hugh wouldn't help *me*," Ann says. Askew, the wig makes her look sad. "But I'll help him. I'll clean out Mimi's closets. Lise wants her apartment by the first. He'll need an army to get that done."

Not knowing what any of this is about, Ivy decides, in a clean-souled burst of decency, that it is none of her business unless Hugh tells her himself.

Then Della comes clattering down the stairs, a breath of fresh wind, some good sense. "Betty says it's all right," she calls. "Oh, hi, Ivy! Are you helping with the sale?"

Ivy is quite relieved to see her. "Burton wanted me to find some stuff for class."

Della is already busy with the keys. "What are you looking for?"

"Boudoir stuff, I gathered. Burton said fifties shoes, nightwear . . ."

Della opens the big sliding doors. Inside—lights clicking on as a powdery scent floats out—is an Ali Baba cave of clothes. Shelves and racks stretching into the distance. There are worse ways to spend an afternoon than looking at feminine trappings. Net gloves, feathered hats; purses and parasols; shoes of every era. White go-go boots, gorgeous chunky heels.

"Out of period," Ivy sighs. Back on the shelf.

Ann takes the boots down again. "I think these were Mimi's."

Ivy asks Della, "Pearls, powder puffs, peignoirs—where will I find the Ps?"

"Hugh's mother had a peignoir and negligée set we loved," Della says, moving down a packed aisle. "Powder blue with ecru lace. Newell wore one and I wore the other, to be twins. She never minded us dressing up. Mimi loved, loved clothes. She knew everybody, all the designers, and she had such lovely things."

An aisle away, clicking through hangers, Ann says, "I was thinking about that leather Halston skirt with the assymetrical zipper—and remember the Afghani velvet patchwork dress with little mirrors all over it?"

Della sketches it in the air, tiny bodice, flowing arms. "And she smelled so good."

"Here's that long purple Halston!" Ann cries. "I forgot that one. It's disgraceful that Betty didn't get these back to us. The clothes are all we've got left of Mimi now—but her career lives on, I got nowhere with the *Ontario Living* editors until I mentioned her."

"Did she work?" Ivy asks.

Della laughs. "Constantly! However sad or sick she was, she hardly ever stopped working. She was an actress first, and a pop/op artist; she spent a couple of months at the Factory, you know the kind of thing. Long, shiny hair like Millie the Model. Crossed with Edie Sedgwick. She sang a little too. In the seventies she was a television interviewer, a star more than a journalist—you'd know her, of course you would: Mimi Hayden."

"Oh, *her*! I was thinking Argylle—of course I do. Micro-mini, white boots, white lipstick—I remember her on TV, down at city hall, demonstrating how to smoke a joint. And being a pretty witch on *Mr. Dressup*."

"Damage control after that joint-smoking thing, I bet. She did *Sesame Street* too. She was the young exciting one on the afternoon show, and she still acted sometimes. She dated Trudeau; she was pals with Glenn Gould before he died—he helped her buy her piano. When she was working she'd take us to shows or into the city to go to the Ex—I can't believe they let us go with her! She drove like a bat out of hell, in a little yellow Karmann Ghia, smoking all the time." Della sounds happy, remembering. "In between the crazy she was so great—funny and sweet. She sprung herself from whatever clinic and came to Ruth's one night, and made us stay up to watch the moon landing. She said we'd have to tell our grandchildren about the first moment humans escaped from Earth, she couldn't let us miss it. Ruth made Jiffy Pop popcorn on the stove."

Ivy laughs. "That silver flower-bulb, bloating and blooming!"

"We were happy." Ann is referring to a completely different *we*. "Hugh and I. It was a good time. I sometimes wonder," she tells Della, wide eyes fixed on her, "if Hugh and I should get back together."

After one quick glance at Ivy's face (which is as perfectly vacant as she can contrive), Della rushes on, "Hey, I promised to go see Mimi today—I'd better get going."

Unable to be left alone with Ann, Ivy says, "Yipes, I'm late—" And in fact, it is three.

She stuffs white marabou mules beside the negligée in her bag, and runs.

Burton's wearing a cape. Following along the hall, Ivy swings her eyes away from his sway-skirted figure. Since she has to laugh, she stops, hand over mouth—never let Burton see you laughing at him—and gives her eyes the great refresher of the whole hot mess of the mural: student angst-love slathered on concrete block wall.

Newell arrives beside her. Does Newell really see Burton? Or is he all angstlove for his old pal, old mentor, old ruination? He is quietly laughing. "We're in Capetown tonight, my darling Mrs. Lovett—and I think you may find yourself Mitch-ing *mallecho* after all."

Ivy's eyes lift. *Twelfth Night?*

His smile is famous because it is beautiful. "It's got a bee in its bonnet."

So all that work on Mrs. Lovett's scenes was wasted. Oh well. Four thousand dollars, her innermost mind murmurs, again. They follow on.

"I've given this a great deal of thought," Burton says, to the assembled masses: twelve students and Terry and Terry. "*Sweeney* is a wonderful opus, Mr. Sondheim's wondrously complex score—its energy, razor wit, and of course the psychological insight. But I think that for this group, *this* cast—for *this* process—another script is needed. I have spent hours in thought, and I emerge, butterfly-like—" (here Burton swings his cape-wings open) "with the conviction that it is Williams we wequire."

Ivy shakes her head, not letting herself laugh, and Burton glares. She nods earnestly.

He continues: "*Streetcar.*"

Then stops, for a considerable time. Nobody moves.

"No more discussion!" (As if there'd been any.) "I don't want us to over-think this, but plunge right in. We'll read scene after scene, as I call them out, and see what pearls emerge."

Burton hands his stack of scripts to Terry, who splits them with Terry, and they dole out the stapled sheets, as per the names scrawled on the top page in Burton's purplest pen. Burton, meanwhile, drapes stockings and filmy silks and slippers along the centre of the table.

Ivy is for a moment overtaken with real joy to be here, witnessing this nonsense. Even in this world of death and pain, we can still sit in a room and connive together to make nonsensical, joyous swipes at something approaching art, with a bunch of students, and somehow, *somehow*— don't leave this out—get paid for it!

Burton orders them into place at the long table so they will be able to look into each other's eyes during the readings: Newell halfway down the table on one side; Ivy on the other, with Savaya on her right. Beside Newell, Orion.

As they all look through their scripts (in the Mitch—Stella scene, as Newell predicted, Ivy's name is purpled in beside Mitch) Burton gives a précis of the reading ethos.

"Of course we ask for commitment and energy during the reading. We are testing to see what will come once we are on our feet . . . And yes," he adds, now that they've all registered who they are reading. "Yes, you'll see—there's a bend in it."

Terry and Terry don't have scripts. None of the students say anything, although Orion does glance quickly up, across the table to Savaya.

Interesting, Ivy finds, to watch Orion's body slightly adjusting, relax- ing—conforming—to, which? Blanche or Stella? He melts a little more, lolls slightly in his chair, smiles a secret, pregnant smile. Stella. Anyway, only Newell could do Blanche. There are other pairings: down at the end of the table giggles break out, kids elbowing other kids and pointing silently to the scripts. Burton stops all that.

"We ask you"—his eye is ferocious—"to take this reading seriously, to honour the text. Cast as a murderous barber, or a woman who cooks people into pie, you would throw yourself into that. Do the same here, even if you find yourself playing against gender."

They read. Burton ignores the tittery end of the table and starts with the beginning of the play, Newell—Blanche coming to find Stella—Orion in the tenement on a street called Elysian Fields. It works, weirdly. Orion is tender; Savaya, six feet tall, broad and flat across the shoulders, is a lovely, taut Stanley. They know each other well enough, Ivy sees, to con- struct (in the ghostly architecture of rehearsal) an entire marriage, a web of compliance and adjustments, a contract between them of strength and sex. But in comes trouble: Newell, with a lightly raised eyebrow, questioning the quality of everything, seeming at first as pure and clean as a bar of fine milled soap.

STELLA: He smashed all the lightbulbs with the heel of my slipper.
BLANCHE: And you let him? Didn't run, didn't scream?
STELLA: Actually, I was sort of thrilled by it.

Orion's sturdy enough to do this, to stand up against the older sister, have an opinion of his own; he's soft enough to still, always, love Blanche. And interestingly, he captures that mysterious superiority that Stella has: the power of knowing that her lover loves her. *He's not just a pretty face*, Ivy finds her mind saying, in just those old-fashioned words.

But it's hard to watch Newell.

Ivy is familiar with that difficulty. The way the eye slides off those who are damaged. She could never watch Michael Jackson either. Or— who else—Lindsay Lohan, combusting; Judy Garland, Marilyn. People who have been broken in public, who are suffering badly, right out in the open. Even the camera's eye seems to glide away.

Now it's Ivy's turn: Mitch meeting Blanche. It's horrible. The hope, the possibility of love, and knowing how it will be dashed, like babies' heads are dashed against the pavement in the Psalms. Men she's known flood through her working mind, fragments of how they spoke or moved that might be useful. Kind plumbers, serious car mechanics, those who help, who are kind. As Mitch ought to be, can be, until that last scene where he has to attack. She herself is Mitch-like—and there's something else in the character, something a bit like Hugh.

Once they're talking to each other, she can look at Newell. Then he gives himself to her. He's a genius, he's an angel to work with, and here's his secret: he knows that you know he's ruined, and he trusts you enough to let you in. He breaks her heart.

They stop, they take a merciful break.

It's absurd, of course, for Burton to have done this, but Ivy can't be sad. Painful, remarkable, to watch the play being made true once again, twisted (or untwisted?) to serve Burton's ends—it's good. Can't do these students any harm to listen to this, she thinks.

Burton thinks so too. He's the Serious Artist, all furrowed brow and deep thought.

"It's so *human*. Wonderful. That was *wonderful*," he says to Orion, as the students disperse to get drinks from the table at the back. Orion blushes. He's very young.

The Terrys don't seem to agree with the *wonderful*. He-Terry stares at the table, maybe bracing himself to object; Her-Terry approaches Burton, clipboard loaded with sponsors' phone numbers: "We do have a responsibility toward those who have so generously—"

Burton forestalls her: "I know, I tossed and turned all night last night. I have great purple circles under my eyes, as do you, dear Terry. Perhaps you too were plagued by the idea that something—something vital—was missing from the master class. But here I believe we have one solution. Perhaps not the *only* . . ." By now, Him-Terry has worked up the courage to join his wife, and Burton folds him into the conversation, waving aside a weak mention of rights negotiations. "Let us fulfill this process—just for today—and see whether it is conceivable that something important may be discovered here—you see, Terry, *It Gets Better*."

Inside her cheek, Ivy laughs at how shamelessly sensible Burton is: twisting the internet campaign meant to console gay teens to his very practical end. Even Terry cannot fight the power of YouTube. Neither can Terry. They confer over folders, darting glances back to the table, more united against Burton than they have been for years. So a little good has been done, Ivy supposes.

Savaya, returning with a bright pink can of cream soda, bursts in with a paean to Dan Savage's genius and his husband and son, his suffering, and *how many people's lives* are being saved by the project to *stamp out bullying*.

Savaya's eyes are sparkling clean, her mouth full of clean sparkling teeth, enthusiasm and animal spirit undamped, unmuffled. Ivy wonders if in fact she might be a "Polack," like Stanley Kowalski. Ivy asks, "What does Savaya mean? Is it a name from your heritage?" (How convolutedly we've learned to ask that question!)

"Doesn't mean a thing!" Savaya says, laughing again. Brilliant teeth. "My heritage is, like, nothing—just white-bread. My parents are, you know, *alternative*. Savaya was a coffee place they liked in San Francisco, sounded kinda yoga-y."

She's a beautiful girl, easy to like. No L, but smart and funny. A shame if that slimeball Pink pollutes her. Ivy laughs too. "Try Ivy," she says. "And my sister's name is Fern. We went through hell. Well, limited hell."

They start again. The second half of the play is worse. Terrible to look up into Newell's eyes again, to watch him peel away the covering from his poor soul and show you the rags inside. Blanche can't even lie properly, can't keep up her pretenses anymore.

"I don't want realism," Newell tells her in the blue light of the third eye, the fourth wall of consciousness not necessary between them, in this working moment. "I want magic! Yes, yes, magic! I try to give that to people. I misrepresent things to them. I don't tell truth, I tell what *ought* to be truth. And if that is sinful, then let me be damned for it!"

All of that is entirely true, Ivy thinks.

As they move through the play Burton gives notes, praising with too much effusion (Orion, mostly). But it's Savaya who surprises Ivy. That's the joy of these workshops, of all teaching: the shock of how good the very young can be. Savaya has headstrong pride as well as kooky, useful humour, and the sexual confidence (or the gall) to bulldoze. Reading Stanley, her head rears back and she stares directly at Newell. Tough thing for a sixteen-year-old girl to do to a minor legend of the big and small screen. Taking on nationality, white-bread or not: "I am not a Polack. People from Poland are *Poles*, not Polacks. But what I am is a one hundred percent American, born and raised in the greatest country on earth and proud as hell of it, so don't ever call me a Polack."

They break again, the tension drops, and the students drift out to get drinks. Savaya and Orion go out arm in arm, kissing each other's cheeks as they sashay, but of course that doesn't mean anything in an arts school.

Only the grown-ups are left. Ivy bends over her script, drawing daisies with her yellow marker.

In the silence Burton lifts his head, saying, "There's nothing there. Nothing."

Newell is watching the students out in the hall. He half-turns back to Burton.

Who sighs, and picks up his script, spiritually spent. Lets it fall again. Staring up at Newell's carved-marble ear, Burton announces, "I was wrong, Boy. They need more of the knife. Like *Spring Awakening*— Wedekind! No one else has touched the soul of youth."

Orion (soul of youth that he is) appears, like Ganymede. He deposits a Diet Coke in front of Burton, and accepts thanks with a slight flush of his lean, silken cheek. Burton returns to his script with much indication of despair: furrowed brow, fierce concentration.

From behind her hair, Ivy watches Orion open the other can, drink from it with his beautiful carved-marble mouth, and hand it to Newell. Who puts his mouth on it and drinks. Whose other hand rises to take a speck of lint from Orion's chest, as Burton lifts his head again and also, Ivy sees, sees what she has seen.

But Burton is a pro. His eyes look west for a brief second and then back down into his script, deep into the dark recesses of *Desire*.

(DELLA)

playing stops the constant barrage
                          the list of all the things that must be done
              pick up Elly / clean up / class tomorrow / pay bills /
                    Mighton all over the dining room table
late but one more piece will keep   has kept, is keeping me from
                    Schumann, *Abschied*
          The Departure   *Le Départ*
                    nicht schnell
everybody is losing everybody   Mimi too losing Hugh
                        losing us, light, air, touch, sound
Gerald, his son, how can he bear it
                          wandering the streets, not thinking
              like I don't think about Elle
a mouth full of broken teeth   don't bite down
        what did you think, Mimi, all those times you lost Hugh?
          my mama lost me too, each time she lost another baby
music helps   thank you, Mimi
should I text an ultimatum?

   >Call or don't come

speaking or not speaking   it is the usual thing, after all
          we're not meant   not built to be monogamous   or loyal
but look at geese   all the geese flying away   each with a single mate
              drawing their Vs along grey paper sky

                              he has stopped loving me
                          that's all, it is the usual thing

              nicht schnell

Getting dark early. At five o'clock, in a fitful wind, Hugh walks the leaf-scuffed, wet sidewalks to Della's to tell her that Ken called. That rising inside-tide of dread: to be the bearer of bad news, the one to trouble your friend. Not the person who did it, but you, Hugh, blamed for saying what is true.

His head hurts, his teeth ache. He climbs the back steps, lightening his heavy tread so as not to give everything away. Why does Della never lock her door? Anybody could come in.

"Hello!" he calls. What a cheerful howl you have, Mr. Wolf.

Nobody answers but music: Della, at Mimi's piano. That rippling thing, Schumann or Schubert, *Impromptu*. Long hours waiting at Della's piano lessons after school, listening to Miss Bick bark at her. He'll sit and listen again.

Out of Della's line of sight, Hugh leans on the dining room table, littered with glossy photos of Mighton, bedroom-eyed, young for his age. We are ego-based life forms. Thank God that didn't last, Della and Mighton. Ken is better. Even now. A better man.

Hugh's head hurts so much. Orange bells on the sideboard, shoved all anyhow into a vase. He shifts a stalk or two to make a more pleasing line. Eye caught by Della's boats, he follows them around the room, trying to see what she's after. Too early in the process to know. Thick work, thick paint. Myriad layers on the ones she has collaged. Della's mind, unrefined.

The house smells of linseed oil, oranges, coffee. Perfume, sharp rather than sweet, vetiver. Not much of Ken—but his law office is bare too. Spare everywhere, guarded, skin stretched thin over long bones. Intelligent, kind, hard-driven. By ambition or dislike of failure? Distant: from having to refrain from relationships with the succession of tragedies he works with, all abuse cases.

He's disciplined. So the wild phone call, the fractured voice, the—breakdown, it sounds like, when Hugh lets himself think about it at all—is more disquieting. To think that Della is, that Ken is, in trouble. It ought to be fixable.

Everything should be. It should be possible to build Utopia. Hughtopia. At least among our friends, in one limited place, like L's *Republic* in the basement. What would fix things for Della? They are careful never to talk about cash—maybe money is what makes her face so white? Money would fix old Jasper and Ruth, who are both essentially happy (business woe makes Jasper crawl inside the bottle, but the bottle creates the woe). Not Newell. Newell has plenty of money, he just lacks . . . peaceful love, or freedom from Burton. But there is nothing you can do about goddamn Burton.

Hugh can't fix Ann's disappointment, her marriage, or the built-in narcissism that makes her so discontented; can't tell young Jason that porn is evil. Can't keep Orion safe.

You can't bring Gerald's wife and son back to life.

L, help L. Talk to Gareth Pindar. Take a piece of L's to show him, without telling her, so that if Gareth laughs she won't be crushed.

From the piano: *Kinderszenen*, Della will be busy for a while. Hugh backs out of the dining room and cat-foots down the basement stairs—then stops, and almost bows before entering L's *Republic*. Fool. Photos the installation with his phone, flash and no flash.

Okay, take the portrait of Newell on rice paper; the roughed-in sketch of Nevaeh. That map of the inner fortress too: intricate, brain-like. He rolls them up together, thinking.

Sound upstairs. The back door opening. Hugh waits for L to come down . . .

Footsteps cross the kitchen, instead. Reprieved!

He heads quietly up the stairs, not wanting L to catch him thieving. Three long steps to the back door. He glances to the dining room arch, his eye caught by a flash of tweed jacket, an elbow—not L, it's Ken, he's back. About to call hello, Hugh catches himself.

Ken stands by the table, staring at the mess of Mightons while the music flows on and on, *Von fremden Ländern und Menschen*. Tense shoulder, neck: he lifts a photo, two more. Flicks them aside like cards being dealt.

You should go in, be glad to see him—find out how he's doing, what's going on. But you can't possibly be there when Della turns and sees him, when they start whatever fight they will have to start.

In the driveway, mist. Hugh tucks L's drawings carefully under his coat. Dizzy, or tired, or is it just sad? He needs some supper.

Staring at his blank-screened phone. No message.

Fuck it anyway.

Give up, go to Savaya's party? Fuck, hard to know. Hard/not hard/
not impossible/I can do it. I can rise above, ride into the sunset, the
blood-orange sun going down on darkness. On silver wheels—a night
Phoebus pulling the moon across the sky.

Orion stands on his back deck, waiting for supper, for something,
whatever his mom might pull together when she stops freaking out on the
phone to someone about something that happened in The Department,
or alternatively the NDP's slide in the polls, and the plight of the
Palestinians and what she said to Jerry Pink about the master-bation
class. When she finally blows her nose and wipes her soft, red eyes and
digs in the fridge for the last edible undead vegetable and the organic,
free-range nest-laid eggs and calls it fritatta.

It might rain before the party.

Bike to the party or drive?

He's no Stella.

He calls softly into the darkness at the end of the yard, "I *do* misrepresent things. I don't tell truths. I tell what ought to be the truth. If that's
a sin, then let me be damned for it!"

Lit by the last orange stab of sun through gunmetal-grey clouds,
Orion shoots up onto the railing, launches from the deck, and flies for a
long moment, everything balanced in air.

He lands by his bike, and goes.

Hugh sits with the windows rolled down in the parking lot of Black Cat Pizza, hoping damp wind will blow his brain into better sense. Waiting for his supper. Disconsolate because of Ken and Della. Also, inappropriately hurt—Ivy hasn't texted. Maybe working still. Maybe he assumed too much.

Stupid head. Tooth hurting again; chew carefully when the pizza's ready. Back molar on the right-hand side: death is waiting for you, first in the falling out of the teeth and the falling out of the hair and then, following, in the incremental death of the rest of the body.

Or else he's just hungry. He checks his phone again. As bad as Della.

Clotted with clouds, grey sky reflects in the grey window where the men are cooking. On the wall-mounted TV inside the grey kitchen, Dorothy has landed in Oz—don't worry, here comes Glinda the Good to solve everything! That other witch, ruby feet sticking out. Now Dorothy's got the shoes, she's setting off. Oz is the only colour in the place: grey steel grey windows grey tiles grey fluorescence white aprons black T-shirts on the pizza guys. Dorothy's brilliant blue-red smile repeats the *Open* sign, red, blue. Grey-white pizza boxes. The men argue among themselves whether a pizza is done, pushing in and pulling out of the red-hot oven with their long-handled peels.

A car door opens near Hugh, and out climbs Newell. That's not—oh, it's Burton's car. Somehow that vintage of Passat is always a little Euro-slime, Hugh thinks. Prejudice.

Newell sticks his head in the passenger-side window.

"Pizza for dinner?" Hugh asks.

"One with everything. Bring yours to my place." At that *my*, Hugh thinks he might go. "Ivy's there," Newell adds, luring him. "Burton kept her working."

Hugh stares at the grey window, the grey men.

"Come," Newell says. "Please come—Ansel's buggered up the master class, they're having a meeting, we might all be fired. It's fraught, but we'll have a party. Come?" He reaches in the window and touches Hugh's arm.

Newell chooses to be kind to Burton, and that is none of Hugh's beeswax.

"Okay," Hugh says. They walk in to pick up the pizzas.

At the condo, Ivy and Burton sit at the long dining room table in drifts of playscripts and student lists. Ivy looks up as Newell and Hugh blow in on a gust of rainy wind.

"It's you!" she says, heavy eyebrows arching in pleasure. "I mean, it's Hugh!"

Her face is open. Honest and clear. He has been looking for her for so long.

Burton adds his own exclamations of *Hugh! HYou!* Ha-ha. His eyes take on a greedy-dog fix as Newell opens the pizza boxes. Anchovies and truffle oil—got to be Burton's. Spinach & feta, Ivy's; one with every-thing (Newell's invariable order, only half Buddhist joke); double cheese, pepperoni and green olives (Hugh's). Too much pizza, but Burton will wolf down whatever's left over. His appetites are famous. *Stop,* Hugh thinks. Look at Ivy instead.

She's looking at him. Not secretly or shyly but with every door, every gate thrown wide.

Hard to be depressed when someone you recognize has recognized you back, when you understand the unlooked-for luck of that. Hugh crosses to her and puts his arms around her, right there, in front of Newell. In front of Burton. Fuck him, anyway.

Plates, wineglasses, pouring, nobody's paying attention to Hugh and Ivy. Newell clicks on music and Burton pulls another cork; one bottle is never enough. "Let's not," Burton says, "let's *not* have salad. Let's pig ourselves on pure pizza, oozing cheese, everything bad!"

The gas fire springs to light. On a cold October night, sitting with Ivy at the fireplace end of the long couch, death is held in abeyance.

Newell eats like he does everything, with detached joy. Burton with gluttonous dispatch, ferocious bad teeth chomping once, twice, per piece, wine to wash it down, between spates of blather on why "we must remain *flexible*" with the master class.

"Tomorrow, we start *Spring Awakening*," Ivy tells Hugh, between neat small-toothed bites. "Plenty flexible. They'll love it."

Newell lies on the rug, head propped vertical, eyes closed, long and flat. His glamour does not ever shut off, but sometimes, like a tiger, is asleep.

"But what about scripts?" Hugh asks.

"Get them couriered from Toronto," Newell says, eyes closed. Having had money for a long time, solutions occur to him.

"I have to run in tomorrow morning," Ivy says. "I have a—a thing—" She drinks, as if wishing she hadn't brought that up. They wait. "My apartment. The dishwasher broke."

"Is that lunatic youth still occupying your apartment?"

Lunatic youth?

Burton's face goes avid when there's something painful in the air. "Yes, yes, I recall him: Jamie, the boyfriend's brother. I suppose you can hardly kick the poor fellow out."

Boyfriend? You know nothing about her, her circumstances—

Hugh turns to take Ivy's plate and his own to the kitchen, and catches her looking up at him, her face frightened. Frightened! That cures his foolish jealousy. No need to know more than he knows: that against all probability or expectation, somehow she is his. He gives her back look for look, as open-hearted as an out-of-practice, fiftyish man can be.

He calls back, to derail Burton, "What will you do if *Spring Awakening* doesn't fly?"

That makes Burton pettish. "Don't be ridiculous, Hugh—*Angels in America*, maybe. Melodrama, but still tediously topical. Or Orton. *Ruffian on the Stair*, remember, Boy?"

Newell laughs. "Try getting that one past Pink."

"*Oh!*" Burton shrieks, suddenly furious. "You never let me do what *I* want to do."

Newell won't take that. "Jesus, Ansel, why not go straight to *Vampire Lesbians of Sodom?* None of it has any relevance to kids from Peterborough. Stick with *Spring Awakening*—it's the only good play you've got up your sleeve that you could possibly get away with in high school."

"They know nothing! Terry! And *Terry!* And that Pink person." Burton scrambles up, last piece of pizza still in hand, his plump body trembling. His face has gone a strange, bad colour. He sweeps half the scripts off the table with the empty hand, the other half with the pizza hand, red sauce staining white pages.

Ivy goes still. Hugh says, trying to manufacture calm, "Burton, you'll get run out of town on a rail if you try to force the gay thing."

Wait, that won't help. But it deflects attention: Burton turns on Hugh, staring, the red bloom rising again in his cheeks. *"Hugh!"* Or was that, probably it was *"You!"* All the scorn and disgust of a long life of constant betrayal. Like Mimi, when you went in this morning.

Everything hurts. Hugh closes his eyes and rubs them. What a headache he has got. It's making him vague and stupid.

Burton laughs, or gloats at him: "I'll tell Hugh one thing, I won't be run out this time. Shall we tell them our secret, Boy?"

"Go ahead," Newell says. His eyes have closed again, Hugh sees. His own eyes open inside the safe cage of his hands.

Burton stands towering squatly over Newell's full-length body, like a lion hunter, tears in his eyes. "You tell them, *you* tell Hugh," he orders, and Newell's eyes open, to stare up at the far-distant ceiling.

"We're engaged," he says. "Congratulate me."

🍃

Ivy doesn't like this development—she hates Burton's dramatics. But it's obviously worse for Hugh. He's stone-still, doesn't speak. Is it a complete surprise? Looks like it, from his face. And from Newell's empty eyes staring up at the fabulous wenge-wood ceiling, not looking at anyone at all. Happy times.

"Wow, fabulous," she says, seeing no alternative. "When did that happen?"

"This very afternoon," Burton says. Too simple to say he simpers. He's watching Newell's quiet face, Newell's eyes that might be counting planks in the fancy ceiling. "We have discussed the possibility before, of course— of course we have, as one does, as *two do*—but we decided this afternoon."

Must have been a doozy of a fight, Ivy thinks, whatever happened over that moment with Orion and the pop can.

"When the people who *are your life* are in need, you step up." Newell says, looking at Hugh. Ivy's insides clench, because who knows how Burton will take that?

She's working up some platitude/lie about how great it is when two people who've known each other for a long time get together, when the doorbell rings. A noble bell, Zen temple with an overtone of pure, deep money.

"Shall I get that?" Ivy asks.

Hugh still hasn't spoken. Nobody else speaks either. Ivy gets up.

Her moving shakes Hugh out of silence. He says, without any discernible difficulty, "I'm happy for you both. I'll—" He balks a bit, there. "I'll tell Mimi. She'll be tickled pink."

Pink comes out just as Ivy opens the door, and there is Jerry Pink, in the flesh.

He pours through the giant wenge-wood doorway. "Newell! Ansel! Great to see you!" As if it's been years.

Burton jerks away from the small tableau at the fireplace. His going frees Newell, who gets to his feet in one lithe cat-move, no gasping, no creaks. Ivy admires his strength, and his social grace. His kindness, too. Pink is a stuffed sausage in a bad suit coat, but Newell shows no disdain. He takes Pink's hand, and as far as anyone would guess, a touch of Pink is just what this place needed.

Ivy leaves them to it, and goes to Hugh. "You okay?"

With Newell's attention diverted, Hugh does not look good. "None of my business," he says.

"Well, yes it is. Newell is your friend, you want him to be happy."

Hugh nods.

The doorbell rings again. Pink is still standing there, and his hand goes out to open the door. A thing Newell doesn't like: Ivy can see his affability erode.

It's kids. Savaya first, and the angry girl, N-something, Never? They'll be very good in *Spring Awakening*. It gives Ivy a bit of a lift to think of that.

Now Orion. When he walks into a room the air practically crackles, she thinks.

She is standing by the long black marble island. There's a cheese-knife there, stubby and strong-looking. She tests the blade; then pockets it, and looks around for Hugh. It strikes her that it's time to go. No good can come of all these whirling egos.

Hugh takes Ivy's hand, which she has flung out to him like a small life preserver. Time to go.

"Okay," he says. "I left the van at the Black Cat—I'll walk you home."

Jacket. Nothing else? His arms feel empty. Pizza, that's what he was carrying. Okay. Hugh nods to Newell and they slide away, out the back door to the terrace and the long set of stairs running down to the street.

Newell follows, seeing them out into the rooftop wind in his shirt-sleeves. He kisses Ivy and she heads down the stairs, going carefully on those pretty, silly shoes.

Hugh pauses for a moment at the brink, moon blinking through the charcoal drama of overwrought, fast-scudding clouds.

"How's your mother?" Newell asks, clearly in no rush to go back inside.

Newell: his strength, his health, his glowing human-ness—and all the misery he carries with him. Hugh asks him, "How can the body die? Tell me. How can the person who is here not be here any longer? How is this—how can it be right, even be possible, that this has to happen?"

"I love her." Newell's voice is gentle, sweet, ordinary. "I'll go over in the morning."

"Okay," Hugh says. He goes down that long, long flight of concrete steps to where Ivy waits.

They walk through misted streets, avenues, a vanished town, to Ann's.

In the quiet, Ivy asks, "Are you upset?"

Hugh tests how he feels, probes down into his inmost heart. No answer there, just lava.

"What made you angry? Do you think gays shouldn't marry?"

"No! They can marry the hell out of each other. It's nothing like that. It's just Burton." Can't tell Ivy the truth. What you think is the truth.

"I know he's kind of hateable. But he's fond of Newell."

Right.

They walk, they walk.

You just don't know. You don't know, you don't know, what is right, what would be best. *Not Burton,* that's all Hugh can think. "I've known Newell for a long time. I don't—Burton is not good for him. Newell's my oldest friend, my Ruth-brother."

"He loves you," Ivy says. "What's the bad part, besides that Burton's an asshole and will be an expensive husband? Newell can afford it. And I don't think, you know . . ." She proceeds a little carefully: "I don't think Newell does anything he doesn't want to do."

Hugh thinks about that, or tries to. All he can see is Newell's lost face, not helped, not saved. He can't tell Ivy what he suspects—okay, never mind suspects. What he *knows.* Knew, when he was twelve. The knowledge of what Burton did all those years ago has been buried deep in his head for a long time. Hurts to think about, not allowed. And it is not simple. Burton and Newell have been together on and off for a thousand years, they have grown into each other by now, have worked out some complicated fucking agreement.

And who is he to say what Newell should think or do.

He kicks through a slump of leaves by the curb. He says, "How can I know anything about it?"

"No. Me neither."

"Hard enough to know about myself."

There's a pause. Half a block of silence.

Ivy stops. "I can't be with you." She just comes out with it baldly. "In case you were wondering, which I thought you might be."

"I know," Hugh says. "I'm too damaged. And my mother is dying. Any day. When she does I'm going to be a mess. You don't need any of this."

Ivy laughs at him. "That's not why!" she says. "All my *own* shit is why."

"I am used to shit," he says. "I can take it."

"You can take it, but you can't dish it out?"

He nods. He's too upset to speak.

Ivy pulls at his arm. "You can cope with a mountain of whatever horrors, but I can't?"

Hugh nods again.

"And your mother— I'm so sorry." She takes his hand.

They go on walking. Their hands fit. The mist hanging over the streets has caused a compression of sound, a minor slapping echo of shoes on sidewalk.

Or wait, no—it's somebody following them. Newell, again?

"Hey," L calls, from behind.

Almost at Ann's walk, they turn and wait for L to reach them.

"Hi," she says, breathy from running. "Hi, hi, Ivy. I saw you at the costume room but I didn't say hi then because we didn't want to see Jason's mom; she was on the warpath this afternoon—she went to see Pink, Hugh, about the—"

Hugh closes his eyes. "I know," he says. "I should have said I'd talk to Jason."

"Now he's got to see Mr. Pink tomorrow, and the appointment is for *forty-five minutes*."

"Where is Jason? Home?"

"I'm not sure—but there's a party at Savaya's tonight. We'll all sleep over there. I'm not telling my mom about the, you know, the magazines. It's not fair, please don't tell her."

"None of my business," Hugh says. "But I bet Ann already has."

"Oh shit, right, thanks." L trots off into the fog.

Ivy hesitates. "I was going to ask you in, but I'm pretty sure there's no coffee, or even a chair to sit on."

Hugh is thinking how to answer that when the door opens.

Ann gleams in the hall light. Her sweater, her hair, perfect. The minimalist thing, she's good at it. "Hey, you." Is she angry? Or no, that's *Hey, Hugh*. "I've been calling you. Don't you ever answer the phone?"

"Usually Ruth gets it," he says, conscious that this is weak-kneed.

He and Ivy move slowly up the walk to the porch stairs.

Ann laughs, sharp as teeth. "I wanted to tell you—Lise Largely says you're clearing out Mimi's place. It's going to be a huge job, poor Hugh. I'm going to go through her clothes for you and decide what to give away and what to sell."

He's taken aback. "I don't think I'll—"

"Some of those things are valuable," Ann says.

Something in her eyes warns Hugh to just agree. Something glassy, not blank but breakable. "Absolutely," he says.

"She was my mother too, for a long time. My creative mother." With that bizarre embroidery, Ann turns to Ivy, eyes on highbeam. "Hugh had to help you find your way home?"

"I'm not lost." Ivy isn't giving ground, the way Hugh always does.

Ann stares at her. A beat. "Are you——?"

Ivy stares right back. Waits for the question to finish.

Ann almost staggers, as if she's missed a step, and reaches for the door handle. She turns to Hugh. "Are you——?"

He weighs the options, decides there aren't any, and nods. "We are."

She's hit.

She had me in her sights again, he thinks. A wave of hot/cold, relief/sorrow washes over him. He puts out a hand to comfort her.

But Jason dashes out between them, slipping past Ann's thin frame in the doorway, jostling Ivy almost off the stairs in his headlong rush.

"Sorry, sorry, late," he calls back, running backwards for a few steps. Making a sorry-face, more lively than Hugh's seen him since childhood.

Ivy megaphones her hands at her mouth and yells, "Watch out for those fan-tailed beavers, mister!"

A great shout of laughter comes back through the mist by the river's edge.

"His dream, this morning," Ivy says to Ann, apologizing, after all, Hugh sees; because you have to when someone has been in the dark, and has stubbed her toe so badly.

Ann nods once to each of them. The ice goddess Freya hammering their heads with her bronze sledgehammer.

She swings away to let Ivy slip inside, and shuts the heavy door in Hugh's face.

(ORION)

The leaves are almost all down. Wind pulling her fingers through her hair, Orion thinks. *The leaves of the trees are for the healing of the nations. No longer will there be any curse,* it says in Revelations. Like, apocalyptic carbon capture. When his mother makes him go to her weird all-denominations church he spends the hour flipping through Revelations, one long acid trip. Not that he has done acid; it's actually quite hard to get around the school.

Savaya's parents are going out—pulling out of the driveway in their '89 Eurovan, held together with duct-tape. Probably going to drive out to Bobcaygeon and do bong hits, that's how hippie they are. Tragically unhip. Orion locks his bike to a wrought-iron fence. Ought to, wrought to, deter thievery. He stands in shadow for a minute, checking out who's already there. Twelve or fifteen guys milling around the lighted doorway—Philip and Coran; there's that fuckwipe Sheridan Tooley, who only drinks Baby Duck, who got the kid lead in *Auntie Mame* in Toronto and quit the master class to go in to the city every night for singing classes with some guy at the opera. Fucker.

Here's Jason running down the sidewalk, not that any of them ought to be in a hurry. Orion puts out a long arm and a jazz hand to stop Jason. "We enter with deliberation, Boy," he says. They're calling each other Boy these days. Burton, you old slag.

Jason nods.

"Where's L?"

"Her mom's driving her—I had to wait till—" Jason's breath is gone.

"You are out of training, my man. Your mom again?"

"Yeah. You sticking around?"

Orion checks his phone. No message yet. "I might."

The crowd around the lighted porch bursts into a clap of laughter. Savaya comes to the door and waves her hands to bring the noise down. The last time the cops came, and her parents said she couldn't have a party if she couldn't control the guests.

"How was it at Newell's?" Jason asks. Hands on knees, getting his breath back.

"You know. Pink told Burton he wants him to go back to *Sweeney* fucking *Todd*, and Burton told him to basically fuck himself. Burton won.

We start *Spring Awakening* tomorrow: two masturbation scenes, onstage sex, and I'm the main guy, Melchior."

"I mean, how's it going with Newell?" Jason says.

"Polyamory is a recognized sexual choice."

"Right."

"How's your own sex life?"

"Right."

"Here comes L, let's go. I need to punch that fucker Tooley, but I am not going to."

"Yeah, Hugh do you think you are?"

Orion laughs. "Jase! Good one!"

They flit, they fly.

(DELLA)

these parties   tell Elly to be careful   don't tell her
Elly DJing   *Short Skirt/Long Jacket*
be acerbic   be witty   and now her Tom Waits impression
                                                          she will be gone
a Hallowe'en party in the 80s walking in to get my coat
Ann fucking some guy on the heap of coats   who was that? not Hugh
Hugh was beside me seeing her   Ken?
                                                  not Ken not Ken

how that hurts
was that the night we met?
or we were already together   and it was Ken
I was busy feeling bad about being with Mighton
All Saints All Hallows old ghosts gone

     Bye, sweetness, turn your phone on . . .

Jason running up   good, he's good
Ann in Mimi's old polyester teagown   *how to talk to your teen about porn*
that's a short skirt   not a long enough jacket
                                            not a baby anymore

no protection from   bareback boys   or girls
I guess it might be girls   how would I know?
the guys hug shake hands   are men   adults   setting out into the world
where no one can humiliate them
                                      only it is all humiliation

drive away
I Will Survive

                          if I'da known for just one second
                              you'd be back to bother me
                              did you think I'd crumble?

The ladder clunks gently against the windowsill, the windowpane. The sill again. In a moment, like a moon rising, Hugh's face rises in the window.

He has a chisel. Ivy laughs, and gets Newell's cheese knife from her purse. She runs it jagging and digging along the dried paint lines inside as Hugh does the same outside. She gets hers done first, and shoves the inner window up. He jimmies more, and mimes for her to shift the metal clasps. He shoves upward on the storm window, hard.

A crack, loud in the darkness. Then silence again.

He grins at her, takes the weight of the storm window carefully, and disappears down into darkness again. The ladder trembles, trembles.

A small cautious thud, the window planted on the ground. Then careful steps, climbing. She backs away from the sill to let him in.

He knows to duck his head for the low ceiling. "A little awkward, knocking on the front door when she's . . ."

". . . hot-tempered?"

"Never hot. In a feverchill." Hugh looks down into the garden. "We'll have to put that storm window back on when it really gets cold. Ices up in here if you don't." He walks quietly around the room, looks at the shelves. In her strong effort to keep the room clear, there are only two things there: her old silver mirror, and a stone.

Neither of them speak. Is he as nervous as she is? It seems so. Ivy's teeth clamp on a small laugh. Then she lets it out.

"I like this room," Hugh says. "I've always liked it."

"Perfect. It's a new bed, Ann tells me," Ivy says.

"Hm. Okay, then." He puts out a hand and touches her face.

They speak to each other in low voices, and in a little while they go to bed.

THURSDAY

❦

With or without Hugh

*Hope and fear are a single coin, one
entity with two faces—on the other side
of a moment in which we hope for more
happiness will be our fear of more suffering.
Until attachment is eliminated, we can be
certain of having both hope and fear.*

The Great Secret of Mind,
Tulku Pema Rigtsal,
translated by Keith Dowman

I entertained her as best I could.

Another Bullshit Night in Suck City,
Nick Flynn

1. HUGHREKA

Hugh crashes down—falls out of the dream-sky. Wide awake. The daily shock of consciousness. How do you keep your mind from eating itself? He reaches for his phone . . . 5 a.m.

He slept.

He looks up, dim light. The old slanted ceiling. For a fraction of a second, confused, he thinks, *Oh no*. But— Oh. This is a change in the program. Letting his head fall to the left he stares at Ivy's dark head, nose, her closed eyelids that slant at the corners and hide her consciousness from him. Her cheek is pale in the still-shadowy room. She brushes her fingers across her mouth. Even in this light, he can see the pores in her skin, he is so close.

You can't know another person. We cannot know each other. It's hopeless.

Her eyebrows are thick, matted, the hairs almost braided together, dark against the white of her skin. Blue veins show in her eyelids. They match the map of blue veins on her breast, slipped from the sheet, pearl or ivory texture. Doeskin, dear skin.

You shouldn't—listen, don't kid yourself. This will never work.

But Ivy, not asleep, not waking, says, "I know you. You are Hugh." Or perhaps she said, "I know Hugh. You are you." Their arms go round each other and they might make love. But instead, because we were up very late, you and I, they fall asleep.

Hugh wakes again; he listens to the hesitating tender percussion of rain, not much of it, eavesdripping, broken rhythm. It's 5:40. Time to go. Of anything in the world, at this moment, Hugh least wants Ann to find him lying here, however new the bed.

On the other hand, his headache is a little better. He turns slowly in the bed, so Ivy won't wake. Kisses her pale cheek. Slides out of sheets, dresses in the cold dawn air. The window will make noise. If he's fast and silent, he can take the stairs.

He finds his phone and texts Ivy: > let me know when your eyes open

Sees the text light up on her bedside table. Good, okay. Bedroom door open, shut. His feet know the treads, know the count of stairs to the empty, black-scribbled living room. The front door opens and closes without appreciably disturbing the silence.

He shuffles into his shoes. First, Mimi. Make her happy too, at least for a moment.

(ORION)

Lying on Savaya's bed in the sunrise after a long party, reading Oscar Wilde—Savaya, what is this doing on your bedside table, crazy girl? Audition fodder?

It's quiet now, everyone tired, Savaya's parents too stoned to yell. While she puts the Desire/Despair costume on again for Jason, Orion reads *Salome* out loud: *"It is thy mouth that I desire, Iokanaan. Thy mouth is like a band of scarlet on a tower of ivory."*

Worrying, really, the volume of porn watched by today's youth. Jason's mom freaking out, as if Jason even— But apparently it's not good for you, makes you dependent. Except that, except, *he* is not dependent. Not incapable. *"O tower of ivory, oh, mouth upon it."*

Savaya glances at the book. "I tried it, but I couldn't do all that *thy moutheth cometh* stuff. Terry gave it to me to look through."

Huh! Was that Terry He, or Terry Her? Like temple acolytes in a weird rite, L holds the gold cloth taut and Jason snips, to underscore the slashes over and under the right breast. Shit, Savaya is a tall, tall girl. She could be so great, if she would just keep her head in the game, and quit fucking assholes like Pink, or whatever's going on there, which she won't talk about. She wields a bright gold lipstick in the mirrored door. She was so good as Stanley Kowalski.

"Thy Mouth is like a branch of coral that fishers have found in the twilight of the sea, the coral that they keep for the kings."

"It's either too early in the morning for lipstick," Savaya says, staring at herself, "or too late at night." She wipes her mouth off. The burnt-black hem trails at the back right down to the red stilts of her Despairing round-heeled, down-at-heel shoes.

There is nothing in the world so red as thy mouth.

Where's the phone?

> Suffer me to kiss thy mouth.

In twenty seconds, it pings back. Always right on cue.

< Never! daughter of Babylon! Daughter of Sodom! never!

He texts, sings, shouts, > I will kiss thy mouth, Iokanaan. I will kiss thy mouth.

In the middle of the night he said *say you love me*. And why not, why not say it? Why make it precious, when it is so precious? "I love you," Ivy tells the slanted ceiling. Meaning *I love Hugh*. If she had a marker she'd write it all over the wall. She stretches in the bed, wondering what what what she will do with this beautiful day.

Then memory comes back: at first a bud of misery—then blooming, fading, falling out of the pastoral, back to the city. It's got to be done. If she leaves by ten, she can get back with time to have a good cry and wash her face and get to the master class before three.

She pats for the phone—email? None from Hugh. Three from Jamie, very long, re: the dishwasher and the water damage. (One from Alex, all caps again, delete without reading.) Prickling duty kicks her up and into the shower.

It's not just fixing the dishwasher. She's got to get serious with them, get Jamie the heck out of her apartment. Alex promised he'd be sent to Winnipeg by September. This is no good for him, he needs real help. Why do so many people have to be crazy? I must have sought them out, her mind says. And what about Hugh? Who's to say he's not crazy too?

Hugh's to say. She laughs. He is *so not crazy*, so sane. His sanity buoys her up, drowning in indoor rain while outdoor rain sluices down the window that's over the tub, water in and out, and a view out to the rainy river where water pours into water like the soul pours itself into the world, over and over, looking for home. He said it—*love*—we said.

Whatever we meant by that. Is it lying, not to have told him about Jamie; about Alex, when she knows about Ann? Avoiding, withholding, that's lying too, yes. Phone on the sink—oh, a text from before! How did she miss that? Sound was off—she flips it on.

< let me know when your eyes open

She answers: > my eyes are open but I do not see you

Half-dressed, she looks at her body in the mirror, how it must have seemed to Hugh last night. It didn't matter, in the night. Our flesh was made one, as the bishop said to the actress. Breast waist bottom thigh— under Hugh's hands all golden. One with everything.

Will it matter in daylight?

A gentle horn from the phone: < but you will, you will

And another: < come to the gallery? ten?

Ten is cutting it fine for getting to the city and back in time for the master class. Dress fast: grey pants and tunic, because who the heck knows what mysteries of Burton are on the menu today, whether she will be man or womankind in *Spring Awakening*.

Now to beard the cold-eyed lioness downstairs.

Ivy takes the front stairs without noise, so Ann doesn't turn from her work: standing on a chair at the front door, she's writing something over the lintel. Ivy reaches the short landing as Ann steps off the chair. In a perfect arch over the doorway, so anyone going out must read it:

Lying is done with words and also with silence. Adrienne Rich

Perfect. So life in this house is now impossible.

Back up the stairs. It is not unheard of for a landlady to change the locks, for people not to be able to get their stuff out later. There's not a lot to pack. Ivy leaves her cases under the window, in case she has to climb the ladder to get them later, and puts on her warmer coat. She opens the door and listens. Nothing. She goes to the top of the stairs, pauses—

Right beside her, Jason says, "You okay?"

She jumps, and turns to him. His face is sharp in the ghostlight of the upstairs hall.

"I think your mom . . ." Feeble. "I was just checking to see if— I guess she's mad at me."

"Because of Hugh?"

Ivy nods, guilty. Jason is carrying his shoes, looks the worse for wear. Sneaking in after a night out? He doesn't seem the tomcat type. He checks the stairs himself.

"She doesn't, she wouldn't, get back with him," he whispers, in a rush. "Don't worry."

She nods again.

"Also, L thinks you guys are good. You and Hugh."

A surging bubble of happiness sings up through Ivy's whole body from foot to head—joy, joy, that other people know about this amazing, unlikely thing. "Thanks," she whispers, not able to look at Jason lest he see the light in her face, even in this dark upper hall.

She slips down the stairs, makes the front door, scoots through with her shoulder bag—and beats Ann's entrance from the kitchen by the kind of quarter inch that gives a person the shudders. Raining still. Ivy dashes for the car, praying it starts.

Reversing down the damp-dark driveway, she sees Ann staring out the open door. Above her head in the doorway, Jason is waving.

(DELLA)

Mighton in the morning might help me forget the disappearing   Ken
at the train station too early   always either too early or too late
Gerald plodding along where's he off to?   sad head sad body sad sack
the rain station   the drops have slowed
                    is it clearing?   glimmering shimmering
thirty years of knowing Mighton   I'm so old he's so famous
what makes one succeed and another not?   his exhibit at the AGO
      cool, hot, too clever, puzzling   boxes, hidden compartments
            brilliantine, bits of glass   a box himself dark glasses
                arrogant, intricate   too bright for his boots
                    surface glitter   shallows, no depth
                                        depth, plunging—Ken
                        his boat half-sunk seen through waves
                                            beyond my ken
train's early too   a miracle—
there's Mighton   always bright   monkey-face   I like him
                               long ago dinner at   where was that cachaça
                               no older   that night him a thin arrow inside me
                               streetlight shining in the round window
Hugh & Ann's   it could have been
Hugh and I walked in   Ann & (who) on the coats   not Mighton
                                            I think it was Ken
      Your new piece, can't wait—let me take that—I've got Hugh's van
      he has a concussion, can't—phew, no ticket!
easy in middle age to be together no self-consciousness   only a gleam
intelligence in his work but he himself is a little stupid   I always forget
Largely kept the mandarin orange door best thing about his house
      Wonderful! I'll come back—All right, if Lise can give you a ride
      to the Argylle? Great!
nice to drive away
best thing about people is driving away from them
                                            I sound like Ken

(L)

Someone's been sleeping in my bed. Somebody walked through the *Republic* and tried to cover the traces. Not Hugh. He'd see half the pieces were backwards and fix them. Not Jason. He has a permanent pass for all L's purlieus—anyway he spent the long night at Savaya's. How to feel about this?

L wanders through the misplaced maze, smoothing, repositioning.

So her dad is back, but not back. Not here, but here, mouse-feet, moving stuff on the dining room table. And searching through the underworld down here. Poor dad, poor dad.

Four are missing. Why would her dad take them? It's—count them: the drawing of her mom; onion skins of Newell and Nevaeh; something else, some map, which, where's the schema . . . The inner fortress. Well that's just weird, and if her father has taken away her vagina, that's a thing that makes L both laugh and want to stomp her feet, thunder them together, drum them on the floor in a fucking tantrum.

No. Always careful, always calm.

We stay very stable in this house. Knowing that any moment, any one fraction of any moment, her father could split apart, husk shedding, and a creature could come out the middle that would frighten you to death. Still her dad, always, always to be relied on. But under that, this problem, such a basic foundation that we've built our whole house on it: careful, careful.

For a bad moment L's hands might stretch out and tear everything down, pull pull rip ruin the whole thing.

But no. On all fours, she crawls out backwards to the door like an olden slave making obeisance, obeised/abased, removing herself from the presence.

Up the basement stairs, coat, bookbag, out. Late for FairGrounds. Will Jason be at school by now? Because she needs some help. She would like to know, for instance, where her dad is sleeping. Why he is not—why her mom is not—dealing with this.

And for this one last year, before she is gone from them pretty much forever, why the fuck the two of them cannot keep it together for just—count them—nine more months until she leaves for good.

Hugh takes the inside stairs two at a time up to Mimi's hall. Racing up is sometimes the only way you can go in. The quietude, the ambient air of death is so thick.

Halt. Ruth's backing out the door with a tray of dishes, tubes, cloths.

"You missed Newell, he brought flowers. I chased him out, though."

Hugh takes the tray from her and sets it safely on a cart left in the hall. No crashing, no broken glass this morning.

"She's not herself," Ruth says, to warn him.

Ah, but she is, Hugh's willing to bet. The door is ajar. From inside he can hear a buzzing droning singsong. The litany streams on without pause, as if breath doesn't pertain. He nods to Ruth, shoulder-clasps her.

In he goes.

"Hugh Hugh Hugh Hugh Hugh Hugh," his mother is saying, broken-hearted. (Or else, of course, "You you you you you you . . .") Tears track down her crepe de Chine cheeks.

Happy time is over, it seems. "What's the deal, what's the deal here," he murmurs, keeps murmuring, a stream of *Yes it's me, it's all right, it's okay.* Heavy scent of Newell's roses, white hearts opening outward, waterdrop halfglobes on the green table.

Leaning over in the familiar partial kneel, since there's no room to sit on the bed beside her, Hugh takes Mimi's hands to stop her fretting with the blankets. Tubes and sticks get in the way, but he is patient. He untangles them all gently, without causing her to cry out.

Today she is not coherent, at least not intelligible. But he's been listening to this language, this deathspeak, for a while now. He can hear the words—not so different from bad racing manic-anxious times he recalls from childhood. "Thank you Ruth. Thank you. Thank Hugh." That for some time, bead-telling, rote-repetitive. Then singsong *Mairzy doats and dozy doats,* also for a good while, over and over, never progressing.

Crouch-kneeling by her side, Hugh joggles the needle of her mind in one of the pauses: ". . . *and little lambs eat Ivy*," he sings. Nibbling lambs circle Ivy's green skirt, her small hands patting their heads. Her lamblike hinder end—he almost laughs.

Mimi falls silent. Then begins the whispered recounting that he's afraid to listen to. One thing that keeps him away from her, away from here. Snatches of memory thrown up from her disintegrating mind, urgent to impart: "She drove us in her little car all the windows open down along the shore he sat beside me our legs touching she told me I was only there to make up to him and no kind of a friend it hurt me so much to have her say that he sat beside me our arms touched all along the upper lengths I shifted on the seat in the heat he'll never amount to anything she said he only . . ."

You can't know another person, can't know anyone. You are alone, alone. No matter what life you construct, no matter what duty you give them or how you love them. She can never know you, or you her. Huge white roses rise from thick green thorns; heavy glass refracts, magnifies the stems and the thorns.

"I knew *him* that's why I went I trailed my hand along the tops of the stones grey lichen green moss stubble graveyard dust the horses the horses were buried under that mound he told us then later he climbed into bed with me when no one was about."

He can hardly bear to hear. It murmurs on and on, so much life to be confessed at last. He thinks and thinks and still she goes on recounting, the tape spooling out of the cassette.

"I pushed him aside I promise I but he was there with me and what was I to I told him I knew all about her and what she'd said it was all so clear, all perfectly all clear I knew I knew it all along I knew it as soon as I saw the blood that they were that I was that it was I who, I did, it was my . . ."

Hugh bends to kiss his mother's cheek. Swollen in the early stages, then shrunken; now a soft husk around her bones, not her face that he has always known. But more her face than ever, the face he now knows best of all. He presses his cheek to her cheek. He hums to her along those *mairzy dozy* lines, floating the song along, easing her. "Never mind," he says to her. "Never mind, never mind, it wasn't your fault, it's all done with now, you don't need to worry now."

"Now no now no thank you, no thank you Hugh thank you, thank you," she whispers.

It gives his head more pain to hear her *thanks*—more pain than he can in any way allow,
    and since she seems quieter he stands and leaves the room
    and there is Ruth outside the door, she nods and trades places with him
    and off he goes blind
    into the long-stretched wet autumn sunlight
    down the hospice steps away

(DELLA)

up the steps to Ken's office: *insist on information*
no Jenny
her assistant says   Ken's assistant has an assistant now
down the steps   down the street
they are not together   they must be together
                —Buckthorn/County Rd 23—
Ken loves her as a friend, who's needed help from time to time
when her boyfriend went off the rails he helped, that was good for him
that's the law, helping people who go before the courts
he loves to help   he loves me
                —Bobcaygeon, 30 km—
still after all this time   who knows why
      he does not have another wife in Toronto and four children
     he is not with Jenny, he could not have kept that from me
he is in pain   distraught
          —having a nervous breakdown—
in the middle of the night   no matter who I am now
how I have failed in everything I've set my hand to   he pulls me to him
to kiss my mouth and body   no erasing that for him or me
he loves me   he is such a fool
       —Echo Bay Road, left at the windmill—
here is a nice leafy road   a quiet place to park
I'll sit and listen to the birds
look there is Jenny driving in trim tidy car
trim tennis figure bending to the trunk
pulling out groceries a carton of Diet Dr Pepper
                        no one else drinks that
                        so there is where he is
Jenny armsful at the cottage door:
    Hey, I'm back! Lunch!
the snap the buckle of the screen such long brown hair, sweet-eyed face
a lovely person, intelligent, kind, on her way up in the law
         axe in the head axeblade in the belly where it hurts the most

Hugh comes to himself again ringing the bell at Newell's big glass door. But the squat shadow strutting across to answer is not Newell. Of course not. Burton's glass-blurred hand fumbles with the lock. His bruise reminds you to be kind——yellow now, a jaundiced eye.

"Hey, Burton!" Hugh says, fake cheer/light beer. "I'm looking for Newell."

Of course. "Of course," Burton says, drawing back to let Hugh in. His sourness may not be personal. The huge Paris clock on the kitchen wall says it's nine, early for Burton. His robe is just the right rich purple to pop that yellow eye. (Wouldn't it be nice to pop that eye again. Sick feeling of fist again on bruise.) To atone for internal loathing, Hugh attempts a smile.

Burton waits. He is a cat. Hugh: mouse or dog?

"I brought Mimi's lease for him to pass along to Hendy," Hugh says. Trying, he is trying, honestly. Head aches, pulses. "Is he out for a run? I could wait."

"I am not quite sure . . ." Burton is careful with the words, "exactly where he is."

"Oh." Now what? "Mind if I——?" Hugh gestures toward the washroom.

"Be my guest," Burton says. And then, "An espresso? I was just about to grind."

Surprise. "Sure, thanks. Be right back."

Huge apartment. High ceilings, all the surfaces hard. Shoes sound down the hall. Past the many pieces Hugh has sold Newell. There's Mighton's portrait, him as Hamlet—not as old as the entwined Newell/Della/Ann thing that Hugh remembers. Wherever that now is.

In the powder room pale glass reaches the zenith. Glass sink, glass tiles on floor and ceiling; like being inside an aquamarine. An aquamarine submarine. He's tired, elation deflated by Mimi's sad condition. Yet she carries on. So you will have to too. Hugh will.

The flush is loud. He shuts the door to contain it; stands for a while in the hallway. The bookcase built into the end of the hall is full now. Burton's books. Hugh looks along the shelf. Pulls out a—oh. Another. Yes. Well. Jason might find these interesting. Hugh is not disturbed by porn, whatever turns the crank. He doesn't (does he?) despise Newell? No, he never could. But he shudders still, however blinkered, bigoted, wrong he is, imagining Burton's crank. Trying to imagine what bond it is that he and Newell— Stop. You can't.

Not your business. How often you'll have to say that. As, presumably, long years go by. In fact, Newell is lost to you. Lost to Hugh. Friendship will be impossible with Burton always here.

Burton is watching from the end of the hall. "Espresso, Americano?" Archness: "Or would you rather browse?"

Hugh puts down the last book. Stupidly quickly. "Coffee, yes. I've been visiting Mimi." Playing the death card, to get out of feeling smutty. He follows Burton to the vast kitchen.

"Bali taught me the art of coffee," Burton says, attending the copper-swathed machine. "*That* is the place to repair the soul. A tarot reader I consult in Ubud—and I very much subscribe to that sort of thing— warned me that the soil in Canada is too new. I need to root myself in ancient soil."

Hugh takes the tiny, perfect espresso from Burton's outstretched hand. He sips. Delicious. Anything he can like about Burton he'd better practise liking.

A wave of Burton's plump palm at the papers and books lying on the black slate counter: "Remounting my one-man Swinburne show for the Edinburgh Fringe—refining my verses."

"Much of a market for Swinburne?"

"Well, it wouldn't play the *Edmonton* Fringe, no!" Burton laughs loudly, Newell not being there to keep him reined in. Vile teeth peep between flexible purplish lips; you don't often see those teeth in the first world. He has an unsavoury habit of allowing his tongue to lie forward on the bottom teeth, his mouth slightly open. "But I have to make my own way in the world, unlike you, dear Hugh. No longer really employable, you know— the school only wants me because Newell is part of my package."

Everything Burton says has a taint. Hugh takes a second sip of espresso.

"We have the privilege of perfect understanding," Burton says.

(*We,* Burton and Hugh? Or Burton and Newell?)

"We have, we've *always* had, an open, mutually supportive relationship."

(Ah. Burton and Newell.)

"And we've had our vicissitudes!" A modest *moue* of the mouth: "We won't get married, in case you were worrying. That was a gesture, an emotional exchange. We have no need of marriage. You hate me, Hugh, and that's all right because I mostly hate you too, but here's the thing you don't take into account: I really do love Boy. I always have. I always have. He and I are all in all to each other. Whoever may, from time to time, come between us."

Hugh drains the cup, welcoming bitter distraction. He can't answer this.

Burton stares at him, waiting. Then gives a bitter chuckle.

"You know, *Hugh* know, there's really something very beautiful in the relationship of an older to a young man—stretching back into ancient history. A rootedness —a way of bringing the young forward into the world and introducing them—not only to the physical, don't think I mean *only* that—to the whole life of the mind, of the soul and heart. A friendship more than ordinary, one that elevates the junior into the society to which he aspires. It is the basis for so much in art, so much in philosophy. Well, the Greeks!"

Hugh looks down into his cup. The dregs. He wants Newell to come home. Burton doesn't spout this kind of shit with Newell in earshot.

"That boy—Orion—he is a very talented young man."

Oh, that's it. Burton is justifying himself, posturing against the long window that looks out over the river.

"A mentor. *You* know—better than I! Every young artist needs a mentor who recognizes talent, who sees the possibility in a young mind and heart and body, whose experience and vision grant the generosity to sponsor—"

Hugh can't listen to any more. He pretends to drink from his empty cup, so he does not have to nod or disagree, or look at the purple dressing gown flapping over Burton's grey old chest, satin clinging to each roll of pompous pitiable belly and butt. *Don't hit him again,* some small voice sings, back behind Hugh's ears. Which are ringing, slightly.

Burton giggles. "I know, some say polyamory is poly-agony! But I refuse pigeonholes. We are what we are, the world can go fuck itself." His yellow-ringed eye wanders, squints. Then zooms in, intense, on Hugh. "*I* lay no blame. I will permit none to be laid by you."

Hugh puts the cup down on the black countertop, where a playscript lies open. Words leap to his eye: *I will kiss thy mouth. . . .*

Burton sees him reading. "Orion is extraordinary, after all. That skin—"

"Don't," Hugh says. It comes out quite softly.

"Ah, you don't like to think of it. Even when he is our dearest friend, we can never think of the older man kindly, objectively, in this day and age."

How can Burton justify himself with this shameless self-serving bullshit?

"But I tell you, Hugh, no one comes into their full glory without a teacher, without being *initiated* into the mysteries. This whole dirty business—well, nobody pretends that it's a nice way to live."

He's gone mad, Hugh thinks. Tears well up—hold on. You can't cry here!

"*Show* business!" An Ethel Merman explosion. Then Burton sweetens, sentimentalizes. "I do understand, I *do*. Orion needs the guidance only an older man can give a younger. I think the good example of Newell's and my continuing—what would you say?—partnership— attests to the value of that."

Where's the lease? Jacket pocket. "I'll leave this," Hugh says. "I can't. Wait."

Burton's puckered neck purples. His age, his sheer old age! He cries after Hugh, "A most intricate, most important relationship—I am his rock, his centre."

But Hugh is out the door.

The light is blinding again. It's rained so long, Hugh can't take in this much light.

Refracted by tears, the world is cellular, universe-huge, distorted. At the brink of the stone stairs he stalls, dizzy, trying to find the van. There, in the shade of the hedge. Okay, railing. Don't fall, don't fall, hold on.

He gets the van door open, and himself inside. Afraid of being sick, of dying of grief—honestly, honestly, stop. You are overreacting. Are you so bound by convention?

Oh no, no matter what the benefit, or whether Orion is old enough to make his own choices, no matter what—this is—this has to be— What is Burton, fifty years older?

Sit still.

The dizziness eases. The sickness. Newell's *whole life*—no—it's none of your business. Newell, Burton—it's not up to you to dictate or judge other people's lives. Orion, even.

Here comes Newell, up the long incline from the river. Loping the last leg of his long-reaching miles. Hugh sits motionless in shadow until Newell has passed, has leapt up the flight of stairs and moved behind the glossy hedgerow.

Then he starts the van.

Ivy dawdles along the riverbank with a coffee, waiting for Hugh, feeling the pressure of time. She's got to head for Toronto by ten if she wants to get back in time for rehearsal.

The river is not in a hurry, it walks along beside her at the same pace, unruffled. Her unreliable memory sends up a clarinet note: a poem she did at a cabaret at I of O in the nineties, a fundraiser for the suicide hotline.

> *The calm, cool face of the river*
> *asked me for a kiss.*

That's it, the whole poem. Langston Hughes, "Suicide's Note." Then she had a long scene with—who? With Bruce what-was-his-name, the second of two Bruces in the show. He had to lift her down from a tree where she was going to hang herself, and he made heavy weather out of the lifting, the stupid old jerk with his tiny girlfriend. Never mind, she won't have to work with Bruce again, because he died of blood poisoning from a sword wound, making a movie in Tunisia. Is it a consolation, being old, that one is safe from some old pain? And some old jerks, because they've moved out of this current vale of tears, into the next.

Thinking of old pains she watches a grey Ford Transit van come along the river side of the road, too close to the curb—hey! It clips a parking meter and the passenger-side mirror flips up into the air, a bright flash, and clangs on the metal arm of a bench facing the river. Ivy runs to pick it up. Pale letters on the unbroken glass: OBJECTS IN MIRROR ARE CLOSER THAN THEY APPEAR. She turns to wave the mirror at the driver: no seven years' bad luck.

The van has stopped. Hugh gets out.

"Hey," she says. "It's you! It didn't break!" Life zings through her chest again, at the sight of his dear head, dear body—but then she sees that he's upset. "Are you all right?"

"I can't—" He stops walking, puts a hand over his eyes.

"Is it your headache? Too much exertion last night, climbing the ladder?"

"I'm all right, I just got dizzy."

"Sit down," she says, and he does, right there on the grass. "I was waiting for you," she says. "I have to go to Toronto, some stupid stuff— how about I take you to the hospital first?"

He looks up, shading his eyes. "It's the light. Not the hospital, but would you take me to the city? I can't—I have to take some of L's, a couple of drawings from her installation. I called my gallery friend and said I'd come in today, could you drop me there?"

"I'll take you anywhere you like." He's worrying her a lot.

"Okay," he says. He closes his eyes again, and presses the heels of his hands on his eye sockets to rest them. "Can we go now?" His voice urgent, anxious; his face hidden.

"My car's at the gallery."

"Can you drive the van? Do you drive stick?"

"Yes, yes, but do you have pills, or anything?"

He shakes his head once, stops. "I had a run-in with Burton and I'm—I don't know how to deal with him, he was trying to tell me things I don't want to know."

Oh, Burton. That explains the wild driving. Burton must have been ranting about Newell and Orion.

Hugh pulls his hands down from his eyes. "Ivy," he says, his voice entirely calm again. "You are making me so happy."

She touches his head, his cheek, checking for fever.

(L)

Every shift she adds a little a little a little. Under the FairGrounds cash register L's sketchbook hides another fragment of the *Republic*. Semi-contaminated now by the thought of her crazy father, roaming through there while she's at work. Empty body feeling.

A while since she ate. NBD. Bran muffins at the school caf too disgusting, pale raisins like maggots wriggling in them; here, too expensive. It is not a *deal*, it is just, one is upset, sometimes, therefore, legitimately not hungry. No deal, but always a worry. Look at Nevaeh (but you can't see her if she stands sideways). It's okay to not eat on shift but if there is dinner at home, eat then.

If anybody comes home. Earlier L ducked below the till to hide from her mother going past the FairGrounds window, mad maenad streaming from the law office to jump into the Mini and roar off down the street, she'll get a ticket—oop, no, reverse—off she goes the other way. Where to in such a rush?

Now Orion's mother trails along, also mad, streaming, thank fuck she did not come in and ask for a decaf quad small non-fat sugar-free cinnamon syrup macchiato three-quarters full, her appalling little drink. The woods are full of them—those boys better watch out, they're supposed to visit Mimi with her on her break. And there goes Jason's mom, also mad as hell and not going to take something or other any more. Going into the gallery—yelling at Ruth—banging out again.

How does a person, a woman, grow up to not go crazy?

Question: is my dad also completely off the rails? Will he have to quit work, and then will they lose the house and will I have to work at FairGrounds forever to support them?

In twenty minutes this shift will be over, this shit shift, the shifting shittiness that is work, but this is not nearly as bad as other shit would be. Nevaeh's not in and neither is Savaya so that makes it boring, and too busy, and here's another fat ass with slumping blood sugar and yes indeedy the one with all the icing, ha ha, you are cute and witty, sir! Thank you for the thirty-cent tip!

6. I CAN'T TELL HUGH WHY

In the elevator hall Hugh stands with Ivy between two doors.

Ivy offers a third option. "Maybe you should wait in the van."

One door is red, the other blue. The elevator clunks down and away, called to do another's bidding.

"I don't want you to come in," she says. She pulls at her lip, the first nervous thing he's seen her do. "I don't want you to know about my stupid life."

"I want to see where you live," Hugh says. He puts out a hand and touches the open plane of creamy skin below the hollow in her neck. Touchstone.

"Right, but I haven't really been here for a couple of—"

The red door opens.

"Jamie?" Ivy turns, keys still in her hand.

A head appears at doorknob height, a narrow face gleaming pale as lard between a small round chin at the nadir and Brillo-pad reddish hair at the zenith. It disappears.

Three lizard fingers grasp the edge of the door. Bitten nails.

"Jamie?" Ivy says the name again, quietly.

"Ivy?" A soft-squeaking disused tenor. The head appears again, higher, between door and jamb. Eyebrows engage in the long face, arched high over pale eyes, looking Ivy over from boot to hat. Jamie speaks slowly—not irritated but bemused. "What are you *doing* out there?"

Ivy glances at Hugh, checking his expression. He gives her a solid, *I'm*-not-crazy kind of look, and a hand at her back. Not to propel, just to bolster. Also for the relief of contact, okay.

Voice pitched to kindness, she says, "Hi, Jamie, I came to see about the flood."

The pale fingers still hold the fort of the door, the door of the fort. The pale eyes shift back and forth from Ivy to Hugh to the blue door to the elevator, evaluating and assessing. Then the door draws back again. "I added a stronger chain," the soft voice says. "Just give me a minute, I have to find the key."

Ivy looks through the slit. Her head turns to catch Hugh's eye. Whole face compressed into a screw of misery, she says, hardly more than a whisper, "It's actually a nice apartment. You have to take my word for that."

From somewhere inside, "I found it!" A small-boy announcement, nervous and proud.

Hasty feet, a scraping, then the lock-twist sound. Ivy pulls back to let Jamie shut the door again, to slide the chain. Then the door is open and the vista clear.

A broad space, a bank of long windows on the far side, thin metal pillars: a reclaimed factory. Old plank floor, what you can see of it; grey walls. The windows are half-masked by sheets of various papers and foil taped haphazardly to the glass and to each other, which has darkened the room. Stacks of cardboard boxes and grey equipment cases litter the space like an obstacle course, like a bad moving day. A long leather couch under the windows has been used as a nest: greyish blankets and sheets tangled all over it, bogged at one end. Several unsavoury articles of clothing litter the floor by the couch, and there are piles in other places. Everywhere, wire and cords. Tangles of wire cross the floor, extra cords cross the counter that separates a galley kitchen from the rest of the big room; wires trail in from two other rooms and a half-open door with a light on, a bathroom? The cords converge at a long work station: four monitors, at least five laptops, a couple of high towers, a synthesizer keyboard setup at one end. Everything is grey with grime and dust.

"Oh, Jamie," Ivy says. "When did Yolanda stop coming to clean?"

"I couldn't let her in, she was moving things." The childish voice is odd, the form odder: he's of medium height, too thin, with wide swimmer's shoulders and a slight paunch. One hand goes up to scratch at his bristly hair, patched with white shocks in the red.

Ivy turns to Hugh. "This is my friend Hugh, Jamie. Hugh, Jamie Carr, my . . . I guess my sort of brother-in-law. My ex-brother."

Jamie gives a conspiring little snicker, heh-heh! Then looks ashamed, or diffident, or just miserable. This guy's a mess.

"Did Alex come over?"

"Well he came *over* last night but I couldn't find the key, so he couldn't come *in*," Jamie says, heh-heh-ing again. He drifts away to the computer set-up by the wall. Under the desk, another cocoon. "He's angry at me, Ivy, he always is, and I didn't think he would be a good guest."

"No, no," Ivy says, slowing her natural speech to match his rhythm. "Not angry, only worried."

"No need! I am *just fine*. In fact, I'm better than fine! I'm working, I'm writing articles all the time, I get paid and it's not a problem."

"Well the *problem*—the problem is the flood, right?" Ivy moves from the entryway now, clapping her hands on her arms to brace herself, around the corner created by the coat closet.

Hugh follows. There's the problem.

The kitchen floor is covered with towels and sheets, all soaking wet, reeking. Dark liquid stains the floorboards outwards in long runnels from the kitchen, ending in a tidemark of paper and towels. Two red pails, assorted cake tins, cups, all full of grey water.

Ivy says, more sad than surprised. "Did you have to use my *linen* sheets?"

The sweet high voice floats over from the computer desk, almost emotionless. "Well the water wouldn't stop coming out, and I knew you wouldn't mind. You're so kind, Ivy. You're kinder to me than my own family ever is. You never mind."

"Actually, I mind this time." But her voice is neutral. "What happened?"

"The water stopped, I don't know how. I think the lady downstairs called the super when it started coming through her ceiling. But now the toilet doesn't flush, I ought to say . . ."

Ivy looks at Hugh. "I can't even think about this," she says.

"Insurance?"

"I don't know. Alex didn't know how much damage there was to the other apartments."

"The super came up this morning, he put a letter under the door," Jamie says, hunching farther over the desk, almost fetal. One white finger points over his shoulder, to the hall shelf. Miraculously unpiled, in all this mess. Just one envelope there. Ivy looks at it.

Jamie's disembodied voice continues in a pallid singsong ramble, punctuated by an occasional small *ha*. "I opened it because I thought you'd want me to but it was—incomprehensible, really it was." His voice goes higher. "And I'm an English major! Ha. The man is *unlettered*, Ivy. It's like he doesn't even, ha, know the language."

Ivy seems to gather herself. Short body tense, her hands clench into fists. Not toward Jamie, just the letter. Three steps to pick it up: she opens it with one quick rip, and reads.

Hugh is sorry, not just for the water, the kitchen damage, but for this hopeless, hapless boy-man suffering at the desk. For Ivy's being tangled up with him at all. Where's the brother—this Alex Carr?

Footsteps in the hall. There, probably.

Nope—it's a woman. She pauses in the doorway. Hugh takes her in; he likes her looks, her manner, her thin face. Plain clothes, mysterious chic.

"Oh, Fern," Ivy says, sighs, sobs. She turns to embrace the woman. "Get this," she says, urgent to appeal to this new mind in the room— then, her hand goes out to him, "Hugh! This is my sister, Fern. Hugh came with me, I wanted you to meet him but this is *not*—"

Fern laughs, same laugh as Ivy. "Stop," she says.

The hunched figure by the window gives a wistful cry: "Hey, Fern."

"Hey, Jamie," Fern says, not sparing him a glance. A harder mind, Hugh thinks. Her eyes are like Ivy's but cooler, acute. "So, Hugh. You drove Ivy in?"

"She drove me," he says. "I have a concussion, she was kind—"

"Ivy's always *kind*," Jamie says from the desk. He's put his head down on a pile of papers, face turned away from them. But still present, unable not to be present.

Ivy sets the letter down. "They'll have to sue me, I guess," she says.

"Alex is on his way, I saw him on the street." Fern takes the letter.

The elevator grinds up again and halts, clanking.

In the silence the doors open, close.

A man in the doorway. Jamie's brother: same lily-white skin, but a lot of snap in the mouth, a lot of bad temper. Avoid this one, Hugh's hackles tell him. Taller than Jamie, same shoulders, the new guy has a bullish bearing that seems unhelpful in the current situation.

He's talking right away, pushing over Ivy's faint *Hi* with, "Don't give me any bullshit about Jamie being responsible, because he's not—that dishwasher was a piece of shit the day you bought it, and if you'd gone for a better brand you wouldn't be in this situation now."

"Hey, Alex," comes from the desk in a whispery wail. Jamie's head burrows farther down, his shoulders cramped flat, as if they could meld right into the table.

The brother doesn't bother responding. He eyes Fern and Hugh as possible combatants, and dismisses them both. Possibly a mistake there, Hugh thinks, watching Fern.

Ivy has turned away, making her way through piles of detritus to a closed door. "Hugh?" she says, half over her shoulder. "Can you . . .?"

He goes; Fern distracts Alex with the super's letter. Ivy opens the door and pulls Hugh in to—her bedroom, it must be. Clear walls except for one big piece on the wall above the bed. A lithograph, a long landscape, shadowed by long clouds.

"He's been sleeping in here too," she says. Hugh checks her face, her eyes: no tears yet. The bed is mounded with blankets and sheets worked into a rat's nest, a dog-basket mess.

"Why are you letting him—" Hugh stops even asking.

The rest of the room is still pristine. Just the bed, greyish and disturbing.

"It's gotten way worse," she says sadly. "This is the worst I've ever seen him."

"How long has he been here alone?"

"He—well, most of the time, since Alex and I split up."

"Like, months?"

Her face is so sad. "I'm sorry, Hugh, I wish you'd stayed in the van. We broke up three years ago. It was civil, mostly, and mutual—I left, I went to the Banff Playwrights Colony for a two-month gig, so he'd have lots of time to get a new place. Then I went to Halifax, three shows at Neptune, I was gone most of that winter, and Jamie came and stayed. So when Alex found a great place but it was a one bedroom, he moved out, and Jamie stayed to house-sit for me . . ."

Hugh laughs. After a second, Ivy laughs too. "And in the spring, he was going to stay with his mom for a couple of months, so that was fine, but she got sick. Then I did a few episodes of a series that shot in Yellowknife, so—it made sense for Jamie to stay, and then—we get along, you know, better than he and Alex do."

"Three years?"

"Turns out, yeah."

"He looks like he needs help."

"Oh, he's *got* help. He sees a shrink three times a week. He's an out-patient at the Clarke. He's *helped* six ways from Sunday. But none of them has a place for him to live, and his mother can't—she's in North Bay, she's seventy-eight, and not well."

So's Mimi, Hugh thinks, before he can push the thought away. Hard to live with someone crazy. This room is unmarred, except for the bed. But the bed is bad.

"He's too sad for you." Hugh means Jamie. "And the brother—I hated him on sight."

"Yes." She smiles at him, accepting his hatred as a love-gift.

"So what's going to happen?"

"Their brother Ray is a doctor in Winnipeg. He's got connections, you know, people who would—if we could get Jamie out there he could stay with Ray for a while and get into a facility. But . . ."

But they're good at taking advantage, Hugh doesn't say.

"Ray's not, not patient with him, so he doesn't want to go." Ivy looks at her bed. "I've been avoiding this— I can't help him, I don't have the skill. His brothers aren't helping either. I've been sleeping on Fern's couch, or house-sitting, or staying with my parents, or getting jobs else-where. I need my place back, but he hasn't got anywhere to go. I don't know what to do. Before I left for Peterborough, Alex swore black and blue he'd be out by the end of October, but it doesn't look like it, does it?"

He wonders if she might cry after all, but she doesn't. He takes her hands. "Okay, listen, the leak, the water damage, we can get that fixed, we'll do that first."

They go back out. Fern and Alex are arguing over the super's letter.

Hugh goes into the hall. He walks past the elevator, past the blue door to the window, and calls the gallery.

"Hell— Argylle Gallery, can I help you?" he hears.

"Good answering, Ruth," he says. "Hey listen, did you get hold of Dave about the basement? Okay, can you tell him I need him for a differ-ent job first? It's here, in Toronto, it's more urgent. I can keep emptying buckets down there for a couple of days. Tell him I'll pay his travel, and get him out here this afternoon, okay? It's Ivy's place, she's got a dish-washer gone bad here, and nobody's doing anything sensible."

Ruth takes the address and promises.

(DELLA)

drive   sickening quickening heart does a loon dive
brain   shrunken to a walnut   pain in the chest
mystery   why he stayed so long: inertia?
no   we are soulmates
Savaya's mother years ago long-legged April at playschool in the morning
leaning languid-eyed against the wall, I *love* my husband—he is my
soulmate, I think we were actually made for each other, I mean it!
languid and lazy too I leaned too laughing at our starstruck luck

but I myself am no April no Jenny no   no Jenny
half-assed at everything
paltry talent lazy teacher poor pianist drifty mother   weak friend
Hugh   suffering with Mimi I've done nothing for him   or her
can't bear to think about my mother   can't help Hugh because of that
I am no Jenny

not telling me
whatever it is between them
Ken

MORAL COWARDICE

MINE   HIS

it isn't true

it's true I know it is it must be true
I know he slept with her I know he did he did it how could he
how could he what is the thing that makes it possible to
betray the other the beloved how could he
he is sleeping with her
say the right word

he loves her

Walking up the alley, Jason tells L, "I miss going to Mimi's, before she got sick." L nods. That apartment in the old house, full of nice/weird things, photographs, clothes; it was a sixties museum. The piano her mom has now—nine feet long, belonged to some dude. Last thing her mom would ever have bought herself, or could ever have afforded, it's worth like fifty grand or something. When they were kids, Mimi would open her closets and get them all tricked out, scarves and wigs and hot pink swathes of psychedelia. Jason loved her too. Loves her. She is not dead yet.

Orion's ill at ease. You don't often see him like that. Moving lightly, knees soft, as if he's afraid they'll all get in trouble—for what? Illicitly visiting the sick? Death scares him.

L too. She feels that barrel-stave/barrel-band feeling, the beginning of an attack, anxiety and claustrophobia leaping and pumping inside her lungs and heart. Go, *go, go*—she makes the stairway door and leaps the stairs three at a time, noisy as fuck in the stairwell but it's insulated from the building and nobody ever uses the stairs, only Joseph the porter sometimes to smoke a joint, beside the one wire-gridded windowflap that opens. He is Trinidadian; so smooth and sleep-possessed, careful when he moves the oldsters room to room, down for their bath, back from the therapy room. This place must cost a bomb. How rich is Mimi? So why does Hugh look pinched all the time? The adult world of money makes no sense. Her dad ought to be rich. Her mom shouldn't have to work. They spend whatever they feel like on the things they feel like; but if she asks for fifty to buy Japanese paper they give her the pinchy look, the *Oh hellish GOD how will I afford this* look. It's priorities, they have screwed themselves.

She does not ask for much. Neither does Orion. They know not to. Jason, OTOH, just calls his dad and five hundred appears in his account. Because his dad is wracked with guilt.

Okay now quiet quiet quiet along the halls. She just wants to see Mimi one more time because what if, what if? The boys follow, their footfalls audible to L's ear. But they are trying. Four doors, five, there's Mimi's. Press the door a little. Peek. Okay. No Ruth to talk their ears off, or shoo them out. L slides in and leaves the door ajar, for Jason to catch.

In the bed Mimi lies mouth-gaped, faintly blue.

L turns to motion the others away, but the air or the sound of her sleeves wakes Mimi and her eyes open wide, afraid. L bends quickly to say, "No, no, it's okay—it's just me, it's L—I came to see how you are doing."

The eyes, clouded, yellowy-grey around the still iris-blue irises, search her face: zip zip zip. How we collect data! Not finished yet, never finished. But the zipping eyes don't recognize her.

L straightens again, touching the petal hand, old white rose-petals, ready to slipslide, slump to the black piano of death. "I'm sorry," she says. "I miss you, that's all."

The mouth shuts, opens, grey tongue inside, grey spittle on the edge. The mouth works, teeth inside sliding as she swallows. "Oh," the old one says. "L."

O L, oh hell, oh well, she tried, LOL.

The hand turns, holds her arm. Not clutching. Velvet skin, a soft surprise. L blinks, and looks—Mimi's eyes are still inside there. At first this was a puppet made like death, a cage for something, but now it is still Mimi again.

"*Fun*," the mouth says, and the mouth is Mimi too: her mouth, her little, far-spaced teeth, not rotted but gone grey. Her mouth, but paler; in real life she is never un-lipsticked.

After a pause, a hiccup of time, L sits on the edge of the bed. There's room.

"How you doing?" she asks. Dumb question.

Mimi swallows, with difficulty. "Missing you, Miss L," she says.

"Well, I could come in sometimes. I was just chicken."

The old head nods a little; the cheek pits. Her dimple. It is still Mimi darling, still her somehow, in this ravagement. But it is hard to sit here.

"We were thinking about your house, how much we love it," L says. "I've been making a big thing, I thought maybe I could bring you some pieces of it to see."

Mimi nods.

"It's so nice to see you," L says, in a sudden flood. Then there is not anything else to say.

Jason seems to be scared to death but is hiding that under a veil of formality. When Mimi's eyes fall on him he almost bows. Orion does bow. He comes forward and bows again, closer to the bed. "This is our friend Orion," L says.

All the ladies like Orion. Mimi twinkles. "Handsome . . . boy," she says.

Boy having new connotations since Burton, Orion's colour rises. Bronze-red sweeps up his neck, front and back, up to the crop of his hair—even his lips go red.

It's funny that he's so sensitive to being called Boy. But then L thinks, wait, why? What have I missed, exactly? She remembers red lips, she puts two with two and two and two, Orion reading *Salome* in Savaya's room that morning and texting—

Now L is herself swept with a wave of red and gets up from the bed so Orion won't see that she knows he's got something happening with, not-Burton, something with *Newell.*

Newell, Newell's eyes, the tiredness in them that is so deep in his mind that he will never recover. That's not so good for someone like Orion, whose eyes are still awake and wild.

Everybody knows Orion is gay, he's been out for like seven years, for ever. Everybody always knew and he made sure we did. And anyway, in our school it's like cooler than not being gay anyway. So but—so it's okay, and anyway, he is okay with all that.

And not that there's anything wrong with it except <*jealous!*> re: Newell, and what about Savaya, who loves Orion partly, because whatever the hell she's got going on with Jerry Pink is stupid and probably arrestable and not real anyway. And also, Newell is, when you think about it, pretty old. So.

L sits on the radiator cover at the window to figure out what she thinks while Orion tells almost-sleeping Mimi about the master class. Jason sits beside her as he always does. Their arms touch all along the length of them, it's helpful.

"My dad," she says in a low voice. "He came back, but he's gone again. He took some pieces of the *Republic* away."

Jason takes his arm away, to put it around her. But they have to go. Mimi will wear out. And Jason's got that date with Pink.

At the Gareth Pindar Gallery, Ivy swoops into a free spot and parks with elegant despatch, her profile snooty. Like her sister after all, Hugh thinks. "She's your twin."

"I know, I look nothing like her, it's God's joke."

"Too bad for her," Hugh says, meaning it with his whole clutching heart. He leans across the stickshift and pulls her to him and they kiss right there in the van like idiots.

"Maybe this whole romance thing is bogus," Ivy half asks.

Hugh laughs as he undoes his seat belt, twisting—and sees, outside the window, Gerald Felker, Saab dealer. Sob dealer. Hugh's hand halts, he puts his left arm out to hold Ivy still.

Gerald is walking away from the Gareth Pindar Gallery.

Hugh's bemused. "He must be buying something big. From Gareth, instead of me."

Ivy shakes her fist at Gerald's departing back.

"No, no, why shouldn't he? But I just thought we had an—" Hugh stops. "What does it matter? The guy's wife killed herself and their child. He can buy his art where he likes."

"Did you know her well?"

"She was a student. Her son was—" He gestures to her, and they get out. He feeds coins into the meter while telling Ivy, "Long story, pretty sad. Their little boy was in Della's art classes, so I knew them, that limited way. He was a sweetheart. Last week she drove into their garage, gassed herself and him; idled the car till they were dead. Gerald found them. He's been walking around like a ghost ever since."

Hugh takes Ivy's arm and they go up shallow, black marble steps into the hallowed halls of GPG. Black glass and metal; a slim platinum plaque the only indication of treasure within.

After the bright white of noon outside, the interior darkness lifts, drifts, light expanding as they stand. Pools of light from focused beams on paintings spread gradually till the whole space is visible. It's very, very quiet. Neutral industrial tile muffles sound.

An elegant man comes down the long room, bending as he nears to keep them in his glance. Hugh is not short, but Léon is very tall. "*Cher Hugues!*" he says, eyes beaming behind small glasses. "How long it 'as been!"

"Too long, Léon, it's good to see you. This is my—" Hugh looks at Ivy. "What am I to call you?"

"Ball and chain? Buttercup? Reason for living, other half?"

Léon looks from one to the other, conveying helpless capitulation to charm.

"This is my Ivy." Hugh kisses her cheek. "It's the birthday of my life, Léon, my love has come to me."

Ivy puts out her hand as Léon laughs, his voice crystal under the high ceiling. She says, "It's all right, we're just punch-drunk, we've been dealing with floods. I'm afraid it's left Hugh light-headed. He's got a concussion too. I think he wants to see Gareth?"

"Léon is Gareth's other half," Hugh says. "Take us to the Master, will you, Léon?"

The inner sanctum (no other word possible for it) is draped. Red silk ceiling, red lacquer walls that Hugh happens to know cost thirty thousand dollars. Black lacquer Chinese cabinets flagrant with birds and lilies fill one wall; the great black desk fills another. Huge and mild, also bespectacled, Gareth Pindar sits in the centre of the spectacle of his room. He rises to embrace Hugh, and on introduction, Ivy also. Léon folds himself down onto a wide leather chaise longue and offers the place beside him to Ivy. Hugh is happy to be here, showing Ivy off to his good old friends; to be with people who make him easy and proud rather than itchy and afraid.

"What's Gerald Felker buying?" Speaking of afraid.

"He came looking for the original of a giclée. Simberg's *Wounded Angel*, in the Ateneum of course. I sensed a tragedy, so did not ask, merely said it was not for sale. As to Aganetha Dyck, he wonders if she would *wax up*, his words, a child's nightlight."

Hugh experiences a bad pain in the left side of his head. He flinches, and Ivy touches his arm. "His wife and young son died recently," Hugh says. "He was at my place the other day looking at a photo based on the Simberg, but didn't want that, or a print—he wanted to pay more than that. To pay, I guess. To forfeit."

"Yes. He is considering a commission." Gareth dismisses Gerald, now that sense has been made of him. "And you, what is it you want?"

"To be one with everything." Hugh gathers himself, shakes Gerald's sadness off, and says, "Okay. I don't do this, bring you artists. But I've seen an installation that you ought to have a look at." He pulls out the small portfolio, the portraits of Newell and Nevaeh, and the map.

"A student?"

"She was, but this is new, nothing to do with me. She's been working on it alone for—I don't know how long. It's extensive, it would have taken months. Years."

"Obsessive?"

"Not in any damaged sense, but certainly."

Gareth accepts the pieces, turns to lay them out on the black length of wood, reaching out a hand absent-mindedly for the white suede back-board Léon proffers, to better reveal the onion-skin drawings. The parchment map glows on the black wood, each alley, each tiny fountain marked. Routes one cannot help but want to walk, through convolute streets. The wind's cheeks (Della's long gaunt cheeks, barely convex) *whoo*-ing from the west.

Hugh stands beside him as he stares.

"You say installed, how?"

"Basement. Not much light, no sound yet, but she plans . . . It's cumulative, hung all over, in a—well, a slaughterhouse kind of track that forces you around, makes you confront, from time to time, or comforts you at odd corners—" Stop talking, stop.

Quiet falls again.

Gareth looks up, looks back to the map. "Her background?"

This is the tricky part. "She's young. Student, finishing high school this year, she'll be going on but I'm not sure where. There's not a lot of money—likely OCAD, maybe even commuting and living at home." Do not say more. Do not say *she's good*.

Another silence.

Then Léon sits up straight. "You will need an espresso," he says.

(L)

Jason slips into FairGrounds like a spectre, and hovers at the side counter.

"Coffee," L orders. She pours one, puts it in front of him; then opens the till, flips a bill-holder for the nanny-cam as if he'd paid, and slams it shut.

He is shivering, though the fire in the fireplace has the whole place overhot.

There's a long wait. She says it for him. "The porn appointment, with Pink?"

He nods.

"You went?"

He shakes his head.

It was for noon. Two now. "He will have called your mom when you didn't show."

He nods again.

"Sugar is good for shock."

Obedient, he takes his cup to the cream table. He puts sugar in it, then pours half the coffee out and pours in coffee cream. She watches his long back, the vulnerable tilt of spine and hip. Why isn't there more of him in the *Republic*? Funny thing. Too close to her, maybe. No need to look at what is right beside you all the time.

"Go sit on Hugh's back porch," she says. "The bench along the wall, where it's hidden, till I'm done. Come to Studio with me, then we'll watch the master class from the back, and you can stay at my house." Maybe he wouldn't want to? "Or at Orion's."

Jason nods again. She goes around the counter and takes his hand, trembling in the fingers, and leads him back down the kitchen hall, scooping a magazine out of the basket. She gives his hand a quick squeeze and shoves him out the back door. "Sit tight and look at *Vogue*," she says.

(ORION)

In another part of the forest, Orion lies back on leaves, leafmulch, leaf-sand, littered. Left.

The look in his eyes, the release, the loving gaze. I am the king and the queen and the boss of him. He loves *me*.

Green on the yellow leaves: a long piece of jade on a cord. His.

Narrow and smooth, dark as his dark green eyes.

The most noble, most talented, kindest and wisest, best, only.

You are not the only, though. No secret about that.

(That's his honour, that's how true he is, that he has to tell me no, it can never be more than this. And it's his honour too that tells him I'm too young.)

Orion slips the cord around his neck, lets the jade slide into place on his bare chest, under his shirt.

8. A CASE OF HUGH

The outskirts of the city flounce away as the van speeds on through the slant-shining rain-impending late afternoon. Hugh asks Ivy, "What does that Carr guy do?"

"Picks up a patchy living, writing online articles about gaming and surveillance. And his mother sends him cheques."

"No, I mean the brother."

"Oh. He's a comic."

Hugh laughs.

Ivy laughs too. "I know! It's the grouchiest profession in the world. He's a grouser. He does Yuk Yuks, Comedy Club, goes round the circuit, you know, gets no respect, et cetera. I left him because—oh, because it was stupid. We didn't love each other, never had. The last straw was when he lost his temper at a dinner party and threatened to slug my friend."

She stops talking. Changes lanes, mouth shut in a cool line.

Doesn't like slugging. Noted. Nothing more to be said, then. Don't do *that* again. Okay, Hugh didn't intend to anyway. His head doesn't hurt, he's at peace. Miles go by, the endless grey of Highway 401, waiting for the diversion, angling north to Peterborough.

It hasn't been an awkward silence, but she breaks it. "I know this road by heart, but I always have to watch carefully for that exit."

There it is, Hugh points: Lindsay/Peterborough 2 km—then the exit, the underpass.

Ivy settles herself. "Okay, so how did you and your mother end up in Peterborough?"

"A friend, a girl she knew from boarding school, lent us a farmhouse in the country near Port Hope. Beautiful place, front porch looking out over farmland. We stayed there several times when I was a kid, peaceful weeks without anyone—"

Without anyone hurting me, he almost said.

"Alone, without anyone else. One of those times, she hit the wall. She went into a frenzy, a manic episode, rearranging all the furniture, boiling jam, trying on all the friend's clothes, tearing everything off. Then she shut down. I couldn't get her to answer me." The smooth road unspools. "The old woman at the farmhouse nearby had a garden. I knew there were things to eat there, so I walked down the road. I was four."

Ivy stays quiet, drives without urgency.

"She found me eating peas." Pea-pod, you still feel the edged mouth of its little unzipping purse, the pea-pearls hung inside there. "I stayed with her while they took my mother to the hospital. Later they arranged for Ruth to take me. Ruth wasn't a permanent foster mother, just did favours, babysat. Her husband died young, and she had no children of her own."

Kaleidoscope of places, the Yorkville apartment, various hotels and houses, the farm—then Ruth's house in the country town, one piece of calm in the changeable world. Dear Ruth. He ought to be with her, up in Mimi's room.

"Did it go on and on? Your mother, I mean?"

"In and out. Breakdowns, manic depression. Various treatments." He stops there. "Out and in. Often out. I lived more with her than with Ruth."

"Do you ever—did you ever talk to anybody yourself? Or—I don't know, get help to work through all that?"

"Not then. I don't think I need help now," Hugh says. "I seem sad, I know, but I'm fine really, better and better. Once Mimi dies I think I'll be— Okay, I'll go into a tailspin, but only for a few weeks. I'm good."

But your dear one is dying. But we all die.

Looking out at the passing countryside, grey ash, grey ground, he says that: "We all die. All of us, and that's a very depressing thing."

Ivy nods. "But also not, at the same time. I mean, since we *all* die, you know, since that's the deal, a) let's have a party first, and b) oh well, we had a very good party."

"That's a very grasshoppery way to live."

"Yes, it is. I am the original grasshopper, fiddling in the summer sun, beginning to creak and worry now that autumn is here. Are you telling me you're an ant?"

"No. You don't find many ants around these days."

"I've noticed that. Must be the banking crisis."

"Gareth is an ant. I admire that about him. He might be the only genuine ant I know—it's not anal or irritating in him, it's comforting and trustworthy, stable. It's good to see those guys. I love them, their long marriage, their finicky ways. We'll have dinner with them next time—they frequent the best restaurants in the city. Léon is a very fine illustrator, does a lot of work for newspapers; he won some big award last year for a kids' book."

"Léon Feldman? I love that book—*Loon Moon*."

"That's the one. They are old friends of mine. I'm glad I met Fern."

"She's an old friend of mine. As well as my sister."

"Della's my sister, as well as my friend," Hugh says. "I'm dropping the ball there." He stares out at the passing scrub, the blur of motion and inevitability.

"What's the deal with her?" Ivy asks lightly, as if thinking he might not want to answer.

Which he doesn't. "Oh, her husband's a mess. Too sensitive for law, probably. He's been working on a long case involving sexual abuse at a school, a nasty case from thirty years ago. Settlements, multiple claimants. Ken's acting for the school's insurance company, deciding how much money for a touch on the breast, how much for a feel, for the thirteen-year-old girl who had an abortion; it's had him in despair for years. Outside the office, Della takes care of him, manages things so he's not bugged. He'll be fifty this winter. Like me."

For a moment, Hugh can't remember if Ivy knows how old he is. Will fifty seem too old?

She doesn't look fazed. "Della has that lovely stability," she says. "But there's something tragic going on in her face."

"Only lately, I think." Or have they been in trouble for a long time?

"I haven't met Ken?"

Hugh half laughs, then groans. "He swore me not to tell Della—he took a week off to figure out whether, when, how to quit his job."

"Oh."

"I'm having a dinner party for them on Saturday, their thirtieth anniversary. You have to come," he says.

"Yes, I'll come," she says.

She turns her head to beam at him, regardless of traffic, of the long-falling light, the long day, whatever fray may come. Then looks back to the road and drives.

(DELLA)

back from Bobcaygeon
sharp hill down from the turn onto 23
eating almonds from a tupperware container   starving gobbling
—the tub slips   hand catches the steering wheel   the car is going—
—veers onto the shoulder   into the gravel   skewing this way   that—

HOW THESE THINGS HAPPEN

brake when the brakes will help—steer   stop   stop stop   stop
hazard lights   open the door   take off the seatbelt
                                          almonds fallen on the mat

nobody in the other lane
the car didn't roll down the bank   the relief of death
never tell anybody   *Ken is not here to tell*
                                          if Elly had been in the car

Jenny on the gravel pad   trim legs
brown hair swinging at the shoulder blade   Diet Dr Pepper
                                          white/red revelation

buckle up, drive off
what could I not have done?   not driven out there
                                          not spied on Ken on them
Elle would come home   not find me   not know
go to sleep without knowing
in the morning   Ruth would come   then the police
to say that I was killed   I need Hugh
no van—he must be with Mimi   Ruth will be here
Mighton might be   my chest cannot break open
                                          while I smile and smile
in the back door   Ruth's cheeriness is not   a thing to bear
                    emptying buckets   it is a blessing
do certificates   snick the glass back in   work eases nerve strain
                    mat paper backer
                    bend the shims   done   6 to go

The lowering sun behind them lends a false glow to the countryside. Twice, they pass fields piled with the last pumpkins, too late for the truck. Tomorrow is Hallowe'en. Ivy worries about Hugh's pumpkin-head. What pleasure is it to become connected to someone, when it means we have to worry about my entanglements, and the state of his head?

They could stop and make wild life-affirming love in the harvest fields, if it was dusk. They would be ghosts, in their pale nakedness. Her cheeks heat, thinking the word *naked*, because after all she is not such great shakes without her clothes on. But the joy of skin/skin, the memory of that comes back to her and she shivers, driving down the straight undangerous highway, so that the van wobbles and Hugh looks up.

She glances left, changes lanes busily so he won't know she's blushing. Inside, skinside. A long time since she . . . No, she has never felt this. Being transported, transcending—even inside the mind, no useful words for all that. Hugh puts his hand on her leg, and the shiver runs through her again. As if she was not a middle-aged woman but a living, ecstatic, conjoined being.

So it's hard to go in to the master class. Doesn't help that she's fourteen minutes late.

Burton! His face is burst-tomato red. Beige eyes lost in swollen flesh under grizzled hair. He usually keeps himself so exquisite—today's sweater is wrinkled, and unpleasantly recalls a flesh-coloured crayon. He leaps up from the table to display plaid golf pants that might be a good joke in another setting, in another mood.

"At last." His sharpest voice cracks like a whip over the heads of the company. "Now that Miss Sage has deigned to grace us with her presence—"

But now Ivy sees the source of his snark: she's only the latest of the late. Newell, eyes grimly down, is still pulling the lid off his coffee. And in the corner where the coats are shed, Orion is tweaking his own sweater into perfection.

They all shuffle to their seats; the agony begins. Ivy knows *Spring Awakening* well, and this is a bad translation. She suspects Burton downloaded it from Gutenberg—the text has a sloggy fake-Germanic feel, unlike the sharp Bond version she's worked on before. Never mind: the twisted unhappiness of the children is freshly astonishing, freshly awful. She, of course, plays all the mamas.

None of the students have seen the modern musical version or read the play; nobody has any inkling of what is to come, except (it seems to Ivy) Orion. Who through some agency or diligence—or insider info—knows exactly what to expect and revels in the rudeness of it. From time to time, rising from the script, his eyes seem to seek out someone or other, but never do more than brush along the company.

It's a good play for teenagers. Orion makes a waking dream of Melchior, his tenderness and wit, the horror and excitement of sex transmogrifying into determination, passion. Savaya sets aside her rampant tigress and puts on Wendla's little girl dress and persona. A new kid, Sheridan Tooley (rejoining the company after his paying gig in Toronto fell through), squeak-squawks Melchior's friend Moritz's lines with the Wedekind whine, griping and grovelling. Orion disdains him, Ivy is amused to see, when not reading; but in their scenes they're bosom companions. The beautiful black girl, Nevaeh, underused so far, reads the wild artist's model Ilse with intelligent abandon.

Behind stacked set pieces Ivy can see L and Jason, shadows in shadows, watching Orion conjure the leaf-strewn graveyard as Melchior escapes from reform school and comes home to find and fend off dead Wendla, dead Moritz. "I was not bad!—I was not bad!—I was not bad! No mortal ever wandered so dejectedly over graves before. *Pah!* I won't lose courage. Oh, if I should go crazy—during this very night . . ."

Ivy is torn between watching the real teenagers and listening to the imaginary ones, fearful for both sets, drawn in (as always) to the pain of the play, its naïve beauty and hopeless frustrated disaster. And conscious of that other pain, real life.

But today Newell phones it in, staring down at his script. Half-asleep for a time, then gusting into bored restlessness that takes the form of striding over to the coffee table and making too much noise there. He has hardly anything to do, playing all the older men, and as they progress through the script the waste becomes painfully obvious. Only the Man in the Mask (who might be Death, and who laughs at morality) sparks his interest at all, it seems.

At the end of the read-through Burton stands, abruptly breaking the spell.

"I—yes." He takes in the company, broods, nods to the table. "I—vy."

Surprised, she looks up again from her script, and he says, briskly, "I've listed scenes, and I'd like *you* to start work on them, script analysis, beats and units. I'm going to take Newell away for a confab."

Newell stands too, and shakes his head in patient reproof.

"A brief consultation," Burton says. He smiles, all his nasty teeth gritted, the bit between them.

Ivy wonders what exactly is going on. Who is the horse and who the master.

"The list," Burton says, needlessly, as he hands her the list. He leans confidingly over her at the table, peers somewhere above her ear. He can never just look her in the eyes. "Only an hour left—split them into groups and run through scenes, will you?" He smiles again, those teeth, and murmurs, "It's all useless. Just busy-work to fill the time. Meet us at the bar, say seven. The Ace, you know it? I'll have worked things out by then."

And without another word said, out they go, two giants of theatre. Or rather, one troll of theatre and one giant of the silver screen, side by side. Conspicuously not arm in arm.

(L)

L brings Jason in the back door. "Hello?"

Nobody. She moves last night's supper plates to the counter, and Jason sinks onto the kitchen table. Advil? Not where they belong . . . Ah, stuck behind the vitamins. She pours a glass of water from the fridge-door tap and takes it to him. "Drink this, take these." He obeys, lies back, skinny arm over his eyes. Shit, his mom is doing such a number on him.

Six o'clock. Supper would help. Not much in the fridge. Eggs.

Gravel—a car in the driveway. Jason springs up, hunted, eyes darting like a two-bit crook at bay. "My room!" she says. Backpack, shoes, he races for the stairs. "I bet my mom wouldn't tell on you anyway."

He's gone. L gets the eggs out and cracks them—nobody here but us chickens. Flicks the stove burner on, just making scrambles, la-la-la! Her mouth is nervous, as if Jason is really being hunted. This is so fricking stupid, over eight old *Playboys*. When you think what everybody can get on the internet any time they—

The back door opens, and hokey jeez, it's her dad. With Hugh.

She stands still, fork arrested in the bowl.

"Hey," her father says. He looks really bad. Rumpled, his hair not nice. There's the band across his eyes, a darkening of the skin or just a darkened look—and his eyes slide sideways, won't look back at her.

"Hey back," she says.

Everybody stands there. Like somebody will break the ice, eventually.

It's Hugh who does, of course. "So!" he says. "I met your dad on the doorstep." Then he runs out of whatever he was going to say.

Her dad drifts off into the dining room. More mess in there. Twelve canvases, still not finished; poster crap all over the table. He hates mess, it gets him all upset. L feels sick deep in her stomach, not throwing-up sick but a deeper horrible pain, the pain of disapproving of her father and his actions.

Hugh puts out a hand. "You okay?" he says, quiet-voiced.

She nods, and is going to tell him about Jason being in her room—but Hugh used to live with Ann, maybe he still has to tell her everything. "More or less," she says. Not looking at the stairs or at the dining room. Down at the bowl of eggs.

"I took a couple of pieces of your installation, I hope you don't mind," he says.

"What? Why? I didn't know . . ." Even surprised, she speaks low so her dad won't hear.

"You weren't here, and I wanted to——"

But her dad comes back, a black cloud, asking, "Where's your mom?" Voice jagged, but he keeps the volume down. They're all practically whispering, cotton wool pressing down from the cotton-white ceiling onto everybody's head, smothering them all.

Then the front door bangs, and her mom's bright voice sings out, "Sorry I'm late! Don't hate me because I'm beautiful—I brought Vietnamese subs, your fave!"

Whatever cheered *her* up won't last. The two men turn, so that when her mom comes through the louvered doors she staggers back as if they were robbers, Perrier bottle and sub bag clutched to her coat. "Sheesh! You scared the life out of me," she says, laughing. Fake laughing. She doesn't look at any one person in the room, like for instance her daughter or her mysteriously absent now strangely returned husband.

Can't take this, can't can't can't, L thinks. She pours the eggs down the sink and turns off the red-hot element. Time to go!

Just as chicken as she is, Hugh's managed to get to the back door, hauling it open. "Great, well, you have those subs, I'll go get Ivy. Don't forget, dinner Saturday!"

"What? Saturday?" her mom asks. How could she forget? It's only every year.

Her dad follows Hugh to the door, host habit, and holds it open. They hear Hugh calling back, "Anniversary! All Saints Day."

The night her parents met; Hugh gives them a party every year. She and Jason are serving, Hugh booked them weeks ago.

He's gone. While he was noisy, L melted away like snow off the driveway, receding gently up the stairs and behind the turn of the wall. Nobody calls after her. She waits.

Her dad shuts the door, goes back. There's a pause, no sound from the kitchen.

This is awful.

Then her mom, saying, "Well."

Her dad: "Here I am."

Her mom: "I see that."

"You've been managing?" he says. "I see the house is perfect, as always." Shithead.

"We've been—I've been pretty worried about you," her mom says.

He laughs.

A thump, a slide. The Perrier and the bag of subs landing on the counter. "So, what's up," her mother says, in a cool, strange voice. Not actually asking.

"I see Mighton's in town."

Her mother laughs. "What tipped you off, the photos? I'm late with the flyer for his class, I have to get it to the shop today." Sounding casual, frozen, angry.

"Handsome guy," her dad says, all arrows and spears himself. "So—I'm working at Jenny's for a few days. Final documents for the abuse case—but you're not interested in that." Another slap in the face for her mom, who has expressed interest many times in L's earshot, and always gets shot down for it—she's not allowed to ask about work because he wants to leave it at the office. Also, her dad: staying at Jenny's?

It seems her mom is not going to question that. Or she is not surprised.

"So the rappelling thing, that was a lie?"

Oh fuck, fuck, on the other hand. Please, don't get into it. When her dad first didn't come home, L searched through the notebook in his bedside table drawer. Because you have to know what's coming. Page after page of lists of things to do:

- books to read
- what must be fixed around the house
- golf swing
- fly-fishing casts
- woodworking tools needed

And the pitiful ones in lower case, followed by question marks:

- remortgage?   • cheque to Hendy?
- rrsp penalty?   • line of credit?

L can't bear to know any more about what's coming. Sicker than ever, fingers in her ears, she turns away.

From the top of the stairs Jason's white face looks down. She goes up a step to whisper. "Don't worry. My dad, he's—my mom—not about you, don't worry."

He comes down the stairs beside her and puts a thin, awkward arm around her neck. Not comfortable, but. She hugs his bony forearm closer to her neck, and kisses the smooth skin.

In her asymmetrical tweed coat, the nice one Fern gave her, Ivy swims through the flood of teenagers to the open door, the exodus policed by the janitor. What a waste of time that was. The door clangs behind her, a *Law & Order* sound, chains and detention. Free!

Hugh is waiting in the gathering dark, leaning against the van. She can't help it, she breaks into a run, trit-trot, gallop-a-trot, straight into his opening embrace.

"Hey!" he says. "You okay?"

"Do you go around the town asking everybody that?"

"Yes," he says. Not smiling, he's been somewhere or other.

"Della?" she asks, thinking through the flip-book of these new people. "L?"

"Both," he says. "Ken's back from the dead, or from Bobcaygeon. Swing by the gallery, we can leave the van there and go for a drink."

Strange to assume, stranger to be right in assuming, that we'll do everything in tandem, she thinks, swinging the van into evening traffic moving riverward. Dark already. Autumn. Another river, of cars: tail lights reddening the right side, headlights whitening the left.

They go in by the framing room door, Hugh calling out, "Ruth?"

Nobody there. In the time it took to park, the lights are off, the front door locked.

Hugh opens it and peers out. "She's got Jasper in tow, heading up the street to the Ace. She makes him go from time to time, to be sure he eats. Want to try it?"

"Oh! I'm supposed to meet Burton and Newell there later on—good thing you said."

Ivy's seen the Ace from outside: fake saloon, long porch and horse-rail, lantern light. Inside, a long L-shaped wooden bar surrounds a pyramid of glittering bottles. Ruth and Jasper sit at the mid-point of the bar, Ruth with a menu, Jasper addressing a glass of red. Hugh's pals are scattered at small tables by the leaded windows, too many, she can't be expected to remember all these people—her head won't hold them all. They chain together, the way people who have known one another a long time do. She has no chains of her own. Well, work chains: Terry and Terry sit huddled close together in a cozy nook, heads nodding in unison against a mutual enemy. They missed the master class. Sad, they'd have *loved* the circle-jerk scene. How that play got produced in 1906 is one of the mysteries of theatre.

Hugh and Ivy stand at the bar listening to Ruth argue with herself about what Jasper ought to eat. He orders, as apparently he always does, steak frites, and Ruth orders a side salad, no dressing, with berries. "For both of us," she tells the waitress, waving her finger back and forth from Jasper's to her own chest. "He needs the greens."

To Hugh, Ruth says, "Long day in the basement. We emptied buckets for a couple of hours, then Della came by to help. We had to stop when Mighton came along, he needed help with his big crate." She sends a cutting glance to the end of the bar.

"There's Mighton—I haven't seen him yet," Hugh says. "Come be introduced."

It's not till they are right beside Mighton that they see Ann is with him.

She gives them a cool glare and turns pointedly on her stool to talk to the woman on her other side. "Lise Largely, the allergy realtor," Hugh whispers in Ivy's ear. He introduces her to Mighton, who sits upright and sneering, like a tall Toulouse-Lautrec: "Ian Mighton, favourite son of Peterborough. At least of the artistic sons—and daughters, like Della."

"*Della.*" Mighton pronounces the name as if it's Meryl Streep or something. Sainted but fallible, teasable, even laughable; honoured all the same. "She picked me up at the train, I thought she was coming here tonight."

"Did she show you the flyer for your class? Must not be finished yet." Hugh shakes his head. "We're behind—it's my fault. We'll sell out anyway, nine spots are booked."

This brings a lift to Mighton's falling face. "They haven't forgotten me?"

"I repacked one of your boxes the other night," Hugh says. "I found a sketch for that portrait you did of Ann and Della and Newell intertwined. I want a new one of them now."

Mighton laughs, and his face breaks from self-absorption into something quite different: sharp, lively, sensitive. Maybe he's just sour because he's unhappy. "Where is that thing? But I don't revisit," he says. "You do it, Hugh. You'd do a better job—you love them."

"Not all of them," Hugh protests, and Mighton sends a sharkish glance to Ann, rapt in conversation with Lise Largely: two fair women pretending (to Ivy's own shark eye) to be unaware, but listening with all their ears to Mighton and his jabs.

Hugh pulls Ivy's elbow to find seats of their own, and they go down the long curve of the bar to empty stools at the other end. "What's his deal?" Ivy asks, nodding back to Mighton.

"He's not so bad. He's got Crohn's disease; gut-ache half the time. Makes him surly, also appealingly vulnerable."

The waitress brings them water and a single malt, neat, for Hugh. She takes Ivy's order for a drink (the same, neat, thanks) and Hugh's for food: calamari for both of them.

"Trust me," he says. "Best you'll ever eat."

Ivy's happy, sitting beside Hugh on old Windsor bar-chairs in this dark-loud-warm room. No demands being made on her, no need for lipstick or chic-er clothes than her nice coat—for anything but the warmth of Hugh's arm, the closeness of his leg beside her own beneath the bar. The whiskey comes, and then the calamari, dredged in Cajun spice, perfect as promised.

That peaceful time ends soon enough: Burton and Newell, emerging from an alcove around the corner, see her before she sees them. Newell puts an arm around her shoulders.

"Sorry we abandoned you," he says. "Burton had a few—notes."

I bet he did, Ivy thinks.

Burton acknowledges Hugh in his usual fractured way, half knowing smirk, half sneer of hatred, and turns to Ivy. "I presume the afternoon proceeded apace, with muffled giggles at every mention of sex or masturbation? *Spring Awakening* is a bust, Hugh."

Mighton comes down the bar and claps Newell on the back. "I saw the musical in New York last year," Mighton says. "Lots of angsty wailing over not much, I thought."

Not giving Newell time, Burton answers. It's unclear to Ivy whether he knows Mighton or just senses and rises to the next-biggest ego in the room. "Glorification of wanking, plus a searing portrayal of sexual awakening et cetera, yes. It is a good play—but problematic: the circle-jerk, we wouldn't get that past Pink. And it's hard to do bare butts in real life, for a company as young as this."

Newell speaks into his glass, behind Burton's bobbing head. "That's the true thing Wedekind catches: shame, and the ignorance it rises from. How shame defiles us, ruins us."

Ivy is perturbed by that, but Burton rides over him: "German stuff— that S&M scene where Melchior whips Wendla, that's the key. One must be beaten into acknowledging one's earthy bestial nature." He pronounces it *beast*-ial, Ivy can't help noting.

Newell's face is distant, thinking, detached from everyone, one arm along Hugh's chair-back. Newell is a sad man, but in these last few days she likes him more than ever.

Mighton asks Ivy over-interested questions about the class, which seems to annoy Hugh as much as Burton's pomposity does. Interesting. "I did the mamas, all of them," Ivy says, to briefly answer him.

"We all have to kill the mother, don't we, Hugh?" Burton lets fly, a random shot.

Hugh doesn't seem distressed. "You can't kill Mimi," he says. "At least this Hugh can't." Then to Newell: "Ruth booked movers for Monday— but maybe a meteorite will hit the earth and I won't have to deal with it."

"Maybe Hendy can find a loophole in the lease," Newell says.

Hugh shakes his head. "She won't be going back—just as well to get it done. I have to deal with it some time."

"I'll help," Newell says. Burton darts him a look, and at the other end of the bar, Ivy sees the Largely woman's head lift. Like a cat scenting the air, catching a wingflutter of bird or breath of mouse.

Hugh stands and flags the waitress. "I've got to run over to Mimi," he tells Ivy. "Wait for me? Or—here." He gives her his keys, speaks into her ear. "If I'm not back when you want to leave, go up to my place, I'll find you there." His hand clasps hers, and he goes out.

Mighton slips into Hugh's chair and prepares to lay heavy siege to Ivy, which makes her laugh at his bravura, and his complete folly.

"I'm not laughing at you," she says, at his affront. "It's just funny because I'm so in love with Hugh."

He looks up, startled, and she says, "I mean, in love with *Hugh*. With Hugh Argylle."

Hugh walks the long linoleum hall in the nightlight-yellow glow. Some doors are open. Old people sitting on beds, relatives visiting. Only occasional sobs. At Mimi's door, he pauses, gathering courage. Relinquishing Ivy's warmth, preparing to bear his mother's deathly cold.

He pushes open the door and sees Della, standing by the window like a ghost.

"She's out. The morphine's working," she says. "I came to spell Ruth off. Come talk for a minute?"

He's downcast. Anticlimactic —sacrifice not required. He goes into the dusk-draped room and stands by the window, close enough for Della to whisper.

But then she doesn't. "What's up," he finally has to ask.

Another minute. "I saw Ken. I saw where he is, out at Sturgeon."

"I know."

"No, he's been there all this time."

Hugh takes a deeper breath. "I know."

Della looks at him. "What do you know?"

"I know he went there instead of to the Elora Gorge thing. He told me he was going out to Bobcaygeon, he asked me not to tell you about it." In the grey night-window light Della's eyes are painfully large, painfully dark, great shadows around them. Hugh feels worse about this than he even imagined he would. "He said he needed a few days to think things through—I saw him coming out of Conrad's office, that's the only reason he told me."

"Told you—what?" Her unnatural stillness makes him think she might fall over, faint.

"Breathe," he says.

She obeys, but only barely.

"He told me he was having trouble deciding what to do, that's all. That he couldn't go on, he had to make a change, and wasn't sure how you would take it."

Della sits on the window ledge, as if her legs won't hold her.

Hugh touches her shoulder, her arm. "Della, don't—it's not the end of the world, it's just—Listen, he was afraid to tell you. He knows it will mean a huge change in your life, he needed a few days to find his courage. I couldn't say no."

She looks away, almost laughs. "You could have."

He's surprised she's taking this so hard. She never wanted Ken to be a lawyer, after all. Wouldn't she'd rather he teach, or whatever he's intending to do, consult?

"I know you want his happiness—when he talked to me, I thought it might even be a case of his life."

She shifts on the ledge. She looks as old as she is. As old as he is too.

"When someone wants so badly not to be—I'm sorry, I'm sorry, Dell. I should have told you anyway."

"You promised," she says, looking down into the hands abandoned in her lap. "He might have changed his mind, or something. Better if we didn't, if I didn't know. It won't make much difference for Elly, she's leaving anyway."

"I'm sure he's figured out the finances, how you can manage."

"Hugh," she says. Her face is flat white. "I don't know what I'll do."

He's beginning to lose patience with her, always crying poor. Everybody's poor. "Look, if it's going to mean hardship, I'll help—we can do more classes, raise the fees."

He stops. Della is shaking her head, tears falling into her loose-cupped hands. He sits, he puts his arm around her.

She takes a couple of hard breaths, then stands. "Thanks. Ken won't talk, can't talk. I'll—I've got to go and think about what to do." She turns and is out the door, made mobile by some awful collision of time and emotion.

Emotion everywhere, exhausting. Ken looked terrible.

Hugh goes to Mimi's bed, to the chair that waits there, his predestined seat. Try not to move from it for an hour. Just in case she comes to life again, out of the sleep that is close, but not close enough, to death.

(ORION)

Sheridan's implement: Sheridan Tooley sent away in the mail for some kind of masturbation aid that arrived yesterday, and he talked about it all through *Spring Awakening* in class. Excellent, apparently. Alone at home, Orion contemplates masturbation, but it's so lonely, so stupid. Like sucking your thumb. Plus he has heard, not that he believes it, that it desensitizes a person. Instead of porn, he shifts the screen to eavesdrop on people he knows, to Facebook and Twitter, finding nothing. Instagram, Tumblr. There's Jason's vidblog from the beginning of term. Half-naked, fake-funny, his soul exposed in the worst way. Wandering around some bedroom, looks like L's. How can you ever help the people around you to not be asswipes?

VidBlog, Jason the Egonaut
"I'm the first person in my class to get their own project. It's down. Working with down. I'm down with that." [Strikes black-culture pose, unsuccessfully.] "So, I'm looking at a slim-line take on the ski jacket. It saves on down, it's wearable in all kinds of climes. Also I know some chunkier girls."

[A pop can hits him in the head, L's arm in frame for an instant; the camera turns on Savaya and Nevaeh: they are twined together on L's trundle bed. While Jason talks, off-camera, they mouth extremely rude things.]

"I've taken the plunge and gone for purple. I figure black is great but . . . But there's room in this world for purple. It's pretty ugly actually. It was all they had left that would keep the down in. I've got a line on that bathing suit stuff, neoprene."

Boring, boring boring. Every person, every thing, every molecule in this world is boring.

Unless part of, attached to, cellularly integral with the loved one.

Orion leaps up the stairs and silent, silent, so as not to wake his zonked-out mother who never does awaken, out the door and onto his bike.

Knowing Ann is safely at the bar, Hugh deviates down the road that runs by her house. Ivy can't go back there, it's ridiculous. He sets the ladder up once more against the wall. Jason probably uses headphones, but Hugh is quiet anyway. At the top of the ladder he pushes the window up, holds on—hands sweating suddenly, because his head really does hurt, a lot—reaches in and gropes for Ivy's duffel in the darkened room. Not too big. It's got a shoulder strap, thank God. He mangles it out the window, steadies himself again, ducks his head through the shoulder strap, and braces as the weight slides down his back.

The ladder shifts under him and he clings unashamed to the window ledge. He shouldn't have done this.

Then he hears Ann calling inside the house, sharp-tongued: "Jason? Jason?"

No answer.

"Jason! Mr. Pink called me—Jason!"

A pause. Hard feet hard on the staircase, coming up. Will she open this door, searching? Hugh ducks below the windowsill, fingers aching on the sill's edge.

"I don't know what you think you're pulling, you can't just *not show up* when I've—" Round the corner of the hall, still talking, getting louder as she goes. "Jason? Answer me!"

Now's the time, creep down. Each rung like a knife under his foot. Ivy's bag clunks against his back, throwing off his balance. There, the ground. Sorry, Jason, Hugh thinks.

He carries the ladder back down by the kayak and makes off into the dark. The bag is heavy—three more blocks, around the alley. He drops the bag on the gallery's back step. Door? Locked. And he gave Ivy his keys. No lights on upstairs, she must still be at the Ace. He shoves the bag into the shadows of the porch and runs. Getting his exercise tonight. But after ten or twelve strides his head hurts, so he walks.

In the pumpkin glow from the Ace's windows, a small crowd of people stands silhouetted on the long wooden porch. No Mighton—his shock of hair would be recognizable. That explains why Ann left. But there's Newell, Burton beside him of course. Coming up to the porch, Hugh thinks Burton looks drunker than Jasper, tonight. Ruth is telling Ivy something, her hand patting Ivy's arm. So they're getting along, that's good.

Hugh has one foot raised to step up onto the far end of the porch when a bicycle zooms past directly behind him. Startled, his balance off, he stumbles forward onto hands and knees.

Ivy's there, like a bird swooping down, touching his head, holding his shoulders.

He laughs, says, "No, it's fine—" and turns to see whose bike that was, riding in the dark with no lights. No, the bike is lit, he just missed seeing it, anxious to get to Ivy.

The rider has pulled up and turned. Orion calls out, "You okay? Hugh! Sorry! I—you cut in front of me!"

"It's okay," Hugh calls back. "I'm fine."

Orion sees who all is there, and glides back, one foot on the pedal, other leg languidly pushing. He's a messenger of the gods, half-bare in the cool of the night, thin skin of T-shirt and shorts. He leans over to give Hugh a peacemaking hand, and a long shard of stone falls out of his shirt front and hangs in air between them, a subtle dark-glancing gleam in the thrown porch light.

There's a little hiss, a breath.

Burton moves. "That's *yours*, Boy," he says. "Your jade."

They all stand still.

Newell leans forward and catches the cord, pulling the jade piece through his hand so they all see how smooth it is, how smooth. "I wondered where that had gone," he says.

Orion stares into Newell's face, his own as open as a lamp. He pulls the cord over his neck, and holds the jade out like a gift.

"I found it," he says, his young voice unstrained. "Lying in the leaves."

That undoes Burton. His face cramps, contorts into a grimace, a rictus. He is instantly, uncontrollably, beside himself, past the red stage of anger and on to the blotched-purple rage that strikes out in all directions. At Newell, now. He turns, fists flailing, slamming, making a drumming noise on Newell's chest and arms. Newell holds him off, then holds him in, binds him close enough that the fists can't swing.

Words bubble out of Burton's sloppy mouth, words and spittle and bile: "It's all perfectly all clear—I *gave* you that! I bought it for you, for *you!*"

It's awful.

Newell doesn't speak. It seems he expends no effort holding Burton. He gives Orion a nod, a motion of the head, to say *go on, go.*

The wheezing shout continues, like foam, like sputum: "I knew! I knew it all along! I knew it as soon as I saw him!"

Orion looks shocked, but not upset. Clear-voiced, even over Burton's raging, he says—speaking directly to Newell, as the sane one— "Sorry, I guess I should have turned it in to the office right away. I was looking for my pencil, in the papers under the workshop table, all the discarded leaves of the other plays, and I just—pulled the string over my head without thinking."

Then, since Burton keeps crying and wheezing, Orion backs the bike with dignity. When Newell nods, he nods himself, and turns to go. He's so young! As he rides off his arm lifts in a gallant wave, a fare-thee-well to all who are not maniacs.

Ruth takes Jasper's hand and walks him toward the store, their heads bent toward each other. Ivy keeps hold of Hugh, as if he might need some protection, but Hugh is mostly worried about Newell. His thoughts are muddled. Burton gave— But Orion— Did Orion steal the jade? He found it in the leaves.

Hugh's head is pounding, shaken again by the stumble onto the porch, or by confusion, or not wanting to know.

He turns away, into Ivy's supporting arm, and says, under or over Burton's sobbing, incoherent yowl, "Okay, goodnight, I guess, goodnight."

Only Newell is left there with Burton, whose wails turn to watery washed-out weeping as they go. Hugh looks back. He watches Newell put the cord back over his neck and pull, persuade, half-carry Burton to his car.

13. I'll See Hugh in My Dreams

She puts him straight to bed. It takes two minutes to find the key, to climb the stairs, to say no no to tea, to find the bedroom and persuade him, like Sweetums, to "lay his ugly head down upon his wretched bed." He closes his eyes, just blinks, and he's out like the famous light. Not snoring, that's a mercy, but breathing slow, asleep. His head can't take much more jangling.

Neither can hers. That was awful, Burton screeling.

Ivy stands at the window looking down on the street, on the Ace in the distance, the stub tower of the Saab dealer, FairGrounds shut up tight next door. Hugh's grey van, just visible, says ARGYLLE GALLERY on the side in an elegant serif typeface. Little black swoops link the interchangeable letters, top and bottom.

He should not lose the gallery, Ivy decides. It is his spiritual home. Plus, the apartment is so nice.

She walks around the rooms, touching the wooden shelves, the clean-lined chairs, the kitchen's shining surfaces. A row of turquoise Le Creuset pots above the cupboards. Someone who likes to cook.

She washes her face with his soap and slooshes water in her mouth to take away the taste of scotch; she takes off her pants and tunic and quietly opens drawers until she finds a T-shirt she can sleep in; she walks once more through the peaceful rooms to turn off all the lights and climbs into Hugh's bed, curling beside him and bending knee in knee.

In the middle of the night they semi-wake and once more make careful, yielding, boundary-dissolving love. Ivy's head fills with unexpected visions: a wolf on a winter hillside, a woman bending near the earth to touch a flower. A great map of all the world, made well.

They sleep.

FRIDAY

⚜

Hughoooooooooo . . .

Someone asked him: *"Why may we not
worship the Buddhas and Bodhisattvas?"
He answered: "Ogres and hobgoblins
can at will assume the outward form of
Bodhisattvas; such are heretical and not
of the true Buddha. There is no Buddha
but your own thoughts."*

Zen Buddhism and Its Relation to Art,
Arthur Waley

1. I SATURATED HUGH

The dawn comes up like wonder. Ivy is not asleep when light begins to leak through shade. Almost six. It's raining again—not a downpour, just a steady-seeping sleep-inducing sound that doesn't break the spell of night. Wide-eyed, she lies under Hugh's arm, flung across her chest. His skin on hers, the whole substance of the lover's person: she had not believed it was true. He is the person of her person.

How can he be so loving and clear of heart, when on his last legs in every other respect? She lies wondering as long as her restless brain will let her, and then slides slowly, slowly, out from under his arm and soft-steps off to the slightly brighter bathroom.

Hugh wakes to the sound he hates most: water running down window-panes, down the downpipes and the downspouts, down into the damned drowned basement. He shudders up in bed, but crossing the warmth of Ivy's side he remembers. Did she leave?

His ear sorts out sounds: shower, rain, falling light. Six-ish. Too early to get up.

Except: the basement, the rain. Coffee.

Okay. Okay. He hauls the covers back. Gets his bearings. Not bad. Turns out, evidence is, you don't feel so bad in the morning if you slept beside Ivy. He finds pants, a clean shirt. Has she locked the bathroom door? No. Not nervous, good. "Coffee?"

"What?" (Her silhouette turns under the water, slicking her hair back to hear better.)

"Coffee?"

"Oh, please." She sticks her head out, holding the curtain round her chin like a movie vixen. "Did I wake you up?"

"I woke from joy. And then I heard the rain."

"This is a good shower."

"I put that rain-head on last month. Probably brought the weather down upon us by that one foolish act."

"It's worth it. Coming in?"

He leans forward to kiss her shining cheek. "Coffee, and I have to check the basement, see if the walls are worse."

Not worse, per se. But wet. All the buckets full—one spilling over, farthest from the drain. He finds a plastic scoop and ladles three cups out before moving the bucket to pour the whole thing through dirt-smeared drain holes. Old basement, old bricks and concrete, muck beneath. One day you will all be gone, you human mites, the water says, chuckling down the drain. Back to water and dirt. And what's so bad about that?

Ivy comes down the wooden stairs, re-dressed in the same clothes.

Hugh smacks his head with the non-bucket hand. "I eloped your bag from your room last night, and then I forgot about it!"

Interested, Ivy cocks her head. "Up that ladder again? Yikes. Where did you put it?"

Hugh blanks. Just . . . blanks.

"Did you leave it in the van?"

"No, I was on foot—I— Shit."

"Was it the big one or the little one?"

"Were there two? It wasn't very big."

"Oh good, then just the little one. Nothing much in there I need."

He can see her flipping through the contents in her mind, and says, "No, no, it's here somewhere. I put it— Oh! I left it, because you had my keys—it's on the back porch, under the seat. I hope it isn't wet."

"No matter if it is, it's just shampoo and socks. Nothing I need."

By the single inadequate basement bulb he looks at her face, a beacon in a damp dead world. "You are the easiest person to love," he says. She blushes, blushes; she puts up her hands to cover her face. "But you could help with the buckets here." A task, to cover her confusion.

They're all empty when the phone begins to ring. Hugh takes the stairs three at a time, unable not to think *Mimi*. He doesn't really think she's dead—he dekes to hit the button on the coffee machine as he goes by, so he must not think it.

It's Dave on the line, Ruth's tame repairman, at Ivy's apartment and already working at seven. Dave talks so loud that Ivy hears it all, even before Hugh hits the speakerphone. The floor is salvageable; her worried look lightens. The ceiling in the apartment below, not as bad as it looked: say, three-fifty for the ceiling, about six hundred for the kitchen floor and dishwasher repair.

"No need for a new dishwasher," Dave announces to the general air. "That was human error. Maybe work on that kid rinsing his dishes? That's a good stainless dishwasher—don't let her get a new one, you'll just be buying trouble."

Hugh gestures to Ivy to take part, but she shakes her head. "I'll tell her. That's all good. And what about my basement?"

"Buddy, that's a bigger job. We're going to have to dig a trench all the way around your store. That's the only way to do it."

"Jasper's side too?"

"Afraid so. Dig down, put in the weepers, seal her all up again, gravel, dirt, pack, you name it. It's not, like, fifty grand, but it's going to set you back."

"I can just imagine."

"And you need better windows in the basement, now'd be the time to do that."

Ivy is looking bleached. When the coffee machine begins its self-cleaning cycle, she goes into the framing room to catch the water, missing the rest of the back-and-forth about when, how long, etc. Not soon enough, too long, is the short answer. But Dave says he'll start on Monday. "Ruth says I got to."

"Whatever she says goes," Hugh says, acknowledging the iron contract of obligation, fondness, and loathing so many people have with Ruth. Especially now she's old.

Empty cup in hand, Ivy is staring at the machine, perplexed.

"It's complicated," Hugh says, instead of thinking about forty thousand plus the windows. "Watch and learn."

(ORION)

Slanted half-conscious in his gaming chair, coming or going from sleep, Orion still feels some bad thing looming. That childish feeling: *I am in so much trouble.*

Oh. Right. Right, he is. And no text.

No text.

What is important, anyway? To work. Not to antagonize fucking Burton. The play is the most important—but what play are they actually doing, after all?

So did he buy that leaves thing?

What is jealousy? Same as it means to say *polyamory* but not mean it.

Don't dare to text now.

Fucking fucking fucking shit.

Well fuck school, anyway.

No text.

Orion gropes for the keyboard, checks email—checks Facebook. Nothing to quell his sick uneasiness. Somebody (Nevaeh, of course, Queen of Darkness that she is) posted a Tumblr of famous photos, and Orion clicks through to it.

Disasters, cruelty, poverty, war. Guys getting shot right in the photo, bleeding out on slanted streets so the blood runs downhill. Climbers, fighters. Stuff he should be doing with his life instead of all this art shit.

Photo after photo. Tears come without bidding. The monk in the bus station, oh man, bending over the dead guy to bless him. Orion cries and clicks through all the hundred shots, like fucking God watching how fucked up we are in *The Fifth Element* or some fucking thing, unable not to look, unable to shut it down, compelled to see what shits we fuckers are.

2. I REST MY CASE

The plaid bag is there, pushed under the bench and down into the bushes beside the porch. Ivy gropes under dripping leaves and pulls it out. Damp, but toothbrush, yay. Foolishly unable to decide whether putting it inside Hugh's door is presumptuous, Ivy takes it with her to the Volvo. Now for the other bag.

The rain is spotty now, stopping? Streets sopping still, black-wet, misty sunshine peeping like a baby, like a lady who stops crying. At the house, she parks a few houses down and slips around to the kitchen door, hoping to sneak up the back stairs and evade Ann.

The kitchen, incandescently clean, glitters under shy watery sunbeams flooding through the sink window. Ivy reaches the door to the back stairs—open, in, shut.

Quiet. The doors at top and bottom make a decompression chamber. A breath in the blackness, then up to the top door.

Ann's room is perfect, as always. Jason's, spotless. Down-storm vacuumed, color-block pillows heaped on a single bed, the magazine ideal of a teenaged boy's room. No flamboyant cloth, no sewing machine, no dressmaker's dummy. No Jason.

Too Marie-Celestial in here. Ivy nips to her room, grabs her bag, and heads for the front stairs. In the living room laid out below, pale sun picks out new writing on the floorboards, words Ivy can't make out from halfway up the stairs. But look—furniture! Two black leather armchairs by the fireplace, looking almost comfortable. On a glass-topped table a vivid slash of colour: full-length pink satin evening gloves and a Lucite head in a strawberry blonde wig, tied with a hot pink headband. An exhibit. Lined up against the French windows to the garden, six dummies in a row, draped in wildly coloured clothes.

It's a museum. Are those—yes, the white go-go boots, on the mantelpiece.

The front door opens. Ann comes in with a half-bearded young man. "Hi, Ivy, there you are." No evil eye, no anger. "This is Stewart—the photographer from *Ontario Living*." She points for him. "Through that arch, to the left."

Stewart heads through the arch to the powder room, and Ann turns back.

"Hi," Ivy says, feeling like a thief, suitcase in hand.

But Ann gives her a sparkling smile. "I hope you're not moving out," she says. Then, in a confiding rush: "I used to live with Hugh, did he tell you? I mean, you know how you always think you could go back—you know, maybe you *should* go back?"

Oh, Ivy knows. Seeing Alex at her place yesterday, for a moment it seemed like she never got away, or was doomed to go back to him. And he's not even a decent, loving, sane-hearted person like Hugh. She sets her case down to rest her arm.

"It was Hallowe'en last year. When Jack told me he wanted out. He left at Christmas." Ann's cool blue eyes fill—overfill, spill over—and one corner of her mouth flutters. But she catches herself, as the photographer breezes back from the washroom.

Stewart is too cool to talk to Ivy, but he bends this one time. "We're doing a feature on Ann and her stunning style. This house, a living statement of her art philosophy. The influence, the legacy of Mimi Hayden, with a TV tie-in. Charlaine and a guy from Farrow & Ball are going to discuss the paint techniques Ann utilizes in her design meditations."

So Sharpie + rage is a paint technique now?

Up the middle of the living room floor along one plank, toward the fireplace:

Behind almost every woman you ever heard of stands a man who let her down. Naomi Bliven

"The betrayal." Waving her arm to include the boots, the psychedelia, the pink-slashing gloves, Ann elucidates her aesthetic philosophy to Stewart, though she talks to Ivy. "Mimi wouldn't have suffered so much if Hugh's father hadn't deserted her. Hugh would say so too."

Ivy doubts that Hugh would say anything at all about that. Does he even know Ann has all this stuff? At the end of the Bliven, the eye runs on to a new one, picked out along the edge of the mantelpiece under the go-go boots:

These boots are made for walking. Nancy Sinatra

Only it was Ann's husband who did the walking.

"I'll let you get back to it," Ivy says.

Outside the front doorway a black noose dangles from the overhanging roof. Perfect. Hallowe'en tonight. It's got a tag on it:

It is the loose ends with which men hang themselves. Zelda Fitzgerald

(L)

Jason is in L's bedroom—sleeping/not sleeping, lying on the trundle bed
left over from childhood that rolls out from under her bed.

"I don't understand your mother," L says.

A foot below her, Jason says, "How the fuck is that any different from
Nevaeh saying, 'What is *wrong* with your *family*?'"

Fair enough, mothers are not fair game. It's early morning still, too
early for Jason's mom to come looking for him. L's mom won't hear them,
she sleeps with earplugs in, and L's dad—wherever he slept—let's not
think about him, okay? She jumps up in her white pyjamas and pushes the
little bed back, forcing Jason to roll out or be trundled under.

She clears the floor of clothes with a few kicks and bows to him, hands
together. They do karate kata, running through *pinan sono ni* and *pinan
sono go*, which mesh really well, bodies almost colliding but not quite, a
punch and a dodge, a block meeting no resistance, kick kick kick in
sequence, the lovely twist-footed one. Once, twice to rehearse, then L
yells *ki-yai!* and they go for it, as fast as they can.

Then again! It is the best. They should never have quit karate. They
wouldn't have, even, but their good sempai left and the other guy was
lame. Jason starts the *Mulan* training song, and L joins him, both as mus-
cled as all get out, *chizuko mae geri*-ing to beat the band:

Be a man!
We must be swift as the coursing river
Be a man!
With all the force of a great typhoon
Be a man!
With all the strength of a raging fire

Orion, climbing in the window, sings too—what's he here for? More
trouble, probably. He has the loudest voice and easily powers over them:

Mysterious as
the dark side of Jason's ass

Ruth is waiting at Mimi's door when Hugh arrives. A bit anxious. "I didn't want to leave till you came," she says. "But I thought you people might of made a late night of it."

He gives her head a tousle. "Not late at all, I fell straight to sleep, too many knocks on the head and too much beer," he says. Neglecting to mention waking or half-waking, making the love of his life.

Ruth shakes her head. "She's a very nice person, that Ivy. I took quite the shine to her. You're a lucky man, even with all that has been happening lately."

Hugh switches places with Ruth, takes the inside and moves her to the outside. "You need your sleep too," he says. "What will I do if you—" (sounds like he's going to say if she dies) "if you don't take care of yourself? Take today off, okay?"

Ruth bridles, then buckles. "Well, I'll trot off home and take a nap. Friday afternoons I do Newell's, and tomorrow Mighton wants me to do his place out good, for selling it. I'm pulling in cleaning jobs hand over fist."

"Tell me you haven't been here all night."

"I ran over early, just to see how she's getting on. Better, you might say—Conrad took her off that, whatever it was, that was causing the you-know."

"So no more crazytown?"

"That's no way to talk about your mother," Ruth says. "But he says it will calm down."

"Thank you, Ruth," he says. Her woes can be fixed with a little cash, now and then. Hugh can do that. What is always holy: patience. The swallowing of selfishness, the gentle tapping of your teeth. He goes in.

The white roses Newell brought are browning along the outer petals. Hugh plucks the brown away.

Patience was his earliest lesson, even before fear and carefulness. Patience whenever his mother recited, as she does now, softly mumbling: "Sorry sorry sorry sorry, for everything I've done, I've left undone, sorry, sorry . . ." At a meal, one of the few, making supper *crash bang I'll show you,* a boiled egg in a teacup, nothing in the fridge but Perrier and a mouldy loaf of Hollywood bread. Going to bed for days. Meanwhile, at Ruth's, calm: macaroni and cheese, tomato soup, Ruth happy to talk to them when he and Newell and Della ran home from school for lunch. But Mimi needed him. Up all night, running down black streets singing— Hugh on the black streets too, chasing her while she sobbed/sang her woes, talking for her to the police. Or that ugly time with the building superintendent.

"Sorry sorry for you sorry I am sorry Hugh, for when you were alone or when I could not sorry—" Eyes blank, she breaks into counting to stave off panic. "One two three four five six seven nine ten eleven twelve, one two three four . . ." Ceaseless movement of her hands and feet beneath above the sheets, afraid to stop since stopping was cessation. God, do not let her cease. "Okay, all right, all right," he says. He says it for hours. The darling one, almost counting right, getting lucid again after those long days of singing. No more crazytown. That's what you think, Hugh thinks. Between Hugh and Mimi and the gatepost, she can always come up with more crazy.

There she lies. *It was not death, for I stood up, and all the dead lie down.* Emily Dickinson, clear-eyed introvert. If he was scribbling on the walls, he'd write that. Or that old Woody Allen thing, *Why are our days numbered and not, say, lettered?* How can he laugh, while his mother is unharnessing herself from the earth? How can he endure it without laughing.

A note on the bedside table: Conrad, saying he'll be in at ten, can he meet Hugh there. *Pleased to meet Hugh, hope Hugh guess my name.* That will be about the new treatment plan, now that they've stopped the hallucinatory agent. Or it will be bad news. But there is no worse news, the news is already final. Now it is just the long unspooling of the last of her thread.

Mimi's eyes open. The pupils move, searching, searching on the ceiling. Hugh makes himself move forward, puts his face in the path of her eyes. Nothing. He's a ghost. The eyes close. *"Living with ghosts and empties,"* he sings to her. Words of others help you fill the silence of dying rooms. When you can't, when Hugh can't bear it any longer. Maybe that's why Ann is writing on the walls.

Nolie glides in, adjusts the drip, glides out. In a moment, false night falling, Mimi sleeps. He could go now. But someone's at the door.

Ann, as if thinking conjured her. Another ghost. Almost panting, she must have run up the stairs. Anxious for Mimi? Affection floods him.

"Hugh! Mimi said I could—" Ann pauses, eyeing the crumpled body in the bed; she turns away. There are tears in her eyes, little sparklers. "I can't take seeing her like this. I feel too much . . . I need her to sign a permission waiver, is she even capable anymore?"

Hugh studies Ann's once-loved face. Hardly seems possible. "Permission?"

"I'm curating an exhibit, the TV guy needs the waiver signed. He's waiting downstairs. You've got power of attorney, right?"

Hugh can't possibly refuse. You can't deny a ghost tribute. He signs the form Ann holds out. No need to read, it's nothing that matters now. She takes it away without another word.

In the quiet he kisses Mimi's sleeping eyes, the blank cheek, blank cheque.

Ghosts and empties. But here's a full: Della is waiting for him on the street outside. She's giving directions to some old homeless guy. Slipping him a ten, looking guilty about it.

"Shut up," she tells Hugh. "I always used to give people food, refuse to give them money, because they'd just—but I got older. I know he's going to drink it, but I can't think of any reason why he shouldn't."

"Because he's an addict. Because it's bad for his health."

"So's sleeping outside when you're seventy."

She takes his arm, and they walk down the street, the way the homeless man went loping to his hidden rain-drenched home.

"He's probably only sixty," says Hugh.

"Living free and easy, the hobo way to happiness."

"Free and freezy, under a bridge in constant rain."

"Whereas Ken is—did I mention this? I think I did—living at Jenny's."

"You did mention that."

Tears bead in her staring eyes, in the slanted corners. For fuck's sake, is she imagining that Ken's got something going on with Jenny, now? Honestly. Impatience rises sharply in him—that hamster-wheel mind of hers, obsessing, creating problems where none exist. She's such an idiot.

"Don't be an idiot," Hugh says, stubbornly refusing to get all verklempt with her. "I'm making a very good dinner for you guys tomorrow night, I don't want it spoiled. Della, really, come on. Give Ken some room to think, let him figure this out. You don't want him to carry on in a life he hates."

Della laughs, like a thin glaze of ice cracking.

"God, it's still early. I've got to go back to the hospice at ten," Hugh says. "Conrad wants to talk about Mimi."

"I'll do the gallery for you this morning—I'm sick of my boats, I was up all hours. I don't know how my mom kept churning them out."

He meets her hollow eyes, blue-bruised below, new threads of wrinkles stretched around them. Looks like she hasn't slept for quite some time. "You'll be too tired. I'll just close for the day."

But she shakes her head. "I said I'd meet Mighton there to help him hang his godforsaken masterpiece, and you don't need to see that. Take Ivy to FairGrounds for a coffee."

She's back to her old generous self, sensible again. He kisses her head, where rain is pearling teardrops on her hair. Cry and the world cries with Hugh, it turns out.

(DELLA)

Hugh's Ivy on the back porch at the gallery   tucked out of the rain
                                                     joy in the morning
he is   they are in love   very good
Ruth bustles to the basement to bail buckets
Jasper a folded grasshopper   on the radiator
bones randomly arranged   coffee in his clutching hand
                             vodka by the lack of smell
                             Dad in the Barcalounger   in a daze, a doze
                             off to school through   turpentine rubble
my mother's rags and palettes and brushes and boats and boats and and
a freshening wind
it might dry up for trick-or-treat
feed Elly drive her to party at eight set alarm for that do this do that
maintain the household   die
even if my husband   disdains me for a narrow face smooth hair
                            candy for tonight   Zellers half price
Mighton blows in   giant piece—too big—Newell will buy it
help with the ladder   slab of concrete wall over his fireplace
                            the darkness of that room
                            internal affliction under his beautiful face

     Of course I can! Got it, yes, got it, handle in the frame, yes, hup!

up the ladder, this is higher than—the last step wobbles—*whoa!*
                           safe—Mighton's hand so warm—not safe
his bright black eyes looking up: we know each other well   we do
his hand moves up
he moves forward   pushing up the skirt   his head darts in   his mouth
he bites my leg
he bites
warm bare flesh above the stocking shocking   is this what Ken feels?

One thing about Burton, Hugh thinks: he is an expert of emotion, having it and digesting it, *Sturm und Drang.* Sated by crisis/catharsis, in sprawling chairs set before the fireplace at FairGrounds, he and Newell recline. The debacle of last night? As if it never happened.

Hugh does not let himself imagine the argument or the making up about the jade—whatever that tantrum was about, Newell dropping the thing in the discarded scripts. The jade's cord shows under Newell's linen shirt, as usual. Burton holds forth, also as usual; Newell drinks coffee with medicinal focus. Hugh's head hurts.

No L at the counter this morning: Savaya and Nevaeh, rapt in low-voiced discussion, arms threaded around each other's tiny waists until Ivy gives a cheerful *hey!* and they detach. Nevaeh takes their order; Savaya adds a log to the fire, then goes back into the kitchen to ferry their muffins forward, tray shoulder-high, shield-maiden Valkyrie.

Burton is burbling about his class. "The Greeks, the original goat-song. *Antigone*—"

Newell stretches out a long arm to set his cup down, and says, "No."

"*Eumenides,* then."

Newell smiles at Hugh. "Hughripides, Hughmenides," he says, and Burton laughs immoderately, latte foam daubed on his loose upper lip.

Stop hating him. Ivy gives you that relief: no need to hate anyone in the world.

He has to go back to Mimi's to hear Conrad's bad news. He can. He rises, floats out of his chair, leans to give Ivy a kiss. "I'll be back. I have to check on my mother."

Can't think when he last said those words *my mother* out loud.

🍃

No excuse to go with him. Ivy's own head hurts, without even falling off a ladder. Partly the drama last night: the undoing of someone's love/life is no fun. Not sure what to think about Newell now, or about Orion. Plus, is she directing those *Spring Awakening* scenes or what? She's done zero work on them and doesn't want to waste time if Burton has something else in mind. Original goat that he is.

Newell downed his coffee fast and asked for another. He has the *New York Times* open, scanning the Arts for dear life. How long can he stick it out in the wilds of Peterborough? He'll have to go back to work soon, if only to maintain Burton's appetite.

Two white chocolate scones disposed of, Burton holds his fat black fountain pen poised over a Moleskine. The Intellectual. "Think, Boy. I won't go back to *Spring Awakening*; the whole play is too much on the nose. Something brilliant, Ivy. Plenty of characters, not a musical, not a tragedy . . ." Burton's eyes light. "*La Ronde!*"

Ivy's least favourite play: ten depressing two-handed sex scenes, lovers trading around the circle. Right up Burton's back alley. He could un-hetero some of the pairs.

"No," Newell says, not looking up from the *Times*. "Not even for a reading. None of us can do *La Ronde* again, after AIDS. It's empty, vapid Vienna froth."

Burton is hard to quell, but that stops him. He sighs. "Well, I don't say you're wrong."

Fine. Ivy will have to think. "*Kennedy's Children?*"

"It's not as hideously depressing as Swados's *Dispatches*—" Burton half-agrees.

Newell stretches his elegant legs. "I've always wanted to play Sparger. Perfect timing: 'I started out the year playing the fixed star Regulus in an astrological Hallowe'en pageant in an abandoned garage—I always start the year with Hallowe'en, I'm a realist.'"

At the counter behind them Savaya laughs, and quickly turns back to the steam-wand.

"You did the other guy, the shell-shocked Vietnam vet, in that Toronto production in the eighties." Ivy saw it four times, star-struck and longing to heal his terrible pain.

"Yeah, but Sparger has all the lines."

"I've always wanted to do *Mother Courage*—I feel I'm the natural heir to Judi Dench."

"You're too kind for Courage, and too original for Dench."

She preens, foolishly pleased.

Burton shakes his head. "Brecht! Beyond these plebeian children."

"*A Chorus Line!*" Ivy cries, jazz hands, but she's going too far in the other direction.

Burton practically stamps his foot. "No music! *No music!*"

"How about with the music pared away? No—there's not much left, is there? Wait, we could do *Les Mis,* only from the book! Let them develop the script."

"I have even *less* desire, if a negative of infinity is possible, to 'develop a script' with donkeys for a solid month."

There's silence, after this definitive statement. Nevaeh seems to have gone off shift, but Savaya leans on her elbows at the counter, listening with both ears up. Burton hits the paper with his pen repeatedly, making a series of black dots.

Try again. "*Cloud 9,*" says Ivy. "If you don't double, there are lots of parts . . ."

Burton shakes his head. "Cross-dressing is built right into it. And Churchill, *ptah.* I'm not interested in rehashing someone else's ideas," he says.

Ivy shuts her eyes, in case they're rolling. She is so bored by Burton's bullshit. Why does she have to be here? Any decision will be his, possibly with Newell's puppeteering. If it was up to her they'd be doing a new play, finding a playwright to come in and work with them, or— No point in stretching the mind to the possibilities, because that won't happen.

"Howard Barker's *The Possibilities,*" she says. Throwing it out like a bad card in poker.

Newell's eyes light up; Burton scowls.

"Im-*Possibilities,*" Newell says, sorrowing. "We couldn't do it with these kids. Nobody could. They couldn't be coached—it's too hard."

Like a fish, gills rippling, rising in green water, Burton says, "Well, it's not *impossible*—it's just always badly done."

Newell feeds the fish, a casual casting of crumbs: "I've always wanted to—but no. Torture, terrorism—timely, but the *Kiss My Hands* piece, that's just too difficult."

Ivy is full of admiration for Newell. "I have a copy," she says, idly. Gentle tickle of worm-fingers, luring the fish. "I don't like it much myself, it's too dark."

Newell's sidelong eye caresses her. (No wonder Orion loves him, she thinks. I do myself. Everybody, everybody does.) Burton's purple lips purse, considering.

But before he can bite, Hugh comes in the door, back from Mimi's, and Ivy jumps up to meet him and take his hand, checking his eyes for news on Mimi's condition.

"Could be any day," he says, without visible distress. "Conrad's taken her off whatever was giving her the jim-jams, so she's calmer, more lucid. She can stop eating now, that's a relief. He's upping the morphine, though, so she'll have fewer periods of . . . I need another coffee," he says. "Savaya, can you make me a—"

Savaya finishes it: "Quad long-shot Americano, three-quarters full."

He puts a ten in the tip jar. "That's the stuff."

"Yikes," Ivy says. "I'll make your coffee, for that kind of money."

"Will you, every day?"

They look at each other with pleasure, long enough for Savaya to set the coffee on the counter. Hugh pulls Ivy into the biggest chair with him, *one for two more to curl up in*, his comforting leg beside hers. Expecting Burton to shoot it down, she says, "Canadian?"

"Hm." Burton ponders. "*Crackwalker*? Ivy cut her teeth on that one, Hugh."

"And then I spent the next five years playing all the broken girls."

"Culminating in a very good Laura in *Glass Menagerie*, as I recall."

It's the only compliment Burton has ever paid her. Ivy puts up a hand to one burning cheek. She likes that Hugh heard Burton say that. Foolish and immodest heart.

"You could do *Taming of the Shrew* backwards," she says. "A woman taming a spoiled-brat boy, a reality-show comedy. Or—or, you could take it seriously. Play it straight, look at domestic violence, what husbands have always been allowed, encouraged, to do to wives." Ivy's scalp prickles, thinking—always a good sign.

Burton purses his lips, and his ankle rotates, the tell that he's engaged. But he has to dismiss the idea, because she thought of it. "I'm thinking about *Twelfth Night*. Full of disguise and deception, and we could double-load it: Orion as Viola and Sebastian, Savaya a corrupt young Duke, you for Olivia, Boy. *Lots* of nice stuff there."

Is he not even conscious, Ivy wonders—has he been able to wash the whole Orion thing out of his mind so well? Or maybe he can compartmentalize it.

Work/love separate. Or perhaps he's so doctrinally aligned with not-faithfulness that he cannot allow betrayal to bother him for more than the initial hurt, the first outrage.

Burton's pen moves across the paper. "And for Malvolio, hm . . ."

"*Some have greatness thrust upon them,*" Newell says. He reaches out one long hand to Ivy's shoulder, and gets up. Session over.

(L)

Down in the Home Ec kitchen, Jason runs a frenzied bee of sewing and
stapling before the costume parade at noon. Between writing up labels for
each dress, L takes photos and video of the milling, half-dressed bodies.
Cut off their heads and they'd fit the Voynich strand of the *Republic*.
Nevaeh's torso, tense in neoprene, strains as she raises her hands to tie the
string behind her rope-tight neck. All her movements are tight today.
She's angry with Savaya because of Pink, and taking it out in lightning
strikes on everyone.

L loves/hates N.

She could write that on a bathroom wall, but she can't put it into the
Republic, why? Because her mom might see? Nevaeh's pink mouth makes
her own mouth itch makes her fingers touch her own lips but but but,
but—*let N be the unknown number.*

It is a problem. For example, Savaya is obviously super hot in the slutty
Desire dress, but to L's eyes, just funny, nothing bothersome. Whereas
Nevaeh is prickly, heartbroken, remote. Putting on a thick coat of MAC
Lovelorn. Something wild about her, ragged, like she knows about the pit,
the worst things—except come on, she's perfectly middle-class, even rich.
Nevaeh's father is a big Marxist guy at the university; she lives in the fanci-
est house they know. Kind of a dichotomy. He's a massive, arrogant,
slow-moving thinker; N's tiny mother jitters around the edges. Her brother
is doing a Fulbright; she's going to have to do something amazing in dance.
Or else. She could never tell her parents the truth.

But neither could L, her stomach in a fist at the prinking thought of
saying anything about Nevaeh, about knowing her, seeing her beauty
and her inside sadness, her lovelorn mouth that is just as beautiful upside
down, her tortured heart, her shyness.

Jason is still getting Nevaeh tied into the thing with feathers, fixing the
eyelashes curled below one breast and above the other—one eye is open
now, Hope half-blind or winking. Where's the Sharpie? *"EMILY DICKINSON"*
Maybe he's doing this quote thing in case his mom comes to see the show.
She's prancing around in Mimi's old clothes today, some skeezy photog
following her around town. There has to be some way to still like Jason's
mom because it is too sad if she's just a narcissist. That's not fair: she's

freaked, she's still crying all the time because Jason's dad left last year. What was feminism even for, if not to make it so you don't collapse without a man? She can be fun, she used to be. L's mom still hangs out with her, sorry for her probably. Hugh's kind to her too. At least she didn't get *him* to talk to Jason about porn, because that would have been the last straw for Jason. L's stomach-fist clenches again, thinking about it.

The party being at Nevaeh's house tonight also fills L with foreboding. The fancy floors, the swimming pool. There's no way Nevaeh's dad will be leaving the premises, and he's scary, with the verbal prowess and the rock-carved face that says: remember, I am an international intellectual. Around him Nevaeh gets nervous, off balance. She needs help or reassurance—so over-needy that L steps back, recedes.

Nevaeh heel-teeters on her stepstool and puts out a hand—Savaya grabs it, not L.

See, L is already pulling herself away, because because, because she wants to work, she needs to stay sane enough to work. Because there is not enough money and it will all be up to her, if her mom goes to pieces. Hugh said he would talk to the gallery guy. She should go home now and finish twenty more things.

Or stay, stay and go crazy with Hallowe'en, which comes but once a year. This school has its faults, every school does, principal among them Pink. But one thing we do well is dress up: costume/disguise, masquerade/reveal.

The Loved One, nice title for a dress, whose is this?—it's attached to a white, drapey tunic thing, a new one. Nice, very nice, feels like silk.

L letters it carefully, thinking of Nevaeh. On the reverse, Jason's sticker says: *"Ah bird, our love is never spent with your clear note. H.D."* She wonders who H.D. might be. Hannah Dixon in grade eleven? But Jason never hangs out with her, he could not love her. He can't love anyone or L would know about it.

Done, okay, got to go—her own costume is still in her room at home, time to run back before Studio class.

Ivy stands at the photocopier in the basement, leafing, pressing, double page after double page. Better than counting sheep to fall asleep. Only the racket of students preparing for the lunchtime costume parade keeps her awake, shriekingly pleased with their finery. Jason is king down here, nice to see. Echoey halls, blue walls, exposed pipes that bang and slosh: this is the underground palace from his watery plague dream.

L trots past, giving Ivy a gleam of grin, quick-flashed and gone. The urgency of every act at school. How restful that this is only for one month. Four thousand, four thousand.

Principal Pink wanders down the hall, gives Ivy the eyeball. "Always read, read, read, eh?" He takes the book and flips through, losing her place. Grunts at Shakespeare and puts it back in her hand, brushing needlessly against her skin. Ivy reminds herself that he is just a natural-born dick, not evil. "Cold hands, warm heart," he says.

"No, I have a thyroid condition," she says.

Pink paces past the door of the Home Ec room, and hearing the din, he pauses. Puts that eye to the crack. Over the next few minutes he moves only to change his angle of view.

Ivy keeps the photocopier going, but principally she watches the principal spying on his charges. Are they getting dressed/undressed in there?

A shout, a slam—the door pulled to. Then it opens again and Nevaeh storms out, half-stripped in high-heeled shoes, cloth clutched to her chest. Slit-eyed, she stares, she glares at Pink. Who stares right back, asshole authority giving him gall. He puts out a hand to arrest her movement; she whirls to go back to the classroom, but stalls—she just rushed out of there.

She turns again to throw a stiff fist at Pink's plaid sportscaster blazer. He moves before the fist connects. Spinning again, Nevaeh runs off down the hall on those dagger-heels, sure-footed and raging. A mad maiden, a young Fury.

Pink smirks at Ivy, woo-woos with his hands, and passes on. The satyr Pan infesting girls with frights and plights.

Hallowe'en is no treat if you are already in the pretending professions.

Over the PA system comes a wild cackling, then the grim tolling of a giant bell—the costume parade, beginning. The scripts are finished. Burton won't notice if she slips out to the Argylle Gallery for a breather, away from this overheated, multi-costumed sweatshop.

The Mighton looms on the north wall, dwarfing the gallery space. Beautiful/dreadful. A thousand dead faces, everything that is lost. Enough to make you weep.

If anyone ought to be gay, it's you, Hugh thinks, surveying his domain: if these things went by love of colour and line, by having too thin a skin, by complicatedly loving your engulfing, badly behaved mother. Being Oedipusly-whipped, as Burton said the other night. What did you say to provoke that? Asked Burton not to compare some beach pickup to your beloved mother. Who in fact has treated Hugh, over the years, pretty much the same as a beach pickup: sunny charm, ice cream, saltwater tears, high-tide abandonment. Repeat.

Della went out the back in a hurry just as he came in, what was that about? Maybe she got a text from Ken—maybe he's made up his mind to talk about his job change, his own abandonment. "No one is alone," that Sondheim song from *Into the Woods*. Another gay marker: life advice from musicals. Equally wrong. Because you are, you will always be alone.

Not that Hugh is alone at the moment: Mighton stands staring at his piece. A discreet card at one side reads, *THE DARK GATES*, *price on request*. They decided on ninety. No red dot, because it has not yet been sold.

The bell over the door tings. Hugh jumps—but it's okay, it's Ivy. He opens his arms and Ivy walks straight in, asking, "Am I too late? All that framing done?"

Shit, the framing. Hugh checks—there's time, still, the Ace guy will be there till six.

Mighton turns from the window and says, "I can keep an eye on the store, if you have back-end work to do."

Grateful that Ivy did not say *certificates*, maintaining the fragile dignity of the gallery, Hugh nods to Mighton and ushers Ivy past the cash desk into the back hall.

"Coffee?" she says, the only word that could make her dearer.

He nods, then stops. Della is still standing out there, on the back porch, leaning her head against the rickety roofpost. He's got to get that fixed.

"You make it," he tells Ivy, pointing silently out the window. She sees, nods, disappears. What a lovely thing a discreet companion is. You are not, in fact, alone.

Hugh opens the door and steps out onto the porch, jingling keys in his jacket pocket as if on his way somewhere.

Della looks up. "I can't go home, I'm afraid Ken will be there."

"Has he talked to you?"

"He doesn't talk. He turns up from time to time, glares at me, and leaves."

Hugh can't think what to offer. "He might need help, might need you to bring it up?"

Della gives a miserable laugh, eyes hidden under cloudy hair. "Jesus, I'm not *helping* him! I don't want to talk—I just want it not to be true." She pulls on the creaking pillar. "Remember when we went to the funeral? I was so happy that day. Because Ken wasn't dead, and neither was I, and we were happy together, with our daughter, our life."

"*You must change your life.*" Then he wishes he could pull that back into his mouth.

Della looks away, probably hating him. She takes the two steps down from the porch as if she will never darken his door again, and walks to her car.

From the spruce trees between the gallery and FairGrounds, Newell springs up the two steps on a quiet foot, watching as Della zims out in her little car. "Ken's giving her hell," he says, not a question.

Which Hugh chooses not to answer. His head hurts all the time. He puts up a hand and presses the spot that hurts.

Newell says, "Hey, Hendy says Lise Largely doesn't just manage that company, it's hers. She wants Mimi's apartment for herself, since she had to move out of Mighton's."

Okay. That makes the haste less weird, at least. Hugh stares into the distance at an invisible list of everything that has to be done, movers, storage, cleaning. At the bottom of the list, Mimi lies dead in the white-clad hospice bed, far from her bright extravagant linens and flowers and treasures and dust. He should be over there.

Down at the street end of the porch, poor Gerald Felker waves to them. "Are you—is the gallery—?"

Hugh waves back. "Yes, open, I'll be right in. Door's open, go ahead."

He tells Newell quietly, "I can hardly stand to talk to the guy, but he wants to buy something big. He'll probably take the new Mighton, have you seen it yet?"

"No, that's why I came. But listen, I wanted to say—last night—"

Then nothing. He stares off into the parking lot.

Hugh is afraid to hear what Newell will tell him about the jade piece and Burton and Orion. Won't let himself think about the possibilities. "Burton was in fine form this morning," he says pre-emptively. "He's a flamboyant personality."

"He's a flamboyant fuckhead. I'm on my way to the class now. Going to Pink's party?"

"Pink's having another party?"

"Hallowe'en Treat, for the board. Some kind of fundraiser, that's why we're invited."

"I wonder if Ruth's working it. She can't keep knocking herself out like this, and then spend all night up in Mimi's room."

"She did my place this afternoon, and she's doing Mighton's in the morning."

"How can we miss her if she won't go away?"

"You'd die without her," Newell says. "You'd go into a decline."

"And you? You keep coming back here."

"Look, this place is Burton's retirement plan."

Hugh laughs.

"He won't let me give him money." Hugh snorts again, and Newell adds, laughing himself, "Not straight out—there always has to be a reason, a gimmick. It's exhausting, thinking stuff up."

Newell slides down the creaking post and sits, stretching his legs along the steps. He sleeps about as little as Hugh does, but it looks better on him. "I leave before Christmas, back to LA, for *Catastrophe*. Burton can stay here safe, and I won't have to worry about him."

"But I will," Hugh says. His head really hurts.

"Well, that's why you're my friend. Why you're my brother."

(DELLA)

drive away, drive
Gerald going into the gallery   death's head lolling at the edges
that's what can happen   people can die on you
Gerald's wife   unfixable because she didn't tell anyone
maybe Toby
what could he do, little boy,   but love her and listen
                                 like Hugh with Mimi in the old days
Elle on the back porch   skipping school? no, it's trouble
glass of milk, slow mouth   thin shoulders rapid-voice

    Nevaeh flipped out at Pink, or maybe at Savaya, nobody knows—
    remember you're driving us to the party tonight, right?
                                 [Nevaeh : heaveN]
        Yes it's in my phone. Hallowe'en is no fun now I don't
        get to take you round the streets.

    Dad's here.

can't meet my eyes as she turns to go
go in   go in   not in the kitchen
                                 dining room   black cloud black gaze
                                 I can't hold any more   anger
                                 but he is suffering   so I will
                                 people can die on you
                                 his eyes pull up from the table
                                 stare at me in silence

    Like the boats? I was thinking of my mother's endless boats, what
    she put in them . . .
                                 he is not thinking of boats
he is thinking   blame blame blame
                                 Mighton photos strewn on the table
right
serves him right   he is suffering   he is in pain

	as I've been	as I am in pain
but in the mind's eye:	Mighton biting	tooth on skin
then a new slide:	Jenny bringing Ken supplies	brown hair
	thin brown tennis-playing arm	lunch
	Dr Pepper dangling	cools my head

Do you have a problem with Mighton being here? He
has an opening at Hugh's and he's selling his house.

long-stretched silence   this again
eyes lasers of black light   after thirty years
refusing to look at me   his old contemptible
                              a thin glaze of ice snaps
                              I can do without him   we'll be fine
                              I'll sell the house   Elly and I can—
                              but Elly and I   does not exist anymore

small homely sound   chick of the back door knob   her step
Elly   blue cascading over   her neck and arm
I could paint that   her stance   flexible slashing blue

Forgot my coxcomb, I had to come back.
I wasn't—I didn't—hear anything.
                              dear liar   worse than anything
                              she has to pity me   smile for her at least
Right, see you later, sweetheart, pick you up at FairGrounds
it's in my phone.

she runs
Elly at 2 sleepwalking   what damage did we do fighting so long?
at our bedroom door

he's walking out   say it before he leaves

I tried to—it's the end of the month, I have to pay the Visas
and the bill for the new windshield—can you transfer
something into the chequing account?

his arm waves backwards   dumping everything   back on me
                               to the ruin   of everything, everything
                               it is all my fault   always   always
                                                                      NO
                                                                 no more
where is he going   fuck you
where has he been all week   your suffering your despair
                                         I hate you with all my heart

whatever is going on
whatever you're angry about
it's not this repeating spread   Mighton's arrogant face
not Mighton   teeth on thigh

hopeless

all the goddamn photos   I haven't made the flyer with   which fatuous
identical face pick one   this one   exacto   tape to the cutting board grab
the ruler hands shaking cut   one wrecked it does not matter   Glenlivet
on the sideboard alcohol is good for shock push the ruler hard slide slide
fine motor control regained   glue to dull unsatisfactory text   add head
photocopy   leave flyers at FairGrounds   at Jasper's

everyone will be satisfied
there! was it so hard?

                                            one crossed off the list

      Hallowe'en candy Zellers fifty percent off after noon

(L)

In Studio class, last stool to the left, L watches the nude model rearrange her pose. Like that old photo of naked women with blue paint on them— the man spreading blue on their pale skin, their breasts and sides, the women laughing from the cold of the paint, from being allowed in to the art, if only as paint rollers. In grade ten, the first year she came in to do AP Visual at school—Mr. Goffer, the teacher then, kind of despisable, but that morning he was pinning a watercolour to the door. A long thing, pale colours on heavy watercolour stock: a lily so beautiful so perfect so meticulously delicately painted she about fainted with joy.

Only it wasn't real. No, it *was* real. It was a real lily, Goffer had run a real lily through the printing press between two sheets of watercolour paper. And then tossed it in the garbage, where it lay splat ruined dead, a lily like a bulldozed glove. Men and manipulation, men copying from nature, with nature, men with women as brushes. A life in art, men and women, what will that mean? Savaya slept with Goffer, also she says with Gordon Lightfoot, yucky because he's like, a hundred. Bones and leather. She might be lying about Lightfoot.

Nevaeh on Hallowe'en last year, crying because she couldn't make herself eat candy. Listening to the parents fighting. Don't think of that. L thinks of Jason lying in the trundle bed, his yielding nature, how he needs to be protected. She draws a set of algebraic diagrams on the paper before her:

L is to J as K is to D? Or as D is to K? Let N be the variable.

Savaya slides in behind L's easel, a minute before the master class, urgent emergency whisper in her ear: "Nevaeh got taken to the hospital after you left to go home. An ambulance came to school and took her away, people are saying she tried to kill herself or she was cutting or something."

L puts down her charcoal and rips off the paper before she runs, because she is always careful about what she leaves lying around. Even if it is in code.

(ORION)

Everybody knew it was coming, anyway—she's been a disaster hankering to happen for the last six months. Why today, what sent her teetering, tottering over the edge on those too-high heels?

"It wasn't you," Jason says, not just to Orion. To Savaya and L and any random others who might hear, milling at the office door. He is usually more contained. His voice tight, blame-dry: "I was pinning her sleeves, I wanted to make one shorter, and she flipped out and ripped the dress right off."

"So it's your fault? *She's* been doing the cutting, the stupid girl."

"Orion!" Savaya pinches his arm.

"I call 'em as I see 'em," Orion says. "She's a stupid stupid girl to mutilate herself and she's stupid not to have come to us a long time ago, she's stupid not to have hidden it better—I'm not saying she's crazy, she's just been very stupid."

Nevaeh, Savaya, L, Jason, who is going to take care of all of them? Only Orion himself has the necessary cool, uncluttered, sociopath's mind to do it. "From now on, everybody has to pass their problems by me," he says. Only one-third joking.

They will be late. "Come on," Orion says, pulling Savaya with him, fingers, hand, arm, away from the rubbernecking grade nine tourists, who aren't going to get any information out of the office anyway.

He still has to brace himself for the master class, for Burton. The risk—Burton's eyes, flat stones in yellow tea, his nose, those pits, the redness. His ugliness that repels/attracts, fascinating to watch, especially if he might attack you. Why does Newell protect him?

And this is my story, as you can plainly see,
Never let a sailor put his hand above your knee.

Ivy senses the seething crisis-juice flooding the halls, but can't see what caused it. Students scatter like frightened mice, here-and-thereing without sensible purpose. She hugs her bundle of scripts to avoid dropping it; the photocopier was out of staples and she does not want to spend an hour on her hands and knees repaginating.

They've all come to the workshop room in a mass. At the door, Orion is saying to Jason, "Also, the party was at her place and now it can't be, so your mission, should you choose to accept it, is to figure out where else we can have it. Your penance."

"Not my place," Savaya says. Her eyes are pink with tears, pretty in pain. "My dad's still frothing at the mouth from Wednesday night."

Burton arrives. "Company, company!" he cries, clapping his plump seal paws. "Desist, take your seats, we are well met by fluorescent light, fair tintinnabulations."

The students scatter and reform instantly at their chairs. The discipline of the class now known to them. Seeing no scripts on the table, they turn their heads to Burton, like flowers to a ghastly sun-lamp. "A frolic Hallowe'en treat, except Hallowmas was for alms-gathering in Shakespeare's day. This post-Christmas holiday, the Feast of Fools, was for disguise, passion, the turning of tables. I'm sure you all know the play: *Twelfth Night*." He pauses. "Or, *What You Will*. As we continue our examination of the plays that inform the Western canon." Flim-flam, thank you, man.

At his arm's wave, Ivy distributes the scripts, enjoying the little stroll around the table.

"We'll read through scenes without explanatory remarks from me, to see what you people understand of the language of the Bard. Orion!"

Orion jumps.

Ivy puts the script in front of him. Not as cool as he hopes, young Orion.

"You will play Sebastian, and his alter-ego Viola, in both manifestations." Burton waggles his eyebrows meaningfully. There's a little frisson of energy at that, but not much. They know their Burton by now. "Animus, Anima. Yin-slash-Yang. With a nod to the rich Shakespearian tradition of boys playing girls, of course. As well as the boy playing the girl, you'll be the girl playing the boy, and the boy she plays at being."

Ivy completes her circuit with a script for Newell and one for herself, and sits, ready to accept the rôle of tedious Maria with equanimity.

Burton swivels his eye from Orion to Newell. "Newell will give us His Eminence the Duke, and Savaya—"

"Oh, sorry! I have to take this text—" Savaya jumps up from the table, leaving Burton fish-mouthed. Perhaps no one has ever done such a thing to him before.

She stops dead in the middle of the room, staring at the screen, and turns to address them all, breast-breath hovering, shimmering; eyes brimming with dew. "Nevaeh's okay! I mean—she broke her ankle really badly, falling down the school steps, her dad is going to sue, and they're operating to put pins in. That's all it was!" How lovely to be young and ardent and full of joy, Ivy thinks. Or full of relief.

Burton, prim: "If you feel able to rejoin us?"

Savaya dances back to her chair, glowing at him.

"Where were we—ah. Savaya, you will read the Countess Olivia. Of her household, Sheridan Tooley will read Aguecheek, the foolish palsied knight, and Ivy—dear Ivy, so flexible, a director's dream, will give us Toby Belch."

Ivy keeps her face perfectly cordial, serene in knowing that whatever happens here will only last one goddamned day. She will pull out all the stops, belch the alphabet at his behest.

"Since it seems Nevaeh will not be gracing us with her presence . . ." Burton's eyes move over the assembled company, searching, discarding. He lights on a grade eleven girl, pretty and bright. "Mikayla, you take Maria. I will myself—" Burton pauses, to regain their whole awestruck attention: "—assay Malvolio. I flatter myself I was born to play the part."

He has thrust the greatness on himself. Newell looks down at his script, the edges of his mouth moving in an ungovernable smile. His hand brushes Ivy's: *we are in this together thank God someone else has a sense of humour.* No gesture could be more different from Jerry Pink's handbrush, that said *I am stalking you, woman-bug.*

Burton accepts the silent awe of the assemblage as his due, and finishes. "You all, in the scenes we read today, will create Feste—not *tout ensemble,* but as a horde, a juggle of jesters. Read line by line as I point to you." Which puts everyone nicely on edge, Ivy thinks. No counting ahead to your next lines. Not that she hasn't done much the same thing, mentally—Belch is only in the Malvolio scenes Burton has chosen. Still, it will be fun to poke fun at ol' Burton's malevolent major-domo. She cheers up a bit. They start: Viola, washed up on shore, disguises herself as a boy to enter the service of the Duke.

But Ivy is distracted. The mystery of Orion and Newell lies underneath every word, every disguised or protective glance. "I have unclasp'd to thee the book even of my secret soul," Newell says down the long table to where Orion sits exiled, close to Savaya.

How can Burton sit and listen, wearing that tiny smile? The innuendos and inside jokes of the script conspire: "They shall yet belie thy happy years that say thou art a man: Diana's lip is not more smooth and rubious . . ." The Duke cannot help flirting with him/her/him, with everything, everyone, making every person love him. Extra meaning conspires, even: Newell smiles to tell Orion, "I know *thy constellation* is right apt for this affair."

Yet Orion's purity of purpose, his clever boy's ambition, has its own morality. He *is* pure, compared to the jaded Duke, whose jade piece knocks gently against his creamy shirt at every gesture. And Newell is the Duke—"For I myself am best when least in company." That inner solitude, that remoteness is infinitely attractive, Ivy thinks. Dean, Brando, all those strange lonely thinkers who become romantic heroes.

Then it's the rascals. Mikayla manages Maria's antique jokes and wordplay far better than Burton deserves from a random choice. She has nice flat eyes and another kind of inner solitude, seeming to be not of the main acting clique, but complete in herself.

The Feste-crowd follows Burton's dreadful pointing finger, but the sense is lost on them and Burton soon stops them with a quick-flashing hand. His eye ranges the table again, coldly, discarding choice after choice. He refocuses beyond the table to where Jason sits at the back wall, hunched over, watching. "You, design boy," Burton says. "You've been listening, what's your name? Jason—come and take part. From, *Take the fool away* . . ."

Ivy experiences a painful lurch, half worry that Jason will be afraid, half fear that Burton might have lighted on new prey.

Jason unfolds himself obediently. He finds a chair beside Mikayla, not visibly anxious. *"Do you not hear, fellows? Take away the lady,"* he says, his voice a dry, shy, fluting echo of Savaya's—unexpectedly funny. He catechizes her on her brother's death and confounds her, lovingly —*"The more fool, madonna, to mourn for your brother's soul, being in heaven. Take away the fool, gentlemen"* —until she must call upon Malvolio for support.

Yipes, the electric charge of Burton reading Malvolio: upsetting and hilarious, authority upturned. Ivy enjoys it very much. This work is dangerous! Burton shows them all how it's done: his greed constrained, his egotistical hunger heightened, made monstrous—then made pitiful by Olivia's delicate distance from Malvolio.

The intimacy between Savaya and Orion lends the first Viola/Olivia scene such free flowing pleasure of instantly recognized love that Ivy thinks of Hugh, of seeing him in the parlour at Pink's and—seeing him. Being seen.

At the end of the little scene there's silence in the room. Burton, even, was caught in the silken net. What a lovely thing acting is, theatre is. Playing at life so well that we believe, we do believe.

Burton calls out page numbers to push the Malvolio plot scenes together. He's right, he was born for this small greatness. The part presents his vast ego like a heart surgeon cuts open a chest: there is Burton's tiny, choked, empurpled, wizened heart, furiously beating. It's not at all fair, what they do to him, but very funny; and Sheridan Tooley turns out to be a heck of a guy, willing to throw himself into poor Aguecheek, to shiver himself silly. So much of the work is seeing what could be—what actors might be capable of, will be, what beauty and transcendence might happen if everything conspires, agrees, conflates. Not that they are good right now, but that they *will* be, could be. This is the kind of day that makes people spend their lives in theatre, Ivy thinks.

Over too soon. Terry and Terry come in promptly at six to hand out Hallowe'en candy and send the students spinning off into the darkening afternoon, with a reminder that Saturday's day-long workshop starts at ten.

Orion murmurs to Savaya as they tidy their scripts; Ivy watches Savaya slip casually down the table to stop by Newell. Burton is consulting some script-note.

Savaya checks to make sure Terry and Terry are out of earshot. "We're, the students are having a party tonight—it was supposed to be at Nevaeh's house, but now . . ."

Jason, reading ahead to the rest of Feste, looks up. "Have it at my house," he says. At the arrested looks of his friends, and of Ivy, he laughs. "Why not? Nothing left in there to break."

8. CAN'T BUY HUGH LOVE

The Mighton has shifted. (*Shifted is not painted.*) Hugh puts out a hand to adjust it, not wanting to climb even the stepstool. The room reels around him as he stretches up his arm. Popping Advil all day, but the headache rises like a wave from time to time anyway. It's the stress, the impossibility of keeping the gallery going—will upping classes help? Largely's offer weights his desk, vibrates at the edge of his eye. He hasn't opened the envelope. Hendy emailed: Newell wants to assume the gallery mortgage at a lower rate. He's a prince, but there is no lower rate, it's already prime minus one, nobody can do better than that. There's no solution except for Mighton to push out vast collages the way Della's mother used to push out identical boats, twelve in a row, so Hugh can sell them all at a fifty percent commission. Who to? Half to Newell, half to Gerald.

Summoned by the power of his name, Gerald walks in. Five-thirty, he must have left his staff to sell. "Like the look of this," he says, hovering at the Mighton.

"A large piece," Hugh says. "Overpowering—not easy to live with."

Gerald steps toward it, backs away, attempting judicious distance. Hugh's heart sags. "My—we—" Gerald's throat works to produce a sound, fails. Hard to watch. Then nothing.

Hugh rushes in. "It's an investment piece, no question—but steep, at ninety. I wonder, Gerald, if you might be happier with something from Gareth Pindar's gallery, something a little less demanding."

Night and day the dark gates stand open, the plaque reads. Around the blazing, ferocious crack of blue-white light down the middle, the dark gates gape. Thousands of shards and fragmentary details woven and soldered into those giant gates, open but not wide open, nothing generous about them. The blue glare down the middle is very hard to take.

Gerald is staring too. Head a-tilt. The patron's stare that after all these years still irritates Hugh—evaluative, cow-eyed pretend-thinking. But maybe Gerald is not-thinking of his wife, or of Toby. Hugh feels tears start into his eyes and turns quickly away, terribly embarrassed. It's his head, the unsteadiness of everything. He's all right when Ivy's there, but otherwise he falls to pieces. All the thousand faces in the gates.

He ought to be with Mimi.

Gerald stands stubbornly planted, silent, staring. Hugh goes back to the desk. He sits holding his head with one cupped hand until a shuffling noise at the communicating door between the stores catches his attention. Jasper. Wisps of white hair straight up on one side, matted flat on the other, like he's been asleep on his desk.

He pokes a full glass through the crack at Hugh. "Care for a taster? A cheeky Malbec."

"No, thanks. Conrad says no booze till my head gets better."

"Your loss, your loss. Here's looking up your old address!" Jasper is well-to-do, as they used to say about drunks. Three sheets to the wind.

Hugh returns the salute, raising his coffee cup.

"Worried," Jasper says, looking up the store to where the Mighton hangs, lessening, cheapening everything else in the place.

"Well, no more than usual, I guess," Hugh says.

"No, no, *I'm* worried." Jasper whispers, hugely: *"About Gerald."*

Hugh shakes his head, motions with it to Gerald, wishes he hadn't tried that motion.

"That he'll — himself. You know." Jasper draws a shaky old finger across his throat.

Even though it is not funny, Hugh almost laughs. "Quit it!" he says, shaking his head. He goes to the framing room to finish.

Ruth is there, stacking the certificates in a box. "Looks like Ivy was a dab hand with these! Lucky you, to find a good apprentice."

Hugh throws his hands in the air, winces again. "Della's with Mimi. You're doing all the work. What's left?"

Ruth looks at him, sparkle-eyed. She's a bucket of vim. "Go put an ice pack on that head, that's what. Did I hear Gerald out there? I'm going out to his place to help him bundle up some things for the Goodwill." She leans forward, like Jasper in her whispering. *"Her things, and the boy's."*

As he goes upstairs, Hugh hears Ruth calling out to Gerald in the front, "Won't be a minute. I brought some Hallowe'en taffy; you never know—might get some trick-or-treaters out at your place."

(L)

Her mom swings into the driveway, late. *It's in my phone,* she always says, and yet she is always late. Grey circles under her eyes. She spent all last night in the dining room working on boats, and now she's been looking after Mimi. After whatever happened with Dad.

Slide in, buckle up, etc. Her mom grinds the clutch and backs out of the driveway. Two lurching turns later, there's Savaya's house. L texts: > **savaya savaya let down your long hair.** Then settles in to wait, because Savaya always takes forever too. The only person in the world you don't have to wait for, in fact, is Jason.

Her mom is fiddling with her phone, so the music keeps changing. *Here Comes the Sun,* that's not going to cheer anybody up. L grabs the phone and dials it round to Hawaiian guitar, which has proved soothing in the past. "We need to stop at FairGrounds for Savaya to get her cheque, 'kay?"

Savaya runs down the walk, waving behind her to April and Justice, whose real name is Scott. April's white-blonde hair is teased, and she's got over-mascaraed, spooky, black tear-stained eyes; Scott is in a sheet with cut-out eyeholes. They've been making sponge toffee for trick-or-treat, and the smell comes pouring out of the house, dark, heavy, burnt. Savaya used to hate it, she wanted to give out bags of chips, but now everybody goes by to get some famous organic sponge toffee and she's proud of it. They make it with fair-trade sucanat. They tried locally sourced sugar beets one year, but the toffee never set.

L's mom waves up at the porch. "Who's April dressed as, Savaya?"

"Courtney Love. On a rough day, I guess. And my dad's Kurt Cobain."

Funny, very funny. Her mom laughs too loudly. But sad too.

"Courtney Love had *plastic surgery,*" L tells Savaya, another piece of tragedy.

Her mom says, "That's not surprising."

"She was a riot grrrl!"

"But she has a lot of money. Money likes plastic surgery. All those grrrls are getting to the age now where they look in the mirror and think, I wouldn't have to look like this if I had a little bit of work done." L's mother has no sense of anything but herself. Everything is filtered through approval/disapproval. Just because she wouldn't do plastic surgery herself or get a decent haircut or use some fucking moisturizer, anyone who does is condemned.

Savaya bubbles over into the gap between the seats, straining her seat-belt. "Nevaeh's mom called me!" L turns to stare at her. "I know! Like, *never before*!" Savaya twirls her head. "Her dad is at the hospital so her mom had to do the calling, we can visit her tomorrow after noon. They're keeping her in till Monday to put pins in her ankle."

As usual, L's mom cannot keep it in. "How many of these girls end up in hospital! I really do have suspicions of the whole cutting thing, these kids need to take up art, find something other than themselves to obsess over."

"Mom, this is not at all helpful." Because a) she knows nothing about cutting, and b) shut *up*. "Anyway, she's not—"

"Reading a book helps with depression better than TV ever could, or the internet."

The car stops, FairGrounds. Savaya springs out, but L can't stop the lava boiling out of her mouth. "You are *so crazy!* Jeez—nobody in the world makes me as mad as you do!"

Shit, shit, shit, there goes the Buddhist vow. Give her a loving, gag-me, big-toothed smile, maybe she won't start sobbing while Savaya can still hear.

L's mom smiles back, in the brave precursor-to-tears way. She says, "Sorry, sorry."

Fuck! L kicks the glove compartment with her flowery vine-laced shoe. "You're doing it again—you're apologizing when you didn't *do* anything! It was me who was crabby. What the fuck, Mom!" Her mom just sits there staring out the window. "*Dad* left, you didn't leave! Anyway you always do that, you just apologize no matter what, so you're not at fault."

"And am I?"

"No! I don't know what's going on, but he's still my— He's not crazy, he wouldn't!"

A person deserves a little faith. Of course he is not having a thing with Jenny, for fuck's sake. L slams the door open and stands on the wet pavement for a second, then leans down into the car. "Fifteen minutes, half an hour? Go see Hugh for a while."

She runs up the stairs onto the FairGrounds porch, shaking the rain from her flying feet, going, going.

(DELLA)

oh L so sorry Mimi says sorry sorry sorry sorry sorry   I say sorry too
nothing to do but wait   don't dare go back to Hugh's   in case Mighton
Jasper's still open   lights on   one light, desk lamp
junkshop shelves shadow into cross-hatch
orange glow holds Jasper's jack-o'-lantern face   devil
his lantern eyes don't change   slow shift refocus

    Happy Hallowe'en! Glass of cheer?

empty mouth empty eyes   hand to glass a puppet moving
hands it across the counter with a leer—   did he see Mighton, biting?
wine dark, strong   drink up

Another? *One for my baby one more for my baby . . .   gloomy listen to me*

he stares into the middle distance
does not recognize me   the stab of hurt is sharp
the store has no floor   because familiar
                                                        because Dad
back out   not fair to look when he is in this state   devil
quarters taped to his skin lucky cat on the counter
spells to draw money to him   hopeless
Ruth frets as stuck with him   as Hugh feels stuck with her
Hugh must be at Mimi's   needs to be   black streets   wind pushes leaves
straggling troops a band of monsters   shepherded by a ghoul
shouts, streets over, short glittery children   each house
                                                        lit and garnished
here, adults running
black leather man and woman   the man's run   is that Ken
                                 running hand in hand   with Jenny?
they turn
their unmasked faces young
younger than Cobain

Mimi's eyes open—searching, beseeching—when Hugh comes into the room. A hand comes from under the blankets, a gesture. Thin-turned forearm half-blue, tape from a needle wound on the back of her blue-ivory hand. Does she know you, though, except as part of herself?

Hugh kneels. He puts the hand to his lips. So smooth it's frictionless, soft as the lining of her old sable coat. The one she wore to get the groceries, when they lived in the highrise on Avenue Road where a cabby delivered the groceries to the lobby. Coat on over her nightgown, feet shoved into boots for the elevator ride: an outing, her hand reaching for him at the door, laughing in fright. He helped with the door, with the buttons. He was her knight. Until someone realized they hadn't left the apartment for a month or three. Who rescued them that time? How old was he, six? He remembers the apartment: creamy white carpet, floor-to-ceiling windows, a white plastic chair like an egg on a chain, where he read. Beautiful books came to the lobby too, and cartons of cigarettes, bottles, a bag of limes. Then she got a little better, a stream of visitors came, then babysitters, then she was working all the time. But still needed help dressing in the mornings and in the evenings, before the other babysitters came. A parade of faceless strange-smelling women showing him their scars.

Forgive her. It's not like she had any choice. Hugh kisses her hand again. This time Mimi motions to the button; he presses to make the bedhead rise. She points, or ghost-points, to a drinking cup with a bent straw. He puts it to her mouth. She drinks dutifully and smiles around the straw. ". . . to the last drop," she whispers, throaty as her old commercial.

Hugh laughs, at her insouciance, at the thread of the well-loved voice back to sense and sanity if not volume. Pushing the cup away, her own hand catches her eye. She spreads the fingers, disapproving.

"Shall I do your hands?"

She nods, pleased, so he pulls the metal bedside drawer open to find her cream and a small glass file, knowing they are there because he packed them at her apartment and unpacked them here. One hand at a time, he covers the frail skin with a veil of Joy, gently pushing the skin down to reveal the moons on each fingernail, as she likes him to do. The hands are the map to her death, coming soon. Pink gone from the nails, but they are still pretty almonds. Her rings, left in the drawer, rattle loose when he pulls it open to replace the cream.

Mimi looks at her hands again, still dissatisfied. She turns her head slowly to the drawer, eyebrows up a little. "Polish?"

He laughs, it's so nice to hear ordinary sense out of her. He shows her a bottle of topcoat; she makes a sad mouth. The deep pink she's always used is not allowed. Nurses need to see the blue of her fingernails. He shakes the topcoat to make the tiny rattle. Mimi spreads a docile hand on the over-bed table. Even strokes, enough bead on the brush. He has been schooled in manicure. He holds each finger in turn and thinks that he might lean his head down on the bed and cry for ten years, except that would not do any good, so he does not.

"It's Hallowe'en," he says, tidying the last finger. "They give you any candy?"

Her eyes reproach him. She loves candy. "Ghost story," she says.

Obediently, he starts off on the first campfire one that occurs to him. "There once was a man who had a beautiful wife, and this wife had a golden arm. They lived happily together, but after a time she fell ill, and he nursed her." He forgot about the necessary death. But there is death in all ghost stories. She's listening.

"Knowing she was near death, the wife said, 'Promise you will bury my golden arm with me,' and he said, 'Of course I will.' When the day came that she died, he did as she had asked. But as time went by, the man thought to himself, here I am poor and grieving, with doctor's bills to pay. My wife is dead, she will not know, she does not need it now. So he went to the cemetery in the dark of night and dug down to her grave. He opened her coffin, and from her body he took the golden arm. He carried it home through the darkness, fearful at every step, because the night was wild and stormy. Twice, he thought he heard someone calling, and stopped to listen: nothing but the wind, or an owl calling *whoo, whoooo*. When he reached his house he ran straight up to bed. He lay the golden arm beside him where his wife had lain for so long, and pulled the covers up over his head. Then he heard the voice again, from far away, calling, *Who, who . . . who has taken my golden arm? Give me back my golden arm.*"

At the trembling in her hand, he checks her face. Is this too scary, now? She moves her mouth into a sort of smile, motions with her hand, go on . . .

"The husband pulled the pillow over his head, not wanting to hear that voice he knew so well. But it came again, *Who, who, who has taken my golden arm? Giiive me baaack my gooolden aaarm . . .* He screwed his eyes tight shut, he put his fingers in his ears. The voice came closer, closer, it was at the bedroom door, it was inside the bedroom—*Who has got my golden arm?*" Hugh pauses, because the story must always pause here, and then pounces tenderly on Mimi's wasted arm: "*You've* got it!"

"*You,*" she says, or maybe *Hugh*. Not frightened. Amused and comforted. She closes her eyes slowly and seems to sleep, mouth falling open a little. Little cat mouth, still. Wide-spaced teeth terrible within, what's left of them.

The good visits are worse than the bad visits. Hugh can't do this any longer, come to this room and watch her dying.

He lets his head fall onto the clean sheet beside her head, to rest with her.

Ruth touches him on the shoulder.

Oh. He fell asleep holding Mimi's hand.

He loosens his hold—her hand is slack, the polish clean except for his thumbprint on the baby finger. It's all right, she won't notice. Dusk in the room, everything is tidy. Nolie must have been in.

Ruth is miming. Hugh blinks and stretches his eyes, not able to make sense of her exaggerated gestures. He gets up, knees creaking. Mimi does not wake.

They go to the door. Ruth whispers, unnecessarily, "I'm back from Gerald's, we put the bags in the back of your van. I said you'd take them to the Clothes Closet, won't you?"

"Of course."

"Well, you go on now, I'm sure Ivy's finished with that class thing by this time. I had supper, I'm set for the evening. Brought my crossword puzzle."

She waves him out, moving away already into the twilight by the bed.

After the post-class consult, Ivy melts into the middle distance, leaving Newell and Burton to their own devices. She refuses an over-lavish dinner, refuses to go with them to Pink's party. You can't look after everyone, you can only keep an eye out. It sometimes seems like the true work of life is to observe and not be asleep.

Bit sleepy now, though. And hungry—almost seven-thirty already. She throws script and coat in the back seat and reaches for her phone with two fingers.

> supper?

In a minute, Hugh comes back.

< pizza? I ought to get the framing packed etc

> I will pick up.

< go to Black Cat on parkhill no anchovies otherwise what you will

> ha! that's the 12th night subtitle!

< okay by that I meant spinach and feta on whole wheat

He remembers what she likes!

> but you like double cheese pepperoni and green olives

< get both we will eat leftover for lunch tomorrow

To be capable of non-compromise/independence already, to be planning tomorrow's lunch—the luxury of that sends Ivy happily down the street. She phones in the order from the number on the sign. The car is warm, thinking is pretty much over for the day, and she likes being alone, since in a minute she will be with Hugh. The thought of him makes her inner works pulse and contract—how hilarious to be in love at this late date. How hilarious that there is no obstacle. No choice, no escape, no question.

A pickup truck pulls in beside her; she glances over. A large cat is driving.

Oh yes. It's Hallowe'en. Three people get out, grown-ups or teenagers, all masked, laughing. They come out in a minute, carrying twenty pizzas, and drive away. Cat, witch, Frankenstein.

(DELLA)

wine seeps down like rain warm rain warms face arms chest warms legs
round the block   twice enough!
up the stairs to FairGrounds   warm light quiet bustle of evening
                                        L behind the till, tallying
stern goddess in a flowing Greek chiton
Jason made that?
                              what she must see in me: a hag, a witch
                              windblown hair, fright, tragedy, old age
she frowns, arrested:
     Have you—been *drinking?*
        I had *a* drink, a glass of wine at Jasper's.
     Well you can't drive us to the party drunk.
        I am not—Elly, of course I can—   what could hurt more?
                                        silence from the goddess
                              angry-eyed Athena she hates me
she doesn't *hate* you, she's *mad* at you

     Never mind, we'll walk. We're early anyway.
she turns   out they go   delicate queens
who will inherit the earth   we are old
everything that once was ours   dying
                                   mine and Hugh's and Newell's
Mighton by the fireplace heard all that
        Need a coffee?
           I am not drunk!
                                        the urge to defend
                                        reveals drunkenness
Mighton = malice but his Dark Gates ≠ not malice   a crack/a crater
ache for all humanity   Hughmanity
     I never thought you were. I wanted company.
he gives up half the settee
moves aside a silver canister helmet   a wooden shield   a sword
   I'm King Arthur. I have to go to that party at Pink's in costume.
   But I'm hiding. Hallowe'en weirds me out. The whole deal of

dressing up, putting on a mask—it takes away identity and
gives us back nothing but wildness.

                                       I forgot this: Mighton holds
                                           conversations by himself

Didn't you worry about Elle running through the streets?
    I went with her, then. Sometimes I dressed up too.
    I went as my mother, one year, in the old beige raincoat
    she used to wear over her pyjamas to drive me to school
    and her blonde wig.
Your mother had a wig?
    It was the seventies, everyone's mother had a wig. Hugh's
    mother had twelve! I stood waiting for Elly like my mother
    used to wait for me, arms crossed across my chest, shoulders
    hunched—spooky.

my mother invades my skin my bones
my mouth my neck my heart braced
for something bad to happen
Mighton sees the transformation   makes a face   still spooky
    Now every time I stand waiting, impatient and tired, I realize
    that I've been trying to peel off that raincoat and that damn wig
    ever since. But I was her on a bad day. I could have worn
    her paint smock, happy at work. Her peacock feather dress,
    when she was beautiful.

Mighton's dark inquiring eye   a nut of old kindness buried in bile
    You don't see angels out on Hallowe'en. You're not your mother
    We choose to look at the hardest parts of ourselves.
                                  wine moves in my chest in my legs
                                  I'll look at the worst of myself
                                        I'll go wild

(ORION)

Candy duty—fuck it, fuck everything. Eight o'clock, the little kids are finished. Orion leaves the bowl of chocolate bars on the step. Jason needs him. Everybody has indoor parties these days anyway, to get away from child molesters. Like those guys only come out once a year, wearing Freddy Krueger masks so you can spot them.

His bike flies through black alleys, skims the river path, skids on gravel round to the back of Jason's. The kitchen door is unlocked. Nobody there. But hark! Voices, up.

Orion slinks up the back stairs, stopping behind the closed door at the top to listen: Jason, somebody else. The Maria, Mikayla? She just came this year, nobody knew she could act. But that was good, today.

"The strap goes through—yes, and—" Jason is dressing her up.

Orion pops the door and slips along the hallway, judges his moment and does a grand-jeté into the room. Stealth-bombs Jason's Despair/ Chastity. Mikayla, half-dressed in Nevaeh's moulted Hope feathers, gives a satisfying *shriek*, upped by the pin Jason shoves into her rump as she jumps.

Jason apologizes, dumbass, and Mikayla sobs for a second but smiles through the rain, saying "I'm so happy to be here" like an idiot. Too bad, it seemed like she might be smart. She hiccups and burps. What's she drinking, Bailey's? Ah. And underage, too, so Orion cops her glass and takes it to Jason's bathroom, pours it down the toilet, and comes back.

He takes Mikayla by the shoulders. "Shhh." She shudders and shuts up.

"You have a chance, here. Don't blow it. Nobody knows you, now suddenly everybody knows you, you get to work with Ivy and Newell, and me—don't drink anymore."

Mikayla nods.

"Don't throw up in the kitchen sink or take off your clothes or laugh like a hyena. For fuck's sake don't *burp* any more. I'm telling you this for your own good. Ivy can do it because she's a trained genius."

Jason laughs his quiet, happy laugh, and Orion feels that the night is already made.

(L)

L goes up the back stairs to find Jason. He's in his bedroom primping the new girl, Mikayla. Weird that he's put her in Nevaeh's dress. Is that okay, actually? Looks entirely different now, of course, especially since Mikayla's like a foot shorter. L leans in the doorway, tilting on her vine-painted shoes. "Better get down there. Savaya put on Facebook that people should bring food and drink and come for nine, and it's nine now."

Orion jumps up, neoprene suit snapping back into perfect form. God, he looks good—Jason's a genius. The cut lingers over Orion's wide shoulders and tapers with his shape, down to where L has to actually look away or her eyes will get stuck. "Savaya's dad is bringing two folding tables, she's waiting for him in the driveway. Hey, Mikayla, I hear you were great this afternoon. Savaya said."

The new girl gasps. Jason flicks her arm and says she's done.

But he takes L's hand at the doorway and pulls her back—what for? Oh, to fix her dress. The tunic has fallen to one side. He straightens it, adjusting the folds, fingers cool on her skin. His breath on her shoulder.

Orion takes the front stairs, so they follow. "Holy shit," he says.

The living room has furniture in it. Chairs, a glass table. And along the wall, a parade of dummies dressed in psychedelic clothes.

"Those are Mimi's pink gloves," L says. She has tried them on many times, on many dull Sundays.

Jason sinks to sit on the stairs. "I don't know about this."

Orion shrugs, neoprene shoulders moving deliciously, his don't-care grin that always means trouble. "Too late to stop the party, we'll just have to work with it." He runs down the rest of the stairs, pulling a black paper mask out of his pocket, which he puts on the wigstand foam-head on the glass table. It looks freaky over the strawberry-blonde afro.

"Okay," Jason says, going down. "But some of this stuff is valuable, I don't want it wrecked or stolen. That Afghani dress, it's like, a relic. L, help me take this one upstairs."

They cart the body up, L holding the foot and Jason at the waist, tending the dress carefully as they go. "Where to?" she asks.

He stops a moment, and turns left. "Ivy's room. It's got a lock."

Savaya's at the back door, shouting for help with the tables. Orion leaves them to it.

He tells Mikayla as they go, "Also, keep your mouth shut. Don't say anything bad about anyone for at least a year—you don't know who's dating who."

Jason and L take the dummies upstairs, one at a time: the backless, black-skirted, paisley-sequined cocktail dress; the Mondrian colour-block; the hot-pink mini that goes with the pink gloves. L puts the gloves in her pocket, rolled together the way Mimi always did. It's kind of a nightmare, because the clock is ticking—they're still on the stairs with a long black satin Audrey Hepburn–type gown when the first bunch of people comes banging at the door. Faster! Ivy's room looks kind of crowded by the time they're done.

"Do you have the key?"

"Nope." Jason pushes the button in and pulls the door of Ivy's room shut. "You can open it from the outside with a skewer in the little hole. Not much of a lock. Used to be the master bedroom, I guess it's for keeping the kids out when the parents are banging." Ghastly thought. "Enough to deter people tonight, though."

L nods. "Want to keep them out of your room too?"

"Doesn't matter—my mom cleaned it out. She had that magazine shoot today, that's why she's been doing the quotes so fast. I didn't know she was going to use Mimi's clothes."

Jason's mom: a continuing enigma. "You ready?"

But at the top of the stairs, he hangs back. Lots of people milling in down there. "Let's go down the back."

Happy to. L loves the back stairs, doors at the top and the bottom. Momentary darkness as you go down, a chamber in a spaceship, or a time machine. All might be different by the time you reach the bottom. That door sticks. Jason jiggles it.

L stands on the step behind him, looking at the barely visible back of his neck, the two cords standing out. He's so concentrated, so exact. She reaches out to touch—

"Got it," he says, and the door opens into a flood of light, the kitchen full of people, bottles, bowls of chips, everyone from the master class and the art people and the tech guys, hubbub. A good party already.

Pink's place is green. Bile-green skull lights along the veranda roof, spooky music. Hugh takes Ivy's arm and mounts the wooden steps again. The bevelled glass of the door frames Burton, scarlet-coated over yellow plaid trousers, hair fluffed, red cheeks chomping.

Ivy whispers, "What is he, Toad of Toad Hall?"

Not even a week since Hugh punched him, in this very house. Phew, because you could have—what if you'd killed him, head on a fireplace fender, some old mystery-novel thing? Burton's bruise has vanished, or been varnished by concealer.

Newell pulls the door wide, grinning above the thick noose around his neck.

"Ah, *Godot*," Ivy says. "Lucky and Pozzo, very good."

Looking remarkably fit, Newell wears a wife-beater over tattered trousers, and carries a heavy bag, a folding stool, a picnic basket and a greatcoat. "No idea why you came," he says into their ears. "But very, very glad." He shifts his burdens to dot a kiss on Ivy's cheek.

She kisses him back. "I made Hugh come. I realized after I left your place, I need to know what's happening tomorrow or I won't sleep tonight."

The rope from Newell's neck stretches taut to Burton's hand, who shouts, flicking his red leather whip: "Is everybody ready? Is everybody looking at me?"

"What were you, eighteen, when you did Lucky?" Ivy asks Newell. "No, you must have been older. I saw you in the Fringe version, before it got picked up."

"Twenty?" Newell looks at Burton, who has stuck his bowler hat back on.

"Nineteen and one-half, I believe. . . . 'Given the existence as uttered forth in the public works of Puncher and Wattmann of a personal God quaquaquaqua. . . .'"

Newell rolls his eyes for Hugh. "He knew the lines better than I did."

Hugh passes a hand over his forehead. Is there punch? Not that you ought to drink any. Takes Hugh a minute to recognize Mighton, by the drinks table, wearing some kind of tin can on his head. A helmet. He's carrying a shield and sword, standing with Della. That old twining portrait, Hugh can't stop thinking about it. Della looks up, sees Hugh. Blinks and turns her head away. Still mad at him? That's ridiculous. Irritated, Hugh makes his way over there. He's saying hi to the back of Della's head when Ann appears, with some guy in tow.

She grabs his arm, crying, "Hugh! This is my photographer, Stewart, he's doing the shoot for my exhibit, for the minimalist—Stewart, Hugh's my ex. My *ex* ex."

As Ivy comes up, Ann adds, "And his current! Oh, you met her this morning."

Hugh nods at the photographer guy, who's wearing a too-tight jacket, too-tight too-short pants, giant boots. Everything coal black. "What are you?" Hugh asks, to be civil.

"A pho*tog*rapher," the guy says loudly, as if he thinks Hugh's deaf.

"I mean, what are you dressed as? More Beckett? Chimneysweep?" The guy just stares at him. Oh, those are his own clothes. Hugh gives up.

"We didn't dress up either," Ivy says, saving his bacon. "Only as old lovers." Her warm voice makes the guy smile, even though baffled.

Ann pulls him away. She's wearing Mimi's purple Halston jumpsuit, the one Hugh always thought of as Virginia Slim. He stares after her. Ghosts.

Mighton tilts the helmet back on his head, a plate of hors d'oeuvres on one arm, Della on the other. He says, "Let's find some place to hide." They process along into the hall, scene of the famous Burton-punch. Hugh rubs his head. A lie-down might help.

Conrad, not costumed, is at the front door. Hugh shies, and tacks left with Ivy, heading up the grand staircase to a clear space above the swarm. They move together like an old couple, like Ruth dancing with Jasper at the Ace. Ruth is at Mimi's. The thought of that quiet room cuts Hugh's breath, makes him stumble on the stairs.

But Ivy is with him; they reach the broad half-landing, a vantage from which to watch the crowd. There's Orion's mother—Hugh points her out to Ivy—wearing a sheer curtain. He feels some kinship with Orion.

Della and Mighton lean into the banisters to let Pink pass behind them, coming down. Pink is Dracula, fake widow's peak vivid against his chalky skin, the freckles a surprise. From below, Burton bounces up the stairs, Newell roped behind him.

Burton seizes the hem of Pink's passing cape. "Everyone seems very pleased with the master class," he boasts. "I'm happy. Not an easy week, by *any* means." Sparkling titter.

Hugh bends away, not wanting to witness Ivy and Newell Pink-pandering too. "Della," he calls, waving to snag her attention from Mighton. "Della—dinner tomorrow. Six or seven?"

She looks at him, finally. "I don't know if Ken's going to be able to make it."

Hugh is shocked. The groceries—the planning. Della's eyes are black and blank. He hates her like this. "Never mind, come anyway," he says, not knowing how else to take the misery out of her eyes. "It'll be a good dinner, no matter what."

"Oh, absolutely." Della turns away again. When things are very bad, you can't bear to be looked at by the ones you love. Hugh knows that feeling.

🍂

Ivy wishes Pink/Dracula wouldn't argue. "Don't know why you're not doing some one-act Canadian plays," he protests. Of course they ought to be, it's the only thing that makes sense.

Burton, exploding: "Dear *God*, they'll be doing Canadian plays the rest of their lives, can we not introduce them to the *canon* here, to the *real* plays?"

Ivy disagrees with this so profoundly she cannot even speak.

"I'm all for gay rights!" Pink's fake fangs chomp. "We're an LGBTQIA-friendly school. But cross-dressing is . . ."

Burton waves his hand, the one with the red whip in it. "Hogwash, it's *entirely* classically grounded—played by a boy in 1602, investigate Original Practices! But you've won already. Viola and Sebastian can't be doubled. Too much of the plot is lost. Film, yes. Onstage, sadly, it simply doesn't *work*. Not without pulling the play *completely* out of true."

Burton's finicky, fustian phrases make Ivy want to wash her own mouth out of anything but plain Americanese. Now he's going on about Mytyl and Tyltyl, technical obstacles-slash-challenges—what's this?

Newell turns, hiding his mouth from Burton. "He was in a production of *The Blue Bird* in Texas as a child."

Ivy asks: "He came from Texas?"

Hugh: "He was a child?"

Behind them, Burton lathers on. "I considered *Our Town*—in drag. And I thought, *yes, maybe,* but *not for this venue.*"

Ivy nudges Mighton's hors d'oeuvres plate closer to the edge of the banister, and coughs, so that it falls to the floor below with a violent crash. Oh dear!

The throng of board members looks up, and Pink, furious, fusses down the stairs to deal with the mess, cape billowing behind him.

(L)

A text bings on L's phone. Her tuned ear catches it through the noise of the party. No pocket in her chiton, she has it wedged under the side strap of her bra.

Her mom.

> when do you need me to pick you up?

< I'm staying at Savaya's

Not that she's going to. Savaya's parents always get wasted on Hallowe'en, the night they first got high or something. Like tomorrow, for L's parents. Not that they—ha ha ha, the very thought of her parents getting high! They just go to Hugh's for dinner every year, since he introduced them, however long ago. L's stomach squeezes at the thought of this year's dinner.

Everybody is so interested in everybody else's business.

Behind her, L can hear a circle of performance-program girls talking about Nevaeh in shocked carrying whispers: "Raped, she was raped." L turns away as another one, that short fat girl who does improv, gives a giggling gasp. "*I* heard she was molested by Terry. She-Terry, not He-Terry." A burst of laughter from the circle. A third one says, "I heard she's been cutting all year."

L ought to interfere. Say something to shut these girls down. The cutting is none of their business. But is it being none of their business any of her business?

"The anorexia got really bad, she fainted in the master class."

"She's a mess. I hear she's in for a thirty-day assessment."

Fuckheads. L turns finally, finally going to say something like they are all *fuckheads*.

But Savaya's already there, in her gold sheath, lips red like they're bleeding: "Why don't you dickwads go down to the hospital and ask her about all this to her face?"

Jason tugs L's hand to pull her away, but she can't abandon Savaya. Another one, a guy, not even from school but some loser from Trent drawn by the excitement, laughs loudly. "What's this I hear? The skeez-ball got all rapey with that black chick Navy?"

Savaya turns to tear into this guy. He sneer-laughs, and Savaya puts out a blood-nailed hand and shoves him to make him shut the fuck up, so he stumbles back toward the fireplace and trips and—slow motion—just lies back, lies down onto the big glass coffee table where the pink gloves used to be.

As he goes down, as the glass is cracking, through that slow-spooling time L is praying that he will not cut an artery.

All the noise of the party stops—the glass makes such a lightning crack! Not deep thunder, but bright and flashing. The boy wallows on his back in the shards like a turtle.

Jason steps carefully over the glass to take his reaching hand. Orion surges through the crowd and takes the other hand, and Jason says, "Put your feet on the metal."

With him braced like that, Orion and Jason pull the guy up and out of all the glass, now crumbled into a rubble of sparkling, dangerous cubes.

Sheridan Tooley bustles in with the broom, his unexpected boyfriend with the long slinky gloves holding the dustpan up like a fan. The circle widens out to make room for the cleanup, and Orion and Jason turn the guy around to see if he's got glass on him.

"Not much—you're lucky, asshole," Orion says. He brushes a couple of square shards off the guy's leather jacket, which saved him from most of it. "Too bad, Jase. But it's a rule: if there's a glass table in act one, it has to get broken by act three. Where's the vacuum?"

The guy is sputtering about Savaya: "She— You pushed me! I was just *asking* . . ."

Savaya barrels in on him, not sorry at all. "Quit saying stuff about Nevaeh, you racist shitpig. She broke her fucking *ankle*, and that's all there is to it."

L is trembling. Why did she not shut those girls down herself? Where is her loyalty, or her love?

Walking away from Pink's party down dark spook-ridden streets, Ivy asks Hugh, "Do we see light and dark differently when we're little? Or is it just that memory darkens it? Scenes from my childhood are so often poorly lit."

"All the scenes from my childhood are poorly lit. I don't remember trick-or-treating."

Ivy hugs his arm carefully, so his head does not jar. "Sorry for yourself? You can have my childhood: running for dear life over damp lawns in a long trippy skirt, fat pillowcase, banging on a spiderwebbed door for stale taffy handed out by a freaking *skeleton*."

"I don't like dressing up."

"Me neither. I spend enough time doing it in real life. Spent." Ivy shivers.

Hugh looks down at her with grave attention. "Do you think you can't work anymore?"

She looks down herself, at the boot-tops appearing and disappearing under her coat. "I think—I think maybe it's like my eye-tic, mostly stress. If I calm down, if I get Jamie moved out of my apartment . . ."

"Or just give it to him and that Alex jackass, and come live with me."

She beams up at him. "Yeah, well—find some solution."

"Dave will get the repairs done quick. Do you have the money?"

"I'll find it. I can borrow from my sister, if I have to. I'm just debating which will be less galling, asking Pink for an advance, or hitting up Fern."

"Money. Fucking money."

"Yeah. Fuck *money*, anyway."

The wind picks up and pushes them along a little faster, throwing leaves at their feet and shivering around their arms, cold as death. Trotting to keep up, and keep warm, Ivy searches for something to distract him: "What did Della say on the staircase?"

"She doesn't think Ken will come to dinner tomorrow. I'll have to go get him. He borrowed his assistant's cabin out at Bobcaygeon, I know the place."

"*It was in Bobcaygeon, I saw the constellations / reveal themselves one star at a time.*" Ivy sings quietly in the darkness. "*Drove back to town this morning with working on my mind, I thought of maybe quitting, I thought of leaving it behind.*"

"Poor guy. You heard him on the speakerphone. He struggles with depression, and the case he's been working on for years is appalling. I don't know how he functions as a lawyer—he can't make a decision to save his life; Della decides. Good marriage. Except now. Della's in a state. I guess Ken knows her better than I do—when he was dithering, trying to decide about quitting his job, I said she wouldn't care, even if they had to sell the house."

"Are you sure that's all that's happening? She looks to me like someone who's lost—well, not her house, but her life."

Hugh throws up his hands. "I can't   Look, nobody else can be sick, nobody else."

The road has taken them to Ann's house—every light on, door wide open, music clamouring out. Ivy draws her coat close to her neck. "A party? But Ann was at Pink's."

"Must be Jason."

"Hm, she had a bunch of your mother's clothes on display this morning," Ivy says, not knowing how Hugh will take this. "I wonder whether they got put away or . . ."

Hugh stands looking at the house. "I don't like to—"

"We'll pretend I'm coming home."

They turn up the walk. Ivy wonders if she should ring the bell—but who would hear? And also, actually, she did pay rent. She pushes the door wider.

There's Jason, dustpan and garbage bag in hand. "Oh!" he says, as if Ivy's the last person in the world he expected. "We just had a little—"

Words fail him. He dives off with the garbage bag, leaving L to explain: "The guy who broke the coffee table left. I hope it wasn't expensive. The metal part is still good."

There's still glass on the floor, crumbled cubes of tempered safety glass. People have left a wide circle around the skeleton of the table. In the empty space Orion swoops on hands and knees with a dustbuster, which accounts for some of the noise. He stands, shuts it off, phew! And wow—he looks fabulous. Tight black neoprene gleams above assertive wing-tips, a black shirt where the jacket opens, red claw-marks on the belly, and a bleeding shoulder in the back, feathers clinging there, like a wing was torn off.

"Fine," he announces to the room. "Just move into the kitchen if you don't have shoes."

Ivy has shoes. "Where did he get that fabulous suit?" she asks L.

L is proud. "Jason made it! This, too—I had a bird one, but he said it wasn't right."

"You're kidding, he made that? That's the prettiest thing!" Ivy's honestly impressed.

Flat-white grosgrain silk in frail folds, held by a belt of braided vines. Persephone, Artemis. L shows off her shoes, too: flowered, with vines lacing round the ankle.

"Like my shoes? Jason embellished them, the vines and flowers."

"It's like a wedding dress!"

L bites her lip, a child trying not to smile—she's as pretty as the dress, suddenly. "Savaya's, too. And see Mikayla from the master class, by the kitchen door? That's Nevaeh's Hope dress. They all have names. Savaya's was going to be Faith, but after the *Streetcar* reading Jason changed it to Desire. Then he distressed it and called it Despair, and made Orion's suit into Desire, with the claw-marks. He calls this one Charity."

"Which means love," Ivy says.

L looks at her.

"You know, faith, hope, charity—the greatest of these is charity. Meaning love."

L looks at Jason, who's back. Ivy puts out her hand and takes his (as a mother-aged woman can, she tells herself), to tell him these clothes are really, really good.

"Yeah, they were meant to be Faith, Hope, Charity," he agrees, oblivious in his obsession. "But I kept fiddling with them, so Faith is like, Despair, right? And so is Desire. They're kind of twins, kind of." He's right, Savaya and Orion look more like twins than she and Fern do: same height, stance, same gall.

"You know," she says, "these clothes are *beautiful*—but they're

charming too, and funny and I guess horrifying—I haven't seen anything else like them."

Jason makes a pleased triangle mouth and ducks his head, trying to
meet her eyes.

"I really mean it!" Ivy says, hearing herself a little over-earnest. "You
have to go on with this. They're—well, I wish you would make me something. I'll commission you."

Leave it there, nod and drift. Don't freak him out. And who's she to
say what's good, what will succeed, anyway? Fashion is hard.

She's lost sight of Hugh. Maybe he went into the garden for relief? She
makes her way out the French doors at the back, to the river-wall. The
garden is full too. A fire in the copper grill, people standing around it or
sitting and smoking along the stone wall. How many? More than when
they arrived, already. Maybe it's going to be one of those Facebook-
announced, police-attending, giant-crowd teenage disasters.

13. IF HUGH CAN'T STAND THE HEAT, GET OUT OF THE KITCHEN

In the kitchen, Hugh finds a beer in Ann's fridge and slips into its shadow, by the door to the back stairs. Almost invisible, he leans there, picturing Lise Largely's offer sitting on his desk. Maybe he should take it. Who knows how much Mimi has left after all these months of bills and care, or how much she's left to him; or how much she had to start with. She has never shown him her will, he could be in for all or nothing. He can't bear to think about inheritance when she lies there imminent, at the dark gate.

Lise, anyway—he hates her most because of the anagram, because she'll change his Argylle Gallery into the Allergy Gallery as if it was a joke, as if it wasn't . . . his *destiny* or something, to run the gallery. She'll one-up him, because Largely. A stupid name. He puts her aside, listens instead to the prattle of the young who have no mortgage, no debt yet.

Orion, clean-lined in that violent black slash of a suit, is laying down the law to a small, quick-eyed girl Hugh doesn't know: "Everyone confesses their old crushes at a party."

Savaya says, "They do to you, because everybody in the world has had a crush on you."

"And couples start disappearing, or fight and make up too much."

"Good thing we don't know any couples," says a lithe young man, who seems to be called Sheridan Tooley. Another slim boy, wearing a frothy black skirt, long black gloves, and quite a lot of eyeliner, shoves Sheridan with his sharp skirted hip. Perhaps they are a couple.

Savaya laughs. "Remember that girl who got drunk and made out with the guy and then she's crying, crying, *I totally made out with Quintin—I shouldn't have!* But people who are drinking a lot for the first time always cry." She's about to cry herself, crystals hovering in those bluebell eyes. "Nevaeh and me at Jerrod's party, in grade nine, we cried all night about how much we loved each other."

Orion shouts, "Man! Jerrod *Schmidt*, the person I most wanted to fight *ever*, he has tricks, like he'll pull out this big ring of keys, describe them to a girl, what each one opens. He plays guitar so people have to *compliment* him. When he's taking a photo, the jerkoff gets out a *reflector*."

Hugh wonders what they're drinking; if he ought to shut this thing down. If he could.

Savaya says, "I like when two guys meet, and one knows he's cooler than the other guy, but he just loves loves loves the dorkier one. Like you, when was that, Hallowe'en last year? Yelling at fucking Charles Elton, man—"

Orion cuts in, "I said 'You should a receive a blow job every day'—"

A general chorus: "*Because you are a handsome Scandinavian man.*"

"Yeah, that was a bit mean," Savaya says.

"I never talk to the guy now. I can't stand to be around him."

Jason comes into the kitchen and Orion calls him Boy, which must be mocking Burton's name for Newell, and Jason says, "*Design* Boy, please." Good to see Jason cocky. And he made that chiton-thing that L's wearing—straight from Schiavone's "Marriage of Cupid and Psyche." Hugh wonders if Jason meant to reference it, or if it is just art coming out in the new age, a pimple on a fresh cheek. The bodice not quite so revealing, mind you. Mind Hugh.

Orion pushes Jason's shoulder. "Feste-Boy, Fester."

"Jealous of my prowess in cold reading, Boy?" He and Orion move into a mock-fight, karate moves, clowning in the kitchen archway.

Mikayla tells Savaya she *loves* Orion. Her quick eyes have gone round and silly.

"Yeah, he likes men," Savaya says kindly.

"But how much, though?"

Savaya laughs and tells Mikayla to drink one glass of water for every glass of punch.

The young, looking after each other. Hugh moves to the back door, invisible as age has made him. Around the lintel, in Ann's handwriting:

No one knows me or loves me completely. I have only myself.
Simone de Beauvoir

(L)

The upstairs hall is littered with people, sitting and standing. L knows none of them. A bunch of people seem to have come out from Trent—as if they didn't have their own parties to go to. Nobody's broken into Ivy's room. There's a lineup at the bathroom door. L goes into Ann's room, where people have been piling coats on the bed, and finds the door that looks like a closet but is really a little washroom. She locks the door and washes her hands and face. She coaxes her eyebrows back into shape and stands staring at her own face, at whether or not. What a person should do. She's had too much to drink. As bad as her mom.

She turns off the light before she unlocks the door. The room light is off too, but she can see people writhing on the bed, on the pile of coats. Yuck, poor taste. Who even is that? Not Savaya. L edges out along the wall, making less noise than the people are making, huffling and moaning. Disgusting, except. Except weird: not pornographic, but suggesting to the primitive lizard mind that it undertake similar action. Except.

Jason is in the hall, organizing the bathroom lineup and tacking a sign on the door: FIVE MINUTES, TOPS / BE CIVILIZED.

Orion watches, applauding. He sees L at the back stair door and comes over. Under the elegant élan, he looks sad, she thinks. Maybe whatever was going on with him and Newell is not going on anymore. Too many people's hearts get trompled on.

Orion shuts the door behind them and says, in the quieter darkness of the stairwell, "Too many people." L agrees. "Too many people are stupid," he says. Halfway down the stairs, at the turn, he says, "Don't open the bottom door yet, let's take a break."

She sits on the wedge-shaped corner stair. "Good plan. It's too— Everybody is too there there. Too here here."

He sits above her. "Everyone is so nice," he says. The saddest voice she's ever heard from him. "And so fucking stupid."

And so familiar, that heart-sunken understanding of falseness and stupidity. "I know, it's like there's a fiction, like, an agreement, that everyone is equal. Everyone is nice, basically, if you understand them— everyone is decent and they just had, like, a rough time, or were abused, or something went bad in their childhood—they'd be just as smart as you, or as good at stuff, except they had this rough time. But that's not true, and everybody knows it. We're different, and some people are just plain—some people are—"

Orion laughs. "Can't even say it, can you? Programmed! Some people are *better than others*. More talented, more beautiful, smarter, more worth loving. Don't say that outside this staircase though."

L hugs herself, since she can't hug anybody better. "The terrible part is, the thing about equality, that everybody knows is a lie—it takes away from the *true* part—that everyone is a human being, a soul, and deserves to be—kinded. Not 'deserves to be loved' because some people don't really seem to deserve that, like Jason's dad, who's an asshole. Or my own dad—not that he doesn't deserve to be loved, but the way he talks to my mom blows the top of my head off. Where do people get the idea it's okay to be *angry*? It's not okay to be angry all the time with the people who love you or depend on you."

Orion never talks about his dad. "My mom doesn't get angry, she cries. I respect anger."

"You don't get angry. You're too smart."

"I might."

"I've never seen you mad. Is that a gay thing?"

He gives a snort. "Have you met Burton? He's on a permanent boil. A gayboil, that's what he is, a giant pus-filled pimple, always about to explode."

Someone at the bottom opens the door and a string of noisy people climb up and over them. The seal on the decompression chamber is broken. They emerge into the dark reaches of the kitchen—three times as many people, ten times the noise.

Ivy finds Hugh, lost in the shadows beside the back door. A stream of kids passing, ignoring him. But she spots him—the shape of his head now printed on her mind's eye.

Hugh looks very tired. Should she drag him home through cold windy streets, or put him straight to bed in her room here? He looks terrible, from this distance. She slides between large young people packed like olives in a jar. Hugh is lost in thought, quiet in the uproar.

"Hi," she says, calling him back from far away. She can just tuck in beside him in the narrow alcove. "Did this little space hold shelves or a phone stand or something?"

"I think so—it was twenty-five years ago that I lived here."

"Crazy-emptying Ann! Does she know about this little party?"

"I doubt it. It's not the sort of thing they do."

They're half-shouting at each other. Hugh points with a jerk of his shoulder at the back stairs. "Care to go up? I haven't been up those stairs for a long time."

They dodge out of the alcove and up the first flight. Hugh shuts the door behind them and the sudden relief of peace is astonishing.

"Oh, let's just stay here for a while." Ivy pulls Hugh down beside her on the wedge-shaped stair and puts an arm around him. With the other hand she touches his closed eyelids, using her cool fingers to soothe his tired face.

"Lise Largely has put in a decent offer for the gallery," Hugh says. He looks at Ivy in the faint light draining in from the cracks in the doors. "Should I even fight her?"

Even last night she thought he shouldn't lose it; here, in the shuffled-off old house he lost, it seems to Ivy that the gallery is his home, his true place.

"You should fight. I think you should."

The party has lost its zing, and it's only midnight. Parties are fucked that way. You're on top of the world—then without missing a beat, without taking a drink, or not taking one, suddenly it's flat.

Jason comes down the back stairs to the kitchen, wringing his hands in a towel. "I hate parties," he says. "I had to put my finger through the puke in the bathroom sink to get the drain to unplug—" He picks up, opens, and drinks a hard lemonade in one gulp.

In the archway, Savaya is taking on Sheridan Tooley. What is he, in those gold shorts, the body builder from *Rocky Horror*? Every word that comes out of the guy's mouth is a lie. An advantage in the working world. Savaya is flattering him, mocking him. She says, with the bright flicker in her eye that makes Orion love her and distrust her, "Wow, I can see almost your whole penis through those spandex shorts."

Sheridan is semi-drunk. "Do you want to see all of it?"

As if thrilled, Savaya says, "Duh, yeah!" And he pulls it out.

Time to go. Orion hooks Jason and L by the elbows and propels them through the arch, into the living room. The flood of bodies has mostly drifted out the French doors. People are standing in clumps in the darkness, the music has hit a soft spot, it's getting late. Midnight.

There's banging on the front door. Jason jumps, and they all do, thinking it's the police. The door swings inward and a large shape looms in from the darkness. Newell.

How the heart leaps up, no matter what, how it quickens —even if . . .

Not the best but not the worst either, to see the love object. He's laden with stuff, a folding chair and a basket, a suitcase, a shabby overcoat, looks like he picked it up at the Mennonite Clothes Closet. Ragged T-shirt shows off his arms and shows, too, how stupid ol' Burton was to cast Savaya as Stanley Kowalski, good as she was, because Newell would have been even more—he makes your legs shake, he's so—

What's that around his neck? A rope?

At least he's on his own.

But no, he's not. Burton sweeps in the door, in a pair of loud-checked yellow Rupert Bear pants and the red generalissimo jacket from the wardrobe room. In a psycho-bullhorn voice that stops the ordinary racket, he shouts, "*I am Pozzo!*" Nobody dares to speak. Even people who are not in the master class know about him. "*Pozzo!*" (A pause.)

From the fireplace, where she is tracking Jason's mother's quotes, Ivy raises her beer to them and says, "Bozzo? *Bozzo* . . ."

Newell tugs at his neck, loosening the leash like he's tired of playing Burton's game. "Hard to find a drink in this dark wood."

Orion slips into the kitchen, snags a couple of beer. He takes one to Newell, and one to Burton, who's coiling up that rope.

"Ah, Ganymede," Burton says, accepting the bottle as his due.

Burton never looks him in the face anymore, just gazes around him. Orion takes the other beer to Newell. Who does not look at him properly either, so Orion lowers his own eyes. Burton coils the leash, pulling it tauter and tauter. It's not a leash, it's a noose.

Orion doesn't like it. He goes to the French doors, where Jason and L are shoring up the door posts, one in, one out in the garden. Sensible positioning for vigilance.

"What the fuck with the noose?" he asks L quietly.

"They're those guys, you know? From the middle of *Waiting for Godot*." L has seen a ton more plays than he has. His mother made him waste too much time on dance. "Master/slave—Pozzo's the boss, and Newell is the silent one. Pozzo drags him around, makes him carry stuff. He doesn't speak except for one long rant at the end of act one."

"What about?"

"I don't know. Freedom?"

"Burton looks like Pink, dressed like that," Jason says.

Savaya has come out of the dark garden. She turns around, gold dress slithering along her sides and legs. "I'm thinking of fucking Pink," she tells them in a trickling whisper.

"Ergo, you haven't yet, *ergo* he is a slimebucket but not a molester nor open to prosecution," Orion says. "Do not do that stupid thing."

"So I just dangle him along? I thought that was bad."

"Not with him," L says.

Savaya pouts. "I would definitely pass Math, though," she says.

She does not know about love, Orion thinks. Not a single fucking single fucking thing.

(L)

L roams the increasing chaos. Down by the riverbank the tech guys are drinking Stuntman shots around the firepit: snort salt, drink tequila, squeeze the lime in your eye. L doesn't have too much to do with them. She's supposed to work on the set—except now there won't even be a performance. Burton gave that to Ivy, like a present. He's stupid and cruel, then he's all-knowing and sensitive. You never know which will pop out.

Sheridan Tooley's sister Cameron, third-year Environmental at Trent, turns up as an organ-grinder with a stuffed monkey, her priceless childhood treasure. Sheridan and his boyfriend kidnap it; it's got long Velcro arms, and they keep playing literal monkey in the middle with her. Then Sheridan sticks the monkey's long hands into his pants, which is rude; then the boyfriend in the long gloves puts the monkey in the oven. That's a tasteless joke.

Some witch in the Trent bunch has a magic wand showering glitter— the glitter is getting in everybody's eyes, and in the splits between the floor boards. That's what finally takes down Sheridan: he gets a grain of glitter in his eye and makes a big deal of it, *take me to the hospital,* etc., and his sister, who still has tears in her own eyes from the fun they made of her monkey, carts him off. The boyfriend, whose name turns out to be Leveret, goes too.

Mikayla has had way too much to drink—who saw that one coming. She moans to L about alcohol poisoning, leaning on one of the folding tables in the kitchen with her (Nevaeh's, really) breast-eyelashes drooping. "That isn't it," Savaya says, coming in from the river. "When you get cold and blue, that's when it's bad." But Mikayla looks pretty bad.

And how long is Jason's mom going to stay out? L finds herself shivering too. She gives Savaya a waggling eye, and Savaya kindly takes the hint. "Hey, Mikayla," she says. "Come on outside. There's a fire going, the fresh air will do you good. You can sit on the wall, then if you have to puke you can do it in the river."

Jason comes up as they go. "Maybe I should get that dress off her."

"When's your mom going to get home?"

He shrugs. "Ideally, Monday or Tuesday."

Oh good, here comes more Trent people, more beer, more noise.

Jason takes L's hand and pulls her to the kitchen stairs. He pushes her up in front of him and closes the door behind them. The dark comes down, the noise recedes, it's so peaceful.

L sits, breaths out a long straggling sigh. She fishes the phone out of her bra and hits the button. "Let's go old school. See who's Facebooking the party." Jason puts out a hand to fix the neckline of her chiton. His fingers give her shivers everywhere. I ought to be living my life, doing my work, she thinks, while her fingers work the phone. Instead I'm stuck being seventeen, stuck here, unable to figure out what, how, who.

"Ha!" he says, looking at her screen.

"What?"

"Look, Sheridan put '*in a relationship* with Leveret.' Whoever that is."

"The glove guy. Good for Sheridan, if obviously a little late."

"You should put that we are."

L laughs. "We are what, '*it's complicated*'?"

Jason has whipped out his own phone and is changing his status as she watches. "Put '*relationship*,' we'll shock people—then we can get divorced or you can be a widow."

"Don't!" She doesn't like that. But it is funny. "It's not even April Fool's."

"We can have April Fool's whenever we like—are we slaves to the mere calendar?"

The phone pings, that was fast. Six likes. Seven. Nine. A comment from Nevaeh, who must be bored out of her mind at the hospital. > oh my god you guys of course you are!

Jason laughs at that. "Told you so."

Another ping: from Savaya, out at the river. > it's like, when are they going to realize?

Nevaeh: > inorite! like like like!

Fifteen likes. Twenty-seven. Forty. They look at each other in the almost-darkness, laughter bubbling up in both of them, springing, springing up. On L's post, a comment from Savaya appears:

> my mom knew months ago.

Nevaeh: > yr mom always has the widsom.

Two a.m. The living room has been abandoned for the fire-pit in the garden, kids letting their smoke wind into the firesmoke and the breeze coming off the river. Ivy plugs her own iPod into the machine and finds some languid Madeleine Peyroux, thinking it might be time to get this wound down . . . *no one but Hugh* . . . And now more ringing at the front door.

She goes, but Newell is closer. Stretching to the end of his rope, he opens the door wide and tells the dark-clad thugs, "These aren't the droids you're looking for." The big shapes look at him for a minute, the arms in the T-shirt, the noose around his neck, and then turn and drift away.

"The tears of the world are a constant quantity," Burton says, tipping his drink. "For each one who begins to weep, somewhere else another stops. The same is true of the laugh."

Jason and L come down the front stairs, laughing together, heads bent over their phones. Hugh heads over and talks into L's ear, trying to make himself clear over the music. One hand goes to his temple, an unconscious gesture. His head, hurting again. He should be in bed.

Ivy goes over to eavesdrop: Hugh is asking L to get him a couple of Della's new boat pictures to frame for Saturday. "I'll bring them over in the morning," L says. "I'm not at the master class tomorrow. I could help you with dinner."

Jason raises his eyebrows to Ivy, wondering whether he will be needed at the class.

"No idea," she says. "Ask the big fella."

But Burton, bored by the quieter music, is disappearing into the kitchen, trailing Newell's rope behind him.

Newell, gagging a little, reaches out a hand to control the pull. Burton resists the tug and hauls on the rope, so Newell needs both hands to protect his neck, and Hugh starts after them as if he's going to tear that rope off Newell single-handed, saying, "Careful!"

That makes Burton change tack and charge back, shouting again: "*Turn him away? Such an old and faithful servant!*"

The room falls still, kids called to startled attention. Something real happening here?

Ivy pulls on Hugh's arm. "He's spouting Beckett," she says. "He's just having fun with you." She begs him, silently, not to lose his temper— "No punching," she mouths, trying to make him laugh, to take some of the strain out of his face.

At the end of his rope, Burton's face has gone livid with booze or rage, hard to tell. Newell raises his arms, surrendering to the noose, to the quarrel, mouthing *quaquaquaqua*.

"What? What is he saying?" Hugh asks.

Burton's voice is rough, drenched in maudlin tears, lost in some old production. "Beauty, grace, truth of the first water, I knew it was all beyond me."

"Stop," Newell says.

Finally, the note in his voice checks Burton, who skips ahead in the script and subsides into pitiful mumbling, "The way he goes on, you've no idea, it's terrible."

The front door opens, and in comes Ann.

Ivy's insides jump so hard she thinks she'll laugh, or die. Standing in the jumbled mass of shoes littering her formerly empty doorway, Ann takes in Hugh and Newell and Burton, their knot of conflict. The iron skeleton of the coffee table. The vanished exhibits, dresses, gloves.

The photographer crowds up behind her, camera slung at the ready. Poser.

"My—" Ann says. "What is this?"

Jason does a brave thing. He detaches himself from L, and says "Hey, Mom. I'm having the class party. Um, a few things got broken."

Ann turns stiffly to face him, like a dressmaker's dummy on a swivel.

At that heightened moment, Orion leaps in from the garden. "Call 911," he says—loud, laughing—"Pumpkin on fire!"

Everyone makes for the French doors in a mass.

Out there beside the small fire pit, a column of flame is shooting into the night sky. One of the jack-o'lanterns, Ivy sees, as her vision adjusts to make out the lumpy shadow beneath the brilliant fire. "Kerosene," Orion says. "One of the tech guys did a torch effect, but it worked better than he—he burned his eyebrows off, and they can't get the fire to go out—"

Everyone would be laughing, except there's a shriek, a real shriek, and one of the girls, Mikayla, runs across the grass to the river, her breasts blinking at the crowd and her feathered tail on fire, flaming feathers shooting out behind her as she runs, tail switching to and fro. Three or four of them run to help her, including Stewart . . . no, he's just taking pictures—

And into the river she goes. Ker-*splash*.

"Hugh?" Ivy takes his arm. "I think we ought to go to bed."

Newell climbing up from the bottom; Orion coming down, smoke and kerosene washed off his hands. "Can't cross on the stairs," Newell says. "Ruth would never forgive us."

Orion stands, heart thumping in his chest. Leaping.

"I slipped my leash," Newell says. His eyes are quiet, his spirit shining out of them in a steady light.

Orion laughs, just as quiet. To know somebody loves you, to see delight in his eyes. Orion shines back. He's been ignoring, suppressing this glorious thing—it washes through him, a painful/exquisite tide of blood. "I—" he says, then nothing more. Newell's hands come up and his own catch them—in the darkness of the stairwell it is enough to stand hand-clasping. Orion's mind/soul/heart is racing, he is a giant again.

Wait. Something is still wrong. They separate.

"Listen, don't be so— Listen," Newell says. "You have to know that Burton will call, and I'll go to him." He looks away, down and to the left. The direction of shame.

Orion's hand goes out, but he sees the blankness in Newell's eyes, and the hand cannot reach him. "Why?" Orion asks. No answer. "Why?" he asks again.

Newell's voice is like water. Serious, honest, pure. "From duty, and love, from long association. I can't explain it to you, I don't— I don't want *you* to feel this way. But I do. I float, I fly, but Burton is the rope. The anchor."

Orion stands there, a stair above Newell, forced into looking down on him, not choosing to. "You are so wrong, so wrong to do this."

"I can't—" To see the great Newell inarticulate, that is weird and painful. He holds the stair-rail instead of Orion's arm. "I know it's not enough. I can't make it whole."

Orion's chest is cracking. He didn't know this pain would be so physical. He feels elevated, looking down on Newell's face, still loving him. But seeing that the one he loves is no king after all. The pain in his chest is fierce.

His eyes are filling, that won't do. Can't cry at this shit, that is *not allowed*. He turns as if he will climb slowly out of this, but his feet betray him and he stumbles and falls down the odd-shaped stairs, past Newell, slipping and turning, and he opens the door and—flees.

Hugh and Ivy carry cans and bottles to the kitchen where Burton is wash-ing glasses, red jacket hung on the doorknob, up to his elbows in soapy water. Easy to clean up empty rooms, turns out—Hugh begins to see method in Ann's madness. It's late, he's tired.

In the lull, a rush: Orion bolts out the back stairs door, a knife in flight.

An instant later Newell emerges, looking like hell.

Orion halts at the back door, turns and tells the room, "I'll go check the—the riverbank, make sure the fire, the others—" A brave stand, a fair recovery of dignity. He smiles, almost an honest smile, and almost-bows to Burton—of all people—before he goes.

You can't blinker yourself forever, bury your head up your own ass. Hugh can't. Burton isn't a danger to the fledgling Orion. Newell is. Your dear friend, your brother.

Burton offers Newell the rope. Newell puts the noose around his neck and starts to dry the dishes.

Ivy leads Hugh out of the kitchen and up the stairs, taking him to bed. Why didn't she take him earlier? His head hurts. The right side pounds and sings, causing a kind of blindness. The living room is empty, empty again; crazy. The writing on the walls makes no sense, he can't get his eyes to focus on it.

Then what is Newell doing to Burton—how can that be justified? By rights, should Hugh want Orion and Newell to get together? His head hurts. No solution. Sleep will be surcease.

Ivy is fiddling with the locked door, doing something, and after a blank space he is in the dark familiar bedroom, crawling in beside her, and asleep.

(L)

Not even 3 a.m. and the garden is empty. The fire truck arriving cleared off the frayed ends of the crowd. Orion ran past L and Jason, said he was going for eggs to make his famous after-party scrambles, but he was crying. So probably lying about the eggs.

Jason's mom is not mad; she's relieved that for once he has a social life. Even about the broken table; she wanted better glass anyway. She asks about Mimi's clothes, and Jason tells her they're locked safely in Ivy's room—then she says she has to get some sleep because TV lady Charlaine is arriving in the morning and Jason says he'll get up and help, which placates her completely. Or else she's distracted by Photog Guy, who is hepped on himself for both getting good pics and putting out the fire with the lid of the pumpkin, he's all whoop-de-doo I'm the man etc. Jason's mom is finding that pretty charming.

The photographer turns out to be called Stewart, which for some reason makes Jason and L laugh so hard, so they pretend to be clearing up bottles and cans, blue recycling bags carried high to hide the hysterical giggling. They fill one bag each, leave them propped up in the kitchen, and drift off up the back stairs.

Taking off her chiton, L hands it to Jason so he can fold it properly. She pulls on one of his T-shirts, stacked by colour and fiber content on his orderly closet shelves.

The thing is, autonomy. She's unwilling to give up her personhood, her autonomy to another person, Nevaeh or anyone. Orion might be worth giving it up for, she can see that, or Newell—there, you see, that's how women (and men) get themselves into trouble. Better to be with Jason who is an extension of herself than to be with the Other who will rule her. But some people choose differently.

He turns off the light, and they get into his big bed, as they have done since the earliest time she can remember.

In the darkness, Jason says, "You know that word *charity* means love, right?"

That makes her heart stop beating, makes her throat unable to take in, to breathe. Then sweet air comes in flooding again.

"Sometimes I want you to touch me," she says.

Oh, the humiliation, if he says no.

(DELLA)

everyone else does   I might   might I   one might Mighton
Ken isn't/won't be home   Elle   isn't/won't be   nothing to go home for
Mighton needs help carrying   sword and shield   3 a.m.
he can drive   he hardly drank   unlike me   mandarin orange door
    Come in, come see what damage Lise has wreaked . . .
copper pots hangledangle from a grid over the island
Mighton's helmet clangs a sauté pan
doesn't want to take it off, that's funny—he likes being king
    Come see—she bought a giant bed—California King, it's called.
Mighton's gazelock   once upon a time
comes close looses his shield   lies his sword   in the centre of the bed
                                                     Lancelot, Arthur

what would it matter to fall into bed again
fall on the sword with my old Mighton   old flame
kind old kindled king kindling
nice new bathroom no barriers   no shower door   nothing but glass
Mighton brushing his teeth
vain mirror-admiring Mighton   both of us
being nothingness   because there is   nothing between us
inconceivable to touch to kiss
anything, nothing there is   nothing between us
                                          but Ken and Jenny
                                        those two together

if my beloved has left me
I will not be the one deceived
not the one the joke is done to
it's *better to be in the right*, my dad said   clothes like leaves
who spent forty years under the yoke of   fall in a heap
being in the right   fall in

Hugh wakes, washed in cool light. Clouds blown away, the floating moon flows through uncurtained windows. Around the room, Mimi stands in various familiar poses. Her backless cocktail dress, glinting redoubling sequins laid over paisley, dazzling as his eyes sweep. The Afghani wedding dress, tiny mirrors making dabs of silver light. The strapless sheath she wore to the American Embassy ball with Trudeau. Hugh zipped it up for her, she bent and kissed you.

The room is full of Mimi, full of her. Her perfume, Joy. The indefinable other smell that is just her, her breath and body. Like her dreams, when she dreamed the house full of people and talked to them all night, only all of these are her.

Hugh sits up. Stares around the room, at each separate form and shape.

Not a dream. It's real, it is her, it is—these are her clothes.

He slides out of bed. Ivy *purrrps* her lips, a baby's noise, but does not move.

He pulls on his clothes. He has to go. Why has he been anywhere but her room, these last few weeks—he can't remember. No, it's Ivy who can't remember. He knows why.

He does not want her to die. He wants her not to die, not ever, never to be gone, never to leave him. All his anger was just clouds, only love left now. He touches the sequins, the mirrored sleeve, the bow at the black sheath's breast. He goes.

(ORION)

Behind the glossy hedge at the big grey condo building, in the shelter of the shadows there, Orion waits. The lights go on, room to room. The men walk through, they move from one room to another, first one and then the other. They pause, drink, one laughs and shakes his head. They speak to each other. He can't hear words. They move back into the darker room.

He turns away, drops down the grey stairs, gets back on his bike and rides away again into the maze of streets.

That lead him once again around, around, around.

To pause without hope by the stairs again.

But Newell comes out of the stairwell, onto the road. "Beauty, grace, truth of the first water . . ." That's from something, not *Twelfth Night*. Godforsaken *Godot* probably.

He walks ahead, down to the river path and in under the overhanging branches. "Intellect is subordinate to the body," he says, waiting for Orion to dismount. And then, "I don't know what to do with you."

Orion feels his mouth breaking into a smile, too big. Too wide open. He begs himself: hold back! But how can he, with the only one?

The noose is no longer around Newell's neck, but Orion's fingers feel it still there, feel the welt it left under the black cord. He crows, sadly.

"That's how it is on this bitch of an earth," Newell says.

SATURDAY

❧

Hugh can't take it with Hugh

Three poisons are the root cause of
dukkha: *ignorance (misunderstanding*
the nature of reality, bewilderment),
attachment to pleasurable experiences,
and aversion (the fear of getting what we
don't want, or not getting what we do want)

entry on Buddhism,
WIKIPEDIA

I. SHE KNOWS HUGH

Empty streets, rain-cleaned, shimmering in half-dark. Not darkest before the dawn, but beginning to fade from black to grey.

Crossing Water Street, Hugh sees Gerald in the distance. Slump-backed, clumsy or drunk, tramping the night streets. A ghost with two ghosts trailing behind him. Hugh does not raise a hand to catch his down-trained eye. Gerald's wife, his son—impossible to take in those deaths.

People die on you. Hard as it is to believe. They are there, and then not there, never to be there again. What it means to be alive: you will be dead.

She's not dead. Her face turns as he enters the room. She is glad to see him, her face is warm and loving. She remembers, she knows Hugh. Through every slight or fight, every abandonment or embrace, she knows Hugh best.

She whispers. Lean close.

"Hugh. You waited so long. I'm always awake, you know."

Her eyes are her eyes, for a moment. Her self.

It won't last, though. They're already closing. She is on her last last legs, her face on its last face. Thinned cheeks, high forehead, hair still spilling but thinning, thinned, lessened as is everything about her. A shell of herself. But still herself, still the woman of the world to him. Always, whatever consolation and comfort others give him. Ruth kept him safe, Della kept him sane, Ivy is his great joy now, but Mimi is the root of his life. Bewilder, betray, frighten him as she may.

When she is dead the root will be torn out, and how will he survive? He's in so much pain already he can hardly stand.

He sits, he sinks at her side. This is his childhood's death, the entry into an empty world. Loyalty to Ivy rises up and scolds him, but it's no use. He loves Mimi best of anything in the world and cannot live through this, this, this great stabbing pain.

(DELLA)

waking from a terrible dream   Ken bleeding
tangled in sheets, strangled   Mighton bleeding   the cremation
in the dream waking waking   it isn't true   no that was a dream
bare skin sheets eyes unglue   empty bed   Mighton's bed
oh consciousness returning   what did I do?   oh memory
                    (it's absurd he isn't never could be not with Jenny
                         not like this if he fell in sudden flaming love but
                         not like this not this   not with Jenny it's absurd)
Mighton! talk talk how he not a word on why I was in his house his bed
drunk and alone not about Ken or me   I'd rather be lonely by myself
nothing between us but old rue   and a toy sword

it's all right   no-one will ever know   he'll never tell
coward me too   coward   out before he wakes   wherever he is
clothes in the bathroom?   close the door   no clothes
bare body in the mirror   turn away!   bare body on the wall
                                 that old painting   me/Ann/Newell
                                 tied in a knot
the doorbell   *key in lock*   *clatter-bang bang-slam*
voice calling

        Good morning! Bright and early, hope I'm not waking you!

Ruth cleaning Mighton's house   no lock on the door no towel no clothes
she always starts with the bathroom   no shower curtain
tin helmet by the sink   nowhere to
helmet on   it hurts my head   into the shower

        Oops! Somebody in here? No rush!
        I'll do the kitchen first.

                                                            water run
                                                            run

(ORION)

Light filters into the basement through last summer's raspberry canes and grass that nobody cut; nobody as in it should have been him. His mother out there in too-short shorts struggling with the eco-friendly blade mower, unsharpened, so noble and so stupid. Who knows where she ended up last night, she wasn't home when he got in at four.

Unsleeping, unslept, Orion sits at the computer crying over the flash mob symphony at Sabadell, *Ode to Joy*, as it builds—fuck he should have kept on with violin, except that he was never going to be good enough, not good enough, not like these people who live and die for their violins, or their oboe, the beautiful woman playing the oboe. People making things beautiful, working together to make art together, to make that one afternoon . . .

He blows his nose again and waits for his eyes to calm down, waits for something to happen.

No text.

No text ever anymore?

The mystery of Burton's value. *Long association.*

In the dark mirror of the computer screen Orion can see himself saying that to some future flashing, ardent boy, about Newell. A vision. He didn't mind being a secret before. But this is sad, to be rejected out loud *and* in secret. He is so fucked. Newell is. Burton is.

Orion is. Stuck, fuck, this so fucking sucks.

(What is he going to do with this cracked and useless heart? Make art?)

(L)

Jason's legs lie empty on the floor. One eye open, she sees them: his pants on one side of her, and (without looking, she knows) his body on her other side. Caught between pants and person.

So what *was that,* last night?

Her phone brrrings.

"L, too early, sorry, but I wanted to catch you—" It's Hugh.

"I remember, boats. I'll bring them."

"Okay, no rush." But there is rush in his voice, because today's the day of the dinner and he likes everything to be perfect.

"All I want to know is, cake? Will there be cake?"

"You have a sweet tooth."

"My dad too. And Jason has a whole sweet head." Jason's arm flails up and whacks her, not in an angry way, in a *yes cake* way.

"Cake first," Hugh says. "Cake second. All cake, in fact."

"Their twenty-what-th?" she says.

"Thirtieth, according to my calculations. And I believe that *is* the Cake Anniversary."

"Happy times."

She clicks off. Jason's arm descends around her, wire and springs, and pulls her back into him while she looks at the bedside table and the clock and the phone in her hand that she is setting carefully on the edge of the bedside table—Jason's new bossiness: how is that going to work? But weirdly she likes him pulling her in and she likes the new crescent shape they make, their bodies aligned and curved together, the springing smooth silk of his et cetera but they have to she has to they ought to go get those boats and it's 9:20 already.

9:40 whoo now they *really* have to go.

Downstairs, coming back to life in the blue light of morning, the living room is strange. Pale, foggy blue with hints of grey. The kitchen gets all the sun in the morning. Ann is tying a garbage bag. Stewart sweeps the floor. He looks a lot younger this morning, still in that stupid black outfit, a zit or two burning bright pink on his pallid forehead.

Stewart empties his dustpan into the last of Ann's garbage bags. He checks his giant technophone. "Right, so Charlaine will be here *stat*," he says.

Pretty gay for someone who stayed the night. A puzzle: did he sleep with Ann? What happened to the chairs?

Jason runs down behind L and jumps the last four stairs, mid-text. "Orion's here. We'll run you over to get the boats and then to Hugh's. I'm going to the class in case they need me."

Seems he liked being Feste after all. Oh great.

At L's house it takes some nerve to go in the back door. Because a) What if her dad is down there? And b) her mom. Nobody there though, the house dead and empty.

Where is everybody?

She picks the best six boats, at least the ones she likes best. Stacks them with paper between.

And then gathers more nerve, to run down the basement stairs. Because it always takes nerve to go down to look at it, to see if it is shit, as so often suspected. The *Republic* that has been her home for so long, two years, three, making and making and thinking, always somewhat thinking about it in the turning gyre of the back of her spacious mind.

And now now will Jason occupy that space—? That can't be right. A person still has to do her work.

He has work, she has work, they can both work?

Look at her parents, though.

She will have to go see Nevaeh. Does a person have to decide permanently, one way or the other? Is the decision made by glands, or growing, or by that which we know as love?

2. WHISTLE WHILE HUGH WORKS

The hall, the stairs; so many stairs in this life. Unfixable. But if, if you could find the force. Okay, some things are unfixable, but—because it is so short, we are here so briefly!—there must be some way to fix, say, Newell's life with the toad Burton, or Della's pain, or at least get L some recognition. Hugh's heart lightens for no reason, rounding the last corner to his apartment, up to the porch, in, home.

The place smells different—something's out of whack. Burnt toast, the smell of having a stroke. Hugh climbs the stairs, slow as his head thumps, wondering who he'll find.

Ken, asleep on the couch, toast-crumbed plate on the floor beside him. Everybody gets to sleep but Hugh. He walks over and stands looking down, wondering what to do. "Everyone knows where you hide your key," Ken says, muffled by couch cushions. "It's not break and enter if I use your key."

"Not calling the police, yet," Hugh says. He picks up the toast plate, the milk glass.

"Thanks for that." Ken moves the cushion. Paper crinkles. He shifts, and pulls a small drawing from under his arm. L's work? He swings his feet down, gropes under the couch—another under there. Pieces from the *Republic*.

Having plundered it without permission himself, Hugh can hardly take him to task.

Ken sees Hugh looking at the drawings: one a small sketchy self-portrait, the other Ken himself. "Do you think she's good?" he asks. Hugh nods. "I didn't see it before. I thought she should do law. This walk-through thing, it's a surprise." Ken rubs his creased, sleep-shadowed face. Strain and unhappiness ironed right in. "Got any coffee?"

"Espresso machine, down in the framing room. Want a cup?"

"For the love of God."

Hugh is unable to gauge exactly what degree of despair Ken is clock-
ing now. "Latte, Americano?" is all he can think to ask. When he comes
back with the coffee, Ken is sitting upright in the blankets, pale and stub-
bled. Unable to meet Hugh's eyes.

Okay. Since it seems there will be a dinner after all, better get cracking. Hugh finds his list. Copper bowl, oven 250. He cracks eggs, saving
the gold yolks in a turquoise bowl.

"I remember the day Dell's mom died," Ken says. Staring into the
mass of untidy half-bare branches overhanging the wooden deck, he
says, "We went down there daily, when things got as bad as they were by
the end. She was torn up. Della."

"I know." Cream of tartar . . . there, behind the vanilla. Salt. Whisk.

"Because she couldn't be sad. She played the piano all day, that half-
size upright in their parlour, not even in tune. All her mom's old music
books, all day."

"Playing helps get rid of pain." Egg whites flick-flick into thickening
mindless foam.

"The thing is, Hugh—you never get rid of your mother."

Has Ken forgotten that Mimi is dying right now? He comes to lean on
the kitchen bar, watching Hugh shake sugar spoon by spoon as the egg-
whites build and stiffen. Strong-arm, concentrated whipping: another
way to shed pain.

Ken says, "You don't know how much you'll miss her."

It feels so lonely when your so-called friends fail to understand anything about you. Makes you wonder if they ever knew you. Knew Hugh.
Hugh who?

"Like I said to Della: she won't ever leave you. In a way." Ken's tight,
dark-shaded eyes are anxious, searching Hugh's face.

"I know," Hugh says. It's okay. Let him search, let him find. "They're
not gone, it's like—a whale listening for another whale across the
ocean—I understand that." He slips a silpat mat onto the half-sheet for
the meringues. "What I don't understand is why you're putting Della
through the wringer like this."

Ken shifts again, moves his hands on the counter—leaving? Not yet.

He pushes away and stands straight. "The trial's coming up, November
third," he says. "The guy is going to take the stand, he's going to say . . .
the things he will say. He's eighty-seven. He's like Della's dad, he's got

that helpless thing. A sweater vest, a *Hang in there!* kitten poster on his classroom door in 1974."

More than Ken has ever said about the case, in the six years he's been working on it. He can't meet Hugh's eyes. He goes to the couch, can't sit; he stands there. "Forty-two plaintiffs over eighteen years. I'll have to talk him through the whole thing. We did a meat chart."

Hugh puts the bowl down. Pay attention, pay attention. "What's a meat chart?"

"This age, and this touch, and this number of occasions . . . a big chart on the wall."

Something looming, a train, or a tree about to fall. On Della, on himself. On Hugh.

"When we have meetings, the client always says a prayer at the beginning."

Hugh remembers that once, Ken was Catholic too. "What do you do?"

"We pray with him, and then we go on."

Hugh wonders if the *we* is Jenny.

"So if it's coming to trial, then it will be over?"

"There are separate actions; some settled, not all. Some of them want, want their day in court. More than the money." Ken's eyelid is twitching. "The trial hasn't done them any good, it hasn't given them closure. One of them—authority issues, tried to go to law school but she couldn't stand being told what to do by male profs, they're all assholes et cetera. She begged me to sign her in as my assistant, take her to the prison infirmary to hear his death rattle. I'm tempted. None of what we do does anything for anyone but the insurance company."

There's a long, quiet space.

"Okay, but I still don't get why you aren't talking to Della."

No answer. Hugh can't leave it at that. "She thinks you're sleeping with Jenny. If you aren't, you have to tell her. If you are, I don't know what to say."

Ken stares at Hugh with panicked intensity, or maybe anger.

Then the door bangs at the bottom of the stairs.

L starts up, singing out, "I got them!"

But Ken shouldn't see the boats—and L can't see Ken, not in this state. Not wasting an instant in thought, Hugh takes Ken's arm and speeds him down the hall. "Bathroom," he says. "Razor in the cabinet, towels, get a clean shirt from my closet." Ken's out of sight by the time L gets to the top of the stairs, blinded anyway by the big cardboard portfolio she's carrying.

Hugh says, "Great, let's take them straight to the framing room." He bundles her back down the stairs. Being young, she doesn't grumble.

She's brought six. "I like this one," she says, fishing among them—the boat/whale.

It's hard to swing back to Della's work, from Ken's.

Hugh pulls another one around, the boat named *Beyond My Ken*. There's Ken in the water, thrashing, or is that the foam of his dive? "Oh good," he says. "This is good."

L spreads the others across the table. Savaya as mariner-figurehead, now with a tiny brass telescope to her eye, finished, very intricate. One with Della's mother painting at the tiller—pale, cherubic babies clinging to the rigging above her. "This is Grampa?" L points to an old man trailing along in the dinghy, looking backward, dangling bare legs in the briny foam. Another: a boat laden with a spilling pile of white and brown eggs, and ha! Kindereggs and Easter eggs and turquoise Araucana eggs.

"But this one," L says, "seemed more cheerful?" It's an ordinary boat, *State of the Union* painted on the side. Della and Ken float naked near the boat, arms wrapped around each other. Clear portraits, they are happy. Is that a shark's shadow in the water, or a dolphin? Never mind. Good piece.

"Okay, I'm glad you found this one," Hugh says. "I was getting worried."

"I know, right?" she says. "I left *The Jenny* on the sideboard."

These are more complicated, more complete, than he'd expected. All the same size, that will make the framing faster.

L picks frame-corners, and they experiment until they're both satisfied: a greyish distressed finish, suggestion of weathered boatboards. Blue-grey linen liner mats, sea-green for *State of the Union*. "I'm happy," L says.

Hugh is too. But the oven is waiting—there's work to do upstairs. Hugh takes the stairs first, checking for Ken as his head lifts over the rail: there he is, cleaned up, presentable. Hugh goes to his egg-white bowl. Okay, the meringue has not deflated.

In the living room Ken puts out an awkward hand, but L walks through that to hug her father. She's a good girl. Meringue mounds gracefully on the Silpat. Hugh hollows yolk-shaped dips with the back of a gravy spoon and slides the pan into the oven. One task down, eighteen to go. . . . "Okay, Ken," he calls. "Help or go. Whichever, be here for dinner at six."

Ken waffles, moves his arms as if conceding an objection at court.

L says, "Put him to work. He did KP in 'Nam . . ."

That makes Ken laugh, a rusty sound. "No, no, I have to go find your—" Tries again. "Got to pack, out at—"

He gives up and goes down the stairs, getting shorter and shorter. L reaches over the banister to pat the top of his head as it disappears. Six more trudging steps, then the back door opening and closing.

L nods to Hugh, her hands wide, helpless.

"Thought he'd never leave," Hugh says. He pulls out his papers: the menu, doodled around the sides like a French restaurant, and eight pages of recipes. "Okay, I've had a lot of stuff going on over the last few weeks. So instead, I thought about dinner."

L comes to the kitchen to look over his shoulder. Foolish, proud of his angular calligraphy, of his cooking, of his cake conceit, he lets her see the front page:

ANNIVERSARY DINNER
TRANSFORMATION ~ TROMPE L'OEIL

aperitif cake
cake salé   mushroom macarons

main cake
sushi cake   seafood crêpe cake
meatloaf petits fours   potato tortilla cake

dessert cake
fried eggs & toast baked potatoes

cake surprise
macaron mushrooms   30-year-old port

He runs down the list, ticking as he goes. "Okay, *cake salé*, that's a French savoury bread with olives, made it last week, thawing now, we'll serve it warm with little fake-beer cocktails. Sushi cake, last thing this afternoon, the seafood filling too; but we'll make the crêpes now. Meatloaf petits fours, ready for warming in the oven—red currant glaze for them, that's easy. Meringue for the fried eggs, in the oven now. Have to make curd for the yolks. Baked potatoes, that will be your job: scoop and shape the ice cream, refreeze, roll in cocoa at the last minute."

"Homemade ice cream?" L asks.

Hugh rolls his eyes. "Okay, look, I've been run off my feet—my *mother*. It's the best bought, they'll never know. Take this, you can start the tortilla cake. Mandoline—be careful."

L takes the recipe, eyes it. "I love potato tortilla. Is it sit-down? Can I do place cards?"

"Perfect. Let's get busy—it's almost nine, and I have to run over to see Mimi at ten."

They get busy.

Freed from the low-ceilinged workshop room because it's Saturday, the master class moves into the theatre. On stage, focused pools of spotlight warm the long table. The students are gathered. Ivy settles into her own name-tagged seat at one end of the table.

The scuffed black-painted stage, dotted with phosphorescent tape for the actors' marks, the ceiling vanishing in blackness high above—this is home, even if it can't be her home anymore. She's on the verge of weeping. Stupid. She sits still and regains control.

Hovering, Jason finds his name and sits across from her. So he's been seconded to the class. At the other end of the table, Orion sits facing Savaya: for the *Blue Bird* brother and sister, Mytyl and Tyltyl? Both subdued, looking no happier than she must herself.

The murmurs die away into the theatre's hush. With a change of the lights, Burton and Newell make their entrance from the wings. Oh, this is no *Blue Bird*.

They're both in black: Newell in a plain leather jacket, Burton in showy black velvet with a Nehru collar. Ivy is amused to see Jason giving it the once-over, and approving. Burton wears a large green scarab ring, jade or aventurine mounted in gold—a beautiful piece Ivy hasn't seen before. His hand moves self-consciously to display it. Must be a new acquisition. He has a sprig of lily of the valley in his buttonhole, and carries a bile-green carnation.

Newell sits at the foot of the long table, beside Ivy.

At the head, with Orion on his ring-heavy right hand, and Savaya on his left, Burton stands to declaim: "Our week of exploration culminates in today's play. Yes, a new play."

Everyone around the table takes this news in character: Sheridan Tooley (still red-eyed from glitter) smirks, Savaya glows, Mikayla (still white-faced from drink) shrinks. Orion and Jason look at the table in front of them. Ivy wishes she'd been so unflappable at that age.

Burton raises his hand, and She-Terry and He-Terry emerge from the wings, bearing a stack of scripts. They split behind Burton and go along the table, delivering scripts to each place, choreographed. The Terrys look a little less drawn than usual. Burton must have calmed their fears. The stacks deplete, until at last a script arrives at Ivy's hand: *The Importance of Being Earnest*. What secret runs under this one? Well, that the boys are gay.

As if hearing her thought, Burton purrs, "The Love that dare not speak its name . . ." He takes the stage, almost noble in a pool of golden light. "Let us embark," he says, "on this darkly, deliciously subversive play, from a writer of genuine genius, leader of the Aesthetic and Decadent movements at the *fin de siècle*. On the surface, a heterosexual draw-ing-room comedy, arguably the pinnacle of that form." Burton pauses to contemplate bliss. "But beneath the froth lies secret depth, a flood of homoerotic reference hidden in plain sight, as it was in their society. A code understood by half the audience." He waves his flower. "Wilde called the green carnation he wore 'the arsenic flower of an exquisite life.' The badge of the Aesthetes' movement, the poisonous colour of absinthe."

A line from a Hemingway story comes into Ivy's head: "Everything tastes of licorice, especially all the things you've waited so long for, like absinthe." Wouldn't it be nice to be in a Hemingway story right now. Cool water, a stab of Anis del Toro.

"Now, to *Earnest*. Wilde himself summed up the play: 'The first act is ingenious, the second beautiful, the third abominably clever.'" Burton bows to his right, green ring gleaming. "Ingenious, beautiful, abomina-bly clever: a pocket guide to the constellation of Orion."

Orion glances up, coolly registering appreciation, even gratitude, for the compliment, and then returns to his script. Watching, Ivy is disturbed both by Burton's strangely placed flattery and by Orion's careful non-reaction. Jason is watching too, she sees. And Newell.

Burton continues, confident in his erudition. "It is a comedy of current manners; better-written than but not unlike *Will and Grace* or *Modern Family,* which also boast gay characters. With this difference: though we still find reasons for concealment—infidelity, or the unsuitable age or station of partner—in those days, the consequence of 'the Love that dare not speak its name' was prison. Wilde was charged with sodomy mere weeks after the play opened, sentenced to two years' hard labour, and died in exile shortly afterward his release, disgraced, poor and broken."

Silence around the table, Burton's desired effect. In the silence, he casts the play. "Orion will play Jack Worthing, also known as Ernest. Sheridan Tooley, Algernon, *also* also known as Ernest. Savaya, cool and lovely Gwendolyn. Mikayla, piquant Cecily. And because there's nothing like a dame, Newell will embody Lady Bracknell, Gwendolyn's ferocious Mama. When we travel to the country in the second act, Jason will undertake Canon Chasuble—and Ivy, my dear, can I trouble you to tackle Miss Prism? Thank you."

Ivy looks down at her script. After all she *is* Miss Prism, to the life. Jewel of the English theatre. It is going to be a long day.

4 . THE VERY THOUGHT OF HUGH

Hugh watches Mimi sleep, watery morning light falling on translucent, blueish skin. Just as he watched when he was a kid, when some pill had had the desired effect. Her mouth a little open. No more foolish-looking now than she was back then. If anything she looks younger now, made child-like by the looming transformation. The fret and fray of life floating away.

Almost too late, now, to tell her how much he loves her. She can't hear, hasn't heard him all day. Lost in chemical sleep, death's waiting-room. Why was he reluctant or shy to say so—what anger, what resentment could still plague him now? Let it drop away. Everything in his heart and body is turning sadly down, dropping as she is dropping away now. All those stupid years of being cruel to her, distant, less than a son. She was never less than a mother. Or at least. Well. Always loving if not always capable.

Ruth tiptoes in. He tries not to be irritated.

"Well!" she whispers. "She's looking lovely." She is not. She looks like death.

"I was at Ian Mighton's first thing this morning," Ruth says, as if explaining where she's been. Her voice lowers: "He had a *friend* over."

Hugh lets that go unremarked. Unlike Ruth to mention that—there's nothing new about Mighton having a *friend*. She trots round the bed to sit on the other side, fidgets with the lines.

Hugh gets up. "Since you're here, I'll go back to work on dinner— Della and Ken's party tonight, remember? L's helping, we're making something specially for you."

Ruth stares down at the taut sheet, smooths it over Mimi's knee. "Well, I just wonder," she says. "I wondered, this morning. You talk to Della, see what she says."

The streets are drying under lemony sunlight. Two kinds of curd to make for the trompe l'oeil egg yolks: lemon and blood orange. Half an hour each, start to finish? He breaks into a jog. Round the corner, there's

Jasper on the porch, sweeping away dead leaves. Okay, as long as he stays off that ladder.

I opened up for you, Jasper mimes. Always a little pale and shaky on a Saturday morning. No sign of him around town last night, he must have fallen into a stupor early on. Once Hugh is close enough: "You have a customer! I kept an eye on him, don't worry."

It's Gerald. "Sorry," Hugh says as he enters the gallery, a little out of breath from running. "I'm actually closed today, what with my mother, and it's Della's——" No need to go into all this. "Something quick I can help you with, though?"

No quick left in Gerald, now. No hale-fellowship, no deal-clinching. He always used to crowd slightly inside your personal shield. Now he is far away. He points vaguely to Mighton's *Dark Gates*. Hugh waits, forcing himself to be patient.

Gerald stares up at the massive piece. "You have another client?"

"Well, Newell has expressed an interest."

Another wait. Then, "There's an empty wall at the house, and this . . ."

Okay, are you a fellow human being? In the presence of someone who has been stabbed by fate, by life, his wife, his son, can you stand separate, apart? Hugh puts a hand on Gerald's big shoulder. "You sure this is what you want, what you need?"

Gerald shifts and trembles. His face does not alter its gaze.

"If you need to fill that space, I'll help you," Hugh says. "But give it time. Newell's not in a hurry. Mighton has work to do here in town, teaching, selling his house. He'll be around. We could talk about a commission, if it's his style you like. Might be more expensive," he forces himself to say. "But I'd hate to see you living with a work so—catastrophic."

"It might be hard to live with," Gerald says. His voice is calm, but his face twists in the effort not to weep.

The door bangs, Della blows in from the front porch. Wild hair, wild eyes. What now?

Seeing Gerald she pulls her own strife inward. Hugh lets him go; the big man moves away, passes Della with a half-raised hand, and wanders out. A drone bee, drunk on lilies. Through the window they watch him halt on the sidewalk, head moving, then turn away from the dealership and walk off toward the river.

Hugh says, "Hope he's not going to drown himself." Then to Della, "How are you?" He can't take her upstairs, or into the framing room, where the boats are all laid out.

L saves the day: she comes running down the stairs and leaps for Della. "*Mamacita*! Can you take me to see Nevaeh before her operation? They're putting six pins in her ankle, she won't be able to do dance for months, can you take me now, please, please?"

Della wraps her arms around her daughter. Speaks over her head, to Hugh: "I want you to know——" To L: "Baby Girl, go out to the car, give me two seconds."

L obeys, giving Hugh one silent *The Scream* behind Della's back.

"About Ken," Della says quickly, when the door closes. "Being at Jenny's."

Hugh doesn't know what to say. You have to say something. "I don't believe it." That took too long. "I mean, I know he's been staying out there, but it's just not——"

She nods. "I know. But look at Jack, with that nice young woman."

"Okay, but Jack was married to *Ann*. As someone who has held that position, I have to say that pretty much any nice young woman would do. Ann is not you. Ken's not Jack. You were horribilizing."

"No. He could," she says, being fair. "Anybody could. But he'd never do it like this."

"No."

"So I just wanted to say I'll try to bring him tonight."

"Good!" Hugh says. "That's good."

At the door, she pauses. "Have you talked to Ruth today?"

"She's at Mimi's, are you looking for her?"

"No! I just wondered if she knew—never mind." She goes out, banging the door again.

He locks it. Puts up the *Closed* sign this time.

Okay, he's got a dinner to make.

(L)

Twenty minutes till Savaya can get here. L's not going up to Nevaeh's room alone. Chickenshit, but what if N's father is there? L stands under the portico where her mom dropped her—*she* was in a hurry. Is she going to Bobcaygeon? Maybe she's painting lake boats now. Down the block, there's the hospice. Mimi's window.

There's time. L sprints the block, springs in through the back door and up the stairs. You have to take the chance to see people who are dying because you never know, and then you'd feel so bad.

She inches open the door. Ruth, in a chair beside the bed, sound asleep. Hey, that vintage corduroy jacket, she finally got it! Go Ruth!

Mimi lies flattened, almost invisible under the sheet. Cheeks old satin, sagged over skull. Thinner than Wednesday, good idea to come today.

The shut eyes look strange without her giant false eyelashes. When her eyes got bad, way back, Hugh screwed a swivel-magnifying mirror to her dressing table. L loved to watch her put them on. Delicate caterpillars. They made her into Mimi; also made her look a little crazy.

Oh Mimi. She was my best friend, when I was little. More than these girls are now.

Ruth stirs, murmurs. She must be Mimi's friend too. Some way. Weird to think about Ruth looking after Hugh and her mom and Newell. Ruth knows about everybody, and never tells. Ruth was in Sullivan's when L stole a tube of stripey toothpaste in grade four. The clerk grabbed L by the jacket, but Ruth was there in two seconds. She marched with them up to the pharmacist's office and made the clerk go away and talked to the pharmacist about when he was a kid, and pretty soon they were out on the sidewalk, and then Ruth gave her a giant talking-to and an ice cream cone at the Dairy Bar. And never told her mom or her dad.

L kisses Mimi's paper-lidded eyes, not worried about waking her, with all the drugs. Then she goes around the bed and kisses Ruth's pink cheek. Ruth wakes, eyes opening quickly, and smiles. "Oh, sweetness," she says. "Don't be worried."

L nods. "About anything, I mean. It'll be all right, your mom and your dad."

L nods again. Ruth turns to find a more comfortable position. Her old-turtle eyes close.

All righty then. Off L goes. She has an idea for place cards. There's the hospital snack store, and she has her trusty X-Acto with her.

(DELLA)

cottage: empty   boat: adrift
hanging on the closet door his shirt
over the bed L's portrait of me   on the table lists   DO PAY FIX
read everything read his mind and heart?   or agree not to look at that
                                                he is not with Jenny
here for some other darker worse thing   to kill himself?
photo stuck to the bathroom mirror   us   the night we met
thirty years gone into air   windspray
me the same   as rudderless   the same me
                                        as buoyed   not buoyed
                                                             where is he
where are you, my beloved, my only one?
don't make me so afraid to see you   not to see you
the ardent man   the one I fought with he would never   have left me
that Ken   the one I love   I loved
the door-spring   there he is
eyes like coals and mine must be the same
we   hate love   each other
                                                                always
I will never forgive him the pain he causes me
that was him fucking Ann on the coats for all the it wasn't him it wasn't
what is this physical bond this mental bond
what terrifying   joy   he is alive
    He says, Hugh says I have to tell you.

                                            (okay tell)

    I've been here all along. I'm trying to—she's been—
    I couldn't talk to—

                    (meaning: I judge you she thinks you're great)
    I don't have any way to—I can't speak to you—
                    (why are we not the only people we can speak to?)
    I try to think what is the worstthing that could happen, that's why
    I got angry about Mighton—I know it isn't true

                            (you don't know what I would have done
                            except that nothing makes any sense
                            no body has any salt but yours)
    I can't go back I don't deserve, I
    I deserve for you to be with . . . I
    I deserve to lose Elle, I, I—
I, I, I, I   make him stop talking like this   such a fucking fake fake fake
garbage of fakeness of false   pretending   not to know me know *us*
    stop stop   again again
          crack my head against the wall because then it will stop
   crash my head on the wall, to make him see what pain he causes me
outside pain is easier to bear   out out into the woods
       into the empty trees and the rainsoaked leafmold under them
       blind with crying   what is the way to get back to my
he comes   run   from him
to get back to my to ourselves in this terrible thundering after me   duck
                  branch—*smack*
it hitting him hitting it   shouting
                stop / turn
hand to eye—torn?   is he blind?
he takes it away   red and white   not bleeding
    I can't, he says.
neither can I   so dark so sad   it is his turn to talk
    I can't go back to work. It's like there is nothing left of life,
    like it is all over for me. Is what I feel.
        Well then don't.   this is all?
   We don't have the money.
      For you to quit? We'll sell the house. Elle can get student
      loans, I'll work, I'll get a real job.
   Not enough—I can't—we can't—
      I'll sell Mimi's piano, it's probably sixty thousand.
   He laughs. That's nowhere near—And no, I like to hear you play.
                           pressing his reddened eye
                           two hands both eyes blind
      It's not the end of the world. Have you already talked to—
never mind can't ask, can't pry can't know
should say / can't say now what the dental insurance didn't pay for

on Elle's teeth and the still cracked windshield on the car from nearly
crashing it will have to be fixed, nothing left in the line of credit so how
will that be managed . . . the car bucking beneath me almost going over
instead touch his bruise his eye his mouth
the relief of touch

                                                    it's all right   wait a while
                                              my own my only my love

           Your eyes are beautiful.
                                        the woods are wet from all this rain
                                              these thirty years of rain

           Help me pack up my stuff?
so we go
I guess we can go back
to dinner with Hugh and the others I guess   I guess

                    (but there is something between him and Jenny)
                         (we will just agree not to look at that)

Orion sings out the tagline on a glad, ringing note, "*On the contrary, Aunt Augusta, I've now realized for the first time in my life the vital importance of being Earnest!*"

And Burton stretches, big old bachelor-cat that he is, and breaks for lunch. Newell raises his eyebrows, pleading with Ivy to stay, but she leaves him to deal with Burton's emotions alone. Enough for one morning. Faster than the students, she flies down echoing Saturday halls, out into the parking lot—sun! incredible after a week of rain—into the Volvo, down the usual flow of streets, to the gallery. A sign on the front door says *Closed,* but he'll be upstairs, getting his party ready. She slides in beside his van, grabs out her suitcases, slams the back door behind her, and runs up the stairs to his crowsnest, treehouse—home. Hugh is pulling a pan from the oven. He looks up.

"Cake?" Ivy says, hoping. Dense aroma of almonds, golden top, perfect.

"All cake all the time, tonight," Hugh says. "This one's marzipan."

He comes to take her tweed coat and suitcases and scarf, hanging them on her hook—hers, already. "Rough day at the salt mine?"

O balm of fondness! She was so right to come. The gristle of her mood clears, melts. "Maybe I'm a sociopath," she says, moving with him back to the kitchen. "I just don't care about anybody—is that it?"

"What's the play of the day—do you seek the Bluebird of Happiness?"

"Not *Blue Bird*, thank God, but *Importance of Being Earnest*. Ugh."

"Ah." Hugh puts a small plate in front of her. "Tester?" Two spoons, mounded with gold and yellow gleams. "Lemon curd on the left, what do you think?"

He regards her with mild anxiety, so she swallows. Even though she has waited so long, it doesn't taste of licorice. Tart-sweetness, smooth and slightly warm, fills the hungry caverns of her mouth and makes her ears ping. "I think I am in paradise at last," she says.

"This one's blood orange."

She swoons, she licks the spoons. Satisfied, he turns back to work, sorting and stemming brown mushrooms. "What's so bad about *Earnest*? I thought it was supposed to be his best."

"Oh it is, it's perfect. Very witty." Sip of tea. The tension of the morning is evaporating. "But here's where my imagination or my sympathy fails me: I think it's tedious. Clever, yes, funny in spots. Stephen Fry, et cetera. But why bother?"

"Too clever? Heartless?" He's chopping stems, graceful in his knife work.

"I don't suppose Wilde was, but the play is. Epigraphs are boring—all substitution, and once you crack the code it stops being funny. And Wilde was horrible to his poor, silly wife. Or maybe he wasn't, maybe he was witty and kind and gentle with her, when he bothered to go over and pat his children's heads."

This must be the first time Hugh has seen her being brittle, theatrical. Makes her sad to let him see her working self this way. Tears threaten her eyes again, *shit*.

"Come," he says, putting down the knife.

He takes her hand and leads her down the hall into his room. Onto the bed. He shuts the door and locks it; when he turns she laughs, seeing what is in his mind. In his heart. He bends to take off her shoes and socks, and takes the tip of one foot in his soft mouth. But his poor head. If she does most of the work, and allows no jarring . . . She sighs, she pulls her tunic up and off, and lies back on the welcoming bed. This is antidote, reward, this is nourishment and sustenance and life. This is the life.

The play has seeped into her anyway, dislike it how she might. When they lie still, replete, Cecily's line comes to her mouth because it is the truth: "*How nice of you to like me so much after we have known each other such a comparatively short time*," she says, kissing him. "But I am going to be late—"

She leaps into her clothes and flies down the stairs and starts the Volvo, still in a dream, in the ecstatic centre of their existential struggle.

As she backs out of the tight spot she's in, the side mirror catches on the fence and pops right off, dangling by wires. No time, no time, she rolls the window down and grabs it, yanks it off, and leaves it on the passenger seat. No looking back.

(L)

Savaya bounds into the hospital snack shop, forty minutes late. L stows the place-card stuff in a take-away Styrofoam box, layers separated by paper napkins. No jarring.

The super smooth elevator is big enough for a couple of stretchers but there is only one in here with them, an old woman being wheeled somewhere to something bad. Her eyes pluck at L's, wanting to be told it will all be okay. Probably it will not. L gives her a half smile and lets her own eyes wander to the keypad. Fourth floor. Okay.

Savaya says, "4108, 4108," and they check the signs and veer to the left, a walkway open to the central atrium. Makes L dizzy to look either down or up, so she doesn't. Savaya stops. "Do you have anything to give her? We can't go in there with nothing." She looks around, then picks six lilies from the planter lining the chasm. "Not even plastic!"

Afraid, L looks up and down the walkway, but nobody seems to notice. Savaya whips the scarf from her ponytail and ties it around the flowers. "There! Nevaeh will be happy."

When they find the room, Nevaeh's head is hanging while her dad delivers a sonorous lecture. But he must be tired; Nevaeh's tiny mother twitches his sleeve and says they might go find tea, since the friends are here, and Nevaeh's dad concurs, slowly. He rises and proceeds out, and Mrs. Nev click-clicks down the hall behind him. She wears four-inch heels everywhere.

"*Fuuuck*!" Nevaeh whispers/screams. Then she starts to cry. Her eyes are always beautiful, but when she cries the fountains overflow in glorious light. Her eyelids are tight-swollen. Her leg must really hurt.

Savaya sits on the wider side by Nevaeh's legs, and L on the narrower. It's actually quite uncomfortable to sit there, L has to make herself count to twenty to stay put. Savaya keeps jiggling the bed, hugging Nevaeh, patting her giant foot wrapped with high-tech fluoro tape.

"No dance til June," Nevaeh says. "They're putting six pins in it, and I'll have a cast till Christmas!" Her bonbon voice is thicker, as if she has cried for days and days.

Savaya might feel loyal about Pink, so L asks. "What did Pink say that set you off?"

"He stared at me through the crack, I saw him, he's such a pervert. Pink freaks me out—but it was *Jason*!" Nevaeh's nervous arms come up one after the other to wipe the tears off her beautiful, blooming cheeks, to flatten out her eyes and stretch the skin.

L looks up at that. "Jason, what?" Savaya asks.

"He looked at me, my arm—I only did it once, to see why people think it works, not because I—" More sobbing. "He cut my sleeve with his scissors, that heavy stuff. He said he wanted to shorten it for the line, but it was to make the scars show," Nevaeh says. Turning the thin arm outward, so they can see a little set of pinkish lines.

Not a lot of lines, only six or seven. But that's not once, either. That's a few times of testing it out, L thinks. Because Nevaeh is a terrible liar and always will be.

Savaya smooths her own smooth golden arm over Nevaeh's, as if she can erase it, the pain or hate or despair. Bending to her shoulder, Nevaeh says, through hiccupping sobs that are still so fucking pretty, "I don't get how you can hang with him, he's cold. I hate Orion too, he thinks he's the shit."

Savaya doesn't say anything.

L feels pretty stiff herself. Not that Jason needs defending because he didn't, he wouldn't, but Nevaeh can't keep on thinking that.

"He didn't mean it like that, Jason didn't—you overreacted," L says.

Nevaeh ignores her and sobs on in Savaya's arms.

Because it's Savaya she loves.

Well, L can't sit there anymore, the bed tilting and nobody believing her. She gets up.

"He *did* mean it!" Nevaeh twists to touch L's leg, not letting her go, all pitiful certainty. "He wants his clothes to look edgy—he was *exploiting* me for the good of—"

L laughs, her loyalty suddenly decided. "If that was true, he'd have painted scars on you. More than a few test cuts." She lifts up her skirt and shows them the inside of her thigh. "If you were really doing anything, you'd know not to talk about it. Anyway, good luck exploiting *you*. You're the most self-possessed, self-obsessed person I know!"

She gets up, finds her box, and goes.

That was unfair. Who cares.

Adios, amoebas.

6. MASTER CLASS: GORGON

"A drawing room romance." Burton tilts his head, thinks deeply. "But vast forces seethe under the surface of this seeming simplicity, this petal-like perfection. Would that the world itself worked as well as the end of *Earnest*! Obstacles removed, love triumphant. Transformation! The cloak-room, the bag, P*rrr*rism herself, no mere educator but revealed as a true artiste, with her failed three-volume romance." He looks fake-fondly at Ivy, who'd like to smack his smirk on behalf of educators everywhere.

Don't hate him. Don't waste effort and energy on an aging acidity with no power.

Now Burton is revealing the hidden meanings, the gay subtext. "Take, for example, Jack Worthing's ward Cecily: a *Cecily* was contemporary slang for a young male prostitute under the protection of an older man."

The students are interested, codes being always cool.

"The cigarette case they fight over: Wilde gave silver cigarette cases to lovers, when delicacy forbade outright cash payment. In the darkness of the seats, imagine those silver cases sliding out of breast pockets, proffered to companions . . . in that audience, imagine the undercurrent of secret smiles and whispers, the thrill of the forbidden."

Listening to Burton, Ivy feels like she's been saying "prunes and prisms" to herself for a thousand years: a prim-mouthed, aged and judgemental spinster.

Burton brings out a new cast list. "So! We'll read the play again, exploring the substrata by judicious casting. Newell will play Jack this time. Jason, raw as he is, will take Algernon. Orion, you will grace us with the urbane Gwendolyn, Jack's inamorata. Sheridan, the young Cecily, boy-ward at the country estate of Jack Worthing. I myself, Dame Bracknell, and Ivy, stout Ivy, remains in Miss Prism's service. The girls: Savaya will chance Chasuble, and Mikayla make hay with Lane and his country counterpart. That's all, I think? Yes."

Savaya seems sulky, understandably; the others look alert, even keyed up. At first, the reading takes on an extra uncomfortable knowingness. But as the boys settle into their roles, as they see what they are saying to each other, the tension in the room gradually calms, replaced by a different tension, the working out of submerged social patterns. There are moments of good comedy: hipster Sheridan as Cecily, telling Ivy, "I don't like novels that end happily. They depress me so much." Ivy has always loved Miss Prism's reply: "The good ended happily, and the bad unhappily. That is what fiction means."

Or Newell to Jason, earnestly, "I don't really know what a gorgon is like, but I am quite sure that Lady Bracknell is one. She is a monster, without being a myth, which is rather unfair." Burton does not react, but the rest of the company finds it necessary to put hands to mouths for various reasons, a cough, an itch, etc.

As the lovers Jack and Gwendolyn, Newell and Orion are a dream. The little proposal scene suddenly thrums with meaning, buried joy delicately overlaid by spiky, glancing, sidelong wit. Aware that this is one of those transforming moments that make it worth working in theatre, Ivy wonders, a little dismayed, exactly what is going on between those two. Something serious. Watching Burton watch them, she feels faintly sick.

"I hope you will always look at me just like that, especially when there are other people present," Orion says, his whole heart on display, but laughing at himself too.

And yet, and yet. It is a long, long afternoon.

After the surprising joy of that proposal scene—his own casting, after all—Burton's worsening temper taints the room. Orion gets paler and paler, Newell recedes farther back into his chair. Burton, eyes darting around the table, seems to have heat-lines vibrating around his form, like those mad cats Wain painted in the asylum. He is horribly good as Bracknell. In the morning reading Newell did Burton-doing-Bracknell, with a faint malicious lisp; Burton simply inhabits her, engorged eyes bulging from his patty-cake face. Ivy has no difficulty paling and quailing as Burton trumpet-calls, "Prrrism! *Where is that baby?*"

Every time Orion speaks, Burton seizes tighter, tauter, his attention pinpointed. False geniality sits like a comedy mask on his face, crookedly hung over rage that darkens as the play winds on. Interesting textual revelations cannot outweigh the strain, which Ivy believes everyone must be feeling. Besides, the male casting is unnecessary. The play exists in its own miraculous atmosphere, straddling both the hetero and gay worlds, the Victorian and the modern. Ivy doesn't believe her dislike of the play stems from prejudice, even given her growing prejudice against Burton.

A surprise, then, when he pushes his chair back at the end of this second run-through. His arm goes up in salute, and he says, "Good. Well done. But no. Here is why we would never produce it this way: blatant all-male casting neuters the hiddenness, the closetedness that was in their time so vital to the green-carnation life. It takes the secret mainspring out of the play, and ignores the truth that many gay men in those days married to disguise themselves, including Wilde himself. In approaching a production, it would be our work to enter into the world behind the world of the play: to research and understand that Victorian culture of propriety and secrets, of rigid class distinction—a culture where the worship of class still edged out the worship of money."

Burton is not an idiot. A clever creature who is the product of his time, of his training, and of the wrongs done to him, no doubt over and over. Ivy cannot hate him. Maybe Orion can.

"We've tested out five plays from the canon," Burton says. "Look up *canon* if you don't know what I mean. We've played rich, poor, clever, stupid, cannibal, German, American, English, Illyrian; that gorgeous brute Stanley, shipwrecked Viola. We've read the musical, the domestic tragedy, the drawing-room comedy—each at the pinnacle of perfection."

The young faces around the table, turned to him like daisies, register various degrees of hope and confusion. Only Orion looks down at his script, thinking his secret thoughts.

Burton surveys them. "All right. On Monday, we go farther back into the canon, to the dawn of the written drama—the Greeks. We will read the original bill of divorcement, the first wronged woman wreaking havoc: *Medea*. With one interesting twist—but I'll save that for Monday. Away, all of you. Thank you for your energy this week. Total rest tomorrow."

Orion looks up. "I don't think so," he says.

Like a ring has been twitched in his nose, Burton jerks his head. "I beg your pardon?"

"I don't think we should do a different play," Orion says, white around the nostrils but calm outside. "No more changing. I think we should stick with *Earnest*. We'd do a great job, we could really work. I don't care about the—I mean, cast somebody else—and I don't care if you can't stick with the cross-casting, but I think we should work on one play, one project, instead of jumping around so much."

He stops talking.

Ivy feels faint. Everyone else is quiet. Even Newell, whose cloudless gaze stays on Orion's face.

Burton's throat works, Adam's apple jumping unpleasantly under the wattled skin. But he restrains, contains himself. "Thank you for your input," he finally says. "I will take that under advisement." The maestro's nod, dismissal.

It's over, no lightning or thunder: Phew.

Anticlimax, in fact. The students gather their wits and papers and begin to drift off.

Terry-She snags Newell to sign some posters for her sponsors. Terry-He and Pink stand chatting at the door. Savaya postures and laughs for them.

Ivy's phone is plugged in behind the curtain leg. She goes to retrieve it.

"Scripts in the recycling, please, *not* under the table again," Burton calls. Then, as the others disperse in clumps, he says, "Orion, a word?"

The plug sticks, it has to be wiggled gently to come out. In the wiggling time Ivy hears Burton, very cool, professional. None of the bombast now.

"I don't want you in my class any longer, Orion." Simple as that.

Orion makes no sound.

"For *Medea*, which you clearly scorn, Mikayla and Newell will take the leads. All the others will be chorus; I wouldn't want to demean you by using you in such a minor way."

Orion still does not speak. Perhaps he is frightened.

Burton huffs. "Your very commercial talent is wasted in this investigative, exploratory work, and your impatience with the class has been crystal clear." (What?) "I suspect you've got a big future, if you learn to submit to direction. You think your working life has already started, but you're banking on the cheap—*facility*—you already have, rather than deepening your work and digging harder for more truth, more grit. I can't work with you, and I won't have your arrogance polluting the group. Your fee will be refunded."

Ivy looks around the curtain. Orion stands on the black stage straight and tall as a shaft of light through branches.

"Are you going to answer me?" Burton's voice betrays him. Choking, fat with fury.

"I think this is a fight between the two of you," Orion says, his voice cool water, undisturbed. "It's not about me."

Ivy can't see Burton's face, only the purple edge of his cheek.

Silence.

Then Burton gestures at Orion's still figure, flaring out, "Go, go! The decision is made."

"All right, old man," Orion says. As if *old man* is the worst thing he can think of.

He walks away.

(L)

Hugh likes the place cards! L is happy with them: each one the bottom half of an Oreo, icing carved away to make a profile of the person, like a cameo. Camoreo. Her mom, the knot of hair behind her head, and the strong nose; her dad was hard to catch, no hair sticking out, just a plain silhouette, Some Guy. L deals out two more: Ivy looking up, eyebrows raised; Hugh, looking down, another nice nose to cut. Then Ruth. Sad to do Ruth but not Mimi. "I brought the bag of cookies, I can do more. I didn't know who was coming."

Hugh makes a face. "I've been avoiding thinking about it. But it's no good, I have to ask Newell, and he has to bring Burton—I'll call them later. And Ann, I asked her. Maybe more, later, but those are the sit-down dinner people."

Newell will be easy, the famous profile, hair flying back. Burton too, piece of cake, piece of cookie. All chins, like a Roman emperor on a coin.

Hugh drags out a large, flat package from under the sofa, all proud. "I couldn't keep this in the framing room," he says. "Your mom is always bustling in there to help—don't let me forget to take those damned certificates to the Ace." He pulls off the masking tape.

Ha! It's a paint-by-number kit, a picture of her mom and dad. A big canvas with pale blue outlines, tiny pale blue numbers, and an assortment of bad acrylic paints in little pots.

"I sent away for it weeks ago, there's a website where you upload a photo. It's them, in 1984. I took it the night they met. All Saints."

"Cool! They'll love it."

Wait—feet on the stairs. Heavy ones. Hugh snatches the brown paper, refastens the tape.

It's her dad. His head rises above the railing, slowly, as he climbs the stairs. He turns to look at them. He's got a black eye.

He stares at them standing awkwardly to block his view of the big parcel on the coffee table behind them. "Hey," he says, after a pause. As if he's out of the speaking habit.

"Hey," L says.

"Had a chat with your mom."

They don't speak, both too busy looking at that eye.

"Looks like we're coming for dinner. So, put me to work." He pulls himself up the last two stairs, using the railing to help. Is he badly hurt?

Just his eye. Black, slashing stripe below the eyebone, purple smudge around it. Wow.

He stands by the kitchen counter. Seeing the tray there, he says *mmm* and goes to grab an Oreo. "No!" L says. "Those are place cards."

"Neat. Now I see—there's Della—neat-o." Oh, the uneasy goofiness. Her dad.

"Do you need an ice pack?" Hugh gestures at the black eye, points at his own helplessly.

"Oh, no, it's fine now. Hurt a bit when—when I walked into that door, though."

Sure, they all agree to let it be that way. Hugh turns to his list: "Okay, rice for sushi cake, the crêpes, we've still got a lot of work to do." Then, bright idea, he asks her dad to run down to the basement to check if the buckets need emptying.

The footsteps fade to the basement stairs.

Hugh points down after him. "What the hell?"

"Do you think my mom punched him? He doesn't seem upset." Lots of punching these days. Must be some astrological conjunction of Mars with Neptune, planet of surprises.

Hugh spreads his hands wide, not knowing. "Maybe it's good. They were legendary for fighting in the old days. Wasn't a party until one of them stormed out shouting. They fought for—how old are you, eighteen?—for twelve straight years. Till they had you."

When her dad comes back from the basement he's got Jason with him. Two heads rising up the stairwell—Jason's hair in a cockscomb, is that what you say? (Aieee, the word *cock*!)

"Buckets emptied, none were full," her dad reports. "You need work done down there—I wonder if it might be the city's problem, though, Hugh?"

Hugh leaps at that and they get into sewers and bylaws and weeping tile and the river, because around here it's always the river. While they blah blah blah, L looks at Jason for his master class verdict.

He shakes his head. "Something with Orion and Burton—I took off."

The timer bings, the rice has finished steaming, and against his protests, Hugh hands her dad an ice pack and makes him go lie down for a while.

"Too many cooks," Hugh says, coming back, dusting his hands. He asks Jason, "Here to work? Okay, you can start on the crêpes."

Ruth doesn't like sushi—how possible?—so they're doing crêpes too. Hugh has drawn a picture: a tower of lacy crêpes, filling oozing between twelve layers, like wedding cake.

"Scallops, salmon, crab. She won't eat shrimp since that documentary. When you're chopped, I'll teach you to make a roux."

He gives Jason an apron and a station, and Jason rolls up his sleeves and gets to work, melting butter and whisking batter. (L can't help thinking of the white apples of his butt, the springing tension of everything, his fingers, hers, *quiver*, everything.)

L wonders if Hugh was always like this, free and happy while cooking, and if so why did he stop and run a gallery instead? When he's framing he's pretty anal, like he's always afraid of screwing up. Here he's good at making an occasion without getting fussed. When her mom has a party she panics and all the joy dies. L likes the casual way Hugh cooks, his effortless order, even the music he plays—not anything you might expect, just weird stuff he likes. Banjo music. *Now at Last,* that's Blossom Dearie. In another life L would like to be Blossom Dearie. Wearing Mimi's pink gloves, which she has in her coat pocket. She's carrying them everywhere now because she can't forget that Mimi is dying.

A bang at the bottom of the stairs—the outside door.

Everyone swivels to see whose head rises next. Satin gold: Orion, lightning-flashing up the flight of stairs. His face is blown apart, eyes wild, not even—

"I'm out," he says to Jason, not even seeing the others. "He kicked me out, I'm gone. It's not—it's *so not fair*—he knows I'm the—" He stops, he can't complete that.

The best, yes.

Jason says, "You are the best, man. What the fuck?"

"He kicked me out. *Cheap facility*, he—" Orion's voice stops working. His great black eyes lock shut and he turns away so they won't see.

Jason pulls the crêpe pan off the stove and turns the burner off, deliberate smooth action, and goes to put his arms around Orion.

Hugh takes his apron off. He gives L the sheaf of recipes.

"Carry on as best you can," he says, heading down the stairs, already gone. "I've got to see a man about a dog."

7. FUCK HUGH

Up the concrete staircase at Newell's place. When these buildings went up, people gasped. Million-plus for a condo?!—this isn't Toronto. But it sort of is, now. Newell's slice of glass and rock, plus the stairs, plus the hedges and the terrace: this one must have been three times that price, Hugh thinks, or four. But he is entirely naïve; he has no real idea what Newell paid, or has, or earns or costs. His head hurts from running. Maybe shouldn't have made love at lunch—but then his head always hurts. He's going to have to confess that to Conrad soon. Maybe he'll beat Mimi to the punch and die on everybody, on Newell and Della and Ruth. On Ivy.

Climbing the endless stairs, Hugh casts his fractured mind backward, trying to think what he knows about this mess, what he could swear to. He witnessed that first approach, in Pink's parlour, whatever it was Burton said to Orion. Orion said it was a line from *Streetcar*. Then he saw—what?— the other night at the Ace: Orion taking off the jade piece, giving it back to Newell. No idea what that meant, or why Burton wept. Hugh's head was in bad shape by then. Ivy took him home and put his sorry ass to bed. Last night at the party, he knew it was Newell who was the problem. And now—

Orion breaking down, kicked out of class. There could be some reason or excuse for that, some acting thing he wouldn't know or understand.

Talk carefully. The point is to fix things for Orion, not to achieve eternal justice.

The doorbell at the terrace door peals like angels coming in chorus, Aa-*ahhhh!* A shadow, a self, emerges from the shadowed glass.

Burton. "Hugh!" he exclaims, with mock delight. "A sight for a sore eye."

"Is Newell here?"

"Not at the moment—I believe he went for a run, to restore the tissues. May I, poor I, be of use?" Burton plays puzzled, one tended eyebrow arching.

"You kicked Orion out of the master class," Hugh says. No more preamble.

Burton purses his purple mouth. "Oh dear, I'm afraid I can't discuss a student with you, Hugh. Confidentiality, the FOIP, you know. Curiosity will just have to kill you."

You won't punch Burton this time, but the sweetness of the memory is sustaining. "I came to tell you," Hugh says, "you need to retract this."

The mouth smiles, the pig-eyes fold. "I'm renowned for the gentleness of my disposition. But I warn you, Hugh, you may go too far."

Hugh shakes his head. That hurts. He puts a hand on the glass. "Burton—I don't know what's going on, but you can't pull this high-handed director stuff. These are kids, they don't need the drama. Orion is their friend, their star. I don't believe you can justify kicking him out. They'll all quit, if you do this. It will make trouble for Newell, as well as for you. It's just not—it isn't kind, and it's stupid."

He has never been so straightforward with Burton. It's kind of a relief, except for the splitting headache it's giving him. Only the memory of Orion's eyes makes it possible to keep standing there, the deep visible wound to his whole tentative, youthful being.

Lazy, content, refusing to fight, Burton stretches out his right hand to the door handle. Hugh puts his own arm out to stop him—not that he could. "Like the bling?" Burton asks, pretending to think Hugh wants to see his lump of green scarab. "From Newell. An antiengagement ring, a consolation prize, I guess you would call it."

"If you don't fix this," Hugh says, his head pounding rhythmically like it will actually break open, "I will make it my business to see that you're investigated for abuse."

The smile again, elongated, if anything.

"Oh no, dear Hugh. *I* never touched the child. Never had the chance. It's Newell's career, *his* life you'd be jeopardizing. I'm sure Pink is putty in your hands, or at least in Ruth's, behind whose apron you all hide so coyly. But here is *my* response," Burton says. "Fuck Hugh."

He allows the great glass door to swing, to glide, to shut.

8. AND THE HORSE HUGH RODE IN ON

Okay, that didn't work.

Hugh steps, staggers, down the concrete stairs again. Dark hedge hides the street from view until he almost reaches the ground—and there's Newell, sprinting the last stretch, sleek and gleaming in running gear.

"Did you know?" Hugh asks. Demands.

Winded, Newell leans against the concrete, waves his arm: Carry on.

"About Orion?"

Newell looks at Hugh then, hands on his knees. Finally, his breath back he says, "Know what?"

Hugh waits. Newell waits too, not speaking. Okay, fine. "About Burton kicking him out of the class. For good."

That makes Newell stand. "No," he says, looking up the stairs. "That I did not know."

"Well, Burton says—"

"You talked to him?"

Hugh is getting angry. "Yes, I talked to him. He's gone too far—Orion's not some sixth-rate kid. Terry will go to bat for him, so will Terry—even Pink. Burton has to—"

Newell waves an arm again, "Shut up, shut up. I know. *Fuck* me."

"That's what Burton said."

"What?"

"What he said to me. Fuck Hugh."

Newell laughs. But he is angry too.

So's Hugh. His head hurts, he can't see very well, he's tired of feeling confused. "I want you to stop this now," he says. Stop what? Burton, his head, the world. Della in pain, Mimi. It's not getting through to Newell, who stands looking up the street to the river path, thinking. Or not thinking, just drifting, like he's done his whole floating life. "You have to do something," Hugh tells him. "For a change. You have to engage, here."

Newell pulls his eyes back from the trees, looks at Hugh. Not angry now. Sad, or something. "You've never known what it's like being me," he says.

"I know you better than anybody," Hugh says. "You just don't see Burton, you don't know how bad he is."

Newell laughs again. "That, I do know."

"Then ditch him."

"It wouldn't be . . . right."

Hiding behind Ruth's apron, Burton said. Like Newell hides behind Burton.

"He's not your friend, not your mentor. Not your father."

Newell's eyes go blank, flat. His version of anger. "Can you ditch Mimi? Or Ruth? Can you stop doing all the things that make you yourself?"

"He didn't make you."

"What do you think is going on, here, Hugh? I'd like to know."

"I think—Burton is jealous of Orion. He's too good, too young, too handsome." Hugh can't say, *and Burton couldn't seduce him*. (But Newell could—Hugh can't think about that.) "He's afraid of losing you."

"He's not. We have a long-standing—we're—"

"What, polyamorous? Yeah, he told me. What a load of horseshit that is." Newell shakes his head.

"Using a fancy label to behave like jerks."

"No," Newell says, as if he's honestly trying to tell Hugh something. "It's the truth. It's—grief, maybe. I don't believe in love, for me. Except in all-love, maybe. Loving everyone."

"Horseshit."

He shakes his head, holding Hugh's eyes, trying. "Reality, for me."

They fall into a moment of silence and hurt. On both sides, both of them feeling it: you misjudge me, you have never understood me.

Newell straightens up first. Maybe he's more used to not being understood. Hugh feels even worse than he did coming out of Burton's vile shadow.

"Well, shit," Newell says. "The class is screwed now, I suppose, and I've been enjoying it, in a mild way. This sucks. You should have kept out of it—now he'll be difficult."

"Can you fix it for Orion?"

He breathes in, head lifting to the sky. "Probably."

Okay. Orion's blazing eyes. It needs to be fixed, no matter what it costs Newell.

Hugh turns to go, turns back. "And you're coming for dinner? It's Della and Ken's anniversary tonight, remember?"

Newell glances up the stairs again. "Shit, yes."

"Bring Burton, if you want." Hugh thinks he's never said anything as difficult, or as kind, to his friend, his little brother.

Newell is never unresponsive, never holds a grudge. He gives Hugh a loving smile. "You went a little overboard with the dinner, and you need someone to show off to? I'll bring him."

"Maybe a little. It's all trompe l'oeil." Hugh turns away, turns back again. One more thing: "Della's in trouble. Ken has a black eye." Newell laughs at that, and Hugh laughs too. "No, you should see it, a big black line, looks like she hit him with a hockey stick. It's swelled up like a plum. I put him to bed with an ice pack."

"I refuse to believe she hit him," Newell says.

"You've never known what it's like being her," Hugh says.

Newell punches his arm, good one. "Or Ken, thank God."

Hugh laughs again. "Yeah, but Jesus, his eye—it's worse than Burton's was."

They fall silent. Time is passing, dusk is coming down. Hugh says, "Okay, look, he didn't sue me over the eye; Orion won't sue him over this. But you have to fix it. It's not okay that he got kicked out. You know he's the best thing in the class."

"He's the best thing in— He's very good, he will be, very."

Hugh doesn't want to say what's in his mind: that any suggestion of— Anything between student and teacher, even a temporary visiting artist, would bring media wolves down on Newell's head. And that notoriety would be bad, really bad, for Orion.

"It's a new world, but it's not very new," Newell says, following Hugh's mind. "I don't want to watch Pink play Marquess of Queensberry."

"You know I have no idea what's actually going on, right?"

"How's the headache?" Newell says, touching him lightly on the forehead.

"Don't ask." Hugh does turn then, to go off down the street. Then switches direction: the certificates to deliver to the Ace, he grabbed them as he went out the door. And after the Ace, there's time—he'll run up to see Mimi.

Run slowly.

Ivy arrives, carrying flowers and a bottle of pretty good wine.

L and Jason stare down the stairwell as she climbs. L looks happy to see her, if fraught: "I don't know—flowers—vase? Hugh's gone."

They're lilies, which the internet said was right for a thirtieth anniversary. A little funerary. Quarter after five. The kitchen is a shambles.

Jason takes the bunch and says, "I'll stick them in the bathroom sink till Hugh gets back." He looks unscarred, even after that long, bad day. No stakes for him; he doesn't want to act. She hopes he doesn't. He was fine, etc., but the clothes he designs are *perfect*. He gives Ivy a half-grin and says, "Hugh has to be back in a few minutes, or we're hooped."

First, the important thing. Ivy asks, fearing the answer, "Have you seen Orion?"

"In the guest room," L says. "Jason made him lie down with the ice pack. My dad was here but he went to change and find my mom. Hugh said he had to see a man about a dog."

All right then. "Did Orion tell you?" From their faces she can see they know. "So that will be what Hugh's gone to fix." Ivy gives them encouraging nods. "You do the dishes, and I'll get myself ready so I can help."

She dashes off to Hugh's bedroom. Ten minutes' fast work and she's back, clean, coiffed, wearing her best linen dress and a cobweb-fine crimson alpaca sweater. Looking like everybody's maiden-aunt drama teacher, but never mind, the crazy beautiful (crazy expensive) Cydwoq heels covered with roses give her verve.

She raises her hands at the now-sparkling kitchen. "Wow! Perfect! Still no Hugh? Okay, don't worry—okay, I'm good at setting table, if that's any use to you?"

L nods. "Sorry, I was panicking. There are leaves for the table and extra chairs in the basement. He only has one kind of dishes, so we know which to use."

Restaurant white, lots of them; heavy linen napkins in a drawer; good wineglasses, good silverware—that makes sense. Holding the knives, the weighted forks, is like holding Hugh's hand. Dinner is such a ritual of communion. Ivy feels a spring of startling desire for Hugh, his body and mind. Beloved!

The country of the dead. Many people, these days, have never gone to those gates. People are old before they learn to deal with death. Not that Hugh has learned.

Conrad's in the hall, his hand on Mimi's door. He turns to Hugh with serious eyes. "Any time," he says. "Could be tonight, tomorrow. Early next week."

Hugh nods. He nods and nods.

"I'm sorry," Conrad says. He is good at saying that. Empathy without sympathy. We have work to do, you and I, he means.

"I am too," Hugh says.

Conrad looks at his eyes, and asks, "How's that head? Taking care of it? No intellectual effort, right?"

Hugh laughs, almost. "None."

"Pain?"

Oh, pain. What is pain? "None to speak of," Hugh says, and goes into the room.

Mimi is still. Then not quite still. A twitching in her hand. He takes her hand. The pain is easier now, is it? She's so far gone. Her skin loose, her bones revealed, her shadow shrunken. Not his mother now but a dying woman, a mystery, almost separated from us on earth.

Ruth is there on the far side of the bed, pink-eyed with weeping. Her old twisted hand holds Mimi's knee. The sheets are yellow today, pale lemon curd, pale yolk. How can he go back to dinner, that foolish feast? He smiles at Ruth although he hates her for being here. She lifts her lids, gives him back a watery smile, and tilts her head slightly in warning.

A sound, a sigh. He cricks his neck, turning. What's Ann doing here? Sitting on the sill, notebook in hand, making tickmarks on a list: at least she's not writing on the wall.

He should apologize. "Sorry I couldn't talk to Jason about the magazines."

"Stewart says they're actually worth a mint, vintage issues."

"Truly, you don't need to worry about Jason."

Her face is calm, close as she ever gets to happy. "I know. L stayed over last night. They're an item, they posted it on Facebook!"

Okay, with her there the room is too full. He'll come back later. After dinner, he'll come.

As he goes past Ann she puts out a long hand to hold him back. "Hugh, stay . . . I was the same, I couldn't take watching her suffer—but she was so important to me, you know, to my work. You'll regret it for the rest of your life if you leave, if you miss her passing."

The sentimentality of that *passing* revolts him. Her cool, predatory uninvolvement. Her manufactured connection, now that stuff will be up for grabs. Mimi is not hers.

No point in hating her. He tells himself that, and some calm descends.

He turns away and talks to Ruth, only. "You want to stay, okay. I'm going home to look after my friends, to celebrate Della and Ken's long solid-sterling marriage and their recent reconciliation."

Ruth is crying again, tears all over her face, giant bug eyes staring up, wanting him to fix the ordinary physics of the world.

"I wish you'd come for dinner," Hugh says to her, and to Ann too. "You're not doing any good here."

Conrad's still standing outside Mimi's room, writing on a chart held against the wall. "Hugh," he begins, turning his head.

Hugh walks on.

Go be with the living, who you might be able to help. Probably not, because everybody he knows is screwed up. It's insufferable. Hugh lopes along the sidewalk, too fast for the state of his skull. In his head he makes a list of what everybody needs:

	What's Wrong?	*What Would Help?*
MIMI:	dying	o—nothing—nada—zip
RUTH:	old, poor	affection, $$
JASPER:	poor, old, drunk	$$ + AA?
DELLA:	sad, afraid	Ken + $$ + work
KEN:	sad, in despair	quitting + Della

L:	too young, talented	work, Gareth Pindar? + Jason?
JASON:	too young, stuck with Ann	L, it seems to Hugh
ORION:	too talented, alone	work, Newell???
NEWELL:	empty, stuck with Burton	Orion?

Nothing can help what ails Burton.

Okay, nobody needs a trompe l'oeil anniversary dinner. Clearly. But that's what they're all going to get.

Then a nice thing occurs to him: Ivy is not on his list. That's because all she needs is you, is Hugh. And she's got you already.

Up the back porch steps, in, up the stairs: everyone's eyes turn as he rises above the rail. There's Ivy. He kisses her in front of them, and she kisses him back.

He tells her, "I went to see—" No, never mind. Death can't enter here tonight. That's the penance for leaving Mimi: he can't bring her with him.

"I saw Burton—Newell's on it," he says instead.

"Right," she says. "Good. I was there when Burton kicked him out."

"Fucking *Burton*, man," Jason says, bursting, and L says, "*Fucking* Burton."

Hugh surveys the rooms. Kitchen cleaned, living room good, table set, all the leaves in. "Okay—table ready too? Beautiful, you guys! Better than I could have done! Okay, red currant sauce, put the crêpe cake together, believe it or not, we're done," Hugh says. "L, cut and plate the *cake salé;* Jason, shoot those mushroom caps under the broiler, and Ivy—"

The world is so fucked. He kisses her again.

(DELLA)

At Hugh's back door
we don't want to go in   we must
a call from the street—what?   *no no no no*
push Ken up the stairs
        You take the wine up, I need to talk to Ruth—
Ruth trotting along up to the porch   curious bird with red eyes
    Well, don't you look just lovely. I left Mimi for an hour,
    couldn't miss the party!

                                                           humiliation
                                                            say it now

        Ruth, that was me this morning, in the shower.
        None of my business!

                                                    bright bird eyes
                                                make her believe you
        But we—   there is no explanation
                                            rough hand clasp warm skin

No, no, I didn't think so!
        I wanted to tell you—

                                                panic / Ken / Jenny
                                                  money / ugliness
                                              nothing that can be told

another confiding squeeze
scratchy overworked hand
    It's spic and span for selling now, hope it goes fast. Doesn't
    need it anymore, does he? I'm just running to get the macaroons
    or what-not Hugh left in Jasper's freezer. Happy anniversary
    to the both of you.

oh Ruth
Aunt Truth

11. HUGH CAN HAVE YOUR CAKE AND EAT IT TOO

aperitif cake
cake salé   mushroom macarons

Hugh looks down the long table in the long room, white and silver. Kitchen: pedestal cake plates in a row. Teen army: L, Jason, Orion (emerged from the guest room, ice-cool in server's black). Wine breathing, glass aglow in candlelight. Okay.

Downstairs, voices: Della and Ken, right on time. Ken climbs the stairs alone, six bottles of extra special wine cradled in his arms. That eye, purple/black, but no longer pulsing. Della's talking to Ruth downstairs, he says. Not wanting to spoil the trompe l'oeil joke, Hugh waves a squelching hand at L and keeps Ken penned at the landing till they hear Della coming up.

It's always like this at a party, the falseness and theatricality of entrance. Stiff chat and laughter between people who earlier that afternoon were telling each other their marital difficulties or making tender whoopie in the lunch hour, were in despair or vertigo, attending at a death. Put it aside, put it aside.

Newell now, climbing the stairs. Freshly elegant in the softest of linen shirts, hair damp-tousled. He doesn't care about it; he doesn't have to care, because it falls in that wild wave as he shakes his head from the shower. A kiss for Della, for Hugh, a warm embrace for Ken, both shoulders held for a moment as Newell studies him, taking in this new black eye. Newell laughs with Hugh in the general direction of Della (who accepts it as anniversary joy), then breaks away gently to move into the living room.

Seeing Orion he salutes, briefly. The ironic gesture of one who has spent the afternoon in the service of the other. Orion nods his head but stays aloof.

So Newell goes across to him, his radiant warmth making a path between them, and says, "Listen, that great ape Burton came to his senses. He'll tell you later what was in his mind, how confused he was when he made that snap decision he now regrets very much."

Does that fix it? Hugh can't say, looking at Orion's iron face.

L breaks the tension, arriving with her tray of tiny, pretty, fake beer cocktails. Jason gives Orion a plate of *cake salé* to hand round; he has napkins and the mushroom fake-macarons.

"Here," Hugh says. "Everyone!"

People come to order, all that are there. Still missing—Burton—but here's Ruth, coming up the stairs with the salted caramel macarons from Jasper's freezer, and Jasper himself in tow, just-shaved, just-shoved into a fresh shirt and jacket. Is there a place-Oreo for Jasper? L catches Hugh's anguished eye and nods happily.

Hugh continues: "First course, *cake salé* and mushroom macarons!" The guests exclaim at mushroom caps sandwiched together with caramel-smooth foie gras. "Welcome to the thirtieth anniversary of the meeting and entanglement of our friends Della and Ken, making possible their offspring, our amazing L, who is even now handing round small beers." Shot glasses of amber liquid, white heads. "The first and simplest toast: to Della and Ken, a little beer!"

Della is the first to drink. Maybe needs a drink the most, next to Hugh. She drinks, chokes, looks at the glass.

"Not beer—trompe l'oeil," Hugh says. He takes a sip. Hm, pretty sweet. "Cuarenta y Tres, a vanilla-citrusy Spanish *licor*, topped with a little cream for the head."

People drink, slowly—if this is not funny, the whole party fails. None of them see Mimi's face every time they close their eyes. It's possible they still could laugh? But they don't.

The party is nonsense, Hugh thinks, and sinks.

But Ivy threads her arm through his, upending her glass with pleasure. "Better than beer! This is like absinthe ought to be."

Okay. Hugh can carry on.

"This evening will be All Cake All the Time, one cake after another. Because you two take the cake for longevity, passionate attachment, and progeny. You take all the beautiful cakes as a shining example of joy in each other and steadfast love in action."

By saying things out loud, you can breathe them into being true.

MAIN CAKE
sushi cake   seafood crêpe cake
meatloaf petits fours   potato tortilla cake

At the table they discover and exclaim over L's place-card silhouettes, Ivy's lilies, and Ken's very good wine; the pleasure of unblemished linens, shining glass and silver.

Brief disappearance of the wait-staff: then L brings in the first big piece, the sushi cake, pink-ginger-petalled on its pedestal. Hugh carries the dangerously mobile seafood crêpe cake, thirty lacy layers, followed by Jason and Orion with tiered plates of petits fours: glossy red-capped meatloaf squares and golden diamonds of potato tortilla, each wearing a saffron aioli rosette. The boys clasp and clamp with their tongs while L and Hugh carve up the larger cakes.

Ruth watches Hugh cut a careful wedge of crêpe cake for her. "All cooked, no shrimp," he whispers in her small pink ear. She darts a grateful look up at him, her nice pursey mouth like a closed rose. If Mimi was there, she'd have the crêpe cake too. Two old ladies, not entirely unalike.

The company sets to. Della's delighted by sushi cake and ginger roses. "So beautiful! Elly, we had this at Zoom, twenty years ago, remember, Ken?—oh, tortilla petits fours!"

Hugh bows modestly. He gestures, and Della's glass refills: wine bottle napkin-wrapped, Jason sommeliers the long table.

Too soon, Ruth takes her plate to the kitchen. Hugh follows, helps her to find a plastic tub, listens to her whispered apologies as she sets off back to sit with Mimi again. Caught in a vision of Mimi's blue-white hands, her cheek like chalk smeared on a yellow pillow, he has to turn away, bend to the empty oven and hide his face for a while.

❧

Ivy surveys the table and the room, pleasure more acute for being tinged with dread. Orion: a tinder-box. What will happen with all that? Fine for Newell to say it's fine, but it can't be. Out on the deck, Orion mans the barbecue with Jason. Grilling something—slices of the almond cake Hugh was pulling from the oven at lunch time, before they made transcendent, headache-conscious, almost-motionless love. She feels her face warming again.

Across the dining table, Ken draws Newell out about his television show. Newell hates talking about it, but is patient. "I think it's Hercules all over again. Our stories are no more absurd than the Nemean lion— I'm just a guy who has not done well by his family, who's screwed up in every conceivable way, trying to do better."

"But the stunts, they're so violent. Do you do it all yourself?"

"They won't let me. It looks like I do, though, doesn't it?" Newell asks, but he speaks out the open doors to Orion. Who also looks like he does his own stunts, Ivy thinks.

"I like *Catastrophe*," she says. "The mental toughness that makes physical toughness possible. Plus, I always love a caper." It's tricky for Ivy to suss out exactly what Newell's position in the fame arcana is these days, now that she's so far off the table herself.

Della asks her, "How are you liking *Importance of Being Earnest?*"

Orion can't hear her disloyalty, out on the deck, and Newell won't mind, so Ivy tells Della the truth, that she is bored by Wilde's epigrams. "They're not true now, anyway. We've unbuckled some old social shackles. Even gay people get to be people."

As if called up by an incautious word, there's a slam and a shout from below, a tromping on the stairs. Satan rising from Hell's mouth: Burton's roosterish head appears over the stair railing, then his bulging eyes, his babbling mouth, already announcing himself to the room.

"*I'm here, I'm here, let the bells ring out—*" he peals. "Ring out, wild bells, and let him die! No, live! Let him *live!*" He corrects himself. "Another thirty years, at least!"

Ivy looks out to the deck where Orion stands, tongs arrested by Burton's voice. He hands the tongs to Jason, turns in one graceful, discus-throwing motion and launches himself up to the deck's railing—and then straight out into air, arms high.

Before volition can catch up Ivy is out through the door; she's with Jason at the railing almost before Orion lands, strong hands and springing feet, on the lawn below.

He looks up, shakes his head, and takes off across the grass.

Wow, impressive. Real-life parkour.

"Guess he had an appointment," she murmurs to Jason.

Who covers a laugh and boasts, "He could jump back up here, if he wanted to!"—then gasps and whirls back to his toasting cake, tongs grabbing to turn the slices.

Inside, Burton is divesting himself of a bottle of Veuve Clicquot champagne (which he hands to L, stage-whispering *"straight onto ice with the Widow"*), and a large box he plumps onto the table in front of Della. "A toast to the happy couple," he cries. He is in his very liveliest mode. "The pearl anniversary, the thirtieth, you know."

"It is not present time," Newell says, removing the box to the kitchen counter. "Sit, Ansel. You have such a gift for disruption."

"Dear Boy, *now* is *always* present time!"

L puts a plate in front of him. He whips his napkin into place and accepts her offer of cake. "Oooh, sushi, please! Scrumptious, Hugh—all of you—I'm sure Hugh must have had help!" He takes a bite, the more to swoon about the food.

Ivy is aware of Hugh's iron control. All his fume stays inside, like a backyard hamsmoker. She elbows his arm as he passes by and sends him a glance to help him cope.

Burton is under control too. He has not once glanced at Hugh, even when complimenting him. Spikes seem to stick up all over him, more medieval mace than hedgehog. Della asks him about *Earnest* too, his current obsession being the only imaginable topic for Burton; he waxes on about Wilde's subtext, his own experience at the Public, and his unproduced one-man show on the friendship between Wilde and Beardsley, until he catches Ivy watching him.

"You, Ivy—what's your take on today?"

He doesn't want to know, but a devil makes her answer, "I don't much like the play."

"You resent playing pruney Prism? Gay nineties banter depresses you? Or is it a deep-seated prejudice?"

"Nope. It's because I believe that people are—that we are humans before gender, or sexuality, and I don't like glorifying the things that set us apart from each other."

Burton gives this a glazed, offended smile and turns away.

But Ivy does not take it back, arrogant or not. I love Hugh because he is *you*, is me, because of humanity, the parts of us that are the same. I love Newell the same way. And I try, I try, to like you that way too, Burton.

On Burton's other side, Ken—the only one here who can talk to him without constraint—is boasting about Della's grand piano. "A gift from Hugh's
mother when she moved into the apartment, last year. A real treasure, once
belonged to Glenn Gould. It's a Steinway D—not the 318, the NAC has that on
display, but an earlier practice piano. Mimi was a friend, as you probably knew."

"An honour, to play in the maestro's fingerprints! I had no idea you
had *real skill*, Della."

"Then you haven't heard her play," Newell says, and down the table
Jasper agrees with a sudden raucous "Hear! Hear!"

Della disguises her painful modesty by clowning, by breezy arrogance: "Oh, I don't play *accurately*—anyone can play accurately."

Burton laughs. Catching Hugh's blank expression he laughs again,
condescending to explain. "A line from *Earnest*, dear Hugh. She panders
to an old man's obsession."

"After Gould died," Ken asks, "was that when Mimi first had electroshock, Hugh?"

It shocks Ivy that he's so blunt, or clumsy—this is the first time she's
encountered Della's husband in real life. She reserves judgement. He'd
better be nice, to be with Della, to be L's father. But that black eye! His
right eye, so it wasn't Hugh who hit him.

Oddly, it's Burton (his left eye's bruise now faded to a yellow memory)
who saves the electroshock gaffe. "Anyone who was *anyone* had ECT in
those days," he says.

"You?" Newell asks from the other end of the table. Ivy is shocked again.

"*Ow*, yes," Burton says, trotting out his horrendous cockney accent.
"'Ad it as a nipper, to cure me kink."

Newell laughs, and then (permission somehow being granted) everybody else laughs too. It's so absurd, such a perfect example of the hope-
lessness of every single thing, they cannot help but laugh.

❧

DESSERT CAKE
fried eggs & toast   baked potatoes

Hugh escapes the shock-talk, makes himself busy in the kitchen. Let the
skies rain down complete histories of unsuccessful treatments, let memory

blind you with Polaroid snaps of raddled fearful/forgetful eyes, cakes must continue to appear.

L announces, deadpan, "And for dessert: fried eggs, toast, and baked potatoes." She and Jason set the plates at each place.

Hugh allows himself to be happy, as his audience applauds. Lemon curd yolks in meringue-nest whites: sunny-side-up eggs. Toast slices of grilled marzipan cake, they turned out well, and ice-cream baked potatoes fat in their sifted-cocoa skin, with a dollop of crème fraîche. Peculiar plates, but pleasing.

"Homemade ice cream is ten thousand times better than bought," Della says.

Behind her, L and Hugh exchange a sober nod.

"Hugh," Ken says, picking up his spoon, "you are a culinary mastermind."

He and Della are behaving well together, tonight. Only his blackened eye betrays the fight they must still be having. Thirty years together makes concealment easier, even as it makes the quarrel deeper. Nice things to eat help too. Down there at the table's end, Ken absorbs Burton's bile, discoursing on some legal brangle Hugh can't bear to think about, because it brings his own brangles back to his brambled mind. He has the vertigo feeling again, avoiding thought/memory/pain.

Della takes a bite of ice cream potato, white horse teeth biting down. "Remember that peach-raspberry ice cream you made once, Hugh—you called it fire and ice?"

Hugh can't remember. His head swirls unpleasantly. "Best I ever made," he says to Della. You can't remember every dish, every summer night, every person of the past. Only a spoon of mango ice cream through the round ports of the old storm window.

Where is Ivy, why is he not sitting beside her? He does.

Newell leans over. "I had some of that, fire and ice. I drove out here after a show, or was it a Monday? Ian Mighton was there with his girl of the moment, which one was that?"

"Ugh, it was the week he spent with Ann," Della says. "Right after she and Hugh split up. Everyone was being so civilized. Hugh was entirely decent. Honourable."

Newell looks around, as if checking for Ann.

You did invite her. Decent of you, of Hugh. Doesn't matter if she hovers over Mimi, waiting for the closet key to drop out of her claw-like hand. Not hard to be civilized about that Mighton thing, he was so relieved to be out of Ann's clutch. Good policy, as it turned out: the commissions on Mighton's work keep this whole putrid disaster afloat now.

"Bohemians," Hugh dismisses it out loud, to Ivy. "Artists. Worse than actors."

Della looks up, eyes suddenly bright. "Hugh! Was it *Mighton* that we found Ann, um, on the coats with, that night?"

Hugh passes a hand over his forehead, feeling like he'll never speak to Della again for bringing that up. Why did she? For Ken's benefit, perhaps? Doesn't make it less painful. Hugh has always secretly known who it was, anyway. It was Newell.

But Ivy slides a hand onto his thigh under the table and tells Della, "You know, I took the side mirror off my Volvo today, it was the craziest thing. I must have been in some kind of dream state. It was right after I'd had a *very* good lunch."

Hugh laughs, misery eased for a moment.

People get up, walk; they disperse for a little while between courses. A breather.

Hugh slides through playlists to change the music. The rules of honourable behaviour. You know when you break them. Laws change, mores, but nobody is confused about honour. Not rules, requirements: being open, having fair expectations—and the simple one, loving the other more than the self. Where does Newell stand on all that now?

Orion has vanished. Probably for the best. Ivy's at the table with Burton and Della; Ken by the fireplace with Jasper, discussing the curio shop's finances and the legal position re flooding; L and Jason are busy in the kitchen, plating the macarons from Jasper's freezer.

Hugh drifts with Newell out the open doors onto the roof deck. Nice night after all the rain. Black branches bend over and around the roof, black crayon against the night sky. They lean on the back railing like they used to do when they smoked. When everybody did.

In the stillness, Hugh is at last able to say, "What's going on with you and Orion?"

Newell doesn't move, or grow shuttered. He looks out into the blue-black dark, the black branches, the few stars over the FairGrounds roof-peak. "I—like him. Since you say I don't love people. This is new for me."

That's true. Newell's never been involved with anyone younger.

"He's brilliant, he idolizes me, maybe it's ego. Do you feel no pull to L, for example?"

Hugh is revolted. "No, none." Images offer, though: the clean dent between nose and mouth, the pure outline of her mouth. You must have seen those things.

But Ivy. Not that she is salvation, or settling. She is destiny, density.

"I might be of some help to him," Newell says. Always diffident about his stature.

Hugh needs to say something else, though. Not about responsibility or morality, that's not it. "I just—aren't you, isn't it a question of—" Good work, that's articulate. "Of honour?"

A silhouette, dark against pale pearl-grey porch rail, Newell looks at him.

Listen carefully, Hugh thinks. Remembering earlier, talking to Ken, how lonely you feel when your friends fail to understand you. When you wonder if they've ever known you.

Something in Newell's face shifts, an inner gate moving from closed to open. "Oh, Hugh. He'd break my heart anyway in a year or two. I know he's too young, but the heart can't help wanting what it wants—"

A voice says, "When you find yourself sounding like Woody Allen, you know that's not a good sign."

It's Della, coming out onto the deck. They turn to her. "In grade thirteen," she says, "I was so in love with my French teacher, I thought I was going to die. He was married, I don't suppose he ever thought about me for a nanosecond. I still love him."

She blushes. The pink is visible on her long white face, even with her back to the living room's pouring light. "Not that this is the least bit useful, I know."

Newell puts out an arm and gathers her in, letting his chin rest on her head as he has done ever since he was first taller than her. "Come back inside," he says. "You're cold."

"Just tired," she says. Hugging close to him, taking warmth from his warmth. She puts out a hand to Hugh. The three of them were the world, all the time they were at Ruth's. Being at Ruth's was— Not their real lives, the real lives were the misery. Ruth's was refuge. At Ruth's they were together, shielded and shielding; strong and smart and unscathed, together. Able to think.

Hugh can't think—he needs a pill or two.

He can't think without thinking of Mimi, and there's no thinking of her now.

CAKE SURPRISE
macaroon cake   macaron mushrooms   30-year-old port

Ivy busies herself, helping L and Jason clear away dessert plates. The whole trompe l'oeil thing makes her love Hugh with every ganglion of her tired mind, every thrum of her tired heart: that he thought it up; that he thought it would be funny; that he got L and Jason to help; that he pulled it off, even though he almost didn't.

Another bang at the downstairs door. Ivy peeks over the banister. Oh, good! A charming bustle, chiming laughter, a gorgeous welling of scent: Gareth Pindar rises, majestic, Léon harrying behind him, carrying his train. They are elegant and happy in beautiful suits, carrying more flowers, brandy, and cigars, half of them chocolate.

"Impeccable timing. Dessert," Hugh says, coming in from the deck to welcome them. Della is kissing Léon, Ken being bear-embraced by Gareth, who must outweigh him by a hundred pounds. Jasper, asleep in a quiet corner, never stirs.

Della says, "We've had dessert! Fried eggs and baked potatoes!"

"No, no, that was joke dessert. There's still cake. There's always more cake."

L appears carrying the rest of the cake and the port, and Jason brings the macarons (bitter chocolate/salted caramel, shaped like fat mushroom caps).

Places are found for Gareth and Léon, Della and Ken shifting their chairs closer together so that Gareth can sit beside her; Léon (who seems to have an eye for what is needful) sliding in to introduce himself to Burton. Hugh takes Ivy away to be his espresso slave, so she spends ten minutes shuttling up and down from the frame room with small cups, while he pulls Della's pictures from their hiding place and gives them a last polish.

He points out the gold fillet he added inside the linen mat on the *State of the Union* piece, obviously proud of Della's work. Ivy would like to know if he still paints himself, but so far has been afraid to ask. Everybody is afraid all the time. Of asking or of knowing. Like about Mimi, how she is faring; and what's the deal with Orion–Burton–Newell?

Another, another, until all the cups are made.

She follows Hugh up the stairs: his very nice backside before her. He is old, as old as she is herself, yet she does not see age and decay, only the answer to her long true question: who am I to love? He is my work, she thinks, following him. That's good. Whether he's painting or not, in pain or out of it, damaged or clear. I like to have a little job.

Hugh's job at the moment is to fête Della, and by extension Ken. Arms full, he takes the head of the table and draws L to him with a cock of the head. "I—we have to confess, we've done the unforgiveable, Della. L and I went over your head and decided that some of your work is finished."

He turns to the long low bookshelf behind him, and begins to deal out framed boats. L looks at her mother, with pride and worry. Della has half risen in her chair, at first just tucking one foot beneath her for more height, then almost standing. "My boats!" she says. She looks to Ken briefly, then to the framed pictures.

Her eyes flick over them until she comes to the middle picture, the sea-green mat, and Ivy sees her face relax. When we give someone else power over us, when we take power over them by loving, what a long string of obligation we begin to unwind through the maze of life.

"As you'll see when you have a chance to examine these pieces closely," Hugh is saying, "the boat in this one is called *State of the Union*—that's what we're here to celebrate tonight, the ship you and Ken have sailed, through all kinds of weather, for thirty years. You can all come and look in a moment, but first I have a present for Ken—in case you are feeling a bit left out, Ken. I know you've always thought you might paint too, once you retire."

He reaches behind the chair and picks up the final oblong: a large white canvas, marked with a pale blue pattern—oh! Ivy laughs. Paint-by-number. Hugh flips the board around, and there is the original photo, a much younger Ken and Della, standing with their arms around each other's waists, staring into the camera, defiant and determined.

Ken hoots, he almost honks. He rushes from his chair to take the canvas from Hugh's outstretched hands, overcome, eyes blearing, napkin up. "I've always—this photo—"

Ivy is taken aback by this display of sheer emotion—the place is crawling with artists, but it takes a lawyer to show a little honest sap.

Almost under control, Ken wants to make a speech.

"I want to tell you all, I've had this photo, the original of this, beside my bed for the last week, while I've been trying to work out what to do. And a couple of my daughter's drawings that I stole. They made my decision harder and easier. I won't go on about all that now, while you're all—but I hope you know, Hugh, that I do—that it, you've—" His throat closes.

Della stands to rescue him. She is calm. "Quick, Ken, drink some of this port with the big fat 30 on the label. It must have been bottled about the same time that you and I were getting bottled that night, All Souls night, when we were babies no older than these babies now bringing cake and port around. I'll help you with the paint-by-numbers—we'll fill in the outlines of each other's faces, as we've done all this time. All my wrinkles, all my beauty, you've given me these last thirty years. And I account for your grey hair at least as much as Elly does. My friends, you are so kind to help us celebrate!"

She's going to lift her glass, but Burton jumps up from his seat. "Boy! *Your* present! Kitchen!" He snaps his fingers, and Jason slides the wrapped box in front of Della.

"Oh," Della says, seeming a little dismayed. "This shouldn't be a present occasion, not really—Newell, honestly, you shouldn't have."

"Open it later," Newell suggests.

"How do you know he shouldn't until you've opened it?" Burton demands. "Open it now!"

Newell lifts his hands to his face, and for an instant Ivy can imagine what it must be like to have Burton on one's back night and day. In his softest voice, Newell says, "Open the little present, Della, and try to be polite."

Della blows him a surrendering kiss. "Okay," she says. "Come help, Ken." Ken moves down the table to see what she's unwrapping: a creamy inlaid box with a silver hook. "Mother-of-pearl! Oh, beautiful." Della pulls the pin on its little chain out of the hook, and opens the lid. It is a travel box. Peach velvet trays hold bottles with silver lids. Pearl-handled nail files and other mysterious implements, each in their ordained place, the ideal of ordered, elegant living. A silver tag on one side, *HERS*, and on the other, *HIS*.

"A marriage in a box," Hugh says.

At that there is a little silence. Della touches the *HIS* pearl-handled knife and the spoon, spooned behind it. She runs a hand along the box, its smoothness conveyed to each observer's hand by the ease of her gesture. She touches the satin ribbons meant to lift the velvet tray out.

"Fine, now back to the party," Newell says. He reaches out a long hand and closes the lid, slowly enough that Della can pull her fingers out of the way. The mother-of-pearl tiles flash, opalescent in the candlelight. "It's nothing, it's a bagatelle. You can examine it later."

"You are so kind," she says to Newell.

"I found it in Jasper's shop, you should thank him."

She goes to where he is slumbering in the corner, leans over the back of his chair, and puts a hand on Jasper's sleeping shoulder. She kisses his head, her eyes more darkly hollowed than Ivy has seen them before. She shakes his shoulder, a little. But it's all right, Jasper wakes and stretches and manages a wavery dentured smile.

"Thank you," Della says and gestures to the box on the table.

"Usually they're broken up," he says, nodding. "Rare to find one intact."

Hugh stands and calls, "Jason! The widows!" Jason runs. "My friends, my family . . ." Hugh pauses, and Ivy looks up, worried that he might be in trouble. But he carries on (as Jason hands him the first bottle of champagne and stands ready with the next), untwisting the wire and foil and taking the cork, hands gentle on the bottle: "I wish our darling Mimi, who loves Della and Ken, was here to help us celebrate—and Ruth, who's sitting with her now."

He turns the bottle and the cork releases with that velvet clonking sound we love so well. He pours and pours and pours, and lifts at last his own glass.

"All of you who *are* here, let us praise our friends, absent and present, and help me raise a glass to the wish that—that you will never die, not one of you."

(L)

Great Pindar's girth expands to take in everything Jason puts in front of him, sampling all the other cakes to see what he and Léon missed.

L likes Léon, but is too scared of Gareth to look at him. Only the outer outlines, the shape sitting at Hugh's table. From time to time she steals a look. Now he's staring over at the framed pictures Hugh left in a line on the bookshelf—the boats her dad didn't even actually look at.

Her dad never looks at her mom's work. As if it is some intimate thing he's not supposed to see, her panties strung on a line in the bathroom. Not that she ever does that, not even in their own bathroom. They are delicate with each other, each keeping private.

I'm not going to be like that. Nobody can be with me, L thinks, unless they *be* with me.

Jason, going by behind her, snakes a hand in under her arm and through to reach around and touch, touch, her breast. Then he is past, carrying champagne bottles back to the kitchen sink. Her breast! Sings!

Gareth gets up. He wanders to the bookshelf to look more closely at the boats sailing in a row. He stands, stops, moves, stops. He pulls different glasses from his pocket. Casts an eye over his shoulder to see if Hugh is watching, then if Della is. Léon strolls over, a long s-curve, sinuous beside him, and they talk a moment.

Strange and interesting. Because those boats are really good, in L's IMHO.

Jason comes from the kitchen, her phone buzzing like a bottled fly in his hand.

At the head of the stairs, L motions to Ivy and whispers that she's leaving—Orion's on the back porch, won't come up. "Will you tell my mom,
I mean, say I'm sorry I had to leave?"

"Something up?" Ivy asks. Some sixth sense says she ought to ask. Not
waiting for the answer, she trots down herself, to talk to Orion.

Nobody there. Black night—midnight already, how did the night go
so fast? L emerges from the back door, whistles a winding tune. Orion
steps out of the bushes.

"She can help," L says.

After a moment, he nods. "Savaya's gone to Toronto. I have to go
get her."

Ivy doesn't say anything, just looks as open and unjudgemental as she
can, waiting for more. He pulls out his phone. She takes it and reads,

> Indo para Toronto

Eu transei con Terry

e eu loitei con Nevaeh

todo é parafuso

She hands it back, eyebrows up.

"Sorry—" he says, sliding a finger on the phone and handing it over
again. "Here's the English side. When she's got something going on, she
Google-translates it into, like, Tagalog or Malaysian and then into
Galician, in case her parents read her phone. Then I retranslate."

Ivy looks down again, forces her eyes to focus on the tiny print.

> I'm going to Toronto

  I trance Terry

  and I struggled with Nevaeh

  everything is messed

"She—tranced Terry?"

"She doesn't mean *trance*. That's why we use Galician."

Oh dear. "She fought with Nevaeh? Why would that make her go to Toronto?"

"It's because of something I told her—I have to go get her." He sounds about ten years old, suddenly.

There's only a minute to think. This doesn't seem seriously bad, but can she take the chance? Orion won't come inside, shouldn't—Burton's still up there. Oh, no more questions.

"I'll get my keys," she says.

"I can drive," he says.

"Yeah, I've seen your car—let's take mine," Ivy says. But really, hers is not much better. Hugh's van might be the best bet.

Newell steps out of the doorway, keys in his hand. "Need some wheels?" When he says things like that they sound funny and cool, not old and sad.

Ivy says, "I think we're okay, we can take the Volvo."

But there comes Jason with L's jacket and his own, and Orion's backpack that he left behind when he jumped. Four, counting Ivy, and then Savaya to bring back—too many.

"I have to go," Orion says.

"How are you going to find Savaya?" Ivy asks.

"An app—it shows me where her phone is, see?" Orion sticks the phone out, at the end of his long arm, remaining infinitely remote from them. From Newell.

Who says, "I didn't think she'd be so sensible."

"She's not. I installed it while I was taking her Scrabble turn in Social."

"How does it—" Ivy stops. Doesn't matter.

Orion explains anyway: "GPS. It's quite neat to watch, actually. See, she's in Queen's Park, in the government buildings." He says this to Newell, as if it means something, then offers Ivy the screen, looking at it with her. "Look, she's walking. We have to hurry. I told her a stupid thing, and I'm afraid she might—" He looks at Newell.

Newell looks back at him. "Take the Saab," he says.

Orion takes the keys from his hand, an odd silent moment. Then the three of them dart off into the darkness. A moment later the car starts, a low-purring, well-heeled engine noise.

"We'd better go too," Newell tells Ivy. "What can that Volvo of yours do?"

"Well—110, anyway." Ivy feels a bit defensive. She loves that car.

A voice speaks in the darkness. "Take mine," it says, a ghost in the shadowy garden. It's Gerald, sitting alone in the dark on the bench on the gallery porch.

Newell turns to him. "Gerry," he says, in his kindest, milksoft voice. "You okay, sitting out here? Lonely tonight? Go on upstairs—Hugh's giving a little party for Della and Ken, he'd love to have you drop in."

"Looking for Jasper," Gerald says.

"He's up there too, he'll be glad to see you. Ivy and I can take you up."

"That's okay." Gerald stands, heavy on his feet, stooping a little under the porch roof. "Here—" He dangles a set of keys. "Out front. Silver Ghost 9-3, basically a Phoenix. Call it a test drive. Except the way things are with Saab, it won't ever get into general production." He tosses the keys.

Newell catches them. "Your house key on here too? We might be late."

"I'm not going out there," Gerald says. "Jasper lets me stay at his place."

They look at him, as well as they can see in the darkness. A shambling beast, a bear of sorrows and acquainted with grief. Then headlights glare in from the parking spot behind the gallery, and Gerald puts an arm up to shield his blinded eyes.

"Look!" A woman's voice. It's Ann. "People are still going in, see. It's fine, I told you it would be."

Three people get out of the car, and walk over. Ann and a tall man and the painter, Mighton. Ivy has decided she doesn't like Mighton.

Okay, perfect—a little outing will be even better now.

Hugh's at the head of the stairs when Ivy runs up. Her pansy eyes big and dark, with a wild look. Whatever she's up to, she doesn't want Burton to hear—she lets Hugh know this with a slight shake of the head and a directed flick of the feral eyes.

"Listen," she says, urgently casual. "I've got to run in to town, all of a sudden. Sorry to skip out on the cleanup, but leave the dishes for me. I love doing dishes in the morning."

"Sure you don't need help?" He's thinking of Jamie, the mad boy-man at her apartment.

Again the warning flick to Burton lounging at the table, the good port anchoring Léon and Ken and Jasper, the air thick with legalese and cigar smoke. Too soft for them to hear, she says, "Newell's going with me. You can't leave the guests—" She reaches for her coat. "And I know you'll want to go to your mother again later." Diffidence in her voice, as always when she speaks of Mimi.

He wishes she could meet Mimi—did they meet? No, that was a dream. Hugh looks at the people scattered around his living room. "Okay, you head out, and I'll head over. Meet you back here whenever." Trying for nonchalance. Not understanding how she can leave him.

Her hand clasps his, warm and brief. "I'll be back. I have to go, right away. Do me a favour, don't drive to the hospice. And *please* don't fall down any more stairs, or climb up any more ladders. Oh, also—Newell's trying to get Gerald to come up, he's not in good shape. And sorry, Ann's here too."

Hugh's face stiffens. Ivy reaches up and kisses him, hand lingering on his cheek for a moment. "I'll text you the whole story," Ivy whispers, her cheek pressed against his. She pulls back to meet his eyes, with a short beaming grin, and goes.

Okay.

He turns to find Della and Gareth deep in conversation at the book-shelf where her paintings stand. Their bodies form familiar triangles, legs apart, one arm up to point, to remark— Hey, is Gareth stealing Della from him? He laughs, pops three Advil, and heads down the stairs to help poor Gerald.

Still blinded from the upstairs light, Hugh steps out onto the porch, saying, "Come in, come in." Then steps back, bewildered, as a train of people advance on him. Conrad's here? And Ann—is this—?

No—Mighton wouldn't come along to tell him Mimi is dead. It can't be that.

His heart feeling like it's been wrung out violently and left spongey, Hugh stands braced in the doorway, looking around for Gerald: there, at the shadowy end of the porch.

"Sorry I'm so late," Ann says. "Ruth came back and I sat with her a little longer." She lets out a poignant sigh. "We never know when it's going to be the last time . . ."

Hugh growls under his breath.

Conrad says, "No change, no need for alarm." He puts out a hand, man-style. Hugh still likes Conrad, or at least needs him; he puts his own hand out in response.

"Con was leaving anyway, so he gave me a lift," Ann says. "Then we saw Mighton on the street and I knew he must be coming to your party too. Where's Jason?"

A prickle of unease at that—but no, it's okay, Jason went off with L. Hugh waves Ann and the two men upstairs. Old Mighton. Might have known he'd turn up.

Then he walks along the porch to where Gerald sits stalled against the gallery wall.

"Hey, Gerald," he says, trying not to use that calm, infantilizing tone the bereaved must get so weary of. "Come on upstairs—we've got a quiet shindig going on. There's cake, if you're hungry."

Gerald lifts his large round head. The curly hair that was so buoyantly part of his persona now seems like a wig. "Not hungry much these days."

No. Hugh tries again. "Jasper's up there, in case you're looking for him."

"Well," Gerald says. "I was."

Then there's a long wait.

"Should I ask him to come down?" Hugh suggests.

Gerald nods. Then stands, abruptly. "No, I'll come up," he says. "Be a man."

The stairs and the landing are full of people, Ann kissing and hugging her way through the throng, her glow intensified by company. She does love a party. Hugh likes her after all, in an antiquated way. She goes to Della, arms out, crying, "Della, Ken! It's a miracle, you're still married—what's your secret. Oh yes! Ken not being an asshole."

Della turns from where she and Gareth are still talking by the array of boats.

She is not all right, Hugh thinks. Whatever was going on between her and Ken still is, somehow. Whether Ken understands that or not. And what's got him going now? He's on his feet, glowering at the end of the long table, hands shoved into his jacket pockets and the hair practically bristling on the back of his neck.

Standing between Della and Ken, Mighton looks from one to the other and laughs, a half-bark that doesn't quite signal contempt. "Modern life," he says to the general air. "We run into old flames and their new flames all the time, don't we?"

"Not me," Ken says. "I only have one old flame."

The room is suddenly full of maleness, swelled to fill all the corners. It's dicey; Hugh is worried. But now Della is at Ken's side, somehow reaching him without passing through Mighton's tight little sphere at all.

"I'm your permanent, everlasting, waterproof lighter," she tells Ken, laughing. Treating him as if he is the way he ought to be: easy, confident, loving, stable. "You're stuck with me, poor guy."

Baulked of an emotional scene, Mighton locates Gareth Pindar by the fireplace and lifts an arrogant arm. "Gare!" he calls. "Hey, you've got to come downstairs and see my big piece, *Dark Gates*. Hugh hung it yesterday."

From the end of the table, where he sits keeping Burton in check, Léon lifts his lazy lean-jawed head to say, "No working tonight, Mr. Mighton."

That makes Gareth laugh. "A purely social occasion, no opinions offered. Send me a jpeg, I'll peek at it while I'm in the loo." He winks at Della and vanishes down the hall.

"At least come to the wine and cheese tomorrow," Mighton calls after him.

The wine and cheese. Hugh's done nothing about it, not the first thing. Not a single block of cheese. He looks at Della, soundlessly begging her to tell him that she sent the invitations to their usual email list, but she's busy rewrapping her mother-of-pearl box. What happened to Gerald? Okay, there at the abandoned table; Jasper's pouring him a tot of port from the almost empty bottle. Nothing like your thirty-year-old port for disappearing.

Léon stretches and stands, matador slim. Burton rouses himself from the plural pleasures of port and art, and lets Léon go, loosening the vise of his attention with a sated look, as if he's prised out everything about Gareth, the gallery, and their whole world, and looks around for Newell. Who did not let him know he was leaving.

That will mean a scene. Mighton might enjoy it, but can Hugh handle another scene?

Stepping back to the kitchen, Hugh almost trips over Conrad's feet.

"Here, give me a look at these eyes of yours," Conrad says.

The light is dim, at least.

"I'm fine," Hugh says. "I didn't drink. I'm being careful."

"You nearly fell just then."

Hugh gives up his face and stares into Conrad's eyes. Clean, cool blue, bright whites, locking on one eye, then the other, back again. "Head hurt?"

The pounding is so bad. Hugh makes his eyes blink slowly; tilts his head as if he's checking for ghostly pain, rather than speaking through hammers. "Not to speak of, nothing much. I'm being careful." Say it often enough and Conrad will believe him.

Gareth comes back down the hall. Hugh puts out a hand. "You'll stay, you and Léon, won't you? The guestroom is ready for you," he says.

Gareth looks over his glasses at Hugh. "Will you still have us if I woo your artist away?"

"Yes," Hugh says, happy for the first time in a long—wait, okay, since that liquifying lunch with Ivy, five hours ago. He laughs. "Towels in the bathroom cabinet. But listen, this is Conrad Frey, Mimi's doctor. I'm afraid I've got to go back over to her now."

Noises of sympathy from Gareth, and from Léon, who weaves his arm into Hugh's.

"It's been a very long time coming," Hugh says. "Conrad can tell you. Make yourselves at home. I'll be back to give you breakfast in the morning." In the morning—when the moving truck Ruth arranged will be arriving at Mimi's, when the apartment must be cleared out.

Okay. But Ivy will be back to help. To do the dishes, she said so.

"Listen, I'll drive you over," Conrad says, already on the stairs.

Back beyond the other guests, Burton has discovered Newell's absence. His pug-pouting face uplifted, he's scouring the deck through the long windows. In a moment he will turn and explode. Fine.

Hugh clasps Gareth's hand, thanks Conrad, and goes.

SUNDAY

Hughtopia

The soul's like all matter:
why would it stay intact,
stay faithful to its one form,
when it could be free?

Louise Glück

1. HUGHTHANASIA

The hospice is entirely still. Long stairs, long corridor. Night light: scallops of creamy light along the baseboards. In the distance the deserted nursing station is lit by one shaded lamp. Not deserted, he doesn't mean that. The nurse is somewhere, seeing to someone.

Not to Mimi. Her door is almost shut, a fissure of dark interior showing.

Hugh pushes it ajar: a shadowed shape in the bed; Ruth, asleep in the bedside chair. He doesn't want to wake her, but she will be very stiff in the morning.

No need, she wakes by herself, at some slight noise or movement of air. "No change," she says. Reassuring him first thing. "She's been so peaceful tonight, I just drifted off."

"You should go home." At her quick head-shake, Hugh shakes his own. "Gerald turned up at the party, looks like Jasper is saddled with him for the night. Might be good if one of us went over there with breakfast in the morning, to check on them."

Obedient to her twin loyalties (food and caregiving) she gives her eyelids a quick rub and gets up. No complaint over the effort in rising, but she is slower than she was—in the old days she never sat down at all. She'd have been puttering, tidying the room, seeing that everything was shipshape. One arm already in her copper corduroy coat, she pulls the other sleeve on, not quickly. It's a long day, a long life. Near the end you get a little tired.

Hugh is tired too. Cooking helps you not to think, but there's a lot he ought to have done.

"I'm sorry to ask, but would you mind calling my place and asking Ken to check the buckets one more time before they leave? They're all finishing the port up there."

"That was a lovely treat for Della," Ruth says. "You're a good friend."

Look who's talking. She buttons her jacket, bends to kiss Mimi's forehead, and goes.

Silence again.

One a.m. Early for the whole place to be as silent as—not the grave, not that—as church. Hugh sits in the chair, shrugs out of his jacket.

Sits.

The dim light grows as his eyes grow accustomed. He looks around the room, yet again. White roses in a glass jug on the table. The window, pale streetlight behind a pale drawn curtain. Escher print above the bed: stairs everywhere. Duty, tasks not done, misperception, the trickery of the world. He hates those endless, hopeless, pointless stairs, and everything else Escher ever made. Ann had Escher all over her room when they met, where they first made love. One trick pony, one stupid joke. He wouldn't let her put them up in the house. Which probably started that whole thing, that frustrated/frustrating writing on the walls.

He's been blaming her unhappiness on selfishness or narcissism. But back then it was his fault they broke up, that she went searching their acquaintances for someone to love her better. Everything about Ann is his fault. He knows this is absurd—but Jason should have been his son. He only loved Ann for a short time, to a small degree; to the same degree that he still loves her, maybe. The problem: not enough love. Because his mother needed him?

And now as her need ends, Ivy arrives.

A sound from the bed. Not as much as a sigh, just an opening of the lips. He leans forward. Mimi's eyes light, lighting on him. In some sense, she's back.

He leans closer, finds the water, straw ready-bent by Ruth. Holds it to Mimi's lips.

She sips.

She smiles, an echo of an echo of her original face. Thrush has spoiled her mouth, makes it another source of pain. He finds the swab and pulls the chair closer in one practised motion. "Swab?" Her eyes nod, her dear mouth opens a crack. The damp swab slides between lips and teeth as she tries to help. Not much mobility left in her jaw or neck, but after the swab's damping, her lips can move.

"Thank you," she says, mere breath as voice.

The rain has started again, Hugh hears as he sits back down. Oversensitive to the sound of rain these days. Beyond the glass it breathes, then rustles into a shattering, chattering rush.

Mimi's eyes move to the window.

"Wet enough for you?" he asks her. "Your hair will be curly."

She turns her eyes to him again, as sensitive to kindness from him as he is to the rain. Perhaps because there's been a lot of it lately.

"I wish I'd been kinder to you, all this time," he says.

Her eyes fix on his, such dark, searching eyes.

"I'm sorry," he says.

Her hand moves, and he takes it, careful of the tubes.

"You were the best mother in the world," he says. No falsehood in that, it is not a lie when you mean it truthfully, when you tell the story that she needs to hear.

"Difficult," she says.

"Well, I *was* difficult," he says, to make her laugh one more time. "But I always love you best." Giving her the gift of what she used to say to him at night, before she went out gallivanting—*I always love you best*.

That's too close to home. To distract her, he asks, "Can I lift your bed-head?"

Her heavy head shakes slowly, no.

"Release," she says. She begs. *Give me back my golden arm . . .*

He looks into her drowned, once-beautiful eyes and wonders if the pillow, or a kink in the tube, or—or if he could make himself do those things. If it will come to that.

"Is the pain very bad?"

Her head shakes again, no. She was always very brave.

They look at each other for a long time.

"When you need me to, I'll try," he says.

Her eyes close, as if that is release enough for now.

Hugh sits, almost alone.

In the silence, he can hear her breathing. Not frightening yet. Breath—breath, breath—ragged un-rhythm. One of the breaths will be the last one.

Someone is at the door, a hand entering first to hold the heavy door and make as little noise as possible. Hugh knows that hand: the small nurse Nolie. He feels a rush of kindness toward Nolie too, to everyone who is not dead, not yet. Her head peeps round. She nods to Hugh, but looks at Mimi. Pads in on silent soles, checks the drip bag, taps the line once, twice.

"Dr. Hoek says we are to use the mask tonight," she tells Mimi softly. Sorrowful things always accompanied by a dimple beside her mouth, offered to take away some pain.

Mimi's eyes move to Hugh, as if she might ask him for reprieve, then back to Nolie. Who is already attaching the hose to the tank, adjusting the mask's straps. With gentle fingers she dislodges the small nostril tubes and places the mask over Mimi's lower face. Her attention brings everything in the room, in the world, down to the little white straps and the mask's tender hissing, almost masked by the rain. Mimi's hand moves up to waver near the mask, and then subsides.

Hugh swallows, his throat dry because the rain sounds so cool and damp. It's clear to him now. He can't leave her to bear all this alone any longer.

"I'm going to sleep here from now on," he says to Nolie, as she turns from the bed.

She nods, unsurprised, and says, "I will ask Joseph to bring up a cot. It's good time." She gives him a small, contained smile—her approval, or her version of mourning.

Mimi's hand trembles, and Hugh takes it in his own.

He won't leave her again. The relief of saying that floods his body, his head. Eases the aching that has dogged him for so long. The gallery can close, people can make their own art for a few days. And if it's weeks, so much the better.

He texts Ivy: > when you get back, please could you please empty basement buckets please?

There's a long text from her, why she had to go, but he can't make his tired eyes focus on it. It doesn't matter. Everything matters less than you think. Only Mimi's breath, in and out, from the white bed.

"How will we find them?" Ivy asks.

Newell stares ahead into the traffic, oncoming headlights gliding over and past his face. "I have Orion on my phone, that app. We can watch him finding her."

Hm. Having Orion on his phone is not surprising, but that Finder app is more personal than a phone number, it's a location system. Oh, she has to text Hugh.

> Orion went looking for Savaya in Toronto, very worried.
L and Jason went too. N and I are following to keep them
out of trouble. Newell drives fast, this is Gerald's good car.
I'll keep you posted. Back as soon as I can.

A text from him, about emptying buckets. She texts back,

> of course

Waits. Nothing more comes. He must be with Mimi.

Oncoming lights flow over the car, a steady stream returning from Toronto, from Saturday night parties. Each sliding beam illuminates the planes of Newell's cheek, the noble set of his nose. Ivy doesn't get tired of looking at his profile, because with all its beauty it has sadness in it. Like Paul Newman or Alec Guinness; however amusing things are, awareness of pain is built into those faces. She remembers driving with Newell another time, several years ago, out to Elora Gorge for an awards dinner. She was in the back seat because Burton had the passenger seat, talking non-stop the whole time, nauseatingly witty. Newell, silent and patient, drove like a well-trained bat out of hell down that bad stretch of the 401. How can she remember that whole drive, but not a few lines of dialogue when she needs to?

She says, "You know what makes people funny? Memory. Comics remember better than we do. They remember and reincorporate things from twenty minutes or twenty years ago."

"Thirty years ago."

"Thirty minutes from now."

He drives. He watches the road, but he's amused, engaged, and that's flattering. Really, charm is just reciprocity—he finds her charming, so she loves him. "This is like *Comedians in Cars Getting Coffee*," she says.

"What?"

"Oh come on."

"I never, never, ever, watch TV. Now you know my dark secret."

"I know, neither do I, but CCGC, as I like to call it, is on the web."

"All right then, I will watch it."

"But what was I saying? Oh, trouble is I can't be funny now, because I can't remember."

"But you are, so obviously you still can, sometimes."

She laughs. Part of his charm: he induces in her a running giggle.

"Are you really freaked out?"

"Livelihood, man."

It can't mean anything to him, that word. He must have made so much money from *Blitzed Craig* that he never ever has to work again, but he still does work, all the time. And now *Catastrophe*, another goldmine. Yet here he is, in a condo in Peterborough.

"Are you staying—do you live here, in Peterborough, really?"

"Maybe a third of the year here. When I'm not in production. You know, childhood home, people know me. And they know Ruth will get mad at them if they . . . oh, make a big deal, cross some kind of line. Nobody thinks I'm that big a shot here, anyway. I'm the kid from high school who talked funny, who got lucky."

"No performing arts school in those days, I'm guessing."

"Ha. No. We had a couple of visiting theatre workshops though. That's why Burton came to town—he came to direct a show; talked to the university about setting up a drama department, but that went nowhere. Then he got a gig doing a workshop at the junior high."

And that's where we met, Newell doesn't say. She wonders what their early relationship was. How they came to be—attached. Co-dependent. Whatever they are. Notice, no more talk about the marriage thing. Not surprising. Burton wouldn't let Newell damage his career. One thing to be casually, unremarkably gay; another to get married, even now.

Newell says, "I did one myself, a workshop—two years ago, when I came out to finalize the condo. Terry asked me to come in and talk to the kids. I spent the day with the grade ten group." Which would have been Orion's class, two years ago. Changing lanes, Newell keeps his gaze on the road. "Then in the summer, after a late-night *Catastrophe* shoot, I'm walking along in Toronto and there's Orion standing on the street, down behind Queen's Park, all strung out. He said somebody had told him that was the place to go for chicken."

It takes her a minute to process that, switching from *dinner* to *coward* to *boy prostitute*.

"Idiot. Whether or not he actually did anything, got paid for sex— I don't think so. We talked, and I drove him back out here. So I've known him for a while," Newell says. Gently explaining, not justifying.

Not that he has to justify anything to her. And neither does Orion.

"He was right," Newell says, after a few miles of silence. "We should be continuing with *Earnest*. Getting some real work done."

Maybe. But the cast was wrong, anyway, Ivy thinks. It ought to be Hugh as the worthy Jack and Newell his wilder, rascally younger brother; with me as Gwendoline, Newell's theatre-cousin. And Orion as Cecily, Hugh's country ward out in Peterborough. Ivy laughs to herself. Hugh is already a bit over-Earnest, but Newell might become Earnest for the sake of Orion. And Burton, naturally, as the impassable Bracknell bramble-barrier.

Newell says, "At least Ansel never suggested we do *Tender Flowers*, his play about a leper colony for nuns, and the conflicted gay priest who serves among the women."

"When you say, his play, you mean Burton's own?"

"Yes, the play he wrote."Almost serious, Newell says, "It's not as bad as you might think. Delicate, moving. He probably ought to have been a writer, with a Tennessee Williams kind of tragic life. Better than fading away as an unhireable has-been."

Only Newell can say the thing that nobody says about Burton.

He laughs.

"What?"

"Just thinking about it. *Tender Flowers*." Newell smiles as he drives, a slight and perfect Buddha-statue smile.

(ORION)

All down the DVP Savaya's blue dot roves the backstreets around Queen's Park. L watches the phone screen. "Ministry of Health and Long-term Care, the Hepburn Block—what's in there?" When Orion can look she shows him. "Now up to Wellesley Street, she's walking up and down in front of St. Joseph's school."

Get out of there, you dope. The blue slides along St. Joseph Street as Orion turns, cutting over on College Street. "She's up to the yellow street," L says. "Oh, it's the road around Queen's Park, and . . . across, and into the park."

He can't just leave Newell's car on the street, like he would if it was his own. He turns right, right, right again, and finds a lot between the Toronto School of Theology, the Jesuits of Upper Canada, and the Marshall McLuhan building. Theme: Canada's conflicted soul.

From the back seat Jason hands forward a sheet of paper with ON DELIVERY in very professional black capitals. He holds up L's eyeliner and says sorry. Orion shoves it in the windshield, not asking what anybody might be delivering in a Saab 9-3.

"Right," he says. Organizing the troops. Then doesn't know what to say, how much to tell these guys. "Right, so, I think you'd better—I think—let me—"

L nods. "You talk to her, we'll just wander around till you need us."

She takes Jason's hand. They cross the lawn, then pause for the traffic before loping across the big road, into the darkness of the park. They're good.

Right.

Orion checks his phone.

Into the woods. The horrible pain of Burton kicking him out comes flooding back for a moment. Rising up like a freak tide from his ankles whooshing up to his hair. It's not just rage, it's raging embarrassment; and the realization that he *is* stupidly arrogant, Burton's right; then lashing pride and determination to be *more* arrogant; annoying pity for an old man who's past it, thrown on the junkyard of theatre history; and misery, and powerlessness.

Flat out running, now, power of the legs at least, following the blue dot on the screen he checks every few seconds. Almost through the park, and she's still not visible. There's the other leg of the divided road—where the fuck is she?

Through the midnight grove he passes shadows, strange lumps and humps of bodies, singly and in clusters. A clutch of workmen bending together in the grass. He's close, warmer, closer. He stops, swirls, emo batshit—checks the phone again: blue dot, stopped. Like a stupid movie.

There's her red-cased phone, lying on the ground.

"*Savaya!*" he shouts, not even meaning to.

The darkness under the trees is quiet, nothing echoes, no one answers. Even the traffic has quieted. It only—the dot was moving, a minute ago.

He sits on the steps of the monument to WWI or something, South Africa—his own phone buzzes.

The voice says, "We're getting there." Velvet, loving. "Ten minutes, maybe fifteen."

"Right," Orion says. He puts his phone away, and stands. He'll go round the park again, L and Jason are down there at the south end somewhere, maybe they'll—

Savaya slides around the big stone block of monument, above him.

"I don't even *know how*," she says, skinny arms blue-white in the night air. "Check my privilege, I can't even work out what to say to somebody. Or a car—how do you get a car to even stop? How do they tell you're up for it?"

"Good thing you can't figure it out." Orion's heart only starts pounding now, with the effort and the relief. "I'm sure if you were like, starving, you'd do it. But not—it isn't a thing to, to be prying into when you don't need to for survival. Maybe for a part, for research," he adds, to be fair. "Otherwise it's dilettante-ism."

"If that even is a word."

"I'm sure it is."

"Fuck-liar." She climbs down the stone shelves to his level.

"Fuck-wipe."

That makes her laugh, and then crumples her face. "Only not, as it turns out."

He's angry with her now that the relief has eased, but he's not going to let that out. She's shivering and hiccuping and there's a lot wrong; it's no time to be scolding someone for drunkenness. She's more slurry than ever, her orthodontically altered bite making her speech sweetly stupid, when she is so smart. "I'm such a fucking mess." She wipes her nose with the inside hem of her short, stupid, frilly dress, and sees her phone on the ground.

"Hey," she says, "I dropped my phone." She bends to pick it up, like a kid, like Ophelia bending for flowers in the stream. Maybe she'll go and kill herself too now.

"So what's this about Terry?" Orion pulls her down and sits beside her on the cold stone. "And BT-dubs, Terry-He or Terry-She?"

Savaya hiccups again and says, "I was fooling all you guys with Pink. I did a good job, huh? Terry and I, and me, are going to get married. Once they get divorced . . . I *totally* think we are. But I am *not too sure*, because they are getting back together."

She is so drunk, so totally plastered, and on top of weed, smells like.

"Have you talked to him about that? Or to her?"

"Yeah, I talked to *Nevaeh*, that was my first mistake."

"Nevaeh's spinning too fast to listen. She just can't because her family—"

"She hates me so much now." Savaya starts to cry again, fumbling with her phone, looking for some heartbreaking text or other. "It was hard enough before."

Orion takes the phone and puts his arms around her, wanting with all his heart to make her feel all right. "You don't have to do this, you know. Any of it. Terry, Nevaeh, anything. You can just stop for a while, wait for a while, till you can handle it better."

"Yeah, same to you," she says. Bleary, sodden voice. "You don't know my life."

"I was just bullshitting, when I told you about going to the chicken walk. I never did anything. I shouldn't have told you. I was just fucked up, being stupid." She's not listening. "Did you come in your parents' van?"

She shakes her head. "It's so strange. I have slept with some majorly revolting people, you'd think I could *easily*— I mean, this one guy yelled something out the window at me and I was telling him to fuck off before I even thought."

"How did you get in to the city?"

"Hitched."

"Right, but hitching is as dangerous as hooking, you know that, right?" It sweeps over him that she's a baby, such a gigantic, mewling baby, and what does that make him? Exactly the same. He cringes inside, his stomach squeezing to think of Newell finding him that night, walking the streets and trying so hard to be so fucking hard. A baby, as bad as Savaya. Newell must have laughed.

"At least I know how to hitch," she says. "I got a ride right away, in a Jaguar."

"You're so stupid."

He takes off his jacket and puts it over her shoulders because she's actually shaking now.

"Get up, walk," he says. "You can walk it off and we'll get some coffee or something. Plus, L and Jason are here looking for you too."

Savaya gets up, and they go into the park, toward the centre where it looks safer. She doesn't speak, she just lets her mouth open a little and keeps on crying. Damp soaking rain coming straight out of her eyes. Who knew there was that much water in a person.

"I heard Newell talking about me tonight," he says, offering other misery to distract her. "At Hugh's. I left when Burton got there, but then I went back and climbed the tree by Hugh's roof deck and listened. Newell said, he said he *likes* me."

Savaya squeezes his arm, says, "That's good though." The distraction is working, she's stopped shaking.

But it means he has to think about it. "Like is for Facebook. He said I fed his ego."

"Who was he talking to? Maybe he couldn't talk honestly with them."

"Hugh. Who else is he going to talk to? He told Hugh he thought he *might be of some help* to me." Now I can't even talk to him, Orion thinks blankly, bleakly. Or be in the same room with him, ever again.

"It's the same with me," Savaya says, and the fountain of tears starts again.

It's nothing like the same, he doesn't say.

She blubbers through the tears, "Terry said that, *be of help*. Like, with what—auditioning for National Theatre School or some fucking thing? It's *nothing*, it was just something to say. Like I'm such a puppy, all I need is help and not, like, an actual human relationship."

She shudders all over, like she's going to throw up—then she tears off his jacket as if it's choking her and runs like a mad thing, racing to get somewhere private before— Whoop, there she goes. Puking and puking, poor kid. Coming up too late, he tries to hold her hair out of the spray. Fuck, that's a lot of intake volume. Where'd she get all that?

Savaya staggers away from the mess and tries to run again but she can't. He takes her arm to help her. She lies down—they've strayed off the path into dark grass, away from other people, all the crouching shapes in the darkness. She sinks, and slumps over, and lies on the dry old grass, burying her face. He stands over her like some Greek hero over a sleeping maiden. Like fucking Perseus and what's her name with the dragon. They need fucking Medea to make it go to sleep. There's a play he'll never read now. And now here come L and Jason, traipsing along holding hands, all *Midsummer Night's Dream*.

Behind them, who?—Ivy. So is Newell here too? Orion's stomach grips again.

But no, it's just Ivy. He holds out a hand so they don't come too close and freak Savaya out. "Hi, guys," he says. "She's taking a rest. She might have had a few pops or something." Not being sure how cool Ivy is with weed.

"What's going on?" L takes a step but stops, she stays outside the dragon's reach. "Is she hurt?"

"She's okay. Just fucked up and also drunk."

L stares at him. "Did her parents find out about Nevaeh?"

"Terry. Not Pink," Orion says, trying to convey the news without giving it to Ivy.

"Holy," Jason says.

As if it's any of her business, L cries, "Shit, *another* one?"

"Another what?"

L doesn't speak.

"Another?" Orion asks her. "Another stupid kid with a crush on a teacher?" Lightning is racing up and down through his body. He could leap and fly with rage. How could they—even Jason, standing there dough-faced. Don't speak to them, don't justify—but it comes anyway, bursting, electric, unpleasant, unstoppable: "Nobody seems to realize, I *love him*. This isn't a PR plan or some star-fucking thing. I know him, and I—"

They're all staring at him, in the fitful tree-blown lamplight, moonlight.

Fine, stare! "If I was a girl, nobody would have the slightest problem with this—you'd all be saying oh about time Newell left that old hag he's been saddled with for so long, and how much more suitable a match this is, a young woman who loves him—if it was Savaya, you'd all be going oh quite understandable, that rogue Newell, heh heh, but of course, that's the way it should be. Like you were with her and Pink, you can't deny it."

They're all staring at him, like he's doing them some fucking *injustice*.

Then out of nowhere comes water, a violent, drenching spray hurtling from everywhere at once, a raging dragon of cold rain.

Orion hauls Savaya up, and they run.

3. A HUGHLOGY

Joseph the porter carries the comforting, nostalgic tang of tobacco. Once he's finished setting up the cot against the window wall, Hugh has an absurd impulse to put his arms around him, but tamps it down. Just gives him a gentle shoulder-clap. Joseph claps him back, as one of the men who look after others, and goes.

Hugh lies down. It's not comfortable, per se, but it is almost long enough. He gives himself up to not-thinking. Not-writing her eulogy in his head. Eulogy, schmulogy. *Élégie*, who wrote that? Massenet. Mimi used to play it.

L, sitting under Mimi's piano last week while Della played. Himself, crouched there as a small child, the man playing for his mother. In his empty room he sang under his breath. Gould, ghouled, haunted and driven like a leaf. Like Mimi was too.

Maybe enough of the crazies now, for a while, for a lifetime. (What do you think, Ivy? Could we be sane together?) Gould sang in his nose as he played, a distracting noise because he was not a good singer. Under the piano you could just listen to the music, not the weird man. Mimi played Schumann, *Von fremden Ländern und Menschen*, and Gould laughed. Hugh liked her playing, not at all expert, better than his. Naturally. You liked everything she did. Her wild face, the vitality that snapped from her fingertips on a good day. Her sadness and exhaustion on a bad day. Because he was her child Hugh loved and wept for her misery, the flatness, the hatred that poured out of her eyes from time to time. Nothing she did was wrong. Of course it was, later. Not wrong, just herself. Lying in the cot under the window's greyish illumination, Hugh wonders if maybe he could not have loved Ivy unless his mother was dying. Making room in the world for Ivy. Does that mean he wishes Mimi dead?

He has wished her dead for a thousand years; he wants her to live for a thousand years more. Those two being two sides of the coin of adoring love. Perhaps he will try not to adore Ivy. He will warn her not to adore him. Well, wait—he wakes a little from this dream state, humility or ordinary modesty returning—he won't have to warn her about that.

A noise, a movement. Hugh is up from the cot and beside the bed. Mimi's hand searches her face, pulling at the mask. She takes it off and stares up into his eyes.

Hugh touches her hand, her hands. He says, "Hey, little mama, what you doing there? Let's put this back on."

He sits beside her, and she takes off the mask again. He puts it on.

She pulls at the mask, fretting it, but leaves it on.

He moves the roses on her table, and a scent releases. The petals are like heavy cream, drawn through the fingers. Her eyes close.

Mask-hiss, machine-hum, monitor ticks. The hours.

Later, her hands pluck, pluck at the blankets, searching for something she has lost. It's not a myth, that plucking of the sheets. She takes off the mask.

He pulls his chair closer, takes her hands in his own, and kisses the fingers. "I loved it when you played for me," he says. "When you played at night, while I was going to sleep. You played so beautifully—it was wonderful. I've never heard a recording or a concert that was half as good." Talking, he puts the mask back on, her eyes watching his mouth. One hand comes up to trace his lips, and he stays still, stops talking.

"Sorry," she says. "Hugh, sorry."

"No, no, don't be sorry—nothing, nothing to be sorry for. This is unhappy now, but we were often happy," he tells her. Willing her to remember it so.

"Often happy," she repeats, obedient to his will.

"I always loved you best," he says.

"Hugh best . . ." She looks into his face. Seeing Hugh?

In this extremity, you can't be sure.

The cot is too far away. Hugh finds a way to rest his aching head, cheek cool on the clean sheets, letting his arm fall on the sheet along her poor thin leg. Lying like that, arm extended, he feels himself extending, expanding, overblowing—a rose opening out into the wilderness, into the world—what Mimi must have felt on her glorious days. He feels himself broadening out, embracing the whole world—the open feeling of loving Mimi without restraint (which Ivy has made possible), the slow unbinding of loving Ivy without fear.

The headache, present all the time for days now, seems to bloom too. Pricking his scalp from the inside like rose thorns. He is unaccountably sleepy. Maybe not unaccountable: how much sleep has he not had in these last few—in a week, in a year, a lifetime of not sleeping?

Hugh dreams that Burton is dead. You must have killed him, yes, Hugh pushed him down the long concrete stairs at Newell's place, head swollen, broken, blood, and there's a funeral procession: Ann hand in hand with Gerald, walking through golden leaves; Ken and Della, reconciled, riding swingboats in the park, her work selling at a Mary Poppins gallery in the FairGrounds; teenagers mysteriously dancing in the cupola in pretty dresses, long evening gloves—that's how Hugh can tell, how you can tell it's a dream.

The funeral procession winds through the park, Newell strewing flowers in front of the casket-catafalque, looking happy. Looking relieved, his burden finally set down. Thank you, Hugh, you are all singing.

4. I CAN'T STAND THE RAIN

They all run from the stinging spray—what is it? what's—oh! the sprinklers have started, all over the park. Horrifying at first, an attack of freezing bees, but then it's—well, you can't help laughing, it's pretty funny, all the drama doused and drenched, all the faces gaping. Ivy gets a bad case of laughter, the helpless kind that makes her snort—so humiliating, older-ladyish, *snort*—she stops behind a tree, which blocks some of the water coming at her, and bends to try to release her diaphragm. *Snort!* Oh dear.

The others find her, and the sanctuary of the big tree's girth, all huddling there as the water changes to a regular cyclic *spat, spat, spat, spat,* calming from the first fervour.

"They must be blowing the lines," Jason says. "Like they do with our underground sprinklers in the fall, before it freezes. There's just way more water to clear out."

Looking around the tree again, Ivy sees Newell coming through the park, dodging the spray. Shit, it's cold, being wet on a windy night. She pulls back into the lee of their tree. L and Jason are huddled together; Orion holds Savaya close to him, trying to warm her up. Doesn't anybody wear a jacket anymore? It's almost winter.

Fury bristles off Orion like a charge; he is still accusing L and Jason of prejudice. He's practically split himself in two, one half still comforting Savaya, the other spitting at L like a sprinkler: "I know, Burton, other people, you name it. It doesn't—it doesn't take away from, from love."

Ivy ought to intervene, re: people are just worried about you, power dynamics, position of influence, etc. "Everybody has just heard too many bad stories," she forces out, being careful, aware of Newell coming closer, listening.

Orion is too busy ranting to notice. He shouts, "It is not the same thing! I'm the one who wants—in the old days things were different. Now it's—*different.* My mother kept me safe, even though she was such a wack job, hovering around the dressing rooms at dance class, never fucking leaving me alone for a minute."

"Well, we worry," Ivy says. Taking the blame for all the mothers, though she is none. Newell gives her a thumbs-up, quietly coming closer.

The water eases again, the stinging spray subsiding.

Orion, calmer, says, "I've been perfectly well aware of myself, who I am, all my life. I tried out the other just in case I was bi because that would be so handy, but I'm not."

"I vouch for that!" Savaya lifts her drowned face to laugh.

From Jason's coat, L says, "Sorry, Orion, sorry, I didn't mean that at *all*, I was being mean about Savaya, not you. I meant another, um, like another Pink, I think—I hate my saying that, it's just what came up from my—"

Everybody has a flooded basement in their mind, Ivy thinks.

"It's okay," Orion says. He's tired, his voice is cracking. Ivy has to get them all home somehow.

Newell appears around their tree, a jacket in his hand.

A rippling shift of dissipating tension. Orion says, reaching out, "Hey, that's my jacket. It's got our phones in it."

Newell hands it over. "How I found you. That and the shouting."

Orion laughs, what a good sound to hear.

Perfect, but how will they all cope now? Ivy says, "We can't get in Gerald's car like this, we'll ruin it."

"I'll get him another one." The sweetness of Newell's smile is a little weird—Ivy often finds it so. Lots of money makes a person strange.

"We can't drive back to Peterborough all wet. My apartment isn't far—we can dry out and then go home. How about I take these guys in Gerald's Saab—I don't dare drive yours—and you two follow along?" Ivy appropriates Savaya's freezing hand. Leaving Newell to take Orion. As seems right to her, never mind the rules.

Newell nods, and lopes off between the trees, Orion running after, swinging around a lamppost and hurdling benches in joyful, elastic, springing leaps over the damp grass. Love made visible. No wonder, no wonder. She and Hugh struggle along earthbound making love, bodies held by gravity. How these two in the glory of their strength must spree.

Narrow. The room, the world. The body narrow in the bed. Replacing the oxygen mask over and over.

A long time ago they promised she would not be in pain. Conrad coming in the darkness promises again, no pain, no pain, but there is pain, there is the pain of leaving.

But there is not any shrieking that would be

that would be

pain we forget so fast we must

We make things up, we tell ourselves the happy story of a life well lived. We must. These things are for a reason, the old people say, Ruth says. They have to say that.

"Nolie, where are you, there is pain, she is—"

Hugh cannot let go of her hand.

this is too hard, his head will

She is laughing, frightened to laugh, at the enormity of this. At the great step on which she perches still, the diving board. Afraid to dive, but there is no way down but death.

After her, nobody can die. Years will go by and he won't let anyone die, the world will fill up with people. Or at least, nobody he knows—nobody he guards will die. Sometime in the night he sees that Newell must love Burton. So Hugh must let them be who they are, leave it, let it go. Be Newell's brother, Della's brother, Ruth's son. Be Ivy's: nobody else will die.

Shivering and shivering, fingers nervous on the sheet, skin shining blue and sheets of water coursing down the pane, the night so blue and black.

6. MOLE END

The red door opens onto darkness. Is Jamie sleeping? He's usually up at night. A clean smell—fresh lumber, plaster dust, paint. Ivy finds the switch and turns it on. She braces herself, not knowing what chaos she may find, and steps around the little alcove wall.

The kitchen is clean. No sign of damage. The floor is clear, unstained—even the counters are clean, and the sink, clean and empty.

"God bless you, Dave, Ruth's pal," Ivy says, deep in her heart.

There's a note propped on the island counter.

> *All fixed, ceiling downstairs needs a coat of paint, we'll do it Tuesday. I got my cousin to come & clean while we were working. Took out your garburetor don't get a new one they're useless. That guy went to stay with his brother for a couple days, guess the noise was too much for him. I'll give the bill to Ruth. Dave C.*

Clean. The kitchen is clean. It smells so good.

And the new order goes beyond the kitchen. The big windows are clean—Jamie's protective foil taken down, glass shiny between interior light and exterior black. The floor, too. Boxes and cases, gone. The computer station denuded, the desk polished clean.

Everybody has trailed in behind her, and now Newell and Orion are at the door. It's not till then, till she's bringing them inside, that Ivy looks down at her feet. The beautiful shoes covered with roses: perfectly ruined from the sprinklers and the grass. All is vanity.

L catches Ivy's cry of sadness, and says, "Oh, your shoes!"

Newell takes one shoe and feels it. "Ruined," he agrees. And Jason, seeing the roses all muck, says, "That's the saddest thing. I loved those."

Their sympathy is enough to snap Ivy out of selfishness. She laughs.

"They're only shoes. Never mind, maybe I can get them cleaned. Okay," she says, Hugh's word. "L, take Savaya to the shower, through that door, and find towels for everyone in the bathroom cupboard. I'm going to make us something to eat."

Maybe she shouldn't have said that—what's in the cupboards? Milk in the fridge, a Styrofoam pack of cheap white eggs, frozen garlic bread in the freezer. She'd forgotten Jamie's thing about white food. Well. Teenagers won't mind. A dusty can of maple syrup in the pantry that she was supposed to send to an old acting friend in England—that never goes bad. She has flour, salt, yes. Okay, perfect. Pancakes, scrambled eggs, garlic bread: there's a comforting supper, or rather breakfast. It's 3 a.m. A long time since Hugh's trompe l'oeil.

Newell cracks eggs, she whisks pancake batter. The stove warms her. Ivy is happier than she's been in this place for a long, long time. This is like Mole End, when she played Mole for Young People's Theatre, bustling to give Rat tea when they stumble on Mole's old home. Old Ratty. Donald's dead now. He was so good—the antiretrovirals did not work for long enough. She bends into the fridge to hide her smarting eyes.

Orion is witty at table; Newell expands, talking to him, easy and loving. A relief after watching him always so careful with Burton—what a toxic little partnership that is, and always has been, Ivy thinks. Bugger the age difference, the problem is that Burton is cruel and jealous. Food gets everyone giddy, making jokes; even Savaya. She sings, only partly under her breath, "*This bread is thick / just like my dick*. Sorry, couldn't pass up the rhyme there."

She has cratered. Ivy leads her to the futon couch and flips it flat. Savaya crawls up and is asleep before Ivy finds a duvet to pull over her.

"I'm taking the last two pancakes. Arrest me," Jason says. "FTP." It takes Ivy a minute to translate that in her head. *Fuck the police*. How rude. She laughs, happy to have her counter stools filled with people she likes. When they're fed and calm, and the dishes loaded into the gleaming, empty dishwasher, she puts them all to bed: L with Savaya on the futon, Jason on the long couch, and Ivy can sleep in her own (clean-sheeted!) bed, alone. Newell says he'll return Gerald's car and take Orion home. So Newell can get back to Burton, and Orion to his mother. Newell didn't tell anyone where he was going, and still hasn't, at least in Ivy's sight, taken out a phone to text or check. Burton will be livid. But when, after all, is he not livid? Can't live with him, can't seem to ditch him.

"Wait," she says, at the door. "I told Hugh I'd empty the buckets in his basement!"

"I'll do it," Newell says.

"I'll bring these guys back out in the morning, and get your car back to you, somehow."

"You'll find me," he says, smiling at her. His lovely sculpted arms envelop her. "I'll be at Mimi's apartment—we're packing it up, she's got to be moved out by five."

"Oh perfect," Ivy says. "Perfect. I'll be there."

Orion has himself collected, his jacket. "No master class, anyway." He gives her a wicked look and a smart salute. "Thanks," he says, and kisses her cheek as he goes past.

(DELLA)

can I let it go?   if I had he could never let it go
he sleeps   I drive over rain-glossed pavement
my soul thirsts after knowledge
like moths fly into the headlights of my car
                    what they did when and for how long   and how
                    and how he turned to her   and what he said
                    what she did then   and how they got undressed
                    what way he came inside what they spoke of later
                    and how his head turned on the pillow
                    looking for me perhaps in that cool room

go home
maybe I won't come out of this all right
climb into bed beside him
how can he sleep
as if he never left it
his baseball bat abandoned by the bed would fit the hand   vision of
                    the eye resists that vision   but there he is asleep
                    I could hit him   end all this
                    I am so full of fury   I can see him
                    the fullness of his mouth   the liquid motion
don't think don't
in the shower in my fucking helmet of purity   hatred filling my mouth
washing the sin off me no sin at all   *but it is him*
what is the thing that makes it possible to betray the other   how could
he look at her taking off her clothes and think yes   yes how could he

7. HUGH ALONE

Hugh wakes, a great gulp of waking, gasping for air because he was drowning. He looks to Mimi.

She was sleeping, and now she is not sleeping.

The mystery of knowing, instantly knowing. How can she not—

How can she not be.

He must have faded out. How long?

How long it has been, this year of knowing she was dying, she would die. She's been dying since he was four. No length of time was long enough.

Everything in the world is empty. Mimi is no longer filling it.

However, there are things to do. So.

Hugh gets up. Her hand, which he lifts, is dead—no sleep can mimic that lack of volition. There is no confusion. No pain, no sorrow, nobody in that body now. He leans over the bed and puts his cheek against hers. Cool, empty.

Still, for a long time she lived in this shell. He kisses it, and runs his hand over the silver hair, pretending she is not gone.

8. HUGH CAN'T TELL

The streets are empty. Strange, on a, what is it . . . ? Sunday morning. So that makes sense.

Hugh walks without intent, automaton, limbs moving/eyes taking in data, unsubjective. Gerald walking along, Gerald too—don't talk to him right now. Hugh steps into FairGrounds, passes the crowd at the counter, walks along the side wall and out the back door, into the garden beside the gallery. In the back door.

Upstairs, Gareth and Léon will be still asleep, not even eight yet. Can't talk to them either. You should make them breakfast.

You could sit in the framing room, no Ruth on a Sunday morning. (Can't tell her, that will be too hard.) But it's cold in there, as cold as.

Into the gallery, down to the *Dark Gates*. Mighton. How does he channel, how can he paint like this? Huge block of blue-blackness rages up the wall, pulls the eye from form to form, takes Hugh in so that he wants to grip the edge and walk inside the frame, be among the dead who are waiting there. *They stood beseeching on the riverbank / yearning to be the first to be carried across / stretching their hands out toward the farther shore.*

A knock on the window.

Gerald, his face close to the glass.

Open the door, of course. You could tell Gerald. Now you are in his club. They are silent.

The computer clock bings. Nine a.m., too early to open.

"Opening early?" Gerald asks.

Hugh shakes his head. Then stops. His head feels pretty bad.

"I'll come this evening, the wine and cheese," Gerald says.

RSVPing. You ought to cancel that. Hugh nods. He puts out a hand and touches the frame. He wants to tell, he has to tell. "My mother— Mimi," he says.

Gerald nods too.

"I can't, I can't," Hugh says.

Gerald touches the frame on the other side. His hand on the grain of the wood. "I dream every night that they aren't dead, that they weren't. I gave up too soon, I shouldn't have called 911, they were just sleeping and I was too stupid to see it."

Yes, that the dead would have waked had he not been so fast to call it death. That he was mistaken, that empty hand not empty.

"The other dream I have is that I'm dead, inside the house. While they're going to sleep out in the garage."

Hugh stands and listens. You can do that.

"I imagine what it was like, what she said. If she told him what she was going to do."

You can answer that. "No. She wouldn't have scared Toby."

"I know. She struggled, I could see. I mean, I knew. I know, she was having a hard time, she said—"

Oh no.

"Not that she would . . . She said she wasn't a good mother. She said sorry."

Mimi saying sorry, sorry.

Gerald says, "I can't listen to anybody tell me anything anymore. In case it's the thing I ought to be listening to, the thing I ought to fix."

"I don't know how you could have fixed that. I don't think you could have."

"No, maybe. You couldn't fix your mom, I guess."

No.

Gerald lets go of the frame. He puts a hand out to the picture, not pointing at any one thing. "So, I'll come back this evening," he says. Almost as definite as a promise.

Now you have to do that wine and cheese after all.

Hugh follows him out onto the front porch and stands in the damp cool air. Pulls out his phone. He can't see the screen properly, but he texts. As he hits send, the moving truck drives past the gallery. In the passenger seat, Ruth waves, catching sight of him.

Right, get that place cleaned out. That's what he's got to do.

Hugh steps off the porch and walks, limbs moving just as always, as if nothing has happened, over to Mimi's apartment.

(L)

Key in lock, scraping, wakes her.

Where? White light, open air, and far away, a ceiling.

A luxury, not knowing where you are. Maybe it's finally the alien abduction. More noise, keys. Ivy's place. On the couch Jason sits up, looking around at the door.

Savaya's arm is heavy on her other arm, she pulls it out, asleep and tingling. Fuck, she slept like a dead thing. It's—what time is it? Phone— it's nine. Shit, she never called her mom. Seven texts waiting, oh freaking frick.

>sorry sorry sorry I fell asleep—I'm ok

L texts as quick as her fingers will move. All this time the murmuring at the door, and now knocking—she looks up: not knocking but banging against the chain, like somebody has lost his temper. Because it always (let us face facts, ladies), it always is the gents who lose the tempers.

Good chain. The door won't open, the guy keeps bang-banging it like he's going to tear the chain right off, but he can't. Is this a home invasion? Two voices, out there.

Ivy comes out of her bedroom half-dressed, dressed enough for students, anyway. Pants pulled on, still doing them up, holding a short Japanese robe around her. She heads for the door. "What, what, what?" she's saying, still mostly asleep, and then she shouts, "Stop it!" She gets to the door and slams it shut. Angry herself, it looks like.

L slips off the futon and runs on bare feet to huddle beside Jason on the couch. Like front row spectators at the fights, they watch Ivy wrestle with the lock and take off the chain.

Two men. A man and a—a boy or something. Not quite. L looks away. She hates this about herself, this retreating from odd people, people with something wrong with them. The two of them come in, both talking. The wormly one blinks, murmurs, repeats, "Hi, Ivy, nice to see you here hi Ivy nice to see you . . ." The louder, less damaged one says, "Where the hell have you been, and what's with the chain? Have you gone paranoid too?"

"Hi, Jamie," Ivy says, giving him a wave of her hand—he flinches backward even though she doesn't go to hug him. Then she turns to the other guy. "I see you got most of Jamie's things out already, that's good. I was going to give you a call to say I'll need the keys back, but this is— perfect, you can give them to me now."

The belligerent one rocks on his feet, forward, like he's going to punch her.

L pinches Jason's leg, feeling everything go tense. They'll have to intervene. She thinks they could take him—except, unless the other guy went batshit. This is very awkward.

But the loud guy pulls back, reins in the rage. He must want something from Ivy. "You can't—The work's done, so there's no reason he can't come back now, right, Jamie? It was just the noise and all the strangers he couldn't take. We've got his equipment in the car, he wouldn't bring it up unless they were gone."

"They're gone now, Alex," the weird guy says. "They're gone, Ivy. They're gone."

Uncomfortable.

Ivy just stands there, somehow pretty strong in her undone pants and her now-tied robe. "No," she says. They all listen to that for a minute. "It won't work anymore," she says. "He's got to get some help, you're going to have to take care of this." She turns and puts her hand out, not quite touching the limp guy. "I'm sorry, Jamie, but you really do have to go stay with your brother for a while, and see about finding a doctor."

The guy, Jamie, stares off into the distance, not at Ivy. "I know, you're right." Such a sad, apologetic voice that L almost cries. "I've really got to get this under—under something. Control, or something." He shakes his head, ashamed of himself, admitting it all, so sorry.

The brother's not taking it, though. "Listen, I brought a cheque. I know it was partially Jamie, the you-know, the water, so we talked it over and we'll pay half." He digs in his coat pocket and holds out a yellow cheque.

Ivy doesn't take it, and that sets him off again, raging: "No way he's moving out!"

"He's already moved," Ivy says.

"No fucking way! He's been here long enough, he has tenant's rights, you can't shove him out. My place is too small, you *know* that." He's saying ordinary words but the anger behind the words makes them come out in tufts, in flares. All threat, all of it. His shoulders are bunched. He can't stop his hands making fists, even though he keeps relaxing them.

Ivy stands where she is. She doesn't make room for them to come farther inside.

As his brother shouts on and on, Jamie sags against the door like he's melting through it. He turns side-on to the door, tries to edge it open without his brother seeing—but the brother grabs his arm and says, "*Fuck*, Jamie, stay put."

"I can't do any more, Alex," Ivy says. "It's not helping."

Jamie stretches his arm out, a thin wrist reaching out of his grey jacket. "Here," he says in a dying-away voice. "Here, Ivy, thank you very much for all this time. You have been a kind and gracious landlady and I know I've outstayed my welcome."

His delicate ET fingers hold out a Pokemon key ring. He drops it into Ivy's hand.

That nearly does it, you can see Ivy's will crumpling. She's going to say stay, L thinks.

But the burly brother wrecks it. He looks like the kind of guy who wrecks things all the time. "Fucking *cunt*," he says. Meanest voice in the world, dripping with bile and blame and everything always being somebody else's fault. "You fucking, fucking cunt. You'd abandon this poor kid now?"

"Not a kid," Jamie says. "Thirty-four." He's turned his back now, staring into the corner of the wall, as if he got there by accident, a Roomba that can't make its wheels reverse.

"Listen, this isn't going to happen. You don't have a choice anymore. I'm going to the landlord/tenant ombudsman—we'll get our rights. Jamie's rights. He's got tenure in this apartment, there's no way you can kick him fucking *out*, you will be so sorry about this—"

The trembling brother is tugging on his sleeve now, tugging and begging. "Sorry about this," he says in the vague direction of Ivy, and she says back to him, "I'm so sorry about this, Jamie—you know I've always, you know I—" And he says, "I know, I know, I—"

Between those two soft people the hard man ranting in the middle just gets eased out, borne backwards and out into the hall until Ivy can shut the door.

Then there's a quiet little space.

Ivy turns. Her eyes are tragically large and miserable. Jason and L don't comment, don't cheer or high-five like they probably ought to do.

After a minute Ivy says, "Perfect. So I guess we'd better get going. Can you get Savaya up?" She walks back to her bedroom and closes the door, like no big deal.

A beep makes L grab for her phone: a text from her mom:

> you at Jason's? if so we have to talk about this

Agh.

> no, I'm with Savaya, we fell asleep—I'm ok, home by noon?

So there she is, lying to her mom, and no real reason for it even. She honestly does not believe her mom would mind. That was so weird, watching Ivy deal with the guy and poor weird Jamie, tangles untangling. Knowing what they don't know, that Ivy is going to be with Hugh now—and she and Jason too, because they suddenly—oh, look at that! Look at the head-splitting smile on his face, because he is seeing her, her, her. Look at that, they suddenly love each other.

There is a beep again, her mom:

> Gareth wants to do a studio visit this afternoon. To see your install. I'm cleaning the kitchen.

She shows it to Jason. He nods, he signs OMG.

Then Ivy's door opens. Staring down at her phone, she says, "Oh no—we have to hurry—Hugh's mother died last night."

Because don't be fooled, there is no good in the world. In this whole life, you will only lose everything you love, one thing at a time, and no matter what good thing might happen it will never be enough to make up for death.

9. I'M LOOKING THROUGH HUGH

All the way to Peterborough the scene replays in Ivy's mind. Jamie, impossible to kick out; Alex, impossible to just kick. She drives, listening to the girls murmuring in the back, thinking about disentanglement. What is the obligation to our fellow crazies? At some point, do we have to cut them loose? It seems to her, driving along, that normal rules of fair dealing don't necessarily apply: Jamie hasn't kept house—isn't capable of it—hasn't paid rent for eighteen months, but she does not tally that. This cutting-loose is not from grievance but from understanding, after way too long, that she isn't doing him any good.

It's time to let go of that apartment, even though it now looks so nice and seems like a safe haven again. You have to be with the ones you are meant to be with, during this short blink of a life, not fritter away years with the wrong people, not helping them anyway.

But it does not seem very likely that Alex or Ray will actually get Jamie help.

Think about something else. There'd be room in Hugh's van for her good oak table. (But is there room for it at Hugh's?) Her bike, her books. (Can she step into his life? Is he too sad to love anyone? What about money, work, the need to be in the city?)

In the back seat L and Savaya keep up a low-voiced colloquy. Savaya is subdued, hasn't said a word to Ivy yet, presumably too embarrassed. Jason, beside Ivy, seems pretty cheerful. He drums on his knees from time to time, darting, dancing complicated rhythms. As they enter Peterborough he turns for a quick consult with the girls and then directs Ivy to Savaya's place, to drop her off.

Savaya gets out of the Saab, newborn-colt legs folding and unfolding, runs up the walk and through her front door, the screen slam-slamming.

"Wouldn't want to be her this morning," Jason says.

L leans forward from the back seat. "Yeah, her dad is all loosey-goosey except then suddenly he's not."

"Okay, get me to Mimi's," Ivy says. "I've got to find Hugh."

Mimi's old apartment is the bottom half of an old brick house on a nice street. The gingerbread porch is already stacked with boxes.

Ruth comes out with another and sets it on the porch swing, which wobbles; Jason darts over to hold it steady. "I started with the sheets," Ruth says, as if they've been talking all morning. "I know what Hugh needs to keep for his place, not much, he's well outfitted. We're going great guns in here. But there's still the china, and the cedar closet is full."

Ann leans out the front door, one foot inside, and asks Ruth, "What was in that box?"

"Linens," Ruth says. She is slightly stiff with Ann, Ivy's noticed it before. Because she hurt her boy Hugh, maybe. So Ivy had better watch her step.

"Any archival quality? I'll just take a look," Ann says, and steps tightly across to the box. Ruth and Jason back away as she pulls apart the interlocked flaps—the box rocks on the swing and topples, Jason not fast enough to stop it. Perfectly folded sheets tumble slowly out, at first in a pile and then out of the pile, while Ann tries to keep them together. "Help me," she barks at Jason, so he bends, and L bends with him. Ann yanks her sweater tighter around her and goes back inside.

They restack sheets carefully, trying to preserve the folds, but Ruth says, "Never mind, they wash them at the Mennonite Clothes Closet anyway; got to, no matter how clean they've been kept. I put Orion to work on the coat closet, Jason, you go help him out."

When Jason's out of earshot she allows her eyes to roll. "Ann's rummaging in Mimi's dressers, I keep chasing her out. I'll put the boys to work there next. Hugh knows what to keep and what to let go to those who need it, which *she* does not. Archival." Her contempt is deep, somehow Buddhist, Ivy thinks. Let go, let it go, *shenpa*. Ruth sends L off too: "You go grab five or six boxes and a stack of packing paper, and meet me in the dining room."

With L safely gone, Ruth says, "Ann took a lot of old things away already. Her and that Largely woman gutted the front hall closet. The cedar closet has a padlock, so they couldn't get in there." Ruth leans over to whisper. "I made like I don't know the combination."

"But they came in last week, because Ann had Mimi's clothes for that display."

"Largely has a key, she let Ann in."

"But—that's not okay, is it?"

"No, it is not," Ruth says, and stomps off to find L.

Where's Hugh? Still at the hospice, arranging, or somewhere in the house? No, because here he is, coming down the street.

His face is blank. It does go blank, when he is hurt. He and Newell share that; Della too. Something they caught from each other during their siblinghood, or a product of their parents' general abandonment.

He's walking oddly, too. The beloved.

Ivy goes down the porch steps to meet him, her hands stretched out.

He catches them and looks into her face. "You can tell me," he says. "Hugh."

His mouth stumbles. Tries again, "You can tell Hugh, I mean. I can tell you." She waits, but nothing comes out of his mouth. He can hardly seem to breathe.

"You told me. I know. You already told me," she says, the only gentle way she knows, putting her cheek on his cheek, merging her molecules with his.

Ivy takes Hugh to Mimi's kitchen where Newell and Della stand packing the way they do everything, elegantly and efficiently: dishes flying from cupboard to wrapping to box. Brother and sister in all but DNA.

They see at once—how could they not?—that Mimi is dead. Della comes straight to Hugh and folds him in her arms. Newell wraps his other side, a trinity.

Ann is going through a drawer by the back door, magpie-picking through the jumble, searching for shiny things. Oblivious, she pecks at him, "About time Hugh got here. We're doing all the work."

Ruth comes from the bedroom hall with two full blue bags too heavy for her. Ivy takes them from her. "Those good boys have the bedroom closet all bagged up," Ruth says. "Good to have that taken care of—put those bags in Hugh's van, will you, my sweet?"

Ivy feels her cheeks pink up—an important honour to be Ruth's sweet.

But Ruth has seen Hugh now, has seen his state.

Ruth's own state changes, solid to liquid, in an instant. Tears bloom in her eyes and her hands begin to tremble violently. She puts one shaking hand up to push something away—death, pain—and slumps forward, but the triangle opens and Hugh turns to her, and she doesn't fall. She doesn't cry out loud, either. She lets them pet her for a brief minute and then straightens her back again.

"I didn't really need to see Mimi again before she died," Ruth says. "But it seems hard that she did not have me there, saying goodbye."

"She knew how much you—how long—" Hugh puts his elbow up to cover his eyes.

"Well." Ruth wipes her own eyes, first with fingers and then her sleeve, until Della hands her a Kleenex. She blows her nose. "These things happen for a reason, one that we can't know till later. I'm going to miss her, and Hugh will too."

Hugh turns to the sink and pours a glass of water. "We'll go back over after we finish here," he says. "She'll be lonely." He drinks the water, not seeming to be aware of them all looking at him.

The boys come trooping through, two bags clutched in each of their hands, and Ivy turns to help them out the door.

Ann says, "Put those in Hugh's van." As if Ruth hadn't said to.

But when Ivy opens the van doors, it is already full of bags and bags of clothes. How many clothes can one old woman have? The big truck's back door is open too, it's only half full, and there's the attic space above the cab.

"Can you guys get these bags all the way up there?" Ivy asks. Foolish to ask! They flow, they leap up over obstacles, tossing the blue bags fire-brigade style, and Orion (perched on a chair on a dresser) packs them in tight. "Perfect," she says. "Safe as houses."

(L)

Anxiety, old friend, we meet again! Mimi's dead—so everything's weird. Gareth Pindar is coming to see the *Republic*. And now her dad is supposedly at Mimi's to help but is just sitting on the porch. It would be better if he came in and got over himself a little bit, but yipes, don't say that. Packing the dining room sideboard, L can see him outside the window. Sitting there suffering. She packs quietly so he does not get mad or give up and go away. How much she hates depression and frailty, even more since it's hereditary and she's obviously got it too and she's often horrible to her mom too.

Who now comes trotting up the sidewalk with a paper bag from Reggie's Burgers. Feed the brute, Ruth always says. The brute looks up, doesn't take the bag. Doesn't move.

They don't know she's watching. Maybe they won't talk at all—maybe she should go pack the kitchen instead. Her mom stands there, holding the bag out. She's angry, or she'd laugh at him and leave it beside his chair.

Then she says, "Fine. Go back to Bobcaygeon."

Stress. L puts her head into the sideboard so she can't hear, and carefully counts a stack of twelve beautiful plates. Cobalt blue, her favourite colour in the world, painted thick around the paper-thin rims, edged with gold. A plain silver bowl. L turns it over to see the hallmark. Jasper should be packing this good stuff.

On the porch they've carried on whatever they're fighting about—she doesn't want to know. Then her dad's voice, raised. She doesn't turn her head, but her hands stop moving. He sounds bad, really bad. Last night at the anniversary party he seemed okay.

"My life has been spent, and I mean *spent*, in that office. It's gone, I wasted it. Worse than wasted, I was suckered. It was important to—I meant to do something worthwhile, but I haven't done one thing that worked, that helped anyone."

Her mom says, "Not fair, not fair. You have." Is she crying? L sneaks a glance. Can't see. Only her dad's profile, staring out to the street, or to hell.

"I'm telling you how I see it," he says.

"You act as if I made you go to law school—you're the one who wanted the mainline."

"Making the world better, that was a capitalist plan, was it?" Now he's even madder. He takes the bag, finally. "So here I am—all the reward I can hope for is a hamburger one up from McDonald's. A fair-trade coffee, to comfort me when there are no more days left."

L slides silently down under the window.

Her dad's making a lot of noise with the wrapper. Her mom tries to be reasonable, in a very irritating tone of voice. "We don't need the house, we can sell it. I need a table to work on, a bed, a chair—they can all be in the same room as far as that goes. We could move—"

"It makes me so angry when you talk like this." He takes a bite, half the burger at once.

L watches his jaw, his profile as he shoves the burger in. She hates, hates him. Because you have to acknowledge how you feel and not swallow your emotions. She leans over for the silver bowl, hugs it to her chest. It covers her breasts and lungs and heart, it's a silver shield. Athena. Born from the head of her father.

"You're describing a life that doesn't exist," he says, as soon as he can swallow.

"Look at Newell, all he's got is a kitchen, a bed, a chair—all right, they're in two giant rooms and a media alcove . . ."

"Yeah, I'd like to live like Newell too." Over another bite of burger. "Selling the house won't help, there's no equity left in it and the mortgage is cheaper than rent."

Her mom leans forward, eyes all tragic. "What are we going to do, then?" It comes out jerky, like she had to push herself to say it.

Licking his fingers (that was quick, he must have been starving), he crumples up the wrapper, puts it in the bag, crumples up the bag. "I'll sell out."

Her mom is quick to defend: "You didn't sell out! You had honorable intentions and you worked with—"

"No, I'm going to sell *out*, sell out my partnership. Cash in. It's enough for a boat."

A pause, while her mother tries to work that out. So does L, crouched by the windowsill.

". . . a *boat* boat?"

"A small one."

"On which you intend to live?"

"A boat and a camper van. Are you in or out?"

Her mother laughs. Gasping, but laughing. Her dad laughs too, and something breaks a little, like weather.

"Fine, then, no boat. But I don't know what else to do," he says. "I do not know."

Agh. How about go back to work and don't expect to solve every problem in the fucking world? How about get some medication for the anxiety you've been suffering my whole life, probably your whole life? How about my mom makes a different choice in the first place, stays single, without anyone blaming or hating her. Like Mimi did, after Hugh's dad.

L leans her head against the wall because honestly, how can people stay together if it's still so hard, so much later on? She has a pencil in her pocket. She scribbles on a piece of packing paper, getting down a cartoon of her mom holed up in a tower, praying to the sky, all alone. One twinkling star in the sky—that's L, unborn, because her mom had a brain in her head.

Her dad has the sense to reach out and take her mom's hand, pull her over while she's crying. Put your arms around her, FFS!

He sits her with him on the swing.

"Mimi died this morning," her mom says, still crying.

"Oh, no. Oh no. I'm sorry for Hugh. And for you."

"I'm selling the piano. Mimi's dead, it won't hurt her feelings."

"Not for a while. Just let me have a few—I just need—maybe I need a vacation."

Her mom shrieks very softly. "With what, buttons?"

"You come too. We'll sleep in the car. You're not selling the piano."

"Yeah, I'm going to buy a boat. And a camper van."

They're okay.

L gets up, no noise, and goes back through the hall to Mimi's bedroom—nobody's there, for a miracle. Will they put her false eyelashes on, in the funeral home?

She opens Mimi's glove drawer and finds the black gloves Mimi wore to the MOMA opening. They are shaped to Mimi's fingers, as if her hands are somehow still inside them.

L puts them in the silver bowl, and wraps it in her jacket to carry out, all casual. Because she has to have some things of Mimi's, some way to still be with her. Maybe that is bad, who cares. She takes the soap out of the dish in the bathroom, and the little bottle of Joy from the top drawer, and Mimi's tiny gold-bladed scissors—and heavy, pouring, salt tears roll down her cheeks, because she will never be with her again, in this or any world.

Ruth cuts him loose to go find some lunch. Which is why he is on the top step of Hugh's mother's porch when Burton puts his pointed hoof on the bottom one. Wandering by whenever it suits him to lend a hand. Burton gives him a cool look, but inside Orion's chest his heart is a giant cartoon jackhammer, rattling and bursting.

"Orion," Burton says. "Just who I hoped I would run into."

Orion keeps going down.

And Burton keeps going up, so that Burton has the higher ground when he says, "Listen, I had a talk with Boy—with *Newell*—and we thrashed a few things out. It's clear I overreacted to your sensible suggestion of a different approach to the work. My qualms are stilled. Since I never got around to informing Pink or processing the fee repayment, there's no tiresome paperwork to do. Procrastination is our friend, at times."

Orion feels tethered. Does he have to say something, answer this? Burton leans in to whisper. Orion can see the blue veins around his nose and eyes. "*Truth* is, your performance yesterday was a little too good. A painful demonstration that I have been eclipsed."

From above, he waves a jazz hand at Orion. "Good then, all settled, see you tomorrow, *ta-ra!*" He pirouettes on the top step and goose-steps in through the front door.

What a piece of work that guy is. You have to admire the sheer fucking gall. It's all too much. This high-test atmosphere. He needs some youth.

> where ru?

< Nev's rm 4108

He turns the other way and runs in a gradually increasing stride to the hospital.

Nevaeh's room is half-full of asswipes including Sheridan Tooley who is not such a bad guy, fine, but is carrying a big bouquet of fucking mums. If there's one thing every man needs to know: no chrysanthemums, women hate them. First thing he learned at his mother's fragile dance-damaged knee. Savaya is sitting up beside Nevaeh on the bed, two of them together taking up about one person's width-worth across the headboard. Those girls are too skinny. Seeing them cozied up he wonders again, Terry-He or Terry-She?

"She's a steel porcupine!" Savaya calls over, seeing Orion. "All the pins in the world are now officially in Nevaeh's ankle."

He slides carefully onto the foot of the bed on Savaya's side, leaving a wide space around the spectacular cast on Nev's leg. "Jesus, you'll need a great big Sharpie to sign that thing," he says, and Savaya says, "That's what she said."

Oh the general hilarity, the stupidity of these immature yo-yos. They're all right, but once he's finished high school he will never see any of them again. Savaya was going to be good but somehow she and Nev have gone straight off the rails, and it's actually not Orion's job to put them back together. He has his own troubles.

Savaya pushes him with her foot. Under the noisy people she says, not how she is herself, which is what he expects, but, "Are you all right?"

The weird thing is that he stood over her like the dragon last night and now, nothing. She's concerned, is she? Neither of them knows the other person, that is the tragedy of everything.

And is he all right? Not knowing what comes next—not Newell. He can't beat Burton, Orion knows that now. Because last night, Newell drove straight back, easy unimportant chat along the road, straight to Orion's house, stopped the car right by the door, put the interior light on, and smiled and said goodnight without anything. "I hope your mother won't have been too worried." When Orion ignored that and asked why, he said, "You are too young." Because Hugh and L's mom told him that. He said, "I can't let you. I was wrong."

"Are you all *right*?" Savaya says, jiggling her foot. "Where were you?"

"I promised I'd help pack up Hugh's mother's place."

There's a burst of laughter at some sally of Sheridan Tooley's, Nevaeh laughing too loud. A beautiful girl but high-strung; too smart for her own heart, clinging tight to Savaya's waist, clamped, but not looking at or talking to her. Can't acknowledge what's going on—fine, so it's too dangerous for her with her family. But how's Savaya supposed to deal with it, except by flailing around the way she does, pretending everything is just another fuck?

The tragedy of love: you finally figure out that you want to be with another person more than anyone else in the world, more than anything, and then you discover that you are always going to be alone. Never more alone—in all the years of living with his gauzy, half-there mother, of not

having any friends who understood the first fucking thing he was
saying—at least until L and Jason—in all the time of never seeing his
goddamn father, he has never felt as alone as when Burton went up the
steps and he went down.

These people are so kind, the army of help turned out for Mimi.

Burton turns out to be an expert packer. He takes over from L and has twelve boxes of china trussed and labelled in no time. "Jasper must take a look at some of these things," he tells Hugh. "You want an appraisal for insurance even if you aren't selling them—of course the second-hand market is a cesspit even *with* an honest dealer on your side. You'll never realize the value on some of these lovely things. Georg Jensen! A set for twelve!" He has more to say, much more, but his phone rings.

He checks the number and, eyebrows mounting, excuses himself and goes through the hall into the garden, a stubby old peacock shrieking unintelligibly into the phone.

In fact, the china and silver are going straight into Jasper's basement (his storage room, farther from the river, is safer than the gallery's), where he can go through them in his own time. It doesn't matter, nothing does. But they'll be safe there.

The cedar closet—Ruth said he has to empty that. Newell leaves the kitchen and comes to help pull out whatever treasures Mimi squirrelled away in there, furs and necklaces. The burden of selling all this hurts Hugh's head—give it all away, give it away. Money has fallen from any form of importance; losing the gallery to Largely would matter no more than losing this apartment to her. Nothing is permanent, nothing is safe.

Newell laughs, or sighs, looking out the back hall window to where Burton prances up and down on the dead lawn, gesticulating. Faint cries carry on the misty air. "He reminds me of Mimi in a way—don't get pissed. He went through a lot, the losses of AIDS, the theatre, his appalling early life. You don't see his damage, his love of art: his whole self."

Hugh's midnight insight into Newell and Burton has evaporated. He keeps himself from snorting by addressing the padlock, the combination coming to his fingers, not his mind. The door opens. Cedar scent clouds out as they enter, and redwood glow: coats one side, shelves on the other, stacked with velvet boxes, envelopes, her pearls in their old red leather case.

"Why are you always so angry with Burton, Hugh?" Newell asks, persisting.

Because his head hurts. Because Mimi is dead.

No point in anything but the truth now. Hugh stops, leaving the boxes where they lie. "Because you told me he was your—your introducer," he says. "Your first."

Newell doesn't speak.

"At twelve. That's a bad thing, I think it was a bad thing he did, that's why I hate him."

"I never told you that," Newell says. "I never did."

Hugh doesn't speak.

So Newell does. "Fuck, Hugh." (Or is that *fuck you?*) "What do you want me to tell you? It wasn't Burton." Hugh shakes his head. "Okay, it was the priest—it was my father, Della's father, some guy in grade nine—it was everybody. I had a hockey coach, a biology teacher, a fucking scoutmaster. Before them all, I had my own self, my heart and mind. Nobody made me be anything. I am who I am."

You don't often see Newell angry. Buoyed by the strange clarity of everything since Mimi died, Hugh says, "You did. You said, 'I was twelve, and he knew what I was.'"

"Well, he did, but I knew long before that. He—" Newell pauses, eyes going left. "He reassured me. He made it all right to be like—myself. In those days, someone just saying *it's okay* was a considerable gift. Even now."

Yes, Hugh wants to be told that himself. It's okay, to be a failure and a poor excuse for a son and a mediocre artist and—and Newell's friend. Impossible to hate Newell. Or, loving Newell, to hate anyone else, merely for being gay.

"Have you been carrying this all this time, thinking Burton abused me?"

Hugh stands on the verge of tears. "No, no . . ." He has, he has.

"Don't be sad! It wasn't—he helped, he—knew what my life already was, the secret things. He made it seem semi-normal. Or only half-freak. Not toxic."

If you're telling the truth, Hugh might as well continue. "Ivy asked me if I was jealous of Burton, first time we talked. Would you really have married him?"

"Oh, Hugh," Newell says. "Would you have married Ann, if she'd wanted you to?"

You would have.

Newell nods. "So why did that bug you?"

"I don't know. Because you're being taken advantage of, because it wouldn't make you happy. Because it's unsuitable."

"Two men getting married? Somewhere underneath, do you think that?"

No. Clear on that, Hugh can laugh. "No, fill your boots. Marry Orion, if you want to, he's over eighteen—I just don't want you to marry Burton. But I don't want to punch him, either. I will treat him with courtesy and respect, because you do."

Newell looks at Hugh, caught by a subtle tone, an expression, some ghost of contempt. "How can you look down on me the way you do? I'm seriously asking: how dare you be so sad all the time, be made unhappy by me? You think I'd be better off if I was more like you—but I think you'd be better off if you were more like me, like Burton, like Orion. You know me better than anyone in the world—better than Burton knows me. But you don't love me as kindly or blindly as he does, as independently, for *myself*. You love me for the sake of your own remembered self, for childhood and safety, for Ruth, for hard days with Mimi. Like I love you, and Della does, for being our brother."

Hugh tries to make his face blank. Not wanting to hurt Newell any more. But he needs to know, he can't stop himself from asking, "What about Orion?"

"You're right," Newell says. "I stopped it. It's not good, absorbing him, taking over—he has to have his own life." He shrugs, turns away to pull another heavy coat, and holds it up to himself, becoming Mimi, showing it off. Burying his face in the glorious collar, he says quietly, "But it's hard. I love him. If that has any meaning."

It does, it does. Hugh's head hurts so much—Newell has to stop stabbing him like this. He runs a hand down the sleeve of the golden sable. Would it fit Ivy? L wouldn't wear fur.

Lifting his head Newell says, "I just think we should *be with* the ones we love, however difficult it is to arrange the practical part, however impossible. With all the ones we love. You came to live here for Mimi's sake, because you understand that."

Hugh shifts his head, tries to ease the pressure. Yes. "Yes. Yes. I'll stay with her as long as she needs me," Hugh says. His head feels weird.

Newell looks at him. He doesn't stop looking.

"However—however long," Hugh says, feeling for what he ought to be saying. He puts the red calfskin pearl case in the box. His hands are heavy. Shelves empty, rod clear—he closes the door. The lock dangles, open. "I'm going to sleep there, they brought me a cot so I could stay overnight."

He's kind of lost the drift of this conversation. Maybe he needs another pill.

Still with the odd look, Newell zips up the coat bag and asks, "How is she?"

"She's good, she's good. Her old self."

"Did you see Conrad today?"

"Yes, I saw him . . . at FairGrounds, having cake, yes, he says she's tough, she'll . . ."

He shakes his head. Touches his hair, on the right side.

Newell takes Hugh's hand, and looks straight at him—makes you realize that he doesn't do that very often. Like you realized it about Della a few days ago.

"I don't look at you guys nearly enough," Hugh says.

"I think we'll go find Conrad again," Newell tells him, with that sweetness of manner that makes Hugh do things you don't want to.

"Conrad again. Okay," Hugh says. That offers an anchor, and you think (as much as Hugh still can think) maybe you need one.

(ORION)

Burton, squealing into his phone, hogs the whole path from back garden to truck. Orion stays in the shadows of the back porch, boxes piled in his arms. Arms aching, eyes aching. He didn't mean to listen, but by then he was already listening.

Of course he listened. Morals are for adults, for people with the luxury of power, of self-determination. Under-rats, victims, have to listen behind doors. Behind the cedar closet door, listening as Newell helps Hugh pack and says no no no no.

Orion shouts inside: *it's not the same.*

All right, Burton's an evil fucker, big surprise. But why should I be put aside? Whatever happened between Newell and Burton all those years ago is *not the same* as what is between Newell and me.

I want this. I'm not being taken over. I get to say, to decide what's right for me, in my own heart, in my own body. Hugh says marry Orion, if you want—like that's a joke. If Newell was strong he'd tell Hugh NO fuck you I love him. Because we should be with the ones we love.

Burton, dancing down there on the gravel path. Whatever—they've worked it out, they've made this long life somehow weirdly together, and if Newell can't leave that, all right. I could have fit alongside it somehow. Somehow.

Fuck off, everybody who wants to protect me, fuck you all.

Holding Hugh's arm, pulling him gently along, Newell tells Ivy, "Listen, sweetheart, I'm taking Hugh back to the hospital. Can you help Ruth hold the fort here?"

Packing done, Ruth's helpers are hauling a steady flow of furniture out to the truck. Ivy backs against the wall to let a large man past. "Working things out about Mimi?" she asks Hugh. Because she is worried, she wants him to say that's all it is. Hugh shrugs, kisses her cheek, then kisses the other cheek. As if forgetting he'd just kissed her.

"Conrad needs to take another look at Hugh." Newell is calm, but sure. He hands Ivy a key chain. "Mimi's keys."

"I'll come too."

"It'll take a while to get hold of Conrad, and there's still a lot to do here. Come in an hour," Newell says, taking Hugh's arm again. They go out the door between a parquetry tilt-top and a Noguchi cocktail table, like disjointed parts of a mobile.

Ivy is so disturbed that she's still standing there when Lise Largely comes up the porch steps a few minutes later. Perfect. Here's some action she can take. Ivy girds herself.

"Hi-i," Largely chimes, all effusion. "What a day! Moving is mayhem."

"I'm Ivy Sage," Ivy says, knowing she's not remembered. "Hugh had to go back to the hospital, but he asked me to get the deposit cheque from you when you came by."

Largely looks blank.

"For Mimi's original deposit and first month's rent. A personal cheque is fine," Ivy says. "I understand that you were in here *inspecting* on Thursday, so you had the chance to assure yourself there's no damage."

That gets Largely. She looks at Ivy for a brief moment, pulls her bag off her shoulder, and finds her chequebook. Ann comes into the hall while she's writing out the cheque, and says, "Lise, good timing—I have a few things set aside to take to the archives."

If by archives you mean your house, Ivy thinks. Then, never mind, it's only stuff.

She takes the cheque from Lise: four thousand! Nice. Might have taken a while, without the inappropriate-entry lever. There's much to be said for listening and remembering, and it's a miracle that she did. Maybe her mind is improving, as Hugh's goes to pieces.

Ann takes Lise out with her, good riddance, and Ivy goes to look for Ruth. She can't wait half an hour.

Before she can find her, Burton gallops in at the back door. Seeing Ivy, he demands Newell, and makes an irritated *tchah!* when she tells him. "The hospital! Couldn't *you* have taken Hugh? Well, never mind, I've had Big News: Louisville wants my play." He says this without ornament or exclamation, so thrilled he's subdued.

"Your play? For the Humana Festival?" (Trying not to sound incredulous.)

"*Tender Flowers,*" he says. "I may have spoken of it. A long project, an obsession, if you will. They want me to direct, as well. I've applied several times in the past—it's come up so suddenly because they had a no-show—a very fortunate broken leg for me!"

Ivy looks at him. Remembers to smile.

"Rehearsals start in two weeks, there's only *just* time, the designers, the team—it's too much to take in, I must talk to Boy—they want me to fly out tonight and—" He blinks, recalls that she is a woman of no importance, and darts out the front door, phone raised.

There's Ruth, at the truck, watching her crew make everything fast. "I'll go with the truck to the storage space," she says. "These are good boys but they're not saints."

Ivy doesn't say what's happening, just that Hugh's gone over to the hospital; Ruth nods, distracted, and says she'll lock up here. Ivy hands her the keys, and runs.

At the hospice the front desk nurse says they're on the third floor. Ivy climbs the stairs, walks the long polished hall floors that Hugh's been walking for so long. Which was Mimi's room? This door, ajar. Newell's voice, yes. A packed box on the window ledge, and a jug of creamy half-blown roses.

On the whiteness of the bed, nothing.

" . . . not himself," Newell is saying.

Conrad asks Hugh, "You've come to pick up Mimi's things?"

And Hugh says, "Yes, yes, if she's dressed we can take her now." Then he seems to rethink that. He glances at Newell, at Ivy. "I mean . . . I'm going to stay overnight from now on, the cot was very comfortable."

Undisturbed, Conrad sits on the empty bed, and pats the sheet for Hugh to sit down too. Conrad leans back, all comfy, one knee held in his knotted hands. "Remember when we slept on cots, you and I, that time at the South Pole? Or was it when we climbed K 2?"

Hugh chuckles. "Loved those cots. Never slept better."

"We drank yak butter tea. You like it, as I recall."

"I liked it, I liked it," Hugh says. "Very refreshing, after a day in the water." No, that's not right—he looks to Ivy for correction.

Conrad lets go his knee and pats Hugh's, getting up. "Right," he says, to Newell, to Ivy. "Confabulation, that's called."

They all look at him.

"Pressure on the brain creates it. Prime test for a late-presenting subdural hematoma. Given that he's functioned fairly well all this time, it must be a very slow bleed. Hugh, you bastard, you lied to me about the headache, didn't you?"

Hugh puts his hand up to his head, the saddest little gesture. Ivy's heart is being juiced by a giant hand, she can't speak. Newell puts his arm around her.

"Watch this," Conrad says. His empty hands, in front of Hugh, pull apart as if he's drawing out a string. "See my coloured beads? What's your favourite bead, Hugh?"

Hugh stares down at the hands, making an effort. After a minute, he points, his finger back and forth along an imaginary line. "I like the blue the best," he says.

"Right. You need a scan pronto," Conrad says. "And you will have to have an op. Being Sunday, better first thing tomorrow than later today. I'll shove you into the neurosurgeon's schedule at 7. You two take him to the CT area now, sub-basement over in the main building, and I'll run by the operating rooms. I'll try to meet you at CT, I'll phone them to expect you."

Hugh sits blankly on Mimi's blank white bed.

"Nothing to alarm. It's a fairly straightforward procedure, just a craniotomy—a hole to drain the blood. Sounds dramatic but as neuro-surgery goes it's pretty good. You'll look like Frankenstein afterwards, where they stitch the little dot of skull back in. Chris Peterson's on tomorrow, she's a champ. We won't have a bed for you tonight," Conrad says, putting out an affectionate hand to help Hugh up. "If I miss you at the scan, just go home, and don't eat or drink anything after 7 p.m."

Standing, Hugh moves his head gently. He seems to recover himself a little. "Can I still do the wine and cheese for Mighton?"

"Oh for Christ's sake, anything you like, you bloody hound. You'll do so anyway, whatever I say." Conrad is out the door, leaving them to follow.

It's more than Ivy can take. It's all right while they're at the hospital, in the waiting room, Newell never leaving them, keeping Hugh calm. The scan itself, being slid into the machine, seems to interest Hugh. She can be stable for him. The conversation about the drill, the—releasing. Watching a video of his head, the marking. For the piercing. The brain inside there, the sleeping snail of mind/memory/life. Then Ivy can't remember where she put her car, or—no, she didn't drive, she just ran over from Mimi's, that's all right.

Newell takes them to the gallery. Hugh is supposed to rest for the rest of—the rest of, what's left of the day. Her eyes feel both hollow and swollen. "I'll find Ruth," Newell says. "She's got the caterer coming at four, what's that, two hours? I'll come back to let him in, or she will. Get Hugh to lie down until then. And you lie with him, you could use a nap."

She takes Hugh up the stairs, her hand on his back. All the stairs in this world.

No sign of Gareth or Léon—oh, Gareth was going over to look at L's *Republic*, wasn't he. They must have gone there. Hugh doesn't comment, doesn't speak, asleep on his feet, or dopey. She leads him down the hall and takes off his shoes. He doesn't want to undress; he seems to hold the wine and cheese as the next necessary part of living, so she lets it go.

He lies back, cradling his head in one hand and lying very still. She covers him with the mohair blanket and closes the curtains.

Then she gets into the shower, where nobody can hear her, and cries for half an hour. Not knowing if Hugh is damaged, is dead.

I waited so long. I waited so long for you.

When the water turns cool she shakes her head and washes the tears off one more time. Now stop being selfish. Conrad said it's a straightforward—*trepan*—terrifying prehistoric word. Calm down. Dress, and wake Hugh; have a good time at this wine and cheese. Charm Mighton so he brings more paintings to keep the gallery afloat, keep watch on Della and Ken so there's no fighting. See that Ruth doesn't do all the work. Bolster Hugh, make sure he doesn't have an absent-minded drink.

Perfect. I can do those things. Okay, perfect.

(L)

They go down the stairs. Her mom stays up in the dining room where Gareth was looking at the other boats and more stuff she pulled, talking in a quiet voice for a long time. Now he and Léon go down the stairs. L feels the worst stabbing contortion-pain, right in her ovaries . . .

I see now—she sees it. It's shit, it's impossible, every piece of art is futile—what did Burton say, Art is useless. I have been fooling myself and I fooled Hugh too.

The gate, the warning, the sign: *THE ISLAND REPUBLIC OF L* DO NOT ENTER Why didn't she get there in time to take that down? Her hands are like wet cakes of soap.

Gareth looks at her, head tilted and mouth considering. Léon taps him. They go in.

It's just a rec room, too full—L closes her eyes, shuts off the voice inside her head. Turns to watch them walking through, like she watched Hugh on Monday. It's not done, it's not ready, *shitted is not painted*. She flicks her X-Acto knife inside her pocket.

Gareth examines the plans; the street of translucent portraits; makes his way through the Mylar brambles. Stops at a photographic print wrapped around a pillar, leans from one side to the other to see the two girls leaping in the air; steps right to get the whole view as they repeat and repeat around. The print watches Savaya and Nevaeh dancing on the street in front of the movie theatre. L's just in it at the side holding the camera in the repeating mirror of the shop door, watching them, jealous. He points to the bra and garter belt display of the lingerie shop, vanishing over and over in the upper corner behind her head: a thought-bubble, she now sees.

This is good because there's no need to talk, he's not talking yet.

Léon holds out a long, black arm, taps once on the big silver frame Mimi let her have. It is suspended in air and Mimi is suspended in the frame, drawn from the back with the bones of her spine showing and her waist taut in a hanging basket chair; the frame revolves like the chair and there she is from the front. Hello!—eyes hollowed and fresh, crone and child, about to dance. One drawing L is sure of. It makes her happy to have this much left of Mimi. The pink gloves and the black gloves, there might be a way to—get inside them, if you had—

Gareth speaks. "The Voynich, of course. This is Jacques Callot you're thinking of here? Walker? Ed Pien? Yes. The Kusama; but are you referencing *Leonardo* in this sector?"

L nods. "The Val di Chiana topographic map . . . colour-drained, bands, haze."

Then she says, "But too, there's this guy Aozaki making a map from directions people write out for him. Faces turning, hands—ways in, ways you find your way—" She stops, because staring at the face/map of Nevaeh she has just figured out that she doesn't *hate* Nevaeh, she's *mad* at her. She can still love her. The relief of that is intense.

Gareth stays in the *Republic* for more than an hour. L goes to sit on the stairs when it gets too hard to take. Her mom looks over the banister, and goes away quietly.

Then Gareth comes to the gate, motioning with his hand as if they've been talking all along, "Yes, undisciplined, ragged thought, ideas simply unspooled, juvenilia interspersed with oddly mature—well. Brilliance is not the same as depth. It's a mess."

L nods. He is entirely correct. She follows him in, in, farther in.

They stand in the core, all the strings leading up to nothing. She seems to be in stasis.

"You don't have room to work here. It's a straitjacket, ridiculous."

Well. Yes.

"A relationship with a gallery is not the only route. You might choose to put your work on a website, YouTube, Flickr, whichever." Gareth looks around the shifting web of paper and string and ribbon. "The structure of a gallery gives you the chance of significant critical response; makes it more likely that you will end up in museum collections, a validation many artists seek; and it will eventually help to raise your prices."

L nods.

"We create a context for solo exhibitions, we connect you to the market. An ongoing conversation—not the mentorship you have experienced with Hugh, although he disclaims any responsibility for this piece. We ask for exclusivity, at least at the beginning."

L nods.

"For our part: you may expect to feature in our inventory, to have prime exposure at the many major fairs we attend, and—eventually— sales. We will be investing in the hope that your work matures, expands, refines. The financial risk we incur justifies our 50/50 split. You might join an artist-run gallery; but we are in a position to spend five years developing both your work and the market for your work. With a piece like this, an installation, we'll be looking at a solo exhibit sooner than later, once individual pieces begin to sell."

L forces her head to stay still.

Gareth nods. "And we may have a room big enough to hold the vision."

The gallery is already hopping when Ivy lets Hugh go downstairs. He finds the world askew, tilted somewhat on its axis. Your mother died, he tells himself. You have a hematoma. Not surprising.

Still, he is surprised: at the spread of savories on wooden boards, at the deep glow of the wine—those greeny yellows! those infinitesimally differing reds!—and at the press of people. Mighton militant, triumphant, posturing before his piece. Ann, that's Ann beside him, the black Sharpie chimney-sweep. Behind them the louse Lise Largely simpers, whimpers *sorry, sorry,* but she has no power over Hugh, no power of attorney.

He shakes or nods his head. Ivy leans in to his ear and whispers, "I got the deposit back from her. For the apartment." O woman in a billion. He is overcome with love.

In the shattering shards of framed and unframed faces one looms close: he knows that nose: it's Ansel Goddamn Burton. Where is Newell, right behind, that's fine. Burton's voice rings in the ears, it's rude to put your fingers in but—oh, there, volume has been adjusted. He is telling secrets.

"All art is *quite useless,* Wilde decreed," Burton says. "Yet it seems a use has been found for mine. My play—at a little place called Louisville."

He's a purring, post-canary cat. Hugh likes him in this state. "Go on," he says—something he's never said to Burton before.

"Have you been drinking?" Burton asks, suspicious.

"Not allowed," Hugh says, and Ivy chimes in: "A drink, Burton? Lots of choice."

He raises his full glass. "You two are odd."

Newell gives Burton back his phone. "You're checked in," he says. "All packed?"

"Like the tents of the Arabs, but I must attend to one last thing. Hark, Pink!" Burton tacks and wends his stately, plump Buckminster Fuller way—Hugh laughs because in fact the I'm-a-director black glasses frames do have a Fuller look. This is a strange world, and everything in it shines.

Another shining thing: L the lovely girl, his niece, his—you could say—protégé, coming in the front door, glass opening in the middle of glass to let in glass: her fair slightness shining in the last late low slant of sun. Her hairline speaks of peace. Behind her a giant bear rears: old Gareth, and his slighter shadow, lovely Léon. So many people are so lovely now.

Hugh goes to them, so happy he's afraid he'll weep. Gareth stretches out one great limb and pulls Hugh in, a little confab. "That's what I'm doing these days," Hugh tells him, in confidence. "Confabulating."

Gareth nods as if this all makes sense; L is too dazed to respond at all. "I'm taking on this startling young woman," he says. "I want to secure your blessing before I do—I know you have been integral to her education thus far." He talks on for some little time, Hugh nodding as he thinks might be polite, smiling most of the time. No idea what Gareth is saying, or what L may be thinking. Hugh hopes she wants this, isn't just bedazzled—

No, that's Hugh, it's you who is confused, contused. Ivy?

There she is. "Hugh's got a headache," she tells Gareth. She hugs L. "Everything working out to your satisfaction?"

L nods, not able to speak either. Hugh hopes she has not had a bump on the head. That's what he has. He sits. There is a chair against the wall, so he sits in it.

Mighton, in front of him now, confabs with Ann. That's not a good idea. Those two too much of two feathers. Ann says she's got a treasure trove of clothes and Hugh says that's just fine, he nods and then stops speaking for a while. She made off with the fine feathers of Mimi's frantic youth, that's good. Feed her till she's finally full.

Mighton leans over and kisses her, what's that about, what's this?

The good thing is that Mighton's leaning reveals the *Dark Gates* he's been blocking, and Hugh can sit and stare at that beautiful, that magnificent thing, that piece of work.

Gerald sits beside him. Two chairs, who knew? Hugh knew there were more, but not where they were. Language has become a serpent slide, no longer a ladder of logic. Ivy? No, no, she's talking to L, that's all right, she'll guard L.

"Gerald," he says. He searches for something to say that will please Gerald. "I need a new car. Or no, wait. I can't afford one. I'm afraid I'm not myself."

"Funny thing about that," Gerald's mouth crooks. "Saab just went under. We knew it was coming," he says. "Might not be able to buy Mighton's picture after all."

"Okay. You've lost everything now. They're puncturing my head in the morning."

"But you'll be all right. Conrad's here—he told me, he said you can be fixed."

Conrad: he's come to check on him, no doubt. You should never lie to the doctor. Hugh never will again. If you live to tell the telltale never, no. Conrad bends to look into his eyes.

"How you doing, Hugh? Time to go to bed, is it?"

A trick question? What time is it? Hugh panics for an instant but there is Ivy, she has not left him. "He's allowed to eat until seven, the O.R. nurse said—I thought I'd give him a quick supper, I don't think he's eaten since last night. Then we'll have a quiet evening."

Conrad nods. "See you in the morning, then, Hugh. I'm on for that picture, if Newell hasn't already beaten me to it."

"Nothing is settled," Hugh says. "I am unsettled."

"You are. You will be much better tomorrow," Conrad promises. Off he goes.

Gerald leans over. "See you tomorrow," he says. "Day after. I'm counting on you."

So that means Hugh can't die. Nobody else can die.

❧

Ivy scans the room. Things are winding down—there's only the one piece, after all. Hurry up, go! The wine has been drunk, the canapés devoured by the pre-supper crowd. Hugh sits against the wall, staring at the *Dark Gates*. Ivy sees that the painting is good, but resists being pulled in. Not liking Mighton, although he likes her. He's swung his searchlight onto Ann, great.

Jason's worried. He tells Ivy that Ruth asked him to bring Hugh's van from Mimi's place. "There were all those blue bags of clothes in the back, but they're gone."

"I took those," his mother says, idling by, Mighton close beside her. "They're all things that ought to be appraised."

Ruth pauses at Ivy's elbow, tugs her aside to whisper. "Ann took the bags I gave you?"

"Not those ones," Ivy says. "There wasn't room. The van was already full of bags, so I got the boys to put the bags you gave me into the big truck, up on the top shelf."

Ruth laughs, a tiny explosion. "Well, doesn't that just beat the Dutch. Those bags she took from Hugh's van, those were poor Gerald's wife's old clothes. I dropped off the other bags at the Mennonite Clothes Closet. They'll have a high old time over there when they go through them. I guess Ann will have to buy the things she wants back from them."

"Oh no!" Ivy says. "I think Hugh was quite happy for her to have Mimi's clothes."

Repaying the deposit cheque of their old relationship, maybe.

Ruth nods, chuckling again, enormously amused. "Well, I'll go explain there was a small mistake, and get them to give her a deal. But let's wait a day or two."

She trots happily off to the door where a delivery man is arriving. And Della and Ken, coming in around the delivery guy—what is that? Ivy goes to help. Four cartons. Ruth signs, signs, while Della and Jason and L and Ken take boxes through to the framing room. Della is signalling— They're for *you*, Ivy.

What? She opens the first box: it's full of other boxes, and each of those is full of shoes. Red velvet shoes, with lovely Spanish heels. 37? Yes. Another box, red suede wedges—another, another—oh, the roses shoes! Sixteen pairs of red shoes.

She looks up. Leaning in the doorway, Newell says, "I asked for all the reds."

It makes him happy to give people things. Ivy will not get weepy again, because what if she can't stop? Will rose red shoes stop Hugh's head from bursting? No. But her ruined shoes, new again! "Roses fix everything," she says, kissing Newell's cheek.

Hugh is at the doorway too, lost without her; she shows him a rosy shoe. He nods, carefully. "Newell's got a gift for gifts. Like the house for Della and Ken."

There's a silence. Ken asks, "The box? The travel box?"

"Okay, but the place. The house."

Della looks up from examining a pair of red leather sandals. "What place?"

Newell sighs. "Bean spiller. What's the use of a travel box without somewhere to go?"

"She left it here, upstairs," Ken says. "I'll get it." He clatters up the stairs and comes back down with the mother-of-pearl box. He hands it to Della, who sets it on the framing table and opens the lid. She finds the satin ribbons, and lifts out the tray. More silver-capped jars below—and resting on top of them, a grey envelope. She pulls out paper, several pages, and a key slides out, clunking on the table. She and Ken look through the sheaf.

Ken's blackened eye pulses, his tic made more visible by the yellowing patch above and the sharp still-black line below. He looks up, not at Newell. "This is too much."

"I had the idea," Newell says quietly, in the direction of the door, "that some time away might be good—kind of a sabbatical."

Della says, to the watching people, "It's a house in the Bahamas. A year's lease."

There's a thick pause.

Newell says, "It's not a big house, nothing fancy. I was on a wait list for it and my turn came up, but now the insurers for *Catastrophe* won't let me go off the mainland. You'd be doing me a favour. Somebody has to use it. There's a boat, there's coral . . ."

He's used to having presents refused, or grudgingly accepted, Ivy thinks. Good thing she's keeping the shoes.

Ken looks at Newell, his usually anxious, drifting eyes are still. "For a couple of weeks, a month—but listen, I have to get back to work. And Della can't be away too long. Pindar—"

"It's vacant now, go now. Take a month," Newell says, not pressing.

Ken straightens his back as if it's been hurting. Lifts the tight forehead, irons the creases with his palm. "No, listen. This is—it's the choice. That's what's good about it. That makes it possible to go back to work, since I can choose not to now, you see?"

Della leans her head on her husband's arm, looking exhausted, but some variety of happy. "Thank you, Newell," she says. "I will paint you some real boats."

Burton steps into the doorway, surveys the little crowd. "I hate to barge in, but I'm going to miss my plane if we don't hustle, Boy."

That breaks the spell. Newell slips out through the crowd to get his coat while Burton, leaning in, tells Ivy that she'll have to take over the master class. "Poor Boy has no interest in leading, you know him, but he promises he will attend and support you, as a favour to me. I suggest that you abandon directing, *per se*. Do a group project within your reach—you might manage a collective creation in the three weeks remaining. Now that you won't be part of the performance team, I think it really *would* be good to have something the parents can come and see. Some recompense, since I won't be there." Catching sight of Jerry Pink, Burton swans away for a last goodbye.

Ivy goes with Newell to the door.

"You arranged that," she says. "You're the fixer."

He's got such bright clear eyes when he's happy. "I may have made a donation. Don't keep me, I have to get Burton to the airport. We don't want him to miss that plane."

Jerry Pink, seeing Ivy emerge into the gallery, says he'll give her a call to work out the details. Newell prompts, "And to change her contract, since she'll run the class now."

"Collective creation, I hear you're good at that," Pink says.

Ivy nods, feeling very tired. It takes a lot of lift to get a collective off the ground. But Newell will be there, and Orion, back in the class, to soothe his soul. And Jason must stay in, and Nevaeh, they can work around her leg—well, there will be a lot to think about.

Newell is at Burton's back, pushing him to the front. He tells Hugh (and Ivy, knowing she's the fully conscious one) that he wants the Mighton. "Gareth says he's not sure L's installation is ready to sell? So keep an eye on that for me."

Della tucks the pearl box under her arm, shrugging on her black coat with the brilliant lining. Ivy loves a suitable coat for the person; this one is Della all through. She still looks tragic, to Ivy's mind; perhaps that's not knowing her very well yet. Or that we are all so tired, and all these people loved Mimi, and mourn for her.

The door swinging, swinging: the place is almost empty, suddenly. Even Mighton has drifted off. Oh, there he is going up the street to the Ace with Ann and Lise Largely.

Ivy gives one little laugh, looking at them, and at its echo turns to see Ruth, still laughing. It is pretty funny—wonder how much of a donation Ruth will get the Clothes Closet to wangle out of Ann.

"We've got to feed you," Ivy tells Hugh. "Less than an hour till seven."

Ruth, buttoning her corduroy coat, pulls a nice brown crackly hundred dollar bill out of her pocket. "I'm taking Hugh to the Duck," she says, to Ivy's surprise. "We have to make some lists before he goes to get that bump taken care of, what to do about the funeral and so on. I made the reservation for three, hoping you'd come along."

She turns the sign and pulls the door to. "When I found this hundred dollars, we didn't even know you yet! It's like it was meant."

(DELLA)

put him to bed   poor man sad eye browbeaten   thirty years
                          a week in the Bahamas   or a month
Burton is Newell's burden
Mimi Hugh's
mine is Ken   in my ken

all night
poetry in the mind going on work death infidelity suicide work
all these years of being   more or less cheerful more or less loving
                             work is what we live for anyway
so work work is that it?   yes and loving
work and more of it   none of this means   I do not love him
                             oh my mother your boats
                             and Hugh & his head
                             and Newell
                             and Elle   my lovely L
all of them will leave me
                             fine   of all of them
                                                          only Ken is mine
                             where is my Sharpie? do not wake, sleeper
                             under Ken's black and sleeping eye
                             in tiny letters: m i n e

He stops, brakes hissing, and looks out over the river. The moon is wading in it, washing her feet, feeling so smirched. Everybody knowing what was secret, what was pure.

Give up, give up on him. The thing is, I thought this was important. Won't be the last mistake, a thousand huge mistakes left to make in a long, boring life.

Flying out of reach of people, beyond the city, down past the Liftlock golf course and out out out Old Norwood, going farther into darkness as fast as flight. Past the last houses onward right up to Burnham Line, fly like a man-witch from *Macbeth*.

The crossroads.

He stops, gets off the bike. Stands there. Not like those guys from *Waiting for Godot*—like Beckett himself, thinking about Godot. That's the difference. He's not art, he's an artist.

Interesting to note that he doesn't want to lie down on the moon-silvered road and die. So there has to be something to live for.

The moon is high in the split sky, finally clawed out from the clouds chasing around her. Rags of clouds drift off. Cold up there. The moon and all the stars, turning above us all. Distance! We are tiny, unknowable, unimaginably unimportant, far from everything, only close to each other. Alone in lonely infinity.

No cars, no sound of cars. He does lie down, to see the sky whole. Black and grey, giant darkness reaching up or down, limitless, forever. Cold darkness at his back, where he lies connected to the earth by gravity alone, or he might fall up into the dark night sky. And look, there he is, Orion. Already there.

(His mom, what a nutbar to call him that. *Orion*! She thinks he's so great.)

Road-cold seeps up into his bones and makes him stand—leaping in one rush to his feet—this body, this good steed, so perfect and obedient. Where you lie in the sky, or on the earth, what your place is at the moment.

Accepting that in time it will, it will be in the heavens.

The climb up the stairs, the last stairs of the day. Takes a while.

"It's not even eight, but it feels like a million o'clock," Ivy says.

He's tired, yes. But will he sleep if he lies down? Maybe the deck.

"You can take a pill, the nurse said." Ivy goes to get water.

"You fixed the tip?" Ruth does not understand restaurant economy.

"I did, I was discreet."

"What's this box?" It's on the counter.

"The stuff from the cedar closet. Newell brought it. It was in his car when he took you to the hospital."

What's in it? The pearls in red leather; a square blue velvet box, garnets or something. Letters, papers. He opens the interleaved cardboard flaps, but can't bring himself to dig through anything more tonight. Beginning to worry about the morning, he swallows the pill Ivy brings him. She shifts the envelopes to read: "Letters—Gould, Trudeau, here's one from the Queen!"

"That's the Queen Mother, some charity ball or something. Just a thank you note. There are a couple of real letters from Kennedys, though. One from Yoko Ono, with little drawings."

Ivy is looking at him as if she can't tell if Hugh is confabulating, or it's real. "What are you going to do with these?"

"Read them, some time. Not give them to Ann, or a university or anyone." This one box of Mimi's heart and mind and the company she kept. He sees Ivy watching him. "The people who loved her."

"You loved her," Ivy says.

"She drove me so crazy," he says. "I think my head will burst."

"Not yet," Ivy says. "You can last the night. Tomorrow I'll be the Bride of Frankenstein for you." She goes to fold the flaps again, and lifts one last big envelope. "This one says Hugh."

He takes it, fumbling with the flap. Pours out a drift of letters on the counter. Ivy picks one up: "*To Mimi love your Hugh love love love forever.* These are all letters from you."

That she kept his letters—Of course. That's what mothers do.

He goes out onto the deck, not even knowing why. He needs the air, before he goes to sleep this maybe last time. It has stopped raining.

Hugh lies down on the chaise. Ivy sits at his feet and holds his knees.

Around the deck small trees, narrow wrist-span saplings, have sprung up without being asked. They'll have to be thinned but they're so pretty now. And above, clouds in tatters streaming away from the moon. A spray of stars far above, revealed again but always there.

We are so small, how comforting. We are not everything. We lose (childish hope) (most loving heart) (everything) but the stars go on.

"The hugeness of everything," he says, hoping she will understand. How can we feel the pain of others and yet be happy for a moment, an island of happiness in an ocean of suffering, he wants to ask her.

"You're asleep," Ivy says, hugging his knees more strongly. "Time to go to bed, I think."

He goes, obedient, but he has a few things he'd like to get straight. "You won't leave me, will you? You'll come and live with me? But keep that apartment, you need it, for working—it's your . . . you don't want to be stuck with me all the time for the next few—you know, while I'm, if I'm sick or, or even if—anyway, maybe I'll have a hard time with all this, Mimi dying, and the head thing—I don't want you to stay because you have nowhere else to go."

"No matter what, I have nowhere else to go now. I have to be with you."

"Maybe I'd like a pied-a-terre in Toronto. You never think about *my* needs."

If the gallery goes. Which it still might.

"We'll talk tomorrow," Ivy says, "When you are back in your right mind. I love you."

"Do you really?" he asks. "Or is it just a story I've been telling myself?"

"I asked Conrad, and he said, Love is not an artifact of the disorder."

"Good." He turns in the bed to sleep, then turns back. "Will you wait here for me?"

"If you are not too long, I will wait here for you all my life."

(ORION)

In the shattering flood of clear-sky stars Orion zooms on his bike, a comet, a constellation. Through streets and alleys, down the canalside, up and down to the riverbank, light speed, silver flaring in the fiery wheels of his steed.

To pause, panting, at the bottom of the steps.

"Newell!"

Arc the voice up over the glossy briar-hedge, up to Rapunzel's window, to where the sleeper lies unsleeping in the glass mountain. Who cares if Burton hears?

"Newell, I am not too young for you. It's not the same."

Nothing.

Send it sweetly up once more, once more, as if he's there, and listening.

"I am—I am yours," Orion says.

The air stirs, moves in silence. A door, opening?

Hugh lies in his bed, awakened, Ivy sleeping by his side. Not dead, only resting. Phrases from past lives rise in the mind, make you feel better in the middle of the night. When waiting for whatever will happen tomorrow.

Sometimes the breath staggers, thinking about what comes next. Thinking about what came before. Mimi, her eyes, her hand on his, and gone.

You'll be fine. You have people to look after.

You won't, Hugh won't abandon anyone. Newell, Orion, damned Burton, wherever he may roam, in whatever permutation those three work out. Jason, Savaya, poor Nevaeh in the hospital—all to be shepherded somehow—Ruth, Jasper, in their varying degrees. L and Della have to be guarded, Gareth Pindar is a shark. Ken to be kept an eye on in the sharkswim of the law. Ann, Mighton; those two are too much alike. The poor kid who was living at Ivy's, his jackass brother. Gerald.

All of them. All of us who will be dead, all of us, if the fabric of the world is not kept whole by constant never-ending vigilance. The weft, the web map of the world in L's *Republic*, strings, a theory of tendrils, connections, onion-skin portraits receding rapidly to some unimaginable ceiling, to godhead.

A saw, or a pick? To make the first, the deepest headcut—maybe a drill?

He shifts, and there is Ivy warm and loving, her arm, breast, leg, her form between him and the formless void. It is better to think of all those people. Ivy will help him think. Turn again, head heavy. It is all up to us, it is all our fault, they are all our responsibility. Saying his prayers like this he might fall asleep, Ivy beside him.

It is not over, not yet, not yet. At least, that is the story you tell yourself.

In the darkness Mimi is sitting on the bed. Not lost. Loved.

"I am always holding your hand," Hugh says.

ACKNOWLEDGEMENTS

This town is a completely imaginary Peterborough—I did once board in a house on the river, with a kayak in the garden, but that was in another century. And this is obviously not the former Peterborough performing arts school, which I hope will re-open. Nothing about *this* school is true of any school I know. All drama teachers are paragons of stability and selfless good sense, and none of them would ever hire Burton.

Unattributed in the text, since we don't need to tell our friends who wrote the songs we're humming, Ivy sings a line or two of the Tragically Hip's song *Bobcaygeon*. Hugh remembers Jane Kenyon's poem "Twilight: After Haying" and Mighton's collage piece makes use of Virgil's *Aeneid*, translated by David Ferry. Della's MFA gold-leaf installation is borrowed from a beautiful piece Beth Morrow made at the University of Calgary. I'm indebted to my friend Pierre-François of Pierre-François Ouellette Art Contemporain, for an illuminating conversation on the inner workings of reputable galleries. Thanks to Patti Shedden for advice and inspiration, and for our long, sustaining conversation over many years. Thanks to Dr Mike Peterson for his advice on subdural hematomas, especially his reassurance about artifacts of the disorder.

As well as those necessary acknowledgements, I give thanks to all the usual saints who keep me company on the road: Sara, Glenda, Thyra, Babar, Jeanne, Steve, Mel, Connie, Lynn, Timothy and Emily. I thank Lynn Henry, whose wisdom and experience I value far above rubies, for being such good company on the rocky climb into and through a book. To my dear Tracy Bohan and Jin Auh, thanks for your graceful, intelligent help. Thanks to Kristin Cochrane at Random House, and to Nicola Makoway and Kelly Hill. I am properly grateful to Gil Adamson, whose kindly piercing eye made everything clearer.

Affectionate thanks to all you legmen for doing the field research: Rachel, Patrick, Will and Sindy. And as always, to you who (Hugh who) waits to read: loving thanks to Peter. He carries the moral compass on our long walk.